A touch in the dark . . .

"I'll help you." She moved closer, gliding an arm around his neck. Her hair tumbled around him, slick and heavy where it fell onto his shoulders and chest, and infused with a sweet green scent that made him think of a meadow.

Bracing one hand on the floor, Graeham went to curl an arm around her. He misjudged her position, and his hand brushed a weighty softness beneath the silk that could only be a breast. Her indrawn breath was barely audible; she stilled. He retracted his hand, but slowly, slowly, his fingertips lingering over the supple curve of flesh as they withdrew. His heart thudded hard against the bandage wrapped around his chest.

Would she get up and leave? She didn't.

Should he send her away? He didn't want to.

Silken Threads

"Patricia Ryan moves *Rear Window* to medieval London and does things Hitchcock never dreamed of! Fresh, swift, and sexy, *Silken Threads* strengthens Ms. Ryan's reputation as an outstanding author of medieval romances." —Mary Jo Putney

"Simply superb! . . . Ms. Ryan weaves the silken threads of her latest medieval romance into a complex tapestry of mystery, suspense and passion. . . . Not to be missed." —*The Old Book Barn Gazette*

"*Silken Threads* stands out . . . a special and original novel from one of romance's finest authors. Don't miss it." —*The Literary Times*

Wild Wind

"Lost innocence, forbidden desires, everlasting love . . . *Wild Wind* is wonderful. Don't miss it!" —Jo Beverley

"This is what historical romance is all about." —*Romantic Times*

Secret Thunder

"A wonderful writer whose talent continues to enchant readers." —*Romantic Times*

"A marvelous love story from the queen of medieval romance. . . . I will buy anything Patricia Ryan writes!"
—*The Literary Times*

"Totally absorbing! . . . Full-bodied and rich, like vintage wine." —*The Old Book Barn Gazette*

Heaven's Fire

"Lusty and exhilarating, this is medieval romance at its best. . . . A splendid tale." Patricia Gaffney

"An intense tale of deception, religion, murder, and romance. Dramatic . . . a unique love story you will not soon forget." —*Rendezvous*

"Pure reading nirvana." —*Affaire de Coeur*

Falcon's Fire

"A richly textured pageant of passion. A grand adventure!" —Susan Wiggs

"A passionate tale of deception and forbidden love. Don't miss *Falcon's Fire*!" —Suzanne Barclay

"A powerful debut novel by an exciting new talent, *Falcon's Fire* will ignite your imagination and passion." —*Romantic Times*

Other Books by Patricia Ryan

Falcon's Fire
Heaven's Fire
Secret Thunder
Wild Wind

Silken Threads

Patricia Ryan

A TOPAZ BOOK

TOPAZ
Published by New American Library, a division of
Penguin Putnam Inc., 375 Hudson Street,
New York, New York 10014, U.S.A.
Penguin Books Ltd, 27 Wrights Lane,
London W8 5TZ, England
Penguin Books Australia Ltd, Ringwood,
Victoria, Australia
Penguin Books Canada Ltd, 10 Alcorn Avenue,
Toronto, Ontario, Canada M4V 3B2
Penguin Books (N.Z.) Ltd, 182–190 Wairau Road,
Auckland 10, New Zealand

Penguin Books Ltd, Registered Offices:
Harmondsworth, Middlesex, England

First published by Topaz, an imprint of New American Library,
a division of Penguin Putnam Inc.

First Printing, June 1999
10 9 8 7 6 5 4 3 2 1

 REGISTERED TRADEMARK—MARCA REGISTRADA

Printed in the United States of America

*For my dear friend
and critique partner, Kathy Schaefer,
with love and appreciation*

Chapter 1

May 1165, London's West Cheap District

How do you tell a man you've come to take his wife away?
Graeham wondered as he knocked on the red-painted dou-
ble door of Rolf le Fever's Milk Street town house.

He'd pondered the matter at some length during his
storm-ravaged Channel crossing and the two-day ride from
Dover to London, but no easy answer had come to him. It
was a tricky business, removing a woman from her husband's home, one that might call for the most silken
finesse . . . or savage force. Graeham automatically touched
the horn handle of the dagger sheathed on his belt, hoping
he wouldn't need to use it.

The iron door knocker was shaped like the head of some
unidentifiable beast with a gaping mouth, from which
curled a long, demonically pointed tongue. Graeham
reached for it again, but hesitated as footsteps thudded
from within, accompanied by a man's voice. "Where the
devil are you, you bloody worthless wench? Didn't you
hear that knocking?"

The door swung inward with a squeal of corroded hinges.
The fair-haired man who had opened it looked about Graeham's age, although Graeham knew him to be, at five-and-
thirty, fully a decade his senior. He was taller than average,
though not as tall as Graeham. Pale, smooth-boned, clad
in a calf-length tunic of emerald silk trimmed in sable and
cinched with a jeweled belt, Rolf le Fever more closely
resembled a royal courtier—or his own notion of one—
than a merchant, however prosperous he might be.

Le Fever looked Graeham up and down with eyes the color of water, his expression that of a man contemplating an insect. Little wonder; unwashed and unshaven, his split-front riding tunic and leathern leggings grimy from the road, his unbound hair hanging limply, Graeham must have looked as if he were there to empty the privy.

"Rolf le Fever?" Graeham inquired, although there was no question in his mind whom he was addressing.

"Tradesmen enter 'round back." Le Fever stepped away from the door and began to swing it shut.

Graeham slammed a hand on it before it could close. "Gui de Beauvais sent me."

At the mention of his father by marriage, le Fever slowly reopened the door. "Lord Gui sent *you?*"

Graeham opened the hardened leather case resting against his hip and suspended by a cord across his chest. He pulled out a folded sheet of parchment bound in gold cord that had been sealed with the baron's insignia and handed it to the merchant. "His lordship's letter of introduction."

Le Fever broke the waxen seal, slid the cord out of the slits in the crisp parchment, and unfolded the letter, his mouth silently forming the words as he struggled to decipher them.

Choosing to be tactful—at least for the time being—Graeham said, "I apologize for my appearance. I've been traveling for the better part of a week, and I've only just arrived in London."

"Indeed." Le Fever refolded the letter and tapped his chin with it. "Where's your mount, then?"

"I left them—"

"Them?"

"I have two." *One for me and one for your wife.* "I left them at St. Bartholomew's." It was on Lord Gui's advice that Graeham had chosen the renowned monastic hostelry, located outside the city wall, over Holy Trinity or one of London's many public inns. His lordship had extolled the priory's hospitality, but Graeham hadn't been there long enough to sample it. Upon his arrival a short while ago, he'd stabled his exhausted horses and proceeded by foot through Aldersgate—one of the seven gates that provided access into London proper—and through the bustling city streets to the retailing district of West Cheap, mindful of his mission. Too mindful, perhaps, for le Fever might have proven more receptive had Graeham taken the time to clean himself up and dress as befitted the emissary of a distinguished Norman baron.

He was overeager. Little wonder, considering the urgency of his assignment . . . and his stake in its success.

"May I come in?" Graeham asked. "I have a matter of some importance to discuss with you."

Le Fever's eerily transparent gaze drilled into Graeham. "Lord Gui describes you as a retainer. That's not very specific."

"I'm one of his serjanz."

"Ah. A military man," le Fever said, as if that explained Graeham's appearance. He tucked the letter beneath his belt. "Come." Turning, he strode through a small entrance hall and up a flight of stairs to a second-floor landing, with Graeham following; the stairs continued upward to a third level, Graeham noticed.

"You're English," le Fever observed as he led the way into a sizable chamber, opulently furnished and bedecked in silken hangings, its floorboards plastered with smooth white clay.

"Aye." Graeham couldn't help smiling, gratified that the eleven years he'd lived in the Frankish county of Beauvais hadn't completely erased the native accent with which he spoke the Anglo-Norman common tongue of his homeland.

Le Fever motioned Graeham into an ornately carved chair, one of two facing each other before a hooded fireplace set into a stone chimney. A hellish blaze roared within it, out of keeping with the mild spring afternoon. The merchant crossed to a corner cupboard painted with leopards and fleurs-de-lis. "Do you have a name, serjant?"

"Graeham."

A ring of keys dangled from a chain attached to le Fever's belt, much like a lady's chatelaine. Sorting through the keys, he chose one and unlocked the cupboard. "Graeham of . . . ?"

"Some in France know me as Graeham of London—I was born here. But I'm also called Graeham Fox."

"For your cleverness?"

"For my hair." *And* for his cleverness, but sometimes it was best to be underestimated. "In sunlight, it has a reddish cast." When it was clean, which it hadn't been since his last bath, back in Beauvais.

Le Fever's expression hovered somewhere between indifference and disdain. "One must take your word for that, I suppose." He removed a flagon and a silver goblet from the cupboard. "Something to cool your throat after your journey?"

"Ale, if you have it. I've missed English ale."

"Wench!" le Fever shouted. After a moment's silence, he snarled, "God's tooth," stalked to a corner stairwell, and shouted, "Aethel! Where the bloody hell are you?"

Something scraped on the ceiling overhead—a chair?—and then came the hurried descent of footsteps on the stairs. A doughy serving wench appeared, clutching her apron in one hand and a spoon in the other. "Beg pardon, Master Rolf. I was upstairs feeding Mistress Ada, and I didn't hear—"

"Go down to the buttery and bring our guest some ale. Step lively."

"Yes, sire." Aethel cast Graeham a swift, curious glance as she darted back into the service stairwell.

"Pointless creature." Le Fever filled the goblet with wine and sat opposite Graeham to sip it. Rings glinted on his fingers and thumbs. When he crossed his legs, Graeham glimpsed, beneath the hem of his tunic, the intricately embroidered garters that secured his chausses just above the knees. The snug hose were fashioned not of wool but of gleaming plum-colored silk—an understandable affectation, Graeham supposed, given that his host was not only London's most prominent silk merchant but master of the newly established Mercers' Guild.

"I can't help wondering," le Fever said as he eyed Graeham over the rim of his goblet, "what 'matter of some importance' could prompt Lord Gui to send a soldier to his daughter's home."

Tread carefully. "His lordship misses Mistress Ada and is eager to visit with her. Given his advanced years and ill health, it would have been unwise for him to attempt such an arduous journey himself. He sent me to escort his daughter across the Channel to him."

Le Fever's eyebrows quirked, just slightly. "He wants you to take her back to Beauvais?"

Slowly Graeham said, "To Paris. He'll visit her there."

"Ah, yes," le Fever sneered. "Ada has never set foot in her own father's castle, isn't that right? Tell me—does the baron's lady wife even know about the twin daughters her husband sired on that Paris whore?"

"Nay," Graeham said evenly. "And, as I understand it, their mother was a dressmaker."

Le Fever snorted contemptuously. "They call themselves all sorts of things." He took a long swallow of wine and wiped his mouth on the back of his hand. "I'm afraid your journey has been for naught, serjant. I have no intention of consigning my wife to the care of a complete stranger, especially . . ." His frosty gaze took in Graeham's disreputable appearance.

"I assure you she'll be entirely safe with me."

Le Fever smiled thinly. "That's really not the point. 'Tis quite irregular for a married lady to travel abroad without her husband. 'Twould reflect badly on me, and I do have a reputation to maintain. I'm a man of consequence in this city, after all, regardless of what his lordship may think of me."

Something clattered on the floor upstairs. Le Fever did not avert his unnervingly steady gaze from Graeham.

"Are you aware," Graeham said, "that your wife has maintained a steady correspondence with her father since your marriage to her last year?"

"What of it?"

"Six months ago, the letters stopped coming."

Aethel reappeared with a stein of ale for Graeham, at whom she smiled shyly before disappearing back into the corner stairwell. A moment later, there came footsteps on the floor above, and another grating of chair legs. Listening closely, Graeham heard Aethel saying something apologetic in muffled tones, followed by the much softer voice of another woman.

Tracking Graeham's gaze to the ceiling, le Fever said, "My wife has been ill since Christmastide. When she's recovered, she'll resume her correspondence with her father. Is that why he wants to see her? Because she stopped writing?"

"That . . ." Graeham gained a moment by taking a slow sip of ale. Too bitter, but it tasted like ambrosia; it tasted like England. "And because of what she communicated to him while she was still writing."

Setting his stein on a little table next to his chair, Graeham reached into his document case and brought forth a short stack of letters. Le Fever eyed them uneasily, as well he might have.

Graeham said, "Your marriage appears to have soured within days of the wedding."

Le Fever made a sound of derision. "We were married in Paris. Three days later, while we were in a boat crossing the Channel, she told me what her father had declined to mention before the nuptials—that the daughter whose hand he'd so generously offered me had, in fact, been born on the wrong side of the bed. He's never publicly acknowledged Ada and Phillipa, never even owned up to their existence. I thought I'd negotiated a union with a baron's daughter, but what I ended up with was a wife I daren't speak of, lest someone inquire after her parentage. How could such a marriage possibly benefit me?"

" 'Twas to protect the delicate sensibilities of his lady wife that the baron chose circumspection regarding—"

"He hid those girls away in Paris like the shameful little secret they were. And still are." Le Fever drained his wine in one swift tilt of the goblet.

"On the contrary, after their mother died, he delegated their upbringing to the care of his own brother, a canon of Notre Dame. They were well provided for, educated, given every possible advantage. He visited them frequently."

"And all the while," le Fever said, gripping the stem of his goblet as if squeezing a throat, "he hoped and prayed that no one in Beauvais would ever learn of them. Is it any wonder he betrothed Ada to an Englishman? The farther away he could keep her, the better. God damn that blackguard to eternal hell for his treachery."

"His lordship realizes he . . . misled you."

"He lied to me," le Fever spat out as a livid flush suffused his face. "If not outright, then by implication. He arranged my betrothal to his bastard daughter as if there were naught amiss, laughing at me all the while. Tell me—were you privy all along to his sordid little scheme to foist one of his by-blows off on a gullible English mercer?"

" 'Twasn't the way of it. Lord Gui was merely trying to provide for his daughter through marriage to a man of means." Although his lordship had, of course, concealed his daughter's illegitimacy during the betrothal negotiations. By the time le Fever discovered it, he reasoned, the marriage would be consummated and the English mercer would be too enamored of his lovely and sweet-tempered young bride to raise any objections. As it turned out, he was wrong. "But no," Graeham added, "I knew naught of the matter until two weeks ago, when Lord Gui asked me to come here."

His lordship's eyes had been damp and red-rimmed when he'd summoned Graeham to his private chamber. *What I'm about to tell you,* he'd said unsteadily, *I've never revealed to a soul—at least not in Beauvais.* Nineteen years ago, while visiting friends in Paris, he'd had a brief liaison with a woman named Jeanne, whom he'd hired to make some new gowns for his wife. Never before had he strayed in his fidelity to his beloved Lady Christiana, but he found himself helpless to resist Jeanne's seductive charms. Nine months later, he received word that Jeanne had given birth to his twin daughters. Four years later, the dressmaker succumbed to an outbreak of typhoid, and Lord Gui made the girls wards of his brother, Canon Lotulf. Phillipa still lived with her uncle in Paris, where she had several suitors vying for her hand, although her studies consumed her complete interest. Ada was united with Rolf le Fever last year in a marriage that Lord Gui arranged, but that he had since come to regret deeply.

"His lordship must hold you in the highest esteem," le Fever said, "to have confided such a secret—and to entrust his daughter to your care for the journey back to Paris." What might have seemed like a compliment from another man struck Graeham as the most oily dissembling.

"I gather he was simply desperate," Graeham lied, ever-heedful of the strategic advantage of being underrated. In truth, Lord Gui considered Graeham by far his most trusted serjant, as skilled in diplomacy as in the combative arts, which was why the baron had chosen Graeham for the delicate task of spiriting his daughter away from her husband, employing whatever means necessary.

"Despite the circumstances of Mistress Ada's birth," Graeham said, "Lord Gui loves her—and her sister—as dearly as he loves his sons by Lady Christiana. He wants only what's best for them. If he erred in not revealing the circumstances of Mistress Ada's birth, he now deeply regrets it."

"He bloody well *should* regret it. He ruined my life, the lying cur. May he die of the bloody flux and roast in everlasting torment." The contemptible turd actually crossed himself.

Graeham held up the top letter from the stack. "Apparently you flew into quite the rage when your new bride admitted the truth of her birth."

"I damn near pitched her over the side of the boat. I daresay you'd have had the same reaction if you'd been hoodwinked as I was. And do you know the most galling part of it? There's absolutely nothing I can do. I can't annul the marriage—there are no grounds. And naturally I can't let it get out that my wife is the product of some sordid tryst in the back alleys of Paris. So I swallow my pride and carry on. Just as Lord Gui knew I would have to."

Quite right, Graeham thought, sympathizing reluctantly— but only fleetingly—with the bastard's dilemma.

"Ada is provided for," le Fever said, "and her reputation remains intact, as does Lord Gui's marriage to the blessedly oblivious Lady Christiana. The only one who suffers is me."

"And your wife." Choosing the second letter in the stack and setting the others on the table, Graeham unfolded it and read a portion aloud. " 'I despair, dearest Papa, over what will become of me in this marriage. I can bear it when he strikes me. Most husbands discipline their wives, do they not, and Rolf is really rather restrained in this respect, except when he is in his cups. It is his endless taunts and insults that wear me down. Yesterday he said, "No wonder the great Baron Gui de Beauvais was willing to wed his daughter into the merchant class and pack her off to England. You're the misbegotten spawn of some Paris whore. He was glad to be rid of you. Oh, that I could discard you so easily.' "

Graeham looked up and met le Fever's frigid gaze. "How often are you tempted to discard her, Master le Fever?"

The mercer smirked. "Is that it? The old man thinks I'm going to bring some sort of harm down on his precious daughter?"

Graeham refolded the letter and put it with the others. "Are you?"

"That, serjant, is none of your affair."

"Baron Gui de Beauvais has made it my affair. At best, your wife is miserable in this marriage. At worst, you do, indeed, intend some harm toward her."

Le Fever leapt to his feet, his teeth showing. "You've got some stones, coming into my home and accusing me of—"

"I'm accusing you of nothing. I'm merely conveying a father's concern for his daughter's welfare."

Le Fever's gaze sharpened on Graeham. "You're not here to escort her home for a visit," he said softly. "You came to take her away for good."

Graeham didn't bother to deny it. "I should think you'd be pleased to be rid of her, considering your feelings about the marriage."

Le Fever's eyes lit with a white-hot fury. "You propose to steal my wife out from under my roof, and I'm supposed to be *pleased* about it? How in bloody hell do you think that's going to look, for my wife to leave and never come back?"

"Ah, yes, appearances." Graeham sighed. "His lordship has authorized me to offer you fifty marks if you let her leave with me."

"He could offer me a thousand marks. Ten thousand. I'm not letting the bitch go. She knew what she was doing when she married me. Let her reap what she's sown."

"Master Rolf?" came a tenuous voice from the service stairwell.

Le Fever wheeled around to face the girl who stood there, a milky-skinned redhead of sixteen or so, dressed in a dark green, hooded mantle and a homely gray tunic, her brow furrowed. She might have been pretty had she not looked so cowed.

"Olive!" le Fever exclaimed. "What do you mean, sneaking in here this way?"

"I-I knocked at the back door," Olive said, looking back and forth between Graeham and the mercer, "but no one heard me. Your man is out back, currying the horses, and he said I could go on in." She shrugged helplessly and held up a phial of thick blue glass that contained a dark liquid. "I've brought today's tonic for Mistress Ada."

"Very well." Le Fever waved her upstairs. "Bring it up to her." He turned back to Graeham, still seated, as the young woman darted up the stairs. "Go back to that conniving whoreson who sent you here and tell him he's not getting his daughter back. He'll never see her again. She's mine now. He gave her to me. Now, get the hell out of here."

With lazy movements, as if he had all the time in the world, Graeham slid the fourth letter from the pile and unfolded it.

"Did you hear me?" le Fever sputtered, his beringed hands fisting at his sides. "Get out—or I'll have my manservant throw you out. Byram's quite the strapping beast, and good with his fists—I guarantee you'll come away from the experience bloodied."

" 'My husband makes no attempt to hide his numerous assignations with other women,' " Graeham said, reading from the letter. " 'Indeed, he boasts of his conquests to his man, Byram, within my hearing.' "

Le Fever crossed to a large window overlooking the stable yard. "Byram!"

"Yes, sire," came a man's deep-pitched voice from outside.

"Put Ebony back in his stall and come up here, will you? I need your help with something."

"Right away, sire."

Graeham resumed his reading of the letter. " 'Rolf seems proudest of his liaisons with the wives of the high-ranking men whose influence he so avidly courts. Perhaps seducing their wives makes him feel more like one of them. Recently I overheard him bragging to Byram that he had slept with

the wives of four of London's aldermen, including that of
our own ward, Fori.' " Graeham looked up from the letter.
"That would be Alderman John Huxley, would it not? Lord
Gui met Master John when he was studying in Paris—did
you know that?"

Two spots of pink bloomed on Rolf le Fever's cheeks.

Returning his attention to the letter, Graeham read,
" 'From what I can gather, Rolf has grown so bold as to
set his sights on the wife of the king's justiciar. Cool though
my feelings toward my husband have grown, I dread to
think what will come of him should it become known that
he has made cuckolds of so many important men.' " Graeham refolded the letter and replaced it on the stack. "I'd
say she makes an excellent point, wouldn't you? 'Twould
go badly for you should your wife's correspondence happen
to fall into the wrong hands."

Le Fever leaned out the window. "Byram, I . . . I don't
need you after all."

There came a pause. "Are you sure, Master—"

"Yes, damn it, I'm sure. Go back to your work." Le
Fever's expression when he turned back to Graeham was
murderous. "You blackmailing bastard. Let me see those
letters."

"You've got the 'bastard' part right," Graeham replied
as he handed le Fever the bundle of letters. "As for blackmail, it needn't come to that."

"I daresay it needn't." With an expression of triumph,
the mercer flung the sheets of parchment into the fire. "It
seems they really do call you 'Fox' for your hair and not
your cleverness. So glad to find I misjudged you."

"Ah, but you didn't," Graeham admitted with a mild
smile. "Those were copies. I penned them myself before
leaving Beauvais. The originals are locked up safely in his
lordship's private chamber."

Le Fever sank into his chair, his face as white as bleached
bone. "The fox has set quite a cunning little trap of his
own, it seems. That's it, then. If I don't let Ada go, you
ruin me."

"Will it ease the sting any," Graeham said, "to know
that Lord Gui instructed me to give you the fifty marks

regardless of your cooperation? I told him he was too generous by far."

"I've been in trade long enough to know that such generosity doesn't come without conditions."

"You're to refrain from discussing Mistress Ada with anyone, ever, especially in ways that may reflect badly on her. In particular, you are to keep your counsel as regards the circumstances of her birth."

"I'm hardly eager to advertise those circumstances, I assure you. But fifty marks isn't enough. I want more."

"It's all I brought with me, and it's fifty marks more than you deserve. Take it or leave it."

A muscle spasmed in le Fever's jaw. "Give it to me, then."

"The prior of St. Bartholomew's is safeguarding it for me. You'll get it when I come back to collect Mistress Ada." Graeham stood. "I'll return this evening at compline."

"She'll be packed and ready." As le Fever rose, he squinted at something in the corner. Graeham turned to find the young woman who'd brought the tonic, Olive, lurking in the service stairwell. "How long have you been standing there?"

"I just . . . I'm sorry, sire. But Mum, she'll light into me something awful if I come back to the shop again without the tuppence for the tonic."

Glowering, le Fever dug two silver pennies out of the purse on his belt and hurled them at the girl. She squealed and covered her face; the coins bounced on the clay floor and rolled away.

"Jesu!" le Fever bit out.

"I'm sorry," Olive muttered, dropping to her hands and knees to scramble after the money. "I'm sorry, Master Rolf. I'm so clumsy."

She found one of the pennies under a chair. Graeham picked up the other, which had come to rest near his feet, and handed it to her. She accepted it with murmured thanks, blushing when he took her hand and helped her to her feet.

"Do you work for the apothecary?" Graeham asked her.
The girl nodded. "I'm her apprentice. She's me mum."

"If she were to make up a week's worth of tonic for Mistress Ada, would it keep that long?"

"Aye. We brew it up in four-pinte batches that last longer than that. Just mind you don't let it get too warm, and it'll keep just fine."

"Good." Graeham untied his purse and counted fourteen pennies into her hand, then added another four for good measure. He could well afford to be generous—or rather, Lord Gui could, for this was the baron's money, provided to cover Graeham's expenses in returning his daughter to him. "There's a shilling and a half. That should more than cover it. See that you have the medicine here by compline."

"Yes, sir. It'll be here, sir. Good day, sir."

"Good day."

After she left, a disconcerting thought occurred to Graeham. "Your wife," he said to lo Fever, "how ill is she? She *is* well enough to travel, isn't she?"

The guildmaster gave him a look of smug contempt. "The way I see it, that's entirely your problem now. As of compline, I wash my hands of her."

Chapter 2

The sun hung low in the sky, gilding the thatched roofs of London, when Graeham returned to West Cheap on the sorrel stallion he'd purchased in Dover, his saddlebags heavy with silver for Rolf le Fever. Having given it some thought, he'd decided not to bring along the chestnut palfrey he'd acquired for Mistress Ada. If she was seriously ill, it would be safer for her to ride pillion behind him. It was either that or a litter, and he didn't know where he'd find a proper one on such short notice.

Graeham couldn't help wondering what Ada le Fever would look like. The baron hadn't described his twin daughters except as "angelic beauties with exceedingly temperate dispositions." Of course, Ada's long illness might have taken a toll on her appearance. Graeham cautioned himself not to be dismayed if she struck him as less than comely. After all, it wasn't Ada he was betrothed to, but Phillipa.

Almost betrothed to. It wouldn't be official until he returned Ada safely to Paris. Then would come the reward Lord Gui had promised him—Lady Phillipa's hand in marriage and a generous holding. Best of all, an English holding, and one of the baron's finest estates—fifteen hides of fertile farmland and rolling pastures just outside of Oxford.

Graeham had been stunned when Lord Gui had offered such a princely reward—especially as regarded the betrothal to his daughter—but he'd known better than to question it, lest his lordship start entertaining second thoughts. For a man of Graeham's modest background, it was the opportunity of a lifetime—land of his own and

marriage to a beautiful woman of temperate disposition.
Phillipa's illegitimacy troubled him not at all, for it was a
curse he lived with himself. Perhaps their shared baseborn
status would even enhance their compatibility.

What would it be like, he wondered, after a lifetime of
never really belonging anywhere, of always being alone, to
have a home and family of his own? How would it feel,
after years of forgettable couplings with serving wenches
and laundresses, to take his ease night after night in the
arms of the same woman, to see her grow great with his
child, to watch her hair gradually turn to silver as the
years passed?

Soon would come his opportunity to find out. All he had
to do was return Ada le Fever to her father. The Devil
himself couldn't stop him; Rolf le Fever hadn't stood a
chance.

Graeham turned onto Milk Street, guiding his mount
around gaps in the crumbling Roman paving stones. From
his boyhood in London, he recalled perhaps a dozen such
old paved lanes among the complex network of dirt roads
that filled the square mile within the city walls. He walked
his horse gingerly across a section that was mostly rubble,
the stones having been torn up to build the house next to
le Fever's.

Except for the Church of St. Mary Magdalene and that
house, all the dwellings and shops on Milk Street were of
thatch-roofed timber, although Rolf le Fever's was, by far,
the most conspicuous. Of course, this part of West Cheap
was the hub of London's silk trade, which was overseen by
le Fever as guildmaster. He was the most important man
for blocks around; why shouldn't he have the biggest, most
ostentatious house? Still . . . painted in garish red and blue,
its portico supported by intricately carved posts, the rest
ornamented with fancy moldings and beams, it struck Graeham as the home of a man who'd gotten too rich too fast.

Eyeing the window of the third-floor solar as he rode
toward the house, Graeham fancied he saw someone sitting
there, silhouetted against yellowish lamplight. Ada le
Fever? He hoped she was packed and ready, as promised,
for he didn't have that long to get her to St. Bartholemew's,
where he'd secured a place for her in the women's guest

quarters. Once night had fully fallen, the churches would ring curfew and the city gates would be locked until dawn. It was well that Lord Gui had steered Graeham to St. Bartholemew's. Not only did the hostelry accommodate women as well as men, but the priory maintained a splendid hospital—although he hoped Ada wouldn't need it. The sooner they could manage the journey to Paris, the better.

As he approached the house, Graeham noticed a burly, baldheaded man in a russet tunic leaning against the tall stone wall that enclosed the front part of Rolf le Fever's property, absently whittling a chunk of wood with a large knife. When he looked up and saw Graeham, he tossed the wood aside. "Graeham Fox?"

"Aye." Graeham reined in his mount.

"I been waitin' for ye, Master le Fever, he said as how you were to come round back for his wife. Says he don't want the whole neighborhood to see her leavin' with the likes of you." He shrugged apologetically.

"Are you Byram?"

The fellow shoved his knife back in its sheath. "That's right. This way, then." Pushing off the wall, Byram motioned for Graeham to follow him into an alley adjacent to le Fever's house. "You might want to dismount. It gets a mite tight in there before you get to the back of the house."

Graeham got down off his horse, his soldierly suspicion of anything irregular raising his hackles. Alert and wary, he led his mount into the alley, a dirt path about a yard and a half wide that connected Milk Street to the street just west of it—Wood Street, as Graeham recalled. Cast into shadow by the buildings to either side, the passageway was dim and littered with debris. The sorrel stallion snorted anxiously.

About halfway down, the right-hand side of the alley opened up into what looked to be a common rear croft of packed earth shared by the houses on Wood Street, from which access could be gained to Rolf le Fever's stable yard via a gate in the low stone wall surrounding it. The croft was deserted for the supper hour, save for a few chickens and pigs in scattered pens. The alley, shaded by dwellings whose upper levels were built out awkwardly over the lower, grew even darker and narrower as it approached Wood Street.

"Where are you going?" Graeham asked as Byram walked past the gate to le Fever's stable yard.

Byram turned around, his gaze shifting from Graeham to something out of sight behind le Fever's stable.

Graeham spun around, unsheathing his dagger as two men—one of them gigantic—emerged from behind the stable. The smaller one seized the horse's reins, while the giant swung a long-handled sledgehammer at Graeham's head. Graeham ducked beneath the sledge, rolled, leapt up. He grabbed his attacker's tangled black beard to hold him still and drove the dagger deep into his belly. The bastard grunted. Without so much as a pause to catch his breath, he jerked away and whipped the sledge around, smacking Graeham in the ribs and sending him sprawling onto the hard-packed dirt.

"Shit, Dougal," Byram gasped at his companion. "Are ye all right?"

Dougal looked down at the horn handle of Graeham's dagger protruding from his belly and shrugged.

As Graeham struggled to sit up, his teeth clenched against the dull pain in his side, he saw his horse being led swiftly down the alley toward Wood Street. *"No!"* He reached into his boot for his spare weapon, a little razor-sharp dirk—for all the good it would do. He was outnumbered, and by brutes who could clearly take a bit of punishment.

As Graeham braced himself to rise, Byram knelt over him, knife in hand. Grabbing a fistful of Graeham's hair, Byram yanked his head back and pressed the giant blade to his neck. "Say hello to the Devil for me, Fox."

"Say it yourself." Graeham aimed his dirk at Byram's throat, but the bastard saw it coming and recoiled; the blade opened a bloody gash across his cheek and chin instead. Byram dropped his knife, swearing rawly.

Keeping a firm grip on the dirk, Graeham reached for the knife, but Dougal stepped on his hand, immobilizing him and all but crushing his fingers. Graeham drew back his foot, encased in a wooden-soled riding boot, and kicked the giant in the groin.

Bellowing like a bear, Dougal slammed the sledge with a jolting crunch on Graeham's left shin. Pain ignited in a searing explosion, racing like Greek fire along his nerves. A roar that must have come from his own throat reverberated in the alley.

From a window somewhere, a man yelled, "Pipe down out there! I'm tryin' to eat me supper!"

Graeham uncurled himself, sucking air, and tried once again to get up, but his lower leg had been smashed; it wouldn't support him.

Byram, using his tunic sleeve to blot his bleeding face, kicked Graeham in his broken ribs. To Dougal he said, "Finish him off and let's get out of here."

Dougal, the dagger still sticking out of his belly, stood over Graeham. His gaze narrowed on Graeham's head as he took aim. He raised the sledgehammer high.

Gripping his little dirk by its ivory handle, Graeham flicked it toward Dougal's massive neck. It stuck there, quivering. Dougal blinked and slowly lowered the sledge.

"Jesus, Dougal," Byram murmured, gaping as the big man patted the dirk's ivory handle curiously. "Give me that." Byram yanked the sledge out of Dougal's grip and took aim at Graeham's skull. Graeham rolled aside as the sledge descended, embedding itself harmlessly in the dirt.

The big knife was once again close at hand, and Graeham grabbed it. Groaning in pain, he holstered himself against the wall behind him and pulled himself to his feet as Byram yanked the sledge free and wheeled on him.

"Good evening, gentlemen." Graeham and his two assailants turned to find a man—flaxen-haired, lean, and long-limbed—striding toward them from the direction of Wood Street. From the tooled scabbard on his belt, he withdrew a gleaming steel sword. "Mind if I play?"

Byram and Dougal looked at each other.

"Because it strikes me you haven't really got enough competitors." He spoke like a nobleman, and there was that handsome sword—although his leather tunic and woollen chausses were worn and dirt-smudged. A wineskin and satchel hung across his chest. "Two against one—that hardly seems sporting, does it? What do you say I even things up?"

"Bugger yourself," Dougal growled, even as he stumbled back against the wall, nudged by the stranger's sword.

"If I could figure out how, I'd probably give it a go." With a nod toward the horn handle emerging from Dougal's stomach, he said, "That smarts, I'll wager. But I've seen men take a knife in the stomach, pull it out, and snap back good as new within days."

"Hunh." Dougal regarded the dagger with an expression of relief.

"The one in your throat's a bit trickier, though. If you take that one out, blood will start pumping from you like a fountain, and it won't stop till you're dead as a stone. Just thought you should know."

Dougal looked at him with slack-jawed dismay.

"On the positive side, it's a very quick death. And not too painful, as these things go."

"He's lying," Byram said.

Dougal turned and started lumbering back up the alley toward Milk Street, crossing himself and muttering softly under his breath.

"Come back here!" Byram screamed. "Damn your eyes, Dougal, he's making it all up! Come back here!" He shook the sledge menacingly. "Get away from here before I smash your brains in."

Ignoring the threat, the stranger tilted Byram's chin up with the tip of his sword and inspected the laceration on his face. "I hope you're already married, because no wench wants a man with a scar like that." To Graeham, he said, "Your handiwork?"

Graeham nodded, shaking all over as he strained to stay on his feet. "I was going for his throat."

"Were you? I've found the best way to cut a man's throat is to plant the blade firmly, right about here"—he pressed the edge of his sword against Byram's throat—"and then just sweep it across, like so." He made an abrupt slashing movement.

Byram yelped and dropped the sledge. The stranger kicked it toward Graeham, who made no attempt to lean down and pick it up, suspecting he would pass out if he did so. "Hands in the air, then."

Byram spat out a few ripe Anglo-Saxon curses but complied.

"I'm going to send for one of the sheriffs and have your miserable arse hauled off to gaol," the stranger said.

"Let him go," Graeham said.

"What? Why?"

Because Graeham had sworn to Lord Gui that he would proceed with the utmost discretion, revealing to no one—save le Fever himself—his true reason for being in London, lest it become known that the baron was Ada le Fever's father. Getting the constabulary involved would open a Pandora's box of inquiry that could expose the secret his lordship had striven for so many years to protect. Besides, any investigation into the "robbery" was pointless. Graeham had a fairly good notion that Rolf le Fever was behind the attack, the point of which had been to relieve him not just of his silver but of his life as well. Le Fever, fearful for his precious reputation, most likely never had any intention of relinquishing his wife to Graeham. But he wanted those fifty marks.

Graeham still had every intention of bringing her back to Paris, of course. Not only was her delivery from the likes of Rolf le Fever a just cause, but Graeham's very future rode on it. Somehow, despite his injuries and le Fever's defiance, he would manage to execute his mission—but without the dubious assistance of the sheriff of London.

Thinking as quickly as he could, given his throbbing leg, Graeham said, "This mongrel's not worth the trouble of bringing him up on charges. We'd have to give statements, testify at the sheriff's court, all that bloody nonsense—just so they can deal him a few lashes and toss him out onto the street again. 'Tisn't worth it."

He must have been convincing, because after a moment's thought, the stranger stepped back from Byram and said, "Why don't you go find your friend and help him get that knife out of his throat?"

Byram hesitated, casting an anxious glance in Graeham's direction—troubled, perhaps, at leaving unfinished business—then turned and sprinted down the alley toward Milk Street.

Graeham shoved the knife under his belt, then slumped

to the ground, gripping his leg and cursing like a sailor. The crisscrossed thong that secured the leather legging was stretched taut over his bulging shin, which thudded with pain.

The stranger sheathed his sword and squatted next to Graeham, frowning at his leg. His right earlobe, Graeham saw, was pierced by a small gold ring etched with an exotic design. Graeham had once seen an infidel in a turban walking down the rue de la Lanterne in Paris who had an earring like that.

"Is it broken?" the stranger asked.

Graeham nodded. "Rather badly, I suspect. I can't tell too much with it wrapped up this way."

"Don't unwrap it. 'Twill act as a splint till you can get a proper one from a surgeon. Is that all they did to you?"

"They cracked a few of my ribs. But they would have done the same thing to my head if you hadn't shown up when you did. I'm Graeham Fox, by the way. And I owe you a debt of thanks."

"Hugh of Wexford—and I'm the one who should be thankful. 'Twas the best sport I've had all week."

"Will that fellow really bleed to death when he takes the dirk out of his neck?"

Hugh grinned and shrugged. "I've no idea. I made that up."

"It sounded good."

"I thought so. Come." Hugh stood up and hauled a woozy and pain-racked Graeham to his feet, pressing the four-foot shaft of the sledgehammer into his trembling hand. "This should serve fairly well as a cane. Let's get you inside where you can lie down."

"Inside?" Graeham rested most of his weight on the sledge, but Hugh aided him with a hand under his arm.

"This is my sister's house," Hugh said, patting the earth-and-straw wall against which Graeham had been leaning. "I was on my way here for a visit when I saw a rather mangy cur leading a handsome sorrel stallion out of this alley."

"A handsome sorrel stallion with fifty marks in his saddlebags," Graeham said, as Hugh guided Graeham's torturous little hopping steps into the rear croft and around to the back of the house—one of a long row of attached two-story dwellings facing Wood Street. Outbuildings dotted the croft; a privy shed had been built against the back wall of Hugh's sister's house, and in the shadow of a tree behind it stood a stone hut, which probably housed a kitchen. She had a little garden plot, bare of plants this early in the spring, but no livestock.

"Fifty marks!" Hugh let out a long, low whistle from between his teeth. "Rotten luck, falling prey to robbers when you've got a fortune like that on you."

Rotten luck had nothing to do with it, Graeham thought, *and one of those "robbers" just happens to be manservant to the master of the Mercers' Guild.*

Hugh pounded his fist on the oaken back door of his sister's home. "Joanna! Joanna, it's me, Hugh. Open up." He tugged on the latchstring trailing from a hole in the door; from inside came the metallic scrape of the bolt being lifted. Pulling the door open, he called down a narrow hallway, "Joanna?" No sound came from within. "She must not be home. Come on in, but step carefully here—it's a sunken floor."

Hugh escorted Graeham down the hallway, which opened into a humbly furnished living chamber with a ladder in the corner leading upstairs. The rushes that blanketed the floor of this modest salle smelled fresh. In the middle of a rough-hewn table flanked by benches sat a sort of poor man's oil lamp—a lump of fat in a clay dish with a burning rush in it—which cast a wavering corona of light. Two deep little iron-barred windows looked out onto the alley; a white cat observed them dispassionately from the ledge of one.

"That imperious creature is Petronilla," Hugh said. "Her brother's around here somewhere. Manfrid—he's the timid type. With the exception of Joanna, he's terrified of people—especially men. There's usually a dog or two in residence, but not at the moment, apparently. Where's your mum, Petronilla?"

Petronilla turned to look out the window.

"Joanna lit that lamp," Hugh observed, "so she must not have left that long ago. The sun has just set."

Through a wide, arched doorway Graeham could see a

small front room—a shop stall, for next to the door that led to the street was an enormous window with horizontal shutters, now bolted shut. Near this window stood a large rectangular embroidery frame laid flat on trestles, on which a length of sky-blue silk, partially stitched in vines and flowers, was stretched taut by means of lacings around the edges.

Noticing the direction of Graeham's gaze, Hugh said, "Joanna's husband is a mercer. He imports silk and they sell it out of the shop—or rather, she does. He enjoys the buying, but he can't bear the peddling."

Graeham nodded politely, straining for composure despite the howling pain in his leg. "You mentioned someplace to lie down . . . ?"

"Right in here." Hugh pushed a leather curtain aside and helped Graeham to limp into a tiny back room with no rushes to obscure the floor of beaten chalk. By the dusky twilight filtering in through the windows, Graeham made out various chests and sacks and implements, as well as some bolts of jewel-toned silk and a few small baskets on a bench. A narrow cot stood against the back wall.

"Who sleeps here?" Graeham grunted in pain as he lowered himself onto the linen-covered mattress of crackling straw and stretched out, searching for the position that was least agonizing for his leg.

"Prewitt." Hugh punched a limp feather pillow and shoved it under Graeham's head.

"Who's that—the apprentice?"

"The husband—Prewitt Chapman. They don't have an apprentice. Here." Dumping his satchel on the floor, Hugh handed Graeham his wineskin. "Have some of this—'twill ease the pain and warm you up. You're shivering."

Graeham gratefully uncorked the skin and squeezed some wine into his mouth, not bothering to sit up. He was tempted to ask why the master of the house had to make do with a cot in the storeroom when there was apparently a solar upstairs, but it would ill repay his new friend's hospitality to start prying into private family affairs. "Won't your brother-in-law be a bit put out to find his bed commandeered by a complete stranger?"

"Prewitt only sleeps here when he's in town. He spends most of his time abroad, buying silks."

"Is that where he is now?"

"I couldn't say. This is my first visit to Joanna in almost a year." Hugh shook out a woollen blanket that had been folded at the foot of the bed and covered Graeham with it. "You rest here. I'm going to go get you a surgeon."

"Is there one in the neighborhood?"

"I seem to recall seeing a shop with a red-and-white-striped pole out front up toward Cripplegate."

After Hugh left, Graeham set himself to the task of draining the wineskin in the hope of inducing a state of numb oblivion before the surgeon arrived. Having held down screaming men more than once while their cracked bones were shoved back into place, he reckoned he'd rather not be in full command of his senses for the procedure.

Time swam; night fell. Just as Graeham realized the wineskin was empty, he heard a door open and close; the sound came not from the back of the house, where he was, but from the front. From his position, he could see through the open storeroom doorway into the lamplit salle and beyond that to the darkened shopfront. A shadowy figure in a hooded mantle moved through the shop. Graeham was about to call Hugh's name when he realized this person was smaller than Hugh—and wearing a lady's kirtle.

The woman—Hugh's sister, no doubt—entered the salle, hung her mantle on a peg and placed a parchment-wrapped bundle on the central table. Drunk as Graeham was, it was taxing to keep her in focus. She was tall for a woman, though not excessively so. He saw that she wore a plain blue kirtle with no overtunic; her hair was concealed beneath a white scarf twisted and tucked around her head, a few golden brown tendrils having escaped at her nape; keys and various small tools jangled on the chatelaine hanging from her embroidered girdle.

The cat jumped off the windowsill and joined another—a large black-and-white tom—in rubbing against its mistress's skirts. One of them yowled something that sounded like "Now."

She chuckled. "It's eel turnovers you smell, but you must wait till I've eaten my fill before you get yours." Her voice sounded young and had a scratchy quality to it that was not unpleasant.

Graeham knew he ought to announce his presence. He raised himself onto an elbow, groaning when things spun sickeningly.

He heard a sharp gasp. The woman stilled, staring into the darkened storeroom with wide, unblinking eyes. "Who's there?" she called out in a quavering voice.

"Don't be afraid," Graeham muttered thickly as he collapsed back onto the cot, squeezing his eyes shut against another wave of drunken disorientation. He heard the rushes rustling beneath her feet; the footsteps grew closer.

"Get out."

He opened his eyes, squinting at her as she stood over him holding an enormous axe with both hands, its blade aimed at his head.

"Did you hear me?" she demanded shakily. "Get out of my house this instant, or I'll split your skull open where you lie."

Chapter 3

❧

"I can explain," the intruder said, his words slurred, a hand raised as if to ward off the blow of her axe. Another drunken vagrant trying to find refuge in her home; she really must get better about locking up when she left the place unattended.

"Get out!" Joanna repeated, cursing her wavering voice; she knew better than to let one of these street rats sense her fear. But he was such a big man—his booted feet, emerging from beneath the blanket in which he was wrapped, extended past the foot of Prewitt's bed—and his face was grimy, and he stank of wine. His drunkenness would only stoke his capacity for violence. If he leapt at her, she must be prepared to strike back, and hard.

"Mistress . . ." he began.

"Get up!" she ordered, brandishing the axe. "Go! I'll use this, so help me God I will."

He took her measure with oddly unruffled calm, his eyes glowing like blue fire in the semidarkness. "No, you won't," he said quietly, sounding almost sober. "You couldn't. Your hands are shaking." He lifted himself on an elbow.

Joanna backed up a step, holding the axe before her like a talisman. Was he preparing to leave . . . or to attack? "My husband's due home any moment now," she lied. Thinking that might not be enough to discourage him, given his size, she added, "And my brother is with him. Hugh's a master swordsman. He'll run you through if he finds you here."

She saw amusement in his eyes, and something else that might, under different circumstances, have almost looked like compassion. "Actually, 'twas Hugh who brought me here."

"What?"

"Aye, he—"

"Liar. You just want me to let my guard down. Hugh's not even in London. He's off fighting in the Rhineland."

The bastard's mouth quirked. "If your brother's not even in London, how could he possibly be on his way here with your husband?"

Joanna cursed inwardly; she'd never been adept at lying. "My . . . my husband *is* coming."

"I don't think so. If he were, you'd leave right now and let *him* oust me instead of trying to do it yourself. He's not in London either, is he? No one's coming. You're all alone."

"Get out of here!" She advanced on him, the axe at the ready, keeping toward the foot of the cot so he couldn't make a grab for her.

"Mistress . . ."

"Get up! Go on!" Flipping the axe in her hands, she whacked him on the legs with its handle.

"Fuck!" He contracted into a ball, clutching his legs. *"Oh, shit! Fuck! Shit!"*

Joanna backed up swiftly to the doorway, unnerved by his reaction.

He growled a torrent of ragged expletives before sinking, ashen-faced and quivering, onto the cot. "By the blood of the saints, mistress," he rasped. "Did you have to do that?"

"If you don't leave right now," she blustered, "I'll do it again."

"If I could walk, I'd leave," he said breathlessly. "My leg is broken."

She narrowed her gaze on him. "You're lying."

He pushed back the blanket. "My left leg. And one or two ribs, I think."

Joanna fetched her makeshift oil lamp from the salle, careful not to turn her back on her uninvited guest. Holding her axe in one hand and the lamp in the other, she winced to see that his left leg below the knee was grossly swollen beneath the leathern legging.

"I really did come here with Hugh," he said wearily. "He

went off to find a surgeon for me. That's his satchel over there." He nodded toward a leather bag in the corner.

Holding the lamp over it, Joanna recognized it as her brother's. He must have returned from the Rhineland. Thank God; every time he went off on another far-flung military campaign, she feared she'd never see him again. She dreaded the day one of his comrades showed up at her door to give her his personal effects—or perhaps there would be no one to attend to such niceties and she would never find out what became of him.

"How do I know you didn't steal that satchel from him?" Joanna asked, her confidence faltering. "Perhaps he broke your leg trying to defend himself."

"I was attacked in the alley next door. They took my horse and a good deal of my overlord's silver—but not all of it, thank the saints." He patted the kidskin purse hanging from his belt. "Your brother came to my assistance and brought me here. He said your name was Joanna. You have a cat named"—he frowned as if trying to remember—"Pieretta? No, Petronilla. And she has a brother who's shy, but I can't remember his name. Your husband is a silk merchant who spends most of his time abroad. He sleeps down here instead of . . ." He looked away awkwardly.

Heat bloomed in Joanna's cheeks.

The man on the cot said, "That's all I can remember of what he told me. I don't know what else I can say to convince you. I know you're afraid of me and you don't want me here. As soon as your brother comes back, I'll leave— I just can't make it out of here on my own."

Joanna regarded him for a long, thoughtful moment. He met her gaze steadily, although it seemed he was having trouble focusing on her. His face, beneath its smudges of dirt and half-grown beard, was the face of a young man, carved with distinguished planes and an appealing symmetry. There was something earnest and direct about his eyes, despite the drunkenness that made them waver slightly. True, his brown riding tunic was filthy, but it was a tunic of good quality—as were his belt and boots.

"Who are you?" she asked.

"They call me Graeham Fox. I'm an Englishman, but I serve as serjant to a Norman baron."

Joanna set the axe and lamp on the bench. "What brings you to London?"

He turned his head on the pillow, raking a hand through his lank hair. A gold signet ring glimmered on his index finger. "I was just passing through on my way to visit . . . kinsmen."

"Where are they?"

After a moment's pause, he said, "Oxfordshire."

"How did you happen to find yourself in West Cheap?" She moved a little closer to the bed.

"I was looking for an inn."

"Most of the public inns are outside the city walls."

"I didn't want to have to worry about being out and about when they locked the gates at curfew."

Joanna contemplated his distended leg uneasily. "That must hurt."

"The wine helped . . . for a while." Until she'd hit him with that axe handle.

"I'm sorry."

He smiled disarmingly. "You handled yourself rather well, I thought. I was impressed."

She couldn't help but return his smile. "Are you hungry? I bought two eel turnovers at the cookshop. You may have one if you'd like."

He shook his head. "I fear I'd never keep it down after all that wine. Thanks all the same."

The back door opened. Joanna heard footsteps and the voices of men advancing down the hallway adjacent to the storeroom; one of the voices belonged to Hugh. She rose and met him in the doorway.

"Joanna!" Hugh lifted her off her feet and swung her around. "I've missed you."

"I've missed you, too." She kissed him on his scratchy cheek, noting with an indulgent smile that he still wore that heathen earring. "And I've been worried about you. Thank God you're home."

"For the present," he said carefully.

Her mood, so swiftly elevated, plummeted abruptly. "Of course. For the present." She nodded toward Graeham Fox, watching them from the cot. "Still bringing home strays for me to fix, I see."

Chuckling, Hugh told Graeham, "She never could resist a creature in need. How are you?"

"Reeling drunk."

"Glad to hear it."

Someone cleared his throat. Hugh stepped aside to let a stocky man of advanced years enter the storeroom.

"Joanna," Hugh said, "do you know Master Aldfrith?"

"By sight and reputation."

Joanna attempted to introduce Aldfrith to Graeham Fox, but the surgeon interrupted her with a brusque string of commands. "More light! Clean water! And clean linen, if you've got it." He shook his head disgustedly. "Wish I had my assistants with me, but they're in Southwark tonight, squandering their pay at the stews and most likely catching the pox in the bargain. You two will have to do."

Hugh lit a horn lantern off the oil lamp and hung it from a ceiling beam while Joanna fetched a bucket of water from the communal well out back. She produced two clean linen sheets and handed them over to Master Aldfrith, reflecting uncharitably that they'd be ruined now and she could ill afford to replace them.

The surgeon sent Hugh to the table in the salle to tear the sheets into long strips and ordered Joanna to undress the patient.

"Pardon me?"

"Boots, leggings, tunic, shirt," Aldfrith elaborated as he donned a leather apron. "Off. He may keep his drawers on." He arched an eyebrow at her hesitation. "Come now. A maiden might blush at such a task, but you're a married woman—or was I misinformed?"

The serjant was observing her with quiet interest. Scalding heat rose in her cheeks.

"I can do it myself," Graeham said, grimacing as he tried to sit up.

"Lie still!" Aldfrith barked as he pulled surgical tools out of his bag and laid them out on the low storage chest next to the cot. "You'll only worsen your injuries."

"He's right," Joanna said, unsure why she'd balked at the request and feeling like a fool for having done so. "You shouldn't be exerting yourself. And I don't mind—really." She leaned over the foot of the cot and unlaced Graeham's left boot; he hitched in a breath when she pulled it off, although she strove to be gentle. The right boot came next, and then she moved around to his side and studied the thong that bound the sheet of leather around his left leg.

"It's tied off up here." Graeham gathered up his knee-length tunic to expose the top of the legging, a short expanse of densely muscled thigh, and the hem of his linen underdrawers.

"Right, then." Joanna tugged at the thong, which had been knotted off and tucked under itself, but the swelling had apparently spread up his leg, because the narrow strip of leather wouldn't budge. She plucked futilely at the knot, all too aware of her hands grazing his bare thigh in an inadvertent caress, the hair there tickling her fingers, and of him watching her with his heavy-lidded, strangely intent gaze. Her skin felt prickly all over, as if it were suddenly too small for her.

"Perhaps you should just cut it off," he said.

"Ah, yes. All right." Joanna retrieved her little dagger from its sheath on her girdle, slid it beneath the thong and severed it. She unwound it carefully, so as not to jostle Graeham, and then peeled away the leather wrapping. Beneath it he wore a woollen stocking, tightly stretched over his lower leg, and this she cautiously snipped away with the embroidery shears attached to her chatelaine.

"Sweet Jesus," she whispered when she saw his shin. It was misshapen where the bone had snapped, the flesh inflamed and mottled with blue-black bruising.

"Hmph." Aldfrith paused in his preparations to peer at the damaged leg. "At least the bone didn't break the skin. I can put these away." He repacked several hellish-looking knives and a saw.

The relief on Graeham's face more than matched her own. Working swiftly, she divested him of the other legging as he unbuckled and set aside his belt. Between them, they managed to wrestle him out of his tunic and shirt. His left side was swollen in the area of the lower ribs, the only imperfection on a torso that was otherwise the epitome of masculine grace and power. His shoulders were wide and packed with muscle, his belly lean, his hips narrow beneath his loose linen drawers. When he raised a hand to push the unruly hair off his face, bands of muscle flexed and contracted in his arms. It was all Joanna could do to keep from gaping at the man.

Hugh came in with his strips of linen, one of which Aldfrith used to bind Graeham's broken ribs, a swift and seemingly painless operation. The rest he placed on the cot next to Graeham, along with two slender ash boards the length of a man's leg, lined with sheepskin.

"How long will it take to set the leg?" Joanna asked.

"Not long for the actual setting," Aldfrith replied. "Most of the time is spent securing the splints. I need someone strong"—he pointed to Hugh—"that would be you, to help me reposition the bone. Normally I like a couple of sturdy men to hold a patient down for this. Perhaps there are some fellows in the neighborhood who'd be willing—"

"No one needs to hold me down," Graeham said, hiking himself up on an elbow.

"Lie still!" Aldfrith commanded.

Graeham obeyed with a grudging lack of grace. "I don't need to be held down. I won't move."

Aldfrith smirked. "You don't think so now, but wait till we start realigning those bones. You'll be thrashing and screaming like you were on fire."

"I'll be fine," he insisted. "Just do it."

The surgeon shook his head, smiling indulgently. "While I admire your optimism, serjant, you really can't imagine—"

"Do it."

Scowling, Aldfrith motioned Joanna toward the head of the bed. "Hold his shoulders down."

Graeham struggled to sit up again. "I said—"

"Consider it a compromise," Aldfrith said mildly. "A sop to appease a grumpy old surgeon. I daresay you could toss her off like a gnat if you were so inclined."

"And it will give me something to do," Joanna said, "besides standing about wringing my hands." She caught Graeham's eye and smiled beseechingly.

Grim-faced, he looked at the ceiling. "Fine."

She sat on the edge of the bed behind his head and tentatively rested her hands on his shoulders; they felt like warm rock beneath her palms.

Aldfrith briefed Hugh as to what was expected of him, then lifted Graeham's leg while Hugh slid one of the splints beneath it. Graeham let out a pent-up breath as his leg settled onto the fleece-lined board.

The two men positioned themselves above and below the fracture, their hands wrapped firmly around Graeham's leg. "Ready?" the surgeon asked.

Hugh nodded. Joanna pressed as hard as she could on Graeham's shoulders.

"Now."

A low, strangled groan rose from Graeham's throat as the two men leaned into their work. He squeezed his eyes shut, bared his teeth, arched his back.

"It won't take long," Joanna promised in a trembling voice. She eased up on his shoulders when it became clear he could keep himself still, as promised. Smoothing stray tendrils of hair off his forehead, she said, "Ride it out."

"Pull harder," the surgeon ordered.

Graeham swore between his teeth, whipped both hands up to grab Joanna's wrists. She slipped her hands into his and squeezed. " 'Twill be over soon."

Graeham's lungs pumped like a bellows; his face was darkly flushed.

Leaning down, Joanna whispered into his ear, "You're very brave. You're doing very well."

He might have smiled, or perhaps it was just a grimace.

"Perfect," announced the surgeon, slightly out of breath. "Or as near as we're likely to get it. Let's have the other splint."

Hugh placed the second board on top of Graeham's leg and held the two splints together while Aldfrith wrapped the strips of linen tightly around them. The surgeon worked with practiced, economical movements, yet still it seemed to take forever. Graeham lay with his eyes closed, his face pale as wax and sheened with sweat. The fierce grip with which he held Joanna's hands did not let up.

"That's it, then," the surgeon announced at long last. Sitting back, he admired Graeham Fox's splinted leg. "Not bad, considering I had amateur help. You've done this before, haven't you?" he asked Hugh.

"Once or twice, but it was sloppy work on the battlefield. I doubt those fellows ever walked properly again."

"Our fearless and stoical serjant will walk properly," Aldfrith promised as he untied his apron, "providing he stays off that leg for two months, with complete bed rest in the beginning, only gradually adding—"

"Two months!" Graeham exclaimed, letting go of Joanna's hands and trying to sit up.

"Lie still!" Aldfrith shouted. "Do you want to ruin my beautiful work?"

"I can't stay off my feet for two months. I have to . . . I have a matter of great urgency to attend to."

"You can write to your family in Oxfordshire," Joanna said, "and let them know you'll be delayed."

"Nay," he groaned, covering his face with his hands. "You don't understand. I can't explain."

"I'll be happy to write the letter for you," she offered diplomatically.

"I can write," he said. " 'Tisn't that. It's just . . ." He shook his head. "Bloody hell. Two bloody months."

"Possibly three," Aldfrith said. "Or even more. It all depends on how quickly those bones knit. The more rested you keep yourself, the quicker you'll heal."

Graeham muttered something under his breath that Joanna was just as happy not to hear.

"Don't take the splints off," the surgeon said as he closed up his bag and gained his feet. "I'll be back to check up on you, and I'll change them when it's needed and bring you a crutch as well."

"I won't be here," Graeham said. "I'm staying at St. Bartholomew's."

"That's convenient," said the surgeon, "what with the hospital being right there. The sisters know what they're doing. They can tend to your leg."

"I don't understand," Joanna said. "If you've got a place to stay, why were you looking for an inn this afternoon?"

Graeham stared at her blankly for a moment. "Ah. Well, it's just as I told you. I decided I'd prefer lodgings within the walls."

"Yes, of course." He *had* said that. Still, it seemed curi-

ous for a man who was just passing through town to go to
such trouble over his lodgings.

Dusting off his tunic, Aldfrith said, to no one in particular, "I get half a shilling for splinting a leg, plus three pennies extra for coming here instead of doing it in my shop."

Hugh started digging into his purse, but Graeham said,
"Put your money away. You've done enough for me." He
pointed to his purse on the floor, still attached to his belt.
"Take it out of here."

Joanna weighed the kidskin pouch in her hand, estimat-
ing it at half a pound or more. Opening it, she saw that it
was all silver pennies. The only time she'd ever see that
much money in one place was when her father would unlock his money chest to calculate his fortune.

Of course, it wasn't the serjant's money but his overlord's. Most soldiers, with the exception of knights, possessed only enough silver to pay for their next horn of ale—
or their next woman.

She counted out nine pennies and handed them to Aldfrith, who recounted them, slipped them into his own purse,
and took his leave.

Graeham yawned.

"Are you tired after your ordeal?" Hugh asked.

"What ordeal?" The serjant smiled gamely. " 'Twas more
trouble for you two than for me—I got to just lie here. I
am hungry, though." He smiled at Joanna. "I wouldn't
mind one of those eel turnovers now."

Joanna pulled the blanket up to cover him. "I'll go get
it."

In the salle, Joanna found both cats on the table, feasting
on the turnovers, having managed to unwrap them. "Manfrid! Petronilla! Scat!" They leapt down and tore off into
the shop stall. She stared at the half-eaten pasties, sick at
heart over having spent one of her last precious pennies to
feed those spoiled creatures.

Joanna lured the animals into the rear yard by clicking
her tongue—the signal that they were to be fed—and
dumped the remains of the turnovers into their food bowl
by the back door. They'd been an extravagance, a final
treat on the eve of complete penury; now they were cat
food. "Enjoy this luxury while you can." She petted the

cats as they hunkered down to eat. "Soon you'll be reduced to catching your own food." She didn't like to think what *she'd* be reduced to.

Crossing the croft to the kitchen, Joanna scrounged up the best supper she could manage, given her meager provisions—dense, dark rye bread spread with honey and a cup of buttermilk—and brought it back to the storeroom.

Hugh held his finger to his lips when she entered the little chamber. Grinning, he cocked his head toward the cot. Graeham lay with his eyes closed, one arm arcing gracefully above his head, fast asleep.

Hugh extinguished the lantern and carried the oil lamp back to the table in the salle, where Joanna joined him after pulling the leather curtain across the storeroom doorway.

"Buttermilk?" Joanna held the cup toward her brother as they sat opposite each other.

He wrinkled his nose. "Wine, if you have it. Graeham drank all of mine."

"Sorry, I'm all out." And had been for months, ever since her circumstances had begun to deteriorate. "No ale, either, I'm afraid. There's the Red Boar on the corner. You could get something to drink there."

"I'd rather stay here and chat with you while I've got the chance. I've got to get to the bridge before curfew."

"London Bridge?"

He nodded. "I'm staying across the river in Southwark." Her disapproval must have shown on her face, because he quickly added, "At an inn, not a stew."

"Why would you want to sleep three to a bed—a flea-infested bed, no doubt—at some dreadful public inn when you can stay here?"

Hugh gave her that too charming lopsided grin that had inveigled its way through her defenses ever since they were children. "The proprietress has been a . . . special friend of mine for years."

"I see." Half the women of London—and of Byzantium, the Northland, the Rhineland, and everywhere else he'd fought these past years—seemed to have become her brother's "special friends."

"I'll be sleeping just two to a bed," he added unnecessarily.

Joanna glanced uneasily toward the leather curtain that separated them from the stranger sleeping in the storeroom. "I'd feel better if you stayed here—just for tonight."

"Better? Safer, you mean? You sleep in the solar, right?"

"Aye."

He chuckled. "Even if Graeham took it into his head to ravish you in the middle of the night—and I don't quite think he's the type—do you honestly think he's capable of making it up the ladder with that leg of his?"

She sighed. "It just feels . . . odd to have him staying here."

"He seems a decent enough fellow, Joanna. I'm sure he's harmless. And it's just for tonight. Tomorrow I'll bring a cart and take him back to St. Bartholemew's and you can forget you ever met him. Now, are you going to eat that bread or not?"

She shoved the bread at him; he tucked into it ravenously.

"I take it Prewitt's in Italy," he said around a mouthful of food.

Joanna drew in a deep breath. "Prewitt is dead."

Hugh choked on his bread. Joanna handed him the cup of buttermilk. He took a long swallow. His face screwed up in disgust, but the coughing and sputtering eased a bit.

"Christ, Joanna." Hugh regarded her with solemn astonishment. "When did this happen?" he asked softly.

"Last September." Joanna rubbed her arms. "I received a letter from an official in the city government of Genoa. Prewitt . . . he was knifed to death."

Hugh murmured an epithet and crossed himself.

"By the husband of a woman he was . . ."

Hugh closed his eyes and rubbed his forehead.

"The letter came in a package that contained his personal effects," she said. "His keys, his mantle pin, his eating knife, his razor, a few other things. That sapphire ring of his wasn't in there, though. And no money, of course, although he must have had some—he'd been there to buy silks from the Orient."

Hugh sighed. "Joanna . . . I can't pretend to grieve for the man." He reached across the table to squeeze her hand. "Are you all right?"

She nodded. "It's odd. I actually mourned him at first. But then I realized it wasn't Prewitt I was mourning, but the man I'd thought he was when I married him. And perhaps even myself, a little."

"Verily? You're not much given to self-pity, that I've noticed."

She smiled. " 'Twas a momentary lapse. I thought about how he misled me when I was young and naive. How he *used* me. And, even worse, how I let him do it."

"As you say, you were young and naive. You were fifteen, for pity's sake. 'Twould never happen today."

"I daresay not. I've learned a thing or two about men—the hard way. If you've got something they want, they take it. They use you for what you can do for them, without regard for your heartbreak when you discover that it wasn't you they wanted so desperately but some small part of you—your body, usually. Or, in Prewitt's case, your position in the social hierarchy."

Hugh frowned. "Have there been . . . other men, besides Prewitt?"

"Nay—never. Oh, they sniff around me from time to time, like dogs. Usually they're married, sometimes betrothed. All they want is to slake their lust and move on. They're quite insistent, some of them."

"Is that why you carry a dagger?"

"It's proven useful." She smiled inwardly, remembering Rolf le Fever's gaping horror when she shoved that blade up his nostril.

"You should move to the country," Hugh said. " 'Tisn't safe for you in London anymore. It wasn't before, I suppose, with Prewitt gone so much of the time, but at least then everyone knew you had a husband to exact revenge if you were ill used in any way."

A gust of bleak laughter escaped her. "Not that he would have. He wouldn't have cared enough."

"But the world at large didn't know that. Marriage afforded you some measure of protection. Most men aren't like Prewitt—they steer clear of entanglements with married women."

Joanna knew that was true, despite the occasional exception, like Prewitt—or like le Fever, who had made one or two subtle but unmistakable overtures toward her while Prewitt was still alive. For this reason, she'd continued to wear her wedding ring after his death. Nevertheless, male interest in her had increased once news of Prewitt's death began to circulate through West Cheap, despite her demure attire and lack of encouragement.

"As a married woman," Hugh said, "you were shielded from unwanted attention. Now that protection is gone. Cities are dangerous places for women, Joanna—especially women who are all alone."

Well she knew it—and city life, with its narrow, teeming streets, its noises and rank odors, had long since lost its charm for her. Increasingly Joanna found herself yearning for the verdant countryside of her youth, but her dream of settling down in a peaceful little cottage somewhere was all the more unattainable now that Prewitt was dead. She could barely scrape by here in London, where there was a market for her embroidery; how would she manage out in the country? And how could she afford to move? The situation was hopeless; it didn't bear thinking about.

She took a generous swallow of the cool, tangy buttermilk. "How long are you planning on staying in London this time?"

Her effort to steer the subject onto another path met with a smirk from her brother, who knew her too well. "I'm expected back in Saxony in the fall."

She grinned delightedly. "Do you mean to say you'll be here through the summer?"

"I mean to say I could, if I wanted to. I probably will. I can use a bit of a respite from the bloodshed."

"But then you'll be going away again. Must you?"

His gaze suddenly melancholy, he said, "You know I can't stay here, Joanna. And you know why."

Father. "Does he even know you're back in England?"

The expression left Hugh's face. "I've only just returned."

"Wexford is but half a day's ride from London, Hugh. Don't you think you should pay him a call this time?"

He cocked a sardonic eyebrow. "Strange advice, considering you haven't been there in six years."

"Not by my choice, as you're well aware. You do have a choice."

"And I choose to exercise it by staying as far away from that son of a bitch as I can manage while I'm in the kingdom."

"Hugh . . ."

"How are you faring, Joanna?" he asked. Now it was his turn to change the subject. "Tell me the truth."

If only she could; she hungered for a sympathetic ear. But Hugh's automatic response, were she to confide her desperate situation, would be to bail her out of her misery with the foreign gold he'd risked his life to earn. She'd taken his charity once before—and had promised herself she would never do so again. If her predicament was dire, it was of her own making; no one had forced her to marry Prewitt Chapman. She'd gotten herself into this plight, and she would get herself out—somehow.

"I'm getting along fine," she said carefully. "I—they won't let me join the Mercers' Guild, so I can't sell silk by the yard anymore."

"Did he leave you anything at all, any money?"

"A little." And she'd lived as frugally as she knew how, but it was almost completely gone now. Unless she could turn things around, she would soon have to sell her shop. In that event, she'd be not only destitute but homeless. "And I've been making small embroidered items—ribbons, scarves, collars, girdles, garters—and selling them."

Hugh's brows drew together. "And you've been making an adequate living from that?"

"Oh, yes," Joanna said, lifting her cup to her mouth so she wouldn't have to look him in the eye while she lied outright.

Hugh shook his head. "I don't like it. I don't like to think of you all alone here, laboring from sunrise till sunset just to get by. A woman like you shouldn't have to live this way."

"A woman like me? I'm the widow of a silk trader, Hugh, and not a very prosperous one. I'm used to hard work. Besides, I enjoy embroidery."

"You're the daughter of one of the most powerful knights in England, Joanna. You should be doing needlework for pleasure, not to put food in your belly. God's bones, you should be wed to a nobleman, living a life of leisure."

"I made my choice six years ago," Joanna said grimly. "I didn't choose a nobleman. I chose a mercer. Now I must pay for that choice."

"You're how old now—twenty?"

"One-and-twenty."

"That's too young to resign yourself to perpetual widowhood, sister. You're a beautiful woman, and accomplished. You can marry again—a man of your own station this time, a knight or the son of a knight. Someone with a good heart, who'll love you. Not some handsome devil with too much charm and too little honor, who's just out to use you."

The words "handsome devil" conjured up for Joanna the image of Graeham Fox, lying half-naked on Prewitt's cot, watching her with a drowsy intensity that made her shiver. Prewitt had been handsome, too, deadly handsome with his coal-black hair and deceptively soulful eyes. She'd been powerless to resist him; so, it seemed, had a good many other women.

"It's late," Hugh said, rising from the table. "I must go." He stole back into the store room to fetch his satchel, then Joanna walked him to the front door.

"You lock yourself in at night, don't you?" he asked, standing in the open doorway. Wood Street was dark and quiet, most folks having retired for the evening.

"Of course. Do you take me for a fool?"

His expression baleful, he said, "I take you for the kind of careless wench who leaves the latchstring hanging out the back door when she steps out to the cookhouse."

"Ah," she said sheepishly. "I learned that lesson well tonight. I won't do that again."

"I fret about you, Joanna."

"I know, but you mustn't. I'll be fine."

He paused, as if weighing his words. "You haven't ruled out remarriage, I hope. I mean, if the right fellow happened along, a man of rank who could offer you the kind of life you deserve—"

"I take it you have someone in mind."

He scratched his stubbly chin, that lopsided smile tugging at his mouth. "Perhaps. Do you remember Lord Suger's second son, Robert? We were boyhood friends. His father settled a grand manor on him—Ramswick, just south of London."

"Of course." She'd always liked Robert, even entertained a childish infatuation with him for about a fortnight one summer.

"A splendid fellow," Hugh said.

"A splendid *married* fellow."

Hugh shook his head. "Joan drowned in a boating accident last summer, along with their eldest daughter, Gillian."

"Oh, no."

"He told me yesterday—I stopped to visit him on my way here. Gillian was only ten, and he adored her. He pulled her body from the river himself. He wept, telling me about it."

"Oh, how awful. Poor Robert."

"On the whole, he seems to be holding up fairly well. He said he can't afford to dwell on what happened, or he won't be able to be a proper father to his other children. There are two of them, younger than Gillian, both girls. He was telling me how they needed a mother, but the right sort."

"Then he'd hardly be interested in me."

"By 'right sort,' he doesn't mean a pampered heiress. He told me he wants a kind, compassionate woman who will be good to his daughters. He's a fine man, Joanna, a devoted father. And I know he was a faithful husband to Joan. Perhaps I should . . . bring him round." He shrugged.

Joanna sighed. "You'd have to supply your own wine."

"But of course."

"And you'd have to give me advance notice so I can bathe and . . ." She looked down at her shabby kirtle with distaste.

"A bit of brotherly counsel?"

"Aye?"

He tugged on the scarf wrapped around her head. "Leave this off when I bring him by. Your hair's your best feature."

"What kind of widow leaves her hair uncovered? I'll look like a harlot."

"You'll look like an angel." Hugh grinned and kissed her on the cheek. "Good night, sister. I'll see you in the morning."

As he was walking away, she said, "You won't forget the cart, will you?"

He turned and cupped a hand to his ear.

"The cart," she called out. "To take the serjant back to St. Bartholemew's. You won't forget, will you?"

"I won't forget. After tomorrow morning, Graeham Fox will be completely out of your hair." Hugh waved cheerily and continued on his way.

"Good," she whispered, shivering.

Chapter 4

~

Where the devil am I? Graeham wondered as he opened his eyes. He lay beneath a blanket on a narrow bed in a room awash with moonlight from two small corner windows, one on the wall to his right and one behind him.

His head pulsed when he turned to look around him; his mouth tasted sour. He'd been drinking; that's why he didn't know where he was.

He saw bolts of silk stacked on a shelf, shimmering in the half-light, and it began coming back to him—the silk merchant's wife, her brother, the surgeon, his leg.

His leg. Oddly, it wasn't until he remembered having broken it that it started hurting again. The pain was intense, but not so overwhelming as to mask the reason he'd awakened in the middle of the night this way. He needed to relieve himself.

He sat up too quickly, forgetting about his cracked ribs, and had to swallow a groan that rose in his chest. On the floor next to the bed he saw a clay jake with a lid. She must have placed it there for him before retiring for the night. Thoughtful of her, but there was something about the lovely Mistress Joanna having to empty and clean his chamber pot that didn't sit well with him. She wasn't some maidservant, and he wasn't her guest. He was a stranger who'd imposed himself on her. She owed him nothing, yet she'd not only tolerated his uninvited presence in her home, she'd done so with considerable grace.

She'd held his hands while they set his leg and whispered reassurances to him in that soft, throaty voice of hers. She hadn't had to do that.

He would get up and use the privy. It shouldn't be too much of a challenge making it there; he remembered having seen the little shed right outside the back door.

The sledgehammer that had both crippled him and served as his cane leaned against the wall next to him. Graeham reached for it and propped it on the floor. Clenching his teeth, he hauled himself by excruciating degrees to his feet—no easy task with his left leg splinted from hip to ankle.

His leg was on fire now. The pain pounded through his entire body; it was all he could do to stay on his feet. With one hand gripping the handle of the sledge and the other buttressed on the wall, he gradually limped around the perimeter of the tiny chamber, through the leather curtain, and down the utterly dark hallway. He was still woozy from the wine, making the trek all the more arduous.

Graeham leaned against the back door for a moment to catch his breath and get his bearings, then fumbled in the dark for the bolt, lifted it out of its slot and pushed the door open. By the light of the almost full moon, he saw the white cat, Petronilla, watching him impassively from the thatched roof of the kitchen hut. Shaking now from his exertions, he staggered into the little privy shed and somehow managed to empty his bladder without tumbling into the pit.

He had to rest his weight against a wall of the shed to get his drawers retied and then he lurched back through the door, managing not to stumble at the drop-off to the sunken floor. But as he was pulling the door closed behind him, the cat darted inside, a blur of white fur that collided with his legs. He pitched forward, splints and sledgehammer clattering as he fell. There were no rushes back here to cushion his fall. Pain exploded in his leg; he cried out once, then hissed a stream of invective at the cat as she bolted away.

He lay panting on the hallway floor, waiting for the pain to subside enough for him to move, when he heard a squeak of wood. There came another squeak, and another—feet descending a ladder.

"Serjant? Are you all right?"

Still facedown, he pushed himself up on his elbows,

groaning as pain shuddered through him. *God, please don't let me have ruined my leg. I don't want to lose it.*

"Serjant?" He heard her footsteps in the rushes and the leather curtain to the storeroom being drawn back. "Serjant?"

"I'm here," he said unsteadily and collapsed onto the floor again, wishing she didn't have to find him like this. "In the hall."

The footsteps neared, and then he heard her sandy, just-awakened voice much closer. "What are you doing back here?" There was no light in the hallway to see her by; she was but a nebulous shape in the enveloping darkness.

"I fell," he ground out, "coming back from the privy."

"The privy! You got up and *walked*? Are you mad?"

He felt her hands in the dark, reaching out tentatively to gauge his position. Her fingertips, warm and pleasantly work-roughened, skimmed his face, a shoulder, an arm—her touch so featherlight that he might almost have imagined it.

Something brushed cool and sleek against Graeham's side as she crawled between him and the wall to his left. Silk. She was wearing something made of silk—a night shift or wrapper, he supposed. It surprised him for a moment that a woman in such modest circumstances would own silken nightclothes, but then he remembered that she was, after all, the wife of a silk merchant.

Graeham felt her airy touch on his back and his good leg, gentle and inquisitive as she took stock of his position. Trails of warmth lingered wherever her fingers brushed. He closed his eyes to savor the sensation, thinking ruefully that perhaps it had been too long since he'd lain with a woman.

"We must get you into the storeroom," she said. "Can you roll onto your back, do you think? Away from me, taking your weight on your uninjured leg."

"Aye." Gritting his teeth, he pushed himself onto his back while she carefully shifted his splinted leg.

He felt the liquid whisper of silk as she hovered over him and a ticklish softness against his chest that could only be her hair. She must sleep with it loose.

"Can you sit up?" she asked.

He tried to, but grunted and fell back. "My ribs . . . I don't think that fall did them any good."

"I'll help you." She moved closer, gliding an arm around his neck. Her hair tumbled around him, slick and heavy where it fell onto his shoulders and chest and infused with a sweet green scent that made him think of a meadow gone to seed.

Bracing one hand on the floor, Graeham went to curl an arm around her. He misjudged her position, and his hand brushed a weighty softness beneath the silk that could only be a breast. Her indrawn breath was barely audible; she stilled. He retracted his hand, but slowly, slowly, his fingertips lingering over the supple curve of flesh as they withdrew. His heart thudded hard against the bandage wrapped around his chest.

Would she get up and leave? She didn't.

Should he send her away? He didn't want to.

Presently she took his hand and guided it over her shoulder, draped in the satin ripples of her hair. "Hold on to me." He held his breath while she pulled him slowly into a sitting position. "Did that hurt?"

Everything hurt. There was nothing but hurt. He slumped forward as the breath left him in a harsh gust, his forehead touching hers. "I'm all right. Just give me a moment."

He felt the heat of her body through the smooth, thin silk, and it struck him that it was the middle of the night and they were virtual strangers, embracing each other here in this dark, confined place like lovers.

Perhaps it struck her, too, for she drew away from him and rose. "I'm going to help you to stand."

"I've got a sledge somewhere that I've been using as a cane."

"You're better off holding on to me." Hooking her hands beneath his arms, she urged him slowly to his feet. "Are you all right?"

"Aye."

"Put your arm around me and hold on to the wall with your other hand."

They made their way slowly and haltingly into the storeroom, clutching each other, as she murmured encouragement. When they got to the cot, she lowered him gradually, trembling with the effort of supporting his weight.

He positioned his splinted leg with both hands and fell back onto the pillow, his chest heaving.

"Do you think you did any more damage to yourself with that fall?" she asked.

"By God, I hope not."

"Let me get the lamp. I'll be right back."

She retreated to the salle, leaving the leather curtain open. He watched her, a spectral figure in the moonlight, as she struck a little fire iron repeatedly against a piece of flint, trying to light the charred rush sticking out of the lump of fat in the dish.

A servant should be doing that for her. The thought coalesced spontaneously out of Graeham's wine-soaked, pain-addled musings, but he knew why it had come to him. The bits and pieces of Joanna Chapman simply did not add up. There was a refined quality to her speech, for one thing, that was more typical of a noblewoman than a merchant's wife. And despite her air of practicality and competence— not traits that Graeham normally associated with wellborn ladies—she comported herself with a gentility that spoke of breeding. And then there was her brother, Hugh of Wexford, with his aristocratic bearing and fine sword.

A spark ignited the rush; Mistress Chapman blew softly on it to encourage the flame. Cradling the lamp in her hand, she carried it toward the storeroom. By its yellowish light, Graeham saw her clearly for the first time since she'd come downstairs. The sight mesmerized him.

She was luminous . . . entirely, breathtakingly luminous. Not just her hair, which hung to her thighs in sinuous waves of bronze and gold, and not just her gleaming wrapper of white silk. *She* glowed—her face, her throat, her hands— like alabaster lit from within.

Of course, he'd known she was a comely woman, even dressed as she'd been earlier, in her matronly head covering and dreary tunic. She had the kind of soft-edged, meltingly pretty face men found themselves gazing at without realizing it. Her eyes were a deep, liquid brown beneath dramatically arched brows, her lips full and seductively pink. Her chin, like her brother's, was distinguished by the merest hint of a cleft, as if a sculptor had touched the wet clay just once, lightly, and left it at that.

Yes, he'd known she was comely. But now, blanketed by that lustrous hair and draped in a whisper of white silk, she was beautiful in a way that was almost excruciating to behold.

If he were Prewitt Chapman, he would spend a good deal more time in London and a great deal less abroad.

Sitting on the edge of the bed, she set the oil lamp on the chest next to it and gathered her great mass of hair behind her, all the while pointedly looking away from him. To his chagrin, he realized he'd been staring at her, all but awestruck. He dropped his gaze as she leaned forward to inspect his leg, her silken wrapper stretching enticingly over her breasts. They were no larger than average, but lush and round, with high, taut little nipples.

Arousal flared in his loins. Closing his eyes, he took a deep breath and mentally recited his Latin drill, loath to grow hard beneath his drawers with her ministering to him this way. Joanna Chapman wasn't one of Lord Gui's wanton little laundresses. She was a wedded woman—moreover, one who'd been kind to him and deserved to be treated with a modicum of chivalry, not as a vessel for his lust. And he was, after all, betrothed, or soon would be, to another woman.

Graeham had best rein in his carnal appetites until his wedding to the lady Phillipa, which Lord Gui had assured him would take place in Paris within a fortnight of his bringing Ada home. Phillipa had consented to the match provided that she be permitted to continue her studies, a condition none of her erstwhile suitors had conceded to, finding logic and philosophy unseemly pursuits for a woman. Graeham, mindful of St. Jerome's counsel not to look at the teeth of a gift horse, and never having had any quarrel with the education of women, had agreed readily. In turn, Lord Gui, eager to please his beloved daughter, had chosen to award Graeham the sprawling Oxfordshire estate for its proximity to Oxford's emerging *studium generale*.

All his life, Graeham had wanted one simple thing, something even the poorest villein could lay claim to—a home and family of his own. Soon he would have that, and more. He would have the ideal wife—beautiful, learned, and agreeable—and a grand estate in one of the most bucolic regions in all of England. After five-and-twenty years of being the interloper, the tolerated outsider, he would finally belong somewhere—and to someone. At long last, he would be content. Perhaps even happy.

Nothing must interfere with the success of his mission and the claiming of his reward.

Nothing.

"Are you all right, serjant?"

Graeham opened his eyes to find Joanna Chapman looking up at him, one hand on his splinted leg.

"You're clenching your fists," she said, pulling the blanket up to his waist. She turned her attention to his swaddled ribs, which she gently patted and stroked, her brow furrowed in concentration. Her hands looked strong and elegant at the same time. He imagined those long, nimble fingers slipping beneath the blanket, untying his drawers. A helpless little moan rose in his chest.

"Am I causing you pain?" she asked.

A mirthless chuckle shook his chest. "Of a sort."

"I'm sorry." She rested a hand gently on his shoulder. "I'm quite sure that fall was agonizing, and I couldn't swear it did no harm—I'm not a surgeon. But if it did, I see no evidence of it."

"That's some comfort. Thank you."

"You'll sleep better if it's darker in here." She stood and reached across the cot to close the window shutters against the bright moonlight, sliding a wooden pin across to latch them in place. Her wrapper shifted as she moved, caressing a lissome curve of waist and hip and leg. That ugly blue tunic had disguised both her slenderness and her deliciously feminine contours. Moving to the head of the cot, she shuttered the window that looked out on the alley.

When she bent over to lift the lamp off the chest, one side of her wrapper gapped open slightly, revealing a pearly slope of inner breast. Clearly she had nothing on underneath; he realized she must sleep naked.

"Is there anything else you need?" she asked.

God, yes. "I think not."

"If anything occurs to you," she said as she crossed to the leather curtain, "just call up to me. I'll hear you." She pulled the curtain closed.

"Mistress Joanna."

There came a pause, and then the curtain reopened. She looked in almost warily. "Aye?"

Words normally came to him without effort, but not tonight. "Thank you. I—'Twas kind of you to . . . take me in this way. I know I've been a great deal of trouble—"

"Not at all."

He grinned skeptically. "You'd be fast asleep upstairs right now if it weren't for me." He pictured her naked in bed, that luxuriant hair spread out around her, and felt desire rekindle within him. "You're a . . . very unselfish woman, to let me impose on you this way."

" 'Tisn't any great challenge to be unselfish for just one night. Hugh will take you to St. Bartholomew's tomorrow, and then you'll be the sisters' responsibility."

"Tomorrow?"

"Aye, in the morning."

"Ah."

"Is that not what you wanted?" she asked. "I thought—"

"Aye," he said quickly. "It's what I want." It was what he *should* want. It was what was best.

"They've got the hospital there."

"Yes, I know. I'm happy to be going there."

She opened her mouth to speak, frowning. Finally she said, "Very well. Good night, serjant."

"Good night, mistress."

Chapter 5

❧

"Serjant?" came a soft whisper from the other side of the leather curtain the next morning. "Are you awake?"

"Aye. Come in."

The curtain parted and Joanna Chapman entered, cradling a large washbasin in one arm and carrying a steaming bucket in the other. She wore a brown kirtle even more shapeless than yesterday's blue one, and her hair was again concealed, this time beneath a veil draped over her head and tied on one side. How sad, Graeham reflected, that a woman must hide such spectacular hair simply because she'd taken marriage vows.

She said, "I thought you might like to wash up a bit before Hugh comes to take you back to St. Bartholomew's."

"Thank you—I most certainly would." Graeham sat up slowly, teeth clenched.

She set the bucket on the floor and the washbowl on the chest next to his bed. In the bowl he saw a dish of soft yellow soap, a wash rag, and a towel. She arranged these on the chest and half filled the bowl with warm water, leaving more in the bucket.

Averting her gaze, she said, "Do you . . . need help or . . ."

"I can manage fine on my own, thanks."

She unlatched the window shutters and threw them open; morning sunlight flooded the little chamber. "Are you hungry? I've started a pot of porridge. I've no ale to offer you, but the water from the well is pure."

"I don't normally break my fast till midday. Thanks all the same."

She nodded without looking at him, clearly ill at ease. Perhaps their nocturnal encounter had disturbed her as well. "How do your injuries feel this morning?"

"Better. They only really hurt when I move."

"Try not to move too much. Hugh's bringing a cart to take you to St. Bartholomew's, so you'll be able to lie—"

"A *cart!*"

"Aye. 'Twas either that or a litter, and I gather he thought a cart would be easier to obtain."

"I'm not bouncing through the streets of London in a cart, like some murdering churl on his way to Tyburn Hill to be hanged."

"You can't very well sit astride a horse."

"I damn well . . . pardon me, mistress. I most certainly can. And will."

"You're an exasperating man, serjant."

He nodded, smiling. "Point taken. But I'm not getting in any cart."

"You may discuss the matter with Hugh when he gets here." As she turned to leave, her gaze lit on the jake, which he'd tucked under the bed. "Does that need emptying?"

"Nay. I . . . went out and used the privy a little while a—"

"*Again?* After what happened last night?"

"I was careful."

"How did you support yourself? That sledge is still by the back door."

"There's a broom over there." He nodded toward the corner. "I used that."

She shook her head, outrage turning her brown eyes to gold. "Exasperating and *maddeningly* stubborn."

"So I've been told. Don't worry, mistress." His voice grew subdued. "You haven't that much longer to put up with me."

She met his gaze squarely for the first time that morning, her expression pensive, perhaps even a little melancholy.

"God's tooth!" came a man's furious roar from outside.

"You haven't got him saddled yet? I *told* you I was late!
What have you been doing out here?"

Looking out the little rear window, Graeham saw Rolf le
Fever in his stable yard, dressing down a hulking redheaded
fellow who was buckling a saddle onto the back of a black
horse. Graeham didn't know which was gaudier, le Fever's
multicolored tunic or the absurd saddle, which had been
plated with hammered silver and studded with gems; the
bridles appeared to be gilded, and rows of tiny gold bells
hung from the breast strap.

"Beg pardon, Master Rolf, but—"

"You bloody well should beg my pardon! Get him saddled up so I can get out of here!"

"That's the master of the new Mercers' Guild," said Mistress Joanna. "Rolf le Fever."

Graeham turned to find her peering out the window with
her arms crossed, watching le Fever's little performance as
if it were a street play.

"Is that so?" he said.

She nodded. "He lives right behind me, so I get to listen
in on his fits of pique several times a day, whether I care
to or not. Luckily for me, he spends most mornings at the
silk traders' market hall, so the hours between terce and
nones are generally quite peaceful."

"That must be where he's off to now."

"Nay, he walks to the market hall. It's right around the
corner on Newgate Street."

After draping the seat of the saddle with a quilted brown
satin *baudré* that hung nearly to the ground, the red-haired
brute assisted his master in mounting.

"Who's the other fellow?" Graeham asked.

"His manservant, the poor, long-suffering Byram."

Graeham looked at her sharply. "Byram?"

"Aye."

The manservant watched le Fever ride off and retreated
into the house. "That fellow's name is Byram? Are you
certain?"

"He's been serving le Fever for the entire six years I've
been living here. I think I know his name." Her brows
drew together. "Why?"

"Nothing, just . . ." *Are you Byram?* Graeham had asked

the bald-headed cur who'd lured him into the alley. *That's right* . . . "Is it possible there are two Byrams working for le Fever?"

She cocked her head as if she hadn't heard him right. "Two Byrams?"

"Aye . . . I know it sounds daft."

"It *is* daft. Le Fever's only got the one fellow over there. There's a maidservant and a kitchen wench, but just the one man. Why would you think there'd be another Byram?"

Graeham shrugged. This woman and her brother mustn't suspect that the attack on him was anything other than a routine robbery, or Lord Gui's secret might be exposed. "It *is* daft. Never mind."

"But—"

"That's quite a house," Graeham said to divert her. By the light of day, he had an excellent view of the back of it. Through the ground-level windows he saw a kitchen wench with shiny red cheeks, singing as she cooked. The second-floor windows were even larger. To the left was the opulently appointed sitting room he'd been in yesterday. To the right he saw an equally grand chamber, in which the maidservant, Aethel, was smoothing the counterpane of a massive, curtained bed with the aid of a long pole. That must be le Fever's bedchamber. The windows of the solar, on the third level, were shuttered.

"A dreadful house," Joanna said. "I gather he thinks it's quite grand. He has . . . aspirations. Likes to play the noble-man, but he ends up looking more like the court jester."

Which was why he'd married Ada, of course—to help propel him beyond his station. No wonder he became so incensed when he found out his new bride was, in fact, Lord Gui's "shameful little secret."

"Is he married?" Graeham asked carefully.

"Aye. Pretty young thing."

Graeham bit his tongue to avoid asking, *How pretty? What does she look like?* His impending betrothal to Ada's twin sister was, of course, tied into the rest of it, so he must needs conceal that as well. "You've met her?" he asked.

"Nay, but I've seen her—from a distance, when he first brought her back from Paris last year. She did a little gardening out back last summer. I understand she's been suffering with a rheum of the head since Christmastide, though. The apothecary's daughter brings her a tonic every day, but it doesn't seem to help. Some people are like that—they nurse head colds all winter and get better once spring comes."

"It's spring now," he said. "It's mild."

She shrugged. "Mayhap she'll show herself soon. It's time to plant her garden."

From the window that faced the alley, Graeham heard a steady clacking that grew louder as the source of it—a leper, undoubtedly—approached. The sorry creature, wearing a black hooded cloak and a tattered straw hat that disguised both disease and gender, shuffled into sight with a walking staff in one hand and the required wooden castanets in the other. A shabby pouch, which probably held all his worldly possessions, was slung over his back.

"Good morrow, Thomas." Joanna approached the window.

The leper paused and looked in, smiling. "Good morrow, mistress." The gruff, thick-tongued voice was the only indication that this was a man, for his face had been so ravaged by thickened skin and discolored nodules as to nearly obliterate its distinguishing features. One eye was clouded and clearly blind and his earlobes drooped with ulcerous flesh, but strangely, it was his complete lack of eyebrows that Graeham found most unsettling. He'd seen many victims of disfiguring maladies, yet still it took an effort of will to regard this man impassively when his instinct was to look away in horror.

"I looked for you when I passed by the stall," Thomas told Joanna. "I got worried when I saw the front window still shuttered." That he spoke like a gentleman, despite his affliction, surprised Graeham.

"I'm just a bit late getting set up this morning," she said.

The leper's one-eyed gaze fell on Graeham, lighting on his bandaged ribs and splinted leg. "You've graduated to taking in human strays, I see."

Joanna's chuckle had a pleasantly rusty sound. "This is Graeham Fox, who stumbled upon a bit of bad luck yesterday. Serjant, I'd like you to meet Thomas Harper."

"Who no longer plays the harp"—Thomas raised the

scaly hand that held the clacker to display his curled-up fingers—"having stumbled upon a bit of bad luck himself." He laughed wheezily at his jest. Graeham found himself yet again at a loss for words.

"I've got some porridge in the kitchen," Joanna told Thomas, "if it hasn't burned to the pot by now. The serjant has refused my offer of it, and the cats won't touch it. 'Twill only go to waste if you won't have a bowl."

Grinning and shaking his head, the leper dropped his clacker, which was tied to one end of the rope knotted around his waist, and lifted a battered tin bowl, which was tied to the other. To Graeham he said, "She has a way of making it seem as if I'm doing her some great boon by accepting her charity."

"You are," she said. "I can ill afford to be throwing food away. I'll meet you at the kitchen."

"Many thanks, mistress. Good day to you, serjant."

"Good day," Graeham said as Thomas walked away, his steps slow and laborious. His toes were undoubtedly as misshapen as his fingers.

"How old do you think he is?" Joanna asked him.

"Sixty?"

"He's six-and-thirty."

"Poor bastard. Do you feed him every morning?"

"Aye. And sometimes he'll come back later, if his begging hasn't gone well—or if he just can't stomach the humiliation any longer. He's a proud man, Thomas. He was a renowned harpist once—he used to play at the Tower of London for King Henry. He'll never play the harp again."

"Not with those fingers."

" 'Tisn't just that they're deformed. He's got no feeling left in them—nor in his feet."

"None at all?"

Joanna shook her head. "He showed up here once with blood pouring from his foot. He'd stepped on something sharp and not even known it. And last winter, a candle set his shirt on fire in back, but he had no idea until he smelled the linen burning. His back ended up blistered."

Graeham winced. "Is there no lazar house where that poor wretch can live?"

"There's St. Giles, and I'm told it's a fine hospital, regardless that it's for lepers. But Thomas likes his independence, and I can certainly understand that." She sighed. "He's waiting for me. I must go. Is there anything you need before I open up the shop?"

Graeham rubbed the sharp stubble on his jaw. "A razor, if it's not too much trouble. That is, if you've got one."

"There should be one upstairs, with my husband's things. I'll fetch it as soon as Thomas has had his porridge."

After she closed the leather curtain behind her, Graeham struggled awkwardly to his feet, got out of his drawers, lathered up the wash rag, and set about scrubbing himself from head to toe. Movement in the croft caught his eye: Joanna Chapman crossing to the kitchen, in front of which Thomas Harper sat on a barrel with his tin bowl, waiting for his breakfast. His feet, Graeham saw, were bound in rags.

Joanna went into the kitchen and came out a few moments later, carrying a big ladle full of porridge, which she poured into his bowl. Evidently she didn't notice Graeham watching her. This was a small, deep window; he'd be hard to see from outside.

Beyond the croft, le Fever's stable yard was deserted. In his kitchen, the wench continued to stir and chop, happy as a plump house sparrow. The sitting room and bedchamber were empty, the solar windows still shuttered.

So . . . the bald-headed man had lied about being Byram. Still, it was possible he and his cohorts had been hired by le Fever—likely, even. He'd known Graeham's name, and had been lying in wait for him; how could that be if le Fever hadn't put him up to the attack? The greedy mercer had wanted those fifty marks—he had pretensions to keep up, after all—but without the indignity of having his wife snatched away from him and returned to her father.

Had those rapacious thugs actually handed the stolen silver over to le Fever? Fifty marks was a great deal of money, especially now that so little of it was being minted. Coinage was scarce of late; folks who had it hoarded it, and the rest relied on barter to get by. Fifty marks might have been just enough of a temptation to make double-crossing le Fever worth the risk. In that event, Graeham's attackers—those who survived—would most likely simply disappear, and le Fever would never find out that Graeham had escaped death at their hands. Even if they dutifully turned the money over to le Fever and admitted having left Graeham alive, the mercer might reasonably assume that they'd at least succeeded in driving him away.

Assuming he stayed out of sight.

Graeham heard a soft thump and turned to find the black-and-white tomcat on the deep sill of the alley window. The animal had a black nose on a mostly white face, making him look rather like a jester Graeham had once seen who'd painted his face like that for comic effect. He began to squeeze his bulky body between the iron bars, then noticed Graeham. Startled, he backed up, leapt down from the sill, and sprinted away.

Graeham took stock of his situation as he dried himself off. Fate, it seemed, had landed him at the perfect vantage point from which to carry out his mission, or at least prepare for it, injuries or no. From the rear storeroom window, he had an unobstructed view of the backs of the surrounding houses and shops, as well as their yards, gardens, and outbuildings. He could see into the windows of Rolf le Fever's house, the stone house next to it, and nearly every house on the west side of Milk Street, without moving from his bed.

The prudent thing would be to recuperate right where he was. At St. Bartholomew's he'd be isolated outside the city walls, but here he could keep his nose to the ground. If he was clever, perhaps he could ascertain the status of Ada le Fever—possibly even arrange for her to return to Paris—despite his shattered leg.

Sitting on the edge of the little cot and leaning over the washbowl, Graeham poured water from the bucket over his hair and reached for the soap.

He could write to Lord Gui and let him know that there were complications, but not so grievous as to jeopardize his assignment. He supposed he could write to Phillipa, as well, assuring her that, although the wedding would be delayed, he was still eager to claim her for his wife. But given that he'd never met the woman, nor communicated with her at all except through her father, perhaps it would be best to let the baron deliver the message for him.

Above all, he must reassure Lord Gui that he had every intention of bringing Ada home at the earliest possible opportunity—and then he must do so. Failing at his mission was not an option; he had far too much at stake.

Kneeling in the rushes in front of the big, iron-banded trunk at the foot of her bed, Joanna twisted the key in its lock. This had been Prewitt's trunk, where he'd kept his valuables even after she'd banished him to the storeroom. All during their marriage, she'd never seen the inside of it; she'd never had the key until the Genoese official had returned her husband's effects to her upon his death. When the shock wore off, she'd gathered up his clothes and belongings from the storeroom, washed what needed washing, and unlocked the trunk to store them away with his other things.

Raising the trunk's heavy lid, she felt the same mixture of grief and anger that had assaulted her the first time she'd done this, eight months ago. Just as it had then, the scent of her husband—or rather, of the herbs in which he'd bathed—rose from within the trunk to sting her eyes and clutch at her throat.

She'd loved that scent when she first met him. It had captivated her; everything about him had. His sleek black hair and long-fingered hands, his dark and yearning gaze when he looked upon her, his easy laughter . . . the charm, the attention, the breathless need, the kisses and promises. He had cast a spell on her.

It hadn't mattered that he was of the mercantile class and she was Lady Joanna of Wexford. Nothing had mattered but that they should marry and be together always.

Always.

Joanna smoothed her hand over the mantle lying folded on top of everything else in the trunk—silky-smooth purple wool trimmed with black lambskin. Prewitt had been wearing this the first time she'd ever laid eyes on him; he'd been so devastatingly handsome she could barely stand to look at him. Someone had complimented the mantle, and he mentioned that he'd gotten it on his last trip to Montpelier, where he went twice a year to buy Sicilian and Byzantine silks—although he'd also been to Sicily several times and Constantinople once. Oriental silks came through Alexandria, and these he purchased at the Italian ports. Joanna, who'd never been farther from Wexford than London, had been aston-

ished at all the places he'd seen. Never had she known a man
more well traveled, more sophisticated, more strikingly
beautiful.

And he wanted her for his wife.

Her. Many times she'd thanked God in her prayers for
bringing Prewitt Chapman into her life.

In the beginning.

Joanna removed the mantle and placed it on her bed.
Beneath it in the trunk were two silk tunics, a sleeveless
wool overtunic, and a felt cap, which she withdrew and set
on top of the mantle. Next came four pairs of silk
chausses—the connected pairs he'd favored, which were
like snug trousers, coming all the way up to the waist. She
set these on the bed, then pulled out two pairs of russet
braies, which she'd made for him right after their wedding
but which he'd never worn; a man who made his living
importing silk, he'd declared, ought not to dress in baggy
homespun trousers like a water carrier.

She added the braies to the stack on the bed, thought
about it for a moment, and set a pair aside. Shirts and
underdrawers came next. She chose her favorite shirt, of
India muslin—Prewitt had bought it in Rome—and put it
and a pair of drawers with the braies.

At the bottom of the trunk, she sorted through belts,
shoes, mantle pins, gloves, and sundry other odds and ends
until she found what she'd been seeking: Prewitt's little
steel looking glass in its leather case, his knifelike razor,
his whetstone, and his oxhorn comb. She put these with the
clothing she'd set aside for Graeham, and then she turned
back to the trunk, contemplating the carved wooden box
at the very bottom.

Joanna had never seen this box until eight months ago. The
first time she opened it, she felt as if she'd been punched in
the stomach. She'd contemplated pitching it into the Thames,
but in the end she kept it. It was, after all, her most meaningful memento of her marriage, and its presence at the foot of
her bed would serve as a constant reminder not to let herself
be used again as Prewitt had used her.

She lifted the lid of the box, steeling herself to its contents: a tangle of ladies' stockings; a dozen or more garters;
a pink kid glove; innumerable locks of hair tied with rib-

bons; hairpins of ivory and silver; a desiccated rose; a little pot of lip rouge; a handful of earrings, mostly cheap glass; and several chemise sleeves, some still redolent with their owners' perfume.

One of the locks of hair was hers.

She slammed the lid on Prewitt's collection of souvenirs. What was it Hugh had called him last night? "Handsome devil," she whispered out loud.

Joanna dumped Prewitt's clothes back into the trunk, re-locked it, and descended the ladder with the things she'd put aside for Graeham. The leather curtain over the storeroom door was closed. She pushed it aside. "I've brought you some—"

She gasped. He stood in front of the cot, completely naked except for the splints on his leg and the bandage around his ribs, toweling his hair dry.

"I'm sorry." She dropped the curtain and backed up into the salle. "I . . . I . . . didn't realize you—"

"It's all right," he called through the curtain. "Here. I'm covered up, more or less. Come back."

Joanna stared at the curtain, hugging the clothing and shaving gear to her chest. It had been five years since she'd viewed Prewitt's unclothed body, but what she remembered of her husband was a far cry from what she'd just seen of the man in the storeroom. Graeham Fox had the body of a soldier, a body that had been molded into a weapon, hard and sinewy. He was a formidable male animal, in every respect. Prewitt, although several years older, had looked—in all particulars—like an adolescent by comparison.

"Mistress?"

"Um . . . I brought you some clothes. I mean, I brought you the razor, of course, but I also . . . I thought perhaps . . ." *Babbling lackwit.*

Parting the leather curtain, she found Graeham sitting on the cot, the damp towel draped over his lap, his splinted leg straight out before him with his heel resting on the floor.

"Um, here." She took a few steps toward him and reached out to hand him the items. *Fool.* Did she think he was going to bite her?

He'd washed his hair, she saw; it was wet and snarled, with tendrils sticking to his forehead. His face, without its layer of grime from yesterday, glowed with vitality, and there was something almost aristocratic about his high-bridged nose and well-carved cheekbones. He looked younger and even handsomer than she'd realized.

He held the braies up. "Perfect. These are just what I need to fit over this splint."

"That's what I thought."

He still struck her as naked, covered by that flimsy towel and nothing else; Joanna was hard-pressed to keep her gaze on his face. His chest was smooth and layered with muscle, his legs uncommonly long. He shifted, and the towel slipped down an inch, uncovering the upper edge of the patch of dark hair on his lower belly.

"There's a favor I want to ask of you." Graeham set the clothing next to him on the bed and laid out the other things on the chest, frowning in a preoccupied way. "Not a favor, precisely. A . . . proposition."

"What kind of proposition?"

"From things you've said, I gather you're in . . . rather difficult circumstances."

A mannerly way of asking whether she was destitute. Joanna lifted her chin; if she wouldn't share her predicament with Hugh, she most certainly wouldn't share it with this virtual stranger. "Not at all. I live simply because I choose to."

Graeham looked at her, his eyes searingly blue in the morning sunlight. "Because I can help you," he said in measured tones. "I have silver, as you know. 'Tis my overlord's, of course, but I have the authority to spend it. Some of it could be yours. Naturally . . . I'd want something in return."

She stared at him, hoping he didn't mean what she thought he meant.

"I'd like to stay here," he said when she didn't respond. "To live here for the next two months or so, while my leg heals. Instead of going back to St. Bartholomew's."

She crossed her arms over her chest. "That's all you'd want of me? To let you stay here?"

"Well . . . no. There would be something more."

She nodded, her jaw set. "I thought as much."

"I beg your pardon?"

"I should have used that axe on you last night," she said, fury making her voice quiver.

"What?"

"Instead, I gave you refuge. And this is how you repay me—insulting me in my own home."

"By what manner did I . . ." His eyes lit with sudden revelation. "Oh." He stood. The towel dropped to the floor.

She spun around and swept the leather curtain aside.

"No, don't leave," he said quickly. "I'm an idiot—I spoke clumsily. I didn't mean . . . that. I would never make such a proposal."

Joanna stood with her back to him, gripping the curtain in her fist. "You're a soldier. Don't tell me you've never paid a woman for her favors."

After a slight pause, he said, "Never a wedded woman."

Never a wedded woman. But he'd have no such compunction if he knew she was widowed.

"Turn back 'round," he said. "I've covered myself."

She turned around slowly to find that he'd wrapped the towel around his hips. "What was the 'something more' you wanted, then?" she asked.

He dragged a hand through his sodden hair; it caught in the tangles. "Well, meals, certainly, seeing as I'm to do naught but loaf about on this cot all day. And there might be the occasional small service or errand—I can't foresee everything I'll need. But I promise I'll try to keep my needs minimal and not trouble you any more than necessary."

Not trouble her? His very presence here troubled her. Seeing him standing before her, virtually naked, in all his dangerous, masculine splendor, made her heart flutter with quiet panic.

"I don't know, serjant. How would it look, to the neighbors, for me to keep a man in my home?"

He sat on the bed and hefted his leg out in front of him with both hands, grimacing. "I can't believe there aren't other matrons in London who take in boarders. There must be hundreds in West Cheap alone."

There were, of course; it was a common source of income for women, sometimes their only source. "Aye, but such arrangements sometimes lead to talk," she said. "I've managed to maintain an unblemished reputation all these years, despite my husband's frequent travels. I can't help but think it would be compromised if folks saw you about. You're a young man, after all, and, well . . ."

"I'm a young *cripple*—at least for the next couple of months. That should help to allay gossip. But who's going to see me? I'll be hidden away back here for the most part. I'm as eager as you not to let my presence here become too obvious."

"Why?"

He looked away, unsettled for some reason. "Let's just say I'm looking forward to a bit of peace and quiet. I've spent the last eleven years of my life living in a barracks with a hundred other men, and before that it was the boys' dorter at Holy Trinity."

"You were educated at Holy Trinity?" she asked, surprised. The Augustinian priory, tucked against London's northeast wall, near Aldgate, housed one of the most celebrated schools in England. An affluent, well-connected citizen might send his son there, but not if the boy was destined for soldiering.

"I was brought up there," he said. "From infancy until the age of fourteen, when I went to Beauvais to serve Lord Gui."

"From infancy! I . . . I thought 'twas just a school. I didn't know babies were sent there."

"They aren't, generally," he said, his expression dimming briefly, as if a cloud were passing over the sun. "I was the exception. This"—he indicated the storeroom with a wave of his hand—"is the first bedchamber I've ever actually had to myself."

"Not much of a bedchamber," she said.

"But it's mine alone," he replied. "Privacy is a rare and precious thing to me."

"If it's privacy you want, you may be disappointed. Folks walk back and forth along that alley all day long, and they like to look in the windows."

"I can close the shutters if I'm so inclined." Graeham lifted his purse from the floor and tugged open the drawstring that secured it. "I'll pay you four shillings, in advance, for two months' room and board."

"Four shillings," she whispered incredulously. "It's . . . too much."

"Gui of Beauvais is a wealthy man," Graeham said as he spilled pennies onto the chest and swiftly counted them. "And generous. He would want me to pay you well. And, as I said, I'm compensating you not just for the room but for various services as well."

"Aye." Joanna couldn't wrest her gaze from the coins. She counted them in her mind as he slid them one by one into a separate little pile. . . . *Four-and-twenty, five-and-twenty, six-and-twenty . . . Holy Mother of God . . . eight-and-twenty . . .*

"In fact, I need to write to Lord Gui and let him know where I am. If you could provide me with a sheet of parchment . . ."

"Parchment," she murmured. . . . *Seven-and-thirty, eight-and-thirty . . .*

". . . and ink and a quill and some sealing wax, I'd be most appreciative."

"Of course."

"Six-and-forty, seven-and-forty, eight-and-forty." He scooped the pennies off the chest into his cupped hands and held them out to Joanna.

Four shillings. Joanna couldn't remember having had that much money in her possession all at once. Most of her customers paid her in bread and milk and the occasional hen, and now that she couldn't deal in yard goods, there wasn't even much of that. Four shillings was enough to live on for a very long time, if she was judicious in her spending. This money meant she wouldn't have to sell her shop, at least not in the foreseeable future. It was a reprieve.

It was a godsend.

He was looking at her, his eyes translucent in the dazzling sunshine streaming in through the rear window.

She took a step forward and held out her hands. He smiled and filled them with the coins. They felt remarkably heavy, and cool. She had nowhere to put them, she realized. Her purse—empty, of course—hung on her girdle, but she couldn't open it with her hands full like this.

"Here." Leaning forward, Graeham reached out with his long arms and loosened the drawstring of her purse. It felt strangely intimate for him to be doing this; perhaps it was just his state of undress that made it seem so. He slid his fingers inside the purse and pulled it open.

She carefully poured the pennies in, so as not to drop any, then he cinched it closed.

"Oh," he said, "and I'd be grateful for a penknife and some cord, in addition to the other."

"The other?" She rested a hand on her bulging purse, savored its weight against her hip.

"The parchment and ink and so forth."

"Ah, yes. Your letter. Are you sure you need just one sheet of parchment? Isn't there anyone else you should write to? What about your family? Have you a . . . a wife back in Beauvais?" Most military men were unwed, but there were exceptions. Would a married soldier continue to live in a barracks, though? Perhaps; how could such a man afford to maintain a home? The life of a soldier's wife must be even more miserable than that of a merchant's impoverished widow.

Graeham looked away, snagging his fingers in his hair again when he tried to push it off his forehead. He lifted Prewitt's comb from the chest and rubbed his thumb over the teeth. "Nay, I'm not married. I'm more or less . . . I'm alone. I've no family."

"No sweetheart?"

"There's no one."

"What about your family in Oxfordshire? You said you were just passing through London on your way to visit kinsmen."

"They weren't expecting me. There's no need to write to them."

"Very well. I'll bring you what you need, but first I must open my stall."

"Of course." As she parted the leather curtain, he said, "Mistress?"

She turned to face him.

He gestured with the comb toward Prewitt's shaving gear laid out on the chest. "Are you sure it's all right for me to use your husband's things . . . to wear his clothes? He won't mind?"

He glanced up at her, his gaze so penetrating, so astute, that she had to look away.

"Nay," she said as she turned to leave. "I'm sure he won't mind."

Chapter 6

~~~

Joanna was outside opening the shutters of her shop window when Hugh drove up in the two-wheeled cart he'd borrowed from the inn where he was staying. He wondered why she was so late getting set up. The other shops overhanging Wood Street—those of the furrier, the rope maker, the apothecary, and the many silk traders—were open for business. The narrow dirt lane was swarming with pedestrians searching for a bargain, street peddlers hawking their wine and milk and soap, and the occasional pig snuffling for breakfast in the refuse littering the drainage channel.

"Good morrow, little sister."

"Hugh." Joanna nodded at him and glanced in a distracted way toward the cart.

Hugh reined in the mules harnessed to the cart, jumped down and kissed her on the cheek. "Fine morning, eh? Not a cloud in the sky."

She mumbled something unintelligible.

Hugh reached up to hold the upper shutter open while Joanna braced it on either side with two short poles, forming an awning. "I trust our new friend was no trouble for you during the night," he said.

His sister, preoccupied with lowering the bottom shutter, which served as a countertop for her wares, didn't answer him. Hugh propped the shutter in place with two more poles and followed her into the shop.

"He wasn't, was he?" Hugh asked.

Joanna crouched down to unlock a sizeable chest with one of the keys on her chatelaine. "Wasn't what?" She withdrew from the chest a folded length of white silk, prettily embroidered around the edges, which she shook out and spread on her display counter.

"Trouble." In an effort to be helpful, Hugh plucked a jumble of embroidered ribbons out of the chest and shook them out onto the silken cloth.

Rolling her eyes, Joanna separated the ribbons and arranged them in a tidy row, smoothing them down. "No trouble to speak of."

Which meant there was something she was choosing not to speak of. Hugh knew from long experience that he would have no luck badgering it out of her, so he said, "I'll fetch him and have him out of here quicker than you can draw your next breath."

He smacked a palm on the wall for emphasis and turned toward the rear of the house, but she stopped him in his tracks by grabbing a handful of his leather tunic. "He's staying here."

Hugh turned around slowly.

She said, " 'Twas a waste of your time, I'm afraid, bringing that cart." She laid three embroidered girdles next to the ribbons and reached into the box for a scarf. "He offered me four shillings to rent the storeroom for the next two months, and I couldn't turn it down."

"Four shillings! That's ridiculous. It's too much."

"I know. He doesn't seem to care." At last she looked directly at him, in that obstinate way of hers. "I accepted the money. He's staying. You'll have to take the cart back to wherever you got it from." Looking away, she muttered, "Sorry for your trouble."

Hugh leaned against the wall, rubbing his prickly jaw. "I don't mind a bit of trouble. What I mind is . . . well, the notion of your being alone with this fellow, *living* with him, for two whole months. You don't even know him."

She turned to glare at him as she spread the rest of her merchandise out on the counter. "You brought him here, Hugh, or don't you remember? You talked me into letting him spend the night."

"Yes, but—"

" 'He's a decent fellow,' you said."

"I said he *seemed* decent."

"You said you were sure he was harmless. Well, now

that decent, harmless fellow has offered me four shillings—
four shillings, Hugh—to sleep in my *storeroom,* for pity's
sake, and I bloody well intend to let him."

" 'Bloody well'? Since when has my lady sister started
saying 'bloody well'?"

"Since I stopped being your lady sister and started being
the wife of a—widow of a—silk merchant. And not a
very—"

"Not a very prosperous one—I know."

"That's another thing," she said, a bit wearily, as she
squatted down to lower the lid on the chest. "He thinks
Prewitt is still alive. I'd appreciate it very much if you
wouldn't disabuse him of that notion."

Hugh closed his eyes and massaged his suddenly aching
forehead. "And why, exactly, is it that he thinks Prewitt is
still alive?"

"Because I haven't told him that he's dead, obviously."

"And why—"

"Because it's wiser to let him think I'm a married
woman."

Hugh opened his eyes to find her staring him down,
hands on hips.

She glanced toward the drawn leather curtain at the rear
of the house and lowered her voice. "Do you remember
what you were telling me last night? About how most men
steer clear of entanglements with married women? About
how marriage protects a woman, shields her from unwanted attention?"

He sighed. "You think Graeham Fox will pester you with
unwanted attention unless he thinks you're married?"

"I . . . I don't know."

He grabbed her chin and forced her to look at him.
"What happened last night, Joanna?"

"Naught of any import," she said resolutely.

"Did he . . ."

She wrenched her chin out of his grasp. "Nay. He did
nothing. I would just feel better if he didn't . . . entertain
any ideas. He's not . . . the type of man I should be
encouraging."

That was true, certainly, and Hugh found it reassuring
that she had the good sense to see it. Graeham Fox, regard-

less of his character, good or bad, was a professional soldier, without property or prospects. He was the very last
type of man with whom Joanna should become involved,
especially given her dire straits—for it was clear that she
was all but penniless, despite her assertions to the contrary.
A woman who was "getting along fine," as she'd claimed,
would not be lighting her home with lumps of kitchen fat.
She would have wine and ale in her kitchen, and ample
food.

She would take no more charity from him, he knew—
she'd made that abundantly clear six years ago. Perhaps it
wasn't such a bad idea, after all, for Graeham to rent the
storeroom from her. His four shillings would go far toward
making life bearable for her, at least until Hugh could get
her married off to the right sort—Robert or someone like
him. And even if Graeham were the type to take advantage
of the situation—which Hugh doubted—his grievous injuries would render him harmless enough.

For the time being. He'd be on the mend soon enough;
what would happen then? Hugh had best have a little chat
with the good serjant and get some things straight right
from the beginning.

"Very well," he said. "I'll go along with your little mystery play, given that it's for a good cause. I hope you manage to pull it off, though. You've never been any good at
lying, sister."

" 'Twouldn't be lying," she said indignantly. "Precisely.
I mean, I never actually *told* him my husband was still alive,
so—"

"It's lying, Joanna." Hugh patted his sister on the cheek.
"At least be honest with *yourself*."

Joanna opened her mouth to deliver some retort, but
Hugh cut her off by saying, "You've got a customer, I
think."

She turned toward the fat matron scrutinizing her wares
and smiled. "Good morrow, Mistress Adeline."

Hugh strode to the rear of the house and knocked on
the frame of the storeroom door.

"Fear not, mistress," came Graeham's voice from within.
"I promise I'm not naked this time."

After a moment's pause, Hugh pushed the curtain aside

and walked in. Graeham, sitting on the edge of the bed
tugging a comb through his damp hair, looked nonplussed
to see him. "Hugh. I thought you were . . ."

"Evidently."

To his credit, Graeham didn't scramble to explain the
"naked" comment; in fact, he might even have looked
slightly amused. "Did you bring the cart?" he asked.

"Aye." Hugh scraped a wooden cask away from the wall
and sat on it, facing Graeham across from a chest set up
with a washbasin and shaving gear.

"Did your sister tell you it wouldn't be needed?"

"She did."

Graeham lifted his purse from the floor, whereupon Petronilla darted out from beneath the cot to take a swipe at
the belt that still dangled from it. "I'd like to reimburse
you for whatever you paid for it."

" 'Twas free. A friend lent it to me."

Graeham observed Hugh thoughtfully as he resumed
combing his hair. "Do you disapprove of my staying here?"

Hugh shrugged. " 'Twould matter little if I did. Joanna
is her own woman. She's always done just exactly as she
pleased." And been sorry about it afterward, more often
than not.

"You do disapprove," Graeham said.

Hugh leaned forward, his elbows resting on his knees.
"In truth, I'm torn in two directions. On the one hand, I'm
concerned for my sister—for her happiness as well as her
reputation. On the other, I don't quite see you as the type
who would exploit her trust—and mine. I've fought alongside enough men over the years to be able to tell the scru-
pulous ones from the blackguards."

"You're some sort of mercenary, I take it."

Hugh nodded. "A stipendiary knight. I wield my sword
for whoever will pay me the most."

Graeham's eyebrows rose, just slightly. Hugh knew what
he was thinking: How did a knight, stipendiary or not, come
to have a sister living above a shop in West Cheap?

Hugh noticed that Graeham had not only cleaned himself
up, he was dressed differently than he had been yesterday,
in a voluminous white shirt and russet braies. "Are those
Prewitt's clothes?"

"Aye. Your sister's been most generous."

"Joanna's a compassionate woman. She was that way as a girl, too. Used to take in wounded animals and tend to them. She has a good heart."

Graeham nodded, gazing at something through the open doorway. Turning, Hugh saw that, with the leather curtain open, the serjant had an unimpeded view of the entire length of Joanna's long, narrow house. In fact, through the big shop window he could see across Wood Street and into the apothecary's shop. Three gilded discs hung above its door. Inside, a redheaded girl was measuring powders on a scale.

But it wasn't the girl who had so captured Graeham's attention, Hugh knew. It was Joanna, backlit by the morning sunshine from the window, holding a ribbon up for her customer to examine. She laid it back down and lifted another one, her movements as elegant as if she were dancing a galliard in the great hall of Wexford Castle.

Graeham was still watching her, the comb forgotten in his hand. "This isn't her world," he said quietly. "She doesn't belong here."

"No, she damn well doesn't."

Graeham looked pointedly at Hugh. "Then what's she doing here?"

"She married beneath her."

"Prewitt?"

"Aye."

Graeham nodded slowly. "She must have been very much in love with him, then."

Hugh studied his steepled fingers. It would hardly do for him to disclose Joanna's true motivation for marrying Prewitt—that it hadn't been so much a question of love but of gullibility . . . and desperation, for she'd been sorely in need of saving at the time. Prewitt Chapman had been a handsome, smooth-tongued charmer, and she'd been as guileless and trusting as any fifteen-year-old girl. His many defects of character had eventually come to light, of course, but it would serve Joanna ill for Graeham Fox to become privy to them.

Graeham assumed that Prewitt was still alive to throttle him if he overstepped himself—an assumption that served to protect Joanna. That protection would evaporate should Hugh divulge the truth of the matter, which was that any interest Prewitt may have once had in Joanna had vanished within days of their wedding. Even if he were still alive, Hugh doubted he would trouble himself to defend her honor, should the need arise.

"Yes," Hugh said without looking up. "I suppose she must have loved him a great deal."

Graeham's eyes shifted once more beyond Hugh, toward the front of the house—toward Joanna. Hugh turned as well and saw her sitting at her embroidery frame in front of the shop window, passing a tiny needle in and out of the blue silk. The sun shone through her veil; it looked as if she were wearing a halo.

"Then why . . ." Graeham began, his gaze straying to the cot on which he sat, as he doubtless wondered why Prewitt had been relegated to sleeping there. "Nay, 'tis none of my concern."

"That it's not." Grimacing, Hugh picked up Prewitt's razor; it looked dull. Reaching for the whetstone, he set about sharpening the blade.

Graeham combed his hair in silence for a few moments, then said, "She runs the shop all on her own, does she?"

"Aye. Prewitt never could bear the retail end of things. And, of course, he's rarely home. I must say, Joanna's done quite well as a shopkeeper."

"Then why is she so . . ." Graeham tossed the comb onto the chest and smoothed his hair back. "Forgive me. I seem to be full of impertinent questions today."

"Why is she so poor? I suppose because most of her trade is by barter, so it's impossible to save any silver, and Prewitt . . . well, he's been gone for quite some time."

Graeham dipped his hands in the washbowl, scooped up a bit of soap, and worked it into a lather. "I wondered why she wasn't selling silks by the yard. She must be waiting for him to return with more."

"That must be it," Hugh said without looking at Graeham. He was no more adept at lying—or comfortable with it—than Joanna was.

"A pity," Graeham said as he rubbed the lather into his half-grown beard, "for a woman as . . . well, for any woman . . . to be left alone by her husband for months at a time."

"She's not alone now. I'm here." Hugh put the whetstone down and ran his thumb along the edge of the razor's blade; it was lethally sharp now, as keen as his sword. "If any man takes advantage of her in any way," he said, capturing Graeham's gaze meaningfully, "I'll slice his ballocks off and feed them to him." He held the razor out to Graeham, handle end first.

Graeham didn't so much as blink. "Well, you won't have to slice off mine." He took the razor, propped the little looking glass open against the washbowl, and calmly scraped the blade over his chin.

"Nothing personal, mind you," Hugh said. "I rather like you, actually."

"And I you." Graeham wiped the blade on a wadded-up wash rag and ran it over his jaw. "You saved my life, after all. I wouldn't repay you by compromising your sister."

"You must understand my concern. You'll be living under the same roof with her for two months or more, and she's a beautiful woman."

"She's a married woman. I make it a practice to steer clear of them. Too many complications." Graeham contorted his lower face as he shaved his upper lip.

Joanna was wise, Hugh realized, to keep Prewitt's death a secret from Graeham. He must cooperate in the charade, though it vexed him to do so.

"My word!" came a woman's voice from the alley. "Look who's home from his adventures."

Hugh looked toward the window to find a sloe-eyed wench in a provocatively low-cut red kirtle peering through the bars. Her great mop of hair, dyed severely black, tumbled loose about her shoulders; her vermillion-stained lips were curved in a coquettish smile.

"Leoda." Hugh rose and crossed to the window. She offered her cheek, which he kissed, noting that she still wore that oppressively sweet perfume. She'd aged over the past year, he thought, dismayed to see little creases underneath her face powder and a slight jowliness he'd never observed before. Or perhaps he'd simply never seen her in bright daylight. Nevertheless, she was still one of the prettiest whores in London.

"Isn't this awfully early for you to be up and about?" Hugh asked her.

She yawned. "I spent the night with a customer up on Popes Lane. He was gone when I woke up, so I never even got paid, and he'd had me twice, the greedy bugger. I'm heading back to my place now, to beg a bit of bread off my landlady. My belly's growlin'."

"Are you still living in that garret over on Milk Street?"

"Aye." Giving him her most lascivious, sleepy-eyed smile, she reached through the bars to brush a fingertip across his lower lip. "You ought to come by sometime so I can show you how much I've missed you."

"A tempting invitation. I might just do that."

Her gaze lit on Graeham; she appraised him with marked interest as he wiped his now clean-shaven face with a towel. "Who's this, then? A mate of yours? He's glorious. Don't he have the loveliest eyes."

"Breathtaking," Hugh said dryly. He introduced the whore to the serjant. "Graeham is renting this room from my sister, Joanna."

"You can bring him along, too, if you're so inclined," she suggested. "We'll have us a jolly little romp, all three of us."

"Alas," Graeham said, "I'm afraid I couldn't even make it as far as Milk Street." He hitched up the left leg of his braies, uncovering the bottom of the splint.

"You poor helpless pup," she cooed. "Well, if you can't come to Leoda, you must let Leoda come to you."

Graeham glanced toward the front of the house. Hugh looked too and saw Joanna chatting with a passerby without pausing in her work.

"Not here," Graeham said. " 'Twould be . . ." He shook his head. "Nay."

"Ah, the sister," Leoda said. "Are you and she . . ."

"Nay," said Graeham and Hugh simultaneously.

Leoda looked back and forth between them with strangely insightful amusement. "Yes, well, if you change your mind, serjant, I pass through this alley at least once each night. You need but tie a bit of string onto the window bar to let me know you're in the mood for a little company. Oh, and leave the latchstring out in back. I'll be quiet as a mouse. She'll never know I was here."

Graeham sat forward. "I really don't think—"

"It's tuppence for the usual," she said, "an extra penny if your taste runs to somethin' a bit fancier." She surveyed him from head to toe and back up again. "You're darling. And you, Sir Hugh—do come see me. We'll make up for lost time."

Hugh bowed. "I tremble in anticipation."

"Lying dog." She blew him a kiss and started sauntering away.

"Wait!" Graeham called out. "Leoda!"

Hugh looked at him curiously as he lifted his purse from the floor and reached into it.

Leoda reappeared at the window, smiling in a self-satisfied way as Graeham handed four pennies to Hugh and asked him to pass them to her. "Change your mind already, serjant?"

"Fourpence," Graeham said. "That's what he owed you, right? The man from Popes Lane?"

She rubbed her thumb over the coins. "You're payin' me for him?"

Graeham shrugged a little sheepishly. "A woman as beautiful as you ought not to be begging for her breakfast."

She stared at him for a moment in evident shock, then blinked and slipped the pennies into her purse. When she looked up, her eyes were soft. "I'll be lookin' for that string tied to the window bar, serjant."

When she was gone, Hugh grinned and shook his head. "You'll have to bed her now. She won't leave you in peace till you do."

"You're not serious."

"I know she's a bit long in the tooth, but she's been making a living on her back for enough years to have learned how to do it right. And from the way she just looked at you, my guess is she'll give you the tumble of your life."

"It's not her age, it's . . ." Graeham shook his head in apparent bewilderment. "Jesu, Hugh, first you threaten to slice my balls off if I take advantage of your sister's hospitality, and then you suggest I bring a whore into her home?"

"Do it late at night, after Joanna's asleep, and she'll never know."

Graeham chuckled disbelievingly. "You've got a strange notion of propriety, my friend."

"Look." Hugh sat on the cask again and addressed Graeham squarely. "I know you promised to . . . keep your distance from Joanna, and I know you mean well. You strike me as a man of honor. But it's been my experience that prolonged abstinence, when it's the result of circumstance and not of free choice, tends to rob a man of such scruples. Most of the soldiers I've fought with, if they go too long without a woman, they'll tup anything their cocks will fit into."

"Give me credit for some small measure of self-control, Hugh."

"I'm not blind, Graeham. I see how you look at her."

Hot color tinged Graeham's cheekbones. "Brotherly concern is making you imagine things."

"Come, now. How could any normal man live in the same house with a woman like Joanna and not become tempted? 'Twould go far to reassure me of your good intentions if you'd tie a string around that window bar every once in a while instead of trying to store your seed the whole time you're living here. Besides—'tisn't healthy to go that long without easing your lust. When I've had to do it, it's damn near made my balls explode."

"I'll think about it."

"You're just saying that to make me stop pestering you."

"*Is* there anything I can say to make you stop pestering me?"

"I shouldn't think so."

Graeham laughed tiredly. " 'Twill be a long two months, I think."

"It will if you persist in playing the monk the whole while. Listen, I'm going to pay a call on Leoda this afternoon . . ."

"Oh, yes?"

Hugh grinned. "She really is most . . . inspired when she's been missing me. I can ask her to stop by here tonight—"

"Nay."

"Graeham—"

"But there is something you can do for me when you've got the chance. A couple of things, actually. Next time you're out by way of St. Bartholomew's, would you mind collecting my baggage?"

"Gladly."

"And do they still trade horses out at Smithfield every Friday?"

"I should say so—except on feast days." The Friday fair, held weekly in a sprawling, grassy field outside the city walls to the northwest, remained the high point of the week for most folks in London.

"I've got a palfrey stabled at St. Bartholomew's. If you could arrange to sell it at Smithfield, I'd be most grateful."

"A *palfrey*." It was Joanna, standing in the doorway holding a deerskin-covered lapboard on which was laid out a sheet of parchment, a quill, a penknife, sealing wax, a clay jar of ink, and a tangle of coarse string. She looked puzzled but amused. "I wouldn't have thought you were the type to ride a palfrey, serjant."

Looking discomfited, Graeham said, " 'Tis a . . . long story. Are those things for me?"

"Aye." She laid them at the foot of his cot. "This isn't proper cord for sealing a letter," she said, indicating the string, "but 'twas the best I could come up with."

" 'Twill serve me perfectly well, mistress. Thank you."

She studied Graeham—his face—with an interest that made Hugh uneasy. "You look different," she said.

His gaze locked with hers, Graeham rubbed his smooth chin. "I shaved."

She nodded, her gaze lighting on his hair, which had looked dark last night, but was drying into light brown waves with a hint of rust. It seemed to Hugh as if there were something more she wanted to say, but instead she turned and glanced back toward her shop stall to find two women perusing her wares. "I must see what they want. I'll be back to empty the washbowl later, and then perhaps I can get you something to eat."

After she left, Hugh said, "I must be off as well. I promised I'd get that cart back to Southwark before nones."

"Many thanks for all your help, Hugh. But as for your advice about Leoda . . ." He shook his head, smiling.

Using the penknife, Hugh cut off a piece of string and handed it to Graeham. "Just think about it," he said, and left.

Chapter 7

～

Graeham looked up from his second reading of Wace's *Roman de Brut,* his gaze automatically searching through the open storeroom doorway and the empty salle to the shop stall, seeking a glimpse of Joanna. He saw her standing at the display window exhibiting her wares to a customer, an ethereal silhouette in a haze of afternoon sunlight.

A full week in this place, and still he had not tired of watching her as she went about her daily business. He liked the way she moved, the languid elegance of her gestures. He liked hearing the soft scrape of her voice as she chatted with passersby while laboring over her embroidery frame. And he especially liked the ephemeral perfume of newly sprouted grass and damp earth and wild blossoms that lingered in the storeroom after she'd been back there—which wasn't nearly often enough.

His leg still hurt, as did his ribs, but the pain had diminished to a sort of tedious ache, more annoying than tormenting. The surgeon had been by yesterday to check his splint and sell him a fine wooden crutch custom-built to accommodate his height—a vast improvement over either the sledgehammer or the broomstick he'd been resorting to. Of course, given that Graeham dared not show his face out-of-doors and was still too infirm to do so even if he'd wanted to, the crutch languished at his bedside for the most part.

Saving his place with the piece of string Hugh had cut for him last week—the one he was supposed to use to summon Leoda but had pressed into service as a bookmark instead—Graeham closed the *Roman de Brut*. He set it on the chest atop the other volumes—a mixture of history, verse, and epic tales—that Hugh had been kind enough to obtain for him from a used-book seller.

With the exception of his one isolated offer to sever Graeham's testicles and serve them up to him, Hugh had proven himself quite a congenial and useful friend. During the daylight hours, when he wasn't visiting his sister, the amiable mercenary seemed more than happy to run the occasional errand for Graeham. At night he occupied himself as did any furloughed soldier, in wenching and carousing till dawn, he and his mates staying one step ahead of the ward patrols who were charged with keeping London's streets clear after curfew. Graeham listened with envy to Hugh's tales of his nocturnal adventures; if he weren't confined to this bed, he'd have joined in at least once by now.

Graeham heard distant voices raised in argument and looked outside, his gaze automatically attracted to a large second-floor window in the stone house next to le Fever's. They were at it again—a stout and opulently garbed fellow of middle years and a dark-haired young man—his son, no doubt—quarreling once more about whatever it was they quarreled about on a nearly daily basis. This time the bird-like wife was there too, her voice a shrill, cajoling contrast to the masculine wrath of her husband and son.

Graeham was tired of listening to them fight. He was tired of the incessant cries of the street vendors out front, the rumble of cart wheels, the squeal of pigs. He was tired of rereading the same books. And he was sick to death of having to lie here on this cot all day like a bloody invalid, his critical mission at a standstill for God knew how long.

The only activity he hadn't grown weary of was watching Joanna Chapman. His fascination with her had nothing to do with boredom and everything to do with her.

Peering through the house toward the shop window, Graeham saw her hand a wrapped parcel to her customer, a sturdy woman who reached into the wicker basket on her arm and thunked a bundle of what looked like candles onto the countertop.

Aside from his books, which he read sitting up in bed with his leg propped on pillows, all the while keeping one eye on the rear window, there was little to keep Graeham occupied. He'd decided to recuperate here because of the location, but so far his observations of the le Fever house had yielded few insights that might prove helpful in the discharge of his mission.

Byram, Aethel, and the kitchen maid appeared to perform their chores as dutifully as any servants, although Rolf le Fever ranted at regular intervals about all manner of real and imagined transgressions on their part. He seemed to grow particularly incensed when he caught the plumply pretty kitchen wench flirting with Byram. Graeham wondered how the guildmaster would react if he knew that most mornings, after he left for the market hall, the couple took themselves off to the stable; it was always some time before they emerged, disheveled and festooned with straw.

In the afternoons, le Fever would often hold court in his sitting room for visitors, other mercers presumably, who came to transact business with him; documents would change hands, and sometimes silver as well.

The apothecary's red-haired daughter, Olive, delivered her phial of tonic to Mistress Ada every afternoon—she was there now—walking from her Wood Street shop to the back door of le Fever's house by way of the alley. Graeham had taken to shuttering the alley window after nones, to prevent her glancing inside and seeing him there.

Joanna had spoken the truth when she'd warned him that folks liked to look in the windows. For the most part he didn't mind this intrusion into his privacy; in fact, his conversations about literature and history with the leprous Thomas Harper had become highlights of his interminable days. Even Leoda, for all that she was an aging two-penny whore, had a certain rough-edged charm that Graeham found diverting when she stopped to chat with him. He didn't worry about Thomas and Leoda seeing him there, for they knew nothing of him or his reason for being in London. Olive, on the other hand, had been in le Fever's home the day he'd come for Ada. God knew what she'd heard or surmised—or whom she'd shared it with. He must not let her see him.

Ada le Fever hadn't shown herself, although the past few days had been unusually warm and sunny, drawing her neighbors—including Joanna—out of doors to plant their kitchen gardens as they shared jests and gossip. The windows of Rolf le Fever's solar, which presumably served as his wife's sickroom, were perpetually shuttered. At dusk, faint light would glow from within, as from a single candle or oil lamp, to be extinguished when the bells of nearby St. Mary-le-Bow rang curfew.

A distant thud, as of a door closing, drew Graeham's attention back to le Fever's house. Olive, having delivered Ada le Fever's medicine, was crossing the stable yard on her way to the gate in the low stone wall. Graeham shrank back a bit from the rear window, although she had no reason to look in his direction and probably wouldn't notice his shadowy form even if she did.

Petronilla jumped onto his bed, rammed her head against his hand, and looked up at him, as if to say, "Well?"

"Voluptuary," he muttered, and turned back to the window to watch Olive duck into the alley.

"Olive," came a young man's voice from the alley. Graeham saw shadows through the slats of the window shutters.

"Damian," she replied softly. "What are you doing here?"

"Waiting for you."

Petronilla head-butted Graeham again, yowling, "Now."

Olive gasped.

" 'Tis but a cat. Olive, I must talk to you."

A pause, then, "You oughtn't to do this. What if someone sees you? What if your *father* sees you?"

"Now."

Damnable creature. Grudgingly Graeham scratched the cat's head.

"I care naught what my father thinks," he said.

"Then you're a fool."

"Perhaps I am. But what he wants . . . what he demands . . . it doesn't matter. Nothing matters but you."

"I'm not . . ." She drew an unsteady breath. "I'm not what you think I am. There are things about me I could never tell you."

Gravely he said, "I have eyes and ears, Olive. There's naught you can tell me that I haven't already surmised."

"Oh, God," she murmured, her voice breaking.

"I love you anyway," he said, so softly Graeham could barely hear. "I love you, Olive."

"Oh, God," she said, her voice thick with tears. "Oh, God, you can't know. I don't believe it."

"It matters not. Olive, nothing matters but us. I love you."

"Nay . . . nay . . . we can never be together. Don't you understand?" She was weeping in earnest now. "Let go of me."

"Olive, no! Don't go—please. *Olive!*" Rapid footsteps receded down the alley toward Wood Street. Presently there came an extended sigh and a muttered curse, followed by footsteps headed in the opposite direction. From the rear window, Graeham saw a figure in a black mantle and felt hat heading toward Milk Street.

"Look!" Joanna held out the candles Mistress Hulda had given her as she entered the storeroom; Petronilla jumped down from Graeham's cot to rub against her legs. "I sold a kerchief to the chandler, and she paid me in candles. Just tallow, not wax, but they're a far sight better than a rush stuck in a lump of fat."

"Excellent," Graeham said distractedly. He wasn't looking at her, but beyond her to the front of the house. Joanna turned and followed his line of sight to the shop window. Her attention was immediately commanded by a young woman sprinting across Wood Street. The hood of her green mantle slipped down, a cloud of coppery hair waving as she ran. She ducked into the apothecary's and disappeared from view.

"That's Olive," Joanna said. "The apothecary's daughter." With a knowing glance at Graeham, she added, "Pretty girl."

His look of concentration faltered; he met her gaze and smiled. "Is she?"

"Is that not why you're staring after her?"

"Actually, no. She's . . . upset."

"Upset?"

"I heard her in the alley, talking to some fellow—a prospective suitor, from what I could tell, but she was resisting him. She became overwrought."

Joanna arched an eyebrow. "Is that how you amuse yourself all day, serjant? Eavesdropping on strangers' conversations?"

"It passes the time." His expression sobered. "She ran away crying."

"Oh, dear." Joanna turned and peered at the apothecary's shop. "Life hasn't been easy for that girl lately. I must find the time to talk to her. Perhaps tomorrow morning, before the fair." And before Olive's mother, who slept till nones more often than not, was up and about.

"Fair?"

"Aye, tomorrow's Friday—they'll be having the market fair at Smithfield. Hugh's arranged to have your palfrey brought over from St. Bartholomew's—he's going to sell it for you."

"I've put your brother to quite a bit of trouble, haven't I?"

"He doesn't mind. He grows bored and restless during his furloughs." She smiled conspiratorially. "And the busier you keep him, the less time he has for his wine and his dice and his . . . easy women."

Somehow Graeham suspected that nothing could keep Hugh from his easy women. "You're going with him to the fair?"

"Aye."

"I wouldn't have thought you'd want to leave the shop closed up for a whole day."

"A week ago I wouldn't have. I couldn't have risked losing any business that might have wandered by. But your four shillings have eased my circumstances a bit, and Hugh . . . he thought it would be a chance for me to get away from the shop for a while." And to renew her acquaintance with the old friend he hoped to betroth her to. *I'll have Robert meet us at the fair,* Hugh had suggested. *I can't very well bring him by the shop now. What would Graeham think, you entertaining a suitor while your husband is overseas? Wear something pretty Friday, and remember, don't cover up that hair.*

She would have to bathe tonight, but Graeham's presence here made that problematic. Perhaps after he was asleep . . .

"I used to love Smithfield," Graeham said, somewhat wistfully. "We used to go almost every summer afternoon— the boys from Holy Trinity. Brother Simon, our prior, he liked to say it wasn't just our minds and souls that needed nourishing, but our bodies. We'd play ball against the boys from St. Paul's and St. Martin's. And on Sundays we'd go and watch the jousting there."

She smiled, trying without success to envision this virile soldier as a boy. He would have been lanky and rather ungainly, she guessed; men of his stature tended to go through an awkward period as youths, before those rangy bones filled out with muscle.

There was nothing awkward about him now, certainly— nor did a hint remain of the derelict she'd thought him to be that night she'd found him in her storeroom, caked with grime and recking of wine. He'd shaved every day since he'd been here, probably more out of boredom than an obsession with grooming. His hair was always combed, his face clean. He had the most extraordinary, intently blue eyes she'd ever seen on a man—on anyone. His masculine beauty unsettled her. She didn't like to look directly at him, fearful that her appreciation would show in her eyes.

His manner was always polite and respectful. Although she knew his days were filled with tedium, and she often sensed that he would like for her to linger when she brought him his meals or tidied up the storeroom—and, in fact, she was frequently tempted to do so—he never pressed her. She had a shop to run, after all, and chores to tend to.

And he unnerved her terribly, all scrubbed and hand- some in Prewitt's clothes, watching her, always watching her. Yes, he was courteous, the consummate gentleman. But she could not accustom herself to his languid, strangely probing gaze.

And she could not forget the lingering glide of his fingers over her breast that first night, when she'd come to him after awakening to his groaning with pain. What had started as an inadvertent brush of his hand had become, in the charged and silent darkness, a breathless and purposeful caress. She could still feel the heat of his touch, as if his fingertips had scorched her very flesh. It filled her with a strange agitation, a turmoil of the senses that was both frightening and exhilarating.

". . . and I'd take off my clothes," he was saying, "and wade in and let the water envelop me. 'Twas heaven."

She blinked at him. "I'm sorry, I . . ."

He chuckled. "I was telling you how I used to sneak away from Holy Trinity late at night in the summer to go swimming in the horse pool at Smithfield. 'Twasn't a very engaging story, I suppose." His smile was tentative, almost bashful. "I'm just trying to keep you here talking to me. When I took it into my head to stay here, I'm afraid I didn't count on being quite so insufferably bored."

"I'm sorry."

" 'Tisn't your fault. You've your own affairs to attend to."

"Yes, well . . ."

"I'm not a guest, after all, merely a boarder. And you put up with a great deal from me as it is."

"Nonsense. You're no trouble."

He smiled dubiously. "You're a singularly poor liar."

Heat rose in Joanna's cheeks. She edged toward the doorway. "Yes, well. I should be getting back to the shop."

He nodded, expressionless. "You'll be gone all day tomorrow, then?"

"Until vespers or thereabouts. I'll leave food and ale for you."

"Thank you."

She paused in the doorway. "You'll be even more bored than usual, I suppose. I'm sorry."

He smiled and shrugged his big shoulders. "I can hardly expect you to stay here just for me."

Joanna fiddled with the string that bound the candles together. "Yes. Well." She turned and started back toward the shop stall.

"Are you happy?"

Slowly she spun back around, her candles clutched to her chest.

He was sitting forward, looking at her with that keen-eyed gaze that sent warm shivers coursing through her.

" 'Tis a presumptuous question," he said. "I've gotten

into the habit of asking them of late. Perhaps it's the boredom."

She nodded warily.

"Are you?" His white shirt trembled just slightly as his chest rose and fell.

"Serjant, I . . . I don't know how to answer that." She glanced over her shoulder toward the shop. "I really must be getting back to—"

"I'd like to eat supper with you tonight."

"Supper?" she said inanely.

"Aye, I'd like to eat with you at the table there instead of having you bring my meal in to me. I'd like to eat all my meals there, in fact—from now on."

"But your leg . . ."

"It's much improved." Reaching for his new crutch, he stood it up and hauled himself to his feet, grinning—although it seemed to Joanna that his teeth were perhaps just a bit tightly clenched. "I can get about well enough to make it to the table at mealtimes."

Supporting himself with the crutch, he took a few halting steps in her direction. She rapidly backed up. "You're supposed to stay in bed. Master Aldfrith said—"

"My body will waste away if I languish in bed for two months. Come—let me eat with you." Quietly he added, "I promise not to ask you if you're happy."

Chapter 8

~

"Are you very unhappy?" Graeham asked as he broke off a piece of hearty barley bread and dipped it in his lamb stew.

Joanna cast him a censorious look from across the table. "I thought you weren't going to ask me—"

"Whether you're happy," he finished. "I never said I wouldn't ask you if you're *un*happy."

"You *are* presumptuous." She refilled their wooden cups from the ewer of wine that sat on the table between them, a luxury, like the lamb, that he insisted on having—and paying for.

He regarded her for a thoughtful moment as he ate the broth-soaked bread. "Well, are you?"

"Do I seem unhappy?"

"Nay—but there are those who have the gift of persevering with remarkable grace in the face of adversity. I've been watching you."

She looked at him as she took a sip of wine, then quickly dropped her gaze. Her cheeks might have heated to a deeper pink, or perhaps it was just a trick of the candlelight. Her hair was veiled, as usual, and she wore her ugliest kirtle, the brown one. The wool was threadbare, with a neat little patch near the neckline, above which peeked about an inch of white linen shift. There was often a hint of dishevelment about her, as if she were simply too busy to keep herself put to rights, and tonight was no exception; the shift's drawstring had come undone, the two cords hanging over the brown bodice of her kirtle. The loosened shift exposed the merest tantalizing swell of upper breast;

he'd struggled all through supper to keep his gaze from straying downward as they conversed.

Graeham ate some more of her excellent stew, washing it down with a generous swallow of wine. The vexatious Petronilla leapt onto his bench for a handout; he grabbed her by the scruff of the neck and tossed her off. His presence at the table had kept the timid Manfrid from showing his face. "You work from dawn till dusk—and beyond," he said. "Often you're still stitching away at your embroidery when I retire for the night."

"The shop keeps me too busy during the day to get much new work done."

"And on top of that, you cook and clean and see to my various needs. And all without the slightest hint of complaint or frustration, as if . . ." He hesitated, then plunged forward. "As if you were born to this life—as if it were your destiny, and not . . . cause for disappointment."

Her gaze searched his. "What has Hugh told you?"

"Only that you married beneath you . . . for love."

She pushed her half-eaten bowl of stew away and lifted her cup to her mouth.

"And that you've made quite a success of the shop. But that your husband is usually abroad. I imagine you must get lonely."

"Well, I don't."

He sopped up the remainder of his stew with the last piece of bread and ate it, dusting his hands. "There's no sin in being lonely. 'Tis a feeling I'm all too famil—"

"I'm not lonely."

She was too proud to admit it, he realized. "Very well. I shouldn't press the issue."

"Why do you, then? Why do you interrogate me so incessantly? Are you really that bored?"

He gave a small shrug. "Perhaps you're that interesting."

A little huff of bitter laughter rose from her. "I'm a West Cheap shopmaid, nothing more."

"You *were* something more, once," he said quietly. "You still are."

She met his gaze uneasily, looking away when Petronilla approached her, yowling for a handout. Joanna clicked her tongue and the cat leapt onto her bench. She fished a morsel of lamb from her bowl and let the animal lick it off her fingertips.

Beyond her, Graeham saw a figure pass one of the two windows that looked out onto the alley from the salle. The passerby paused and glanced inside; Leoda, in a rust-colored kirtle so snug as to thrust her generous bosom into ripe display. With a glance at Joanna, Leoda smiled and blew Graeham a kiss.

The whore must have captured his attention for a moment too long, for Joanna noticed and turned toward the window.

"Evenin', Mistress Joanna," greeted Leoda.

Joanna smiled politely. "If you're looking for my brother, Leoda, he left here in the early afternoon. I'm afraid I don't know where he is."

"I'm that sorry to hear it, mistress," Leoda replied, though Graeham was fairly certain it was he she'd come looking for; they frequently chatted during the supper hour. "You'll tell Sir Hugh I was askin' for him, then, won't you?"

"Of course."

"Many thanks." Leoda sauntered away without a glance in Graeham's direction. A good whore didn't greet a man familiarly if he was in the company of another woman—unless the other woman happened to be another whore, but nobody could make that mistake about Joanna Chapman. In truth, Graeham wouldn't have cared if Leoda had greeted him. He wasn't ashamed of having befriended her, whore or not, and their relationship was innocent. But then, Joanna would almost certainly assume otherwise. Perhaps it was best that Leoda had been circumspect.

"That was one of the neighborhood . . . women of the town." Joanna pulled Graeham's empty bowl across and nested hers inside it. "She's a favorite of Hugh's when he's in London."

"I wondered how you'd come to know . . . such a woman by name."

She smiled in a way that looked indulgent. "Hugh could have any woman he wants, but he prefers women like that—women who don't expect anything from him but a few pennies. He's a hard man to rein in."

"Is that why he became a mercenary? For the freedom?"
A knight who sold his services to the highest bidder, Graeham reasoned, would enjoy a great deal more autonomy
than one who'd pledged an oath of fealty to any one lord.

Joanna frowned into her wine cup as she thought about
it. "Well, he likes the freedom, certainly. But more than
that, he loathes being forced to live up to someone else's
expectations. It's because of how he was brought up—how
we were both brought up. There were a great many demands placed upon us." She collected their spoons and
swept up the crumbs of bread with a napkin, her troubled
expression giving way to a surprisingly winsome smile. "I
went to the bakeshop today, as you asked. They had
cream tarts."

"Excellent." Sweets were a staple at Lord Gui's table,
and Graeham missed them. As Joanna cleared the table,
he said, "It surprises me to hear you speak of demands. I
was under the impression you and Hugh came from quite
a privileged background."

"It was . . . well, certainly it was privileged in many ways.
Wexford is a grand castle—"

"Castle."

She unwrapped the two little tarts, served one to each of
them, and took her seat. "Our father is William of Wexford. He's a very great knight with a vast holding half a
day's ride to the south. Our lady mother died of childbed
fever after I was born, but Lord William is still living."

"Is Hugh heir to his lands?"

"We won't know that until Father dies. He holds Wexford for his overlord—who may or may not choose to grant
it to Hugh when the time comes." She took a bite of her
tart, and Graeham followed suit; it was sinfully good.

"Doesn't it nettle him," Graeham asked, "not knowing
whether such an important holding is to be his?"

"I'm not certain he even wants it. His recollections of
Wexford, like mine, are . . . not pleasant, by and large. Our
sire is a man very sure of what he wants and how to get
it. The day Hugh turned four, Father handed him over for
military training to his master-at-arms—a monster by the
name of Regnaud. Father's goal was to mold Hugh into
the most celebrated knight in Christendom—a distinction

that would reflect glory upon himself, of course. And . . . well, he felt a boy needed discipline if he was to be a great soldier, and he gave Regnaud a free hand with the whip. 'Twasn't much of a childhood for Hugh."

"And you," Graeham said, frowning, "were you . . . disciplined?"

"Not with the whip." She broke off a bit of the tart's crust and nibbled it. Without looking up, she said, "Father would have me brought to him for beatings when I displeased him. He'd have Hugh locked up in the cellar so he couldn't interfere." She drew in a breath, still avoiding his gaze. "I'm afraid I often chafed at his notion of ladylike behavior. I'd go exploring in the woods when his clerics were expecting me for lessons—that sort of thing."

Graeham found himself asking, "How badly did he beat you?"

She raised her eyes to his. "You're interrogating me again."

"I'd like to know," he said softly.

Her throat moved. "He never struck me on the face. He didn't want to mar my appearance, because he planned to advance himself by marrying me off to a son of Baron Gilbert de Montfichet."

"You were betrothed to a son of Lord Gilbert?" he asked incredulously. Gilbert de Montfichet and his cousin, Walter fitz Robert fitz Richard, held the only true baronies within the city of London. Their castles, Montfichet and Baynard, tucked right up next to each other against the westernmost stretch of city wall, were the only fortressed dwellings in London aside from the Tower. As the city's only true barons, Lord Gilbert and Lord Walter were its most powerful citizens, wielding considerable influence with the king.

"The younger son," Joanna said. "He has two—*had* two. His older son, Geoffrey, died of measles about two years ago. Nicholas was the second son. I wasn't officially betrothed to him. But when I was eleven, Father sent me to London to serve the baron's wife, Lady Fayette, at Montfichet Castle. It was understood that a marriage to Nicholas would be negotiated if I was found suitable. Of course, I bristled at being a pawn for Father's advancement, but I was happy to be away from Wexford. And to be in London!''

Joanna broke off another, larger, piece of the tart and ate it. Finding her fingertips coated with custard, she slid them one by one between her lips to suck them clean. A surge of arousal ambushed Graeham.

"You like London?" he asked, trying to ignore the small pink tip of her tongue as it darted out to sweep a drop of custard from her lower lip.

"I did then. It was so big and grand, and everyone seemed so sophisticated. And I liked Lady Fayette. 'Twas she who taught me to embroider."

"She should be commended. You're very gifted at it."

Joanna smiled shyly. "Thank you."

Graeham finished his tart. "Why didn't you marry the baron's son? Did his parents reject you?"

"Nay, they seemed to adore me. And Nicholas was willing. 'Twas I who balked. The betrothal contract was drawn up when I was fourteen, but I just . . . couldn't consent to it. I stalled for almost a year, puzzling how to get out of it."

"Did you despise Nicholas that much?"

"In truth, I liked him. And he seemed to like me—to a point. Nicholas was one of those men who . . . prefer the charms of their own sex."

"Ah."

"Everyone knew it." She took a deep breath. "And I'm afraid I just couldn't reconcile myself to such a union. But at the same time, I dreaded being made to return to Wexford should I refuse it outright. My sire . . . he threatened to beat me to death if I was sent back home."

Graeham had lifted his wine cup; he lowered it. "Would he have done it, do you think?"

" 'Twas possible—he had an ungovernable temper. There was pressure from all fronts for me to acquiesce. I felt all adrift. I had no one to counsel me, no one to turn to."

"What of Hugh?"

"Oh, he'd turned mercenary as soon as he was knighted, at eighteen. 'Twas around the time I was sent to London. He told me he knew I didn't need him there anymore, for protection, because I'd be away from our sire. And he would have gone mad if he'd tried to remain at Wexford, under the thumb of our father."

"So, you were fifteen, and alone, and distressed . . ."

"Terrified," she corrected.

He nodded. "Is that when you met your husband?" How else could she have gotten out of such a fix?

She looked down and fiddled with her half-eaten tart. "Prewitt came to Montfichet Castle to show some silks to Lady Fayette. I was . . . instantly smitten. He was older, urbane, and he dressed like a gentleman. He wooed me in secret." She shrugged. "We were married within a fortnight."

"That can't have pleased your sire."

"It didn't. He banished me from Wexford. I haven't seen him in six years."

"A pity."

"No, it's not. I'd be happy never to lay eyes on the man again."

"Ah, we come back to happiness." Graeham leaned forward on his elbows and captured Joanna's gaze. "Are you going to tell me whether you're happy?"

She rolled her eyes and began collecting bowls and cups and bits of tart. "I'm going to take our supper dishes out to the kitchen and wash them. And then I . . . I have some things to do."

"More embroidery?"

She nodded without looking at him.

"You'll go blind, doing work like that at night."

"I'll go out of business if I don't."

"But surely your husband will return soon with more silks to sell. And in the meantime, you've got my four shillings to keep you going. You shouldn't work yourself so hard."

She rose and carried the ewer of wine to a crude cupboard fashioned of planks on posts. " 'Tis a difficult habit to break."

Graeham felt a tugging on his splint and looked down to find Petronilla sharpening her claws on it. He swatted her away, whereupon she settled down just out of reach, watching him with what looked like amused contempt.

"Cats make no sense to me," he said. "Meaning no disrespect, mistress, but I can't fathom why anyone would bother keeping one as a chamber animal."

Retrieving a tray from the cupboard, Joanna returned to the table and began piling their dishes on it. "You're not afraid of them, are you?"

"*Afraid* of them!"

"Some people are."

"I don't fear them—it's just that I'd rather have the company of a nice, agreeable dog. Cats are selfish, calculating beasts, useless save for mousing."

"Manfrid never catches anything, but Petronilla is quite the fine mouser. She eats spiders, too. You'll never find anything scuttling about in these rushes."

He drained the last of his wine and handed her the empty cup. "At least she serves some purpose, then. But her brother is too nervous and timid to be of any use, as far as I can tell. 'Tis a mystery to me why you keep him."

"He's not shy with me—although he was in the beginning. It's men he's truly frightened of. I think some man must have mistreated him when he was a kitten, before I got him. He's happy when it's just me here. He likes to sit on my lap when there's no one else about."

"Dogs can warm laps, too, and they can also be trained. They can fetch things for you, flush out small game . . ."

"Manfrid doesn't exist to serve me," she said, a bit testily. "He just exists. I like him for what he is—a big, sweet, shy tomcat. Does he have to be of some use to me for me to want him about?"

"To my way of thinking, yes."

"Perhaps," she said coolly as she carried the trayful of dishes toward the back door, "that's where you and I are fundamentally different." At the entrance to the hallway, she turned and asked, "Will you be needing anything else before you retire for the evening, serjant?"

"Nay, there's nothing I need." He rose awkwardly and reached for his crutch, leaning against the bench. "Good night, mistress."

"Good night."

Graeham awoke to the muffled thump of the back door closing. He lay still in the dark, his ears tuned to the sound of soft footfalls in the hallway next to the storeroom. Someone was entering the house.

An intruder? Perhaps. Whoever it was clearly was endeavoring to make as little noise as possible.

Joanna's upstairs. And Graeham was all but completely crippled. Could he defend her if he had to?

He sat up, heart hammering, and used both hands to lower his splinted leg off the bed. Pulling himself up with his crutch, he grabbed the big knife he'd appropriated from the cur who had lured him into the alley last week, the one who'd called himself Byram. And if the knife was taken from him, there was that axe Joanna kept tucked away in the salle for protection, the one she'd threatened him with that first night.

As Graeham hobbled slowly to the leather curtain, a thought occurred to him. Perhaps the intruder was Prewitt Chapman, home from his latest sojourn. How would the silk merchant react, he wondered, upon finding a crippled, half-naked stranger—for Graeham slept in naught but his underdrawers—accosting him with a knife in his own home in the middle of the night?

How late was it, anyway? He remembered hearing the bells of curfew as he was readying himself for bed, and then he'd fallen asleep. Prewitt couldn't have gained entrance through the city gates after curfew, so it probably wasn't him.

Striving for silence, he parted the leather curtain, just slightly, with the tip of the knife, and peered into the candlelit salle. His breath caught in his throat.

Joanna, standing in profile to him, her single braid draped over one shoulder, was shimmying out of her unlaced brown kirtle. It pooled on the rush-covered floor, leaving her in her undershift of thin, worn linen, which was sleeveless and came only to her knees; her legs, exquisitely shapely, were encased in black stockings.

The drawstring that gathered the shift's neckline, he saw, was still untied. When she bent over to pick up the kirtle, it slid down one shoulder and fell open, baring a softly gleaming breast for the interval of a heartbeat.

Graeham's hands twitched; desire settled heavy in his loins.

She was preparing for a bath, he saw. The table had been dismantled, its top leaning against the wall while the round base had been overturned to form a bathtub. Next to it sat two steaming buckets. The benches that normally flanked the table still stood to either side of the tub. Joanna's white silken wrapper, a towel, a dish of soap, a large ivory comb, and a small phial lay on one of them.

She draped her kirtle over the other bench, next to her girdle and veil, then sat and kicked off her slippers.

Graeham knew he shouldn't watch her unawares. It was dishonorable. There was no excuse for it. He would close the curtain and turn around.

Soon.

Raising her shift to mid-thigh, she slid the garter off and set it aside, then began rolling the stocking down over her knee and calf. The hosiery gleamed with silken luster in the flickering candlelight. There was something oddly touching about this humbly clad woman with her luxurious silken hose and wrappers that only she ever saw—and, of course, her husband, when he deigned to come home for a visit.

Close the curtain, you pathetic bastard. Yet he could not wrest his gaze from her as she slowly peeled off first one stocking, then the other. The shift slipped off both shoulders as she leaned forward to work the snug hose over her feet. The movement exposed the satiny upper slopes of her breasts almost to the nipples. Her legs parted for a fleeting moment; the black shadow at the juncture of her thighs appeared and vanished in a blink.

Graeham closed his eyes, clenched his jaw.

When he looked again, she was on her feet, lifting one of the buckets with both hands, her arms quivering with strain as she poured the hot water into the tub. By the liquid splashing, he could tell there was already water in there—probably cold water from the well that she was heating up with water she'd boiled in the kitchen. She poured in the second bucket, then unstoppered the phial and carefully added two drops of its contents—thick oil—to her bathwater.

Leaning over the tub, she swirled the water with one hand while holding the other pressed to her chest to keep the shift from slipping down. She closed her eyes and smiled as the fragrant steam rose around her. Graeham inhaled as the flowery scent wafted toward him, and he smiled, too; so this was how she managed to smell like a wild, rain-washed meadow in the middle of London.

Graeham didn't think he'd ever seen anything more captivatingly sensual than Joanna Chapman at this moment— her eyes closed, her smile one of dreamy anticipation. She straightened, her smile fading, her gaze unfocused as she contemplated the steaming water. She stood absolutely still, her hand resting on her upper chest, for so long that Graeham wondered what she could be thinking that absorbed her so.

Gradually her hand drifted downward over the curve of a breast, her fingers lightly shaping its roundness through the flimsy linen of her shift. Absently, as if she were mesmerized, she stroked her thumb across the nipple, which stiffened.

Graeham stood rooted to the spot, his heart pumping painfully in his chest, heat flooding his loins as he grew erect.

Joanna's dreamlike countenance never altered as she skimmed her hand downward, over her stomach to her lower belly. Her eyes drifted closed as her hand came to rest between her legs. She didn't caress herself, merely stood in heated silence, lost in thought.

When she opened her eyes, Graeham was unnerved to find them glimmering wetly. Her expression suddenly troubled, she whispered something that sounded like "Fool."

She swiped her hands over her eyes, then swiftly untied her braid and unwove the plaits. Standing with her back to Graeham, she combed through her rippling dark gold hair until it hung in a luxuriant sheet nearly as long as her shift. Tossing the comb onto the bench, she shrugged out of her loosened shift, which fell in a puddle of linen at her feet.

She was naked now, entirely naked, although the silken blanket of her hair concealed all but her legs from view. Graeham closed the curtain with a sigh of disgust at himself. Only a week ago he'd promised Hugh he wouldn't compromise his sister, and already he'd spied on her toilette, like some callow youth who'd never seen a woman

in his life—a callow youth of base character, for only the
lowest churls peeked at women while they undressed.

Graeham had always prided himself on his soldierly
sense of honor. But abstinence, as Hugh had pointed out,
tended to rob a man of his scruples. *How could any normal
man live in the same house with a woman like Joanna and
not become tempted?*

Graeham limped back to the little cot and sat, carefully
so as not to rustle the straw in the mattress and call attention to himself; God forbid Joanna should discover that
he'd been peering at her through a gap in the curtain! He
grimaced as he lay on his back, his broken ribs and leg
grousing about all this activity in the middle of the night.

Straining, he could just make out the hushed liquid
sounds of Joanna bathing—soft trickles, little splashes. He
pictured her reclining in the perfumed steam, naked but
for wet tendrils of hair clinging to her like golden snakes,
gliding her soap-slicked hands down her chest, over her
breasts, and lower . . .

"By the Rood," he whispered into the darkness as he felt
himself grow harder still, "I'll never make it two months."

He took a deep, calming breath and closed his eyes, com-
manding himself to sleep . . . but all he could see was
Joanna, her head thrown back on the edge of the tub,
arched and trembling as she gave herself the pleasure her
husband wasn't here to give her. Did she touch herself that
way? he wondered. It excited him to think of a woman
pleasuring herself. Once, in Paris, he'd even talked a pretty
little whore into bringing herself to climax while he
watched; it had cost him half a sou.

But as arousing as it was to imagine a woman gratifying
herself, Graeham could not bring himself to ease his own
lust, no matter how frustrated he became. Partly it was
because of all those ceaseless lectures by the brothers at
Holy Trinity about the sin of self-abuse. But mostly it was
simply that he'd slept in dormitories his entire life; if threats
of hellfire won't teach a man to sublimate his sexual hunger, lack of privacy generally will. In the past, Graeham
had found tourneys and sport fighting useful in diminishing
his physical passions—when no accommodating woman was

available, of course. But such exercise would be impossible for quite some time.

'Twould go far to reassure me of your good intentions, Hugh had said, *if you'd tie a string around that window bar every once in a while instead of trying to store your seed the whole time you're living here.*

Graeham had tried to imagine tupping Leoda, but despite her brazen flirtatiousness, he didn't find her that desirable. Perhaps it was that he'd come to view her as a friend of sorts. Or perhaps he'd simply had enough of "women of the town," as Joanna so quaintly referred to them. Whores and laundresses had pleased him well enough when all he'd wanted was a bit of indifferent bedsport. But he wanted more now . . . so much more than a woman like that could hope to give him.

By September at the latest, he would be married to Lady Phillipa and settled in Oxfordshire, and then he would not be lying awake nights pondering the problem of how to vent his lust.

From beyond the leather curtain he heard a musical little splash of water and then something that sounded like a sigh.

"Go to sleep, you sorry bastard," he muttered to himself. "Dream about tournaments."

But he didn't dream about tournaments. He dreamt that he was back at Holy Trinity, awakening in the middle of the night in the boys' dorter. He knew it was a dream. Odd, he thought, that he should dream of Holy Trinity after all these years. Perhaps it was because he was back in London.

"Serjant?" The voice was an airy whisper, distant, pleading. But it was a woman's voice, and women weren't allowed in this part of the priory—not ever, but certainly not at night.

Graeham sat up on his little cot, one of many—hundreds, perhaps thousands, for he couldn't see where they ended in either direction—lined up in two long rows against the dorter's east and west walls. Moonlight poured through the narrow, arched windows, illuminating the cavernous chamber in strips of hazy silver-blue.

He was all alone, he realized with a childish surge of alarm. The other beds—the innumerable little neatly blanketed cots—were empty, every last one. They were gone, all the other boys. Where had they gone? Why had they left him here alone?

He drew his legs up and hugged himself, shivering; for some reason his was the only cot without a blanket.

Had the other boys taken his blanket? No—they'd never even been here. They hadn't left him here. He'd always slept here alone. He'd been alone since the beginning— from as long as he could remember. How could he have forgotten?

"Serjant?"

A bench stood in the middle of the dorter, between the two rows of beds. There was something tossed onto it, something made of white linen. His nightshirt?

Graeham looked down at himself; no, he was wearing his nightshirt. He squinted at the linen garment on the bench and saw that it was a lady's undershift.

He felt a quickening—down there. Squeezing his eyes shut, he whispered his Latin drill in an effort to make the feeling pass, as the brothers had advised. When he opened his eyes, the bench was gone. So were the cots, except for his. The dorter was filled with water; it lapped at the walls like a lake. His cot swayed slightly, and he realized it was floating.

His sense of panic worsened when he saw that the stone walls no longer existed. The sky had turned dark and bruised and moonless; the water, which extended endlessly in all directions, was black as ink. His cot rocked on the suddenly bucking waves; he clawed at the straw mattress, trying to keep from falling in.

A thick mist rose from the turbulent water, and from somewhere in its vastness, Graeham heard her again. "Help me, serjant."

"Are you drowning?" he called out.

"I'm unhappy."

He had to go to her. He had to save her. He'd learned to swim in the horse pool, when he was a boy. He was a man now, and he hadn't swum in years, but surely it wasn't the sort of thing you forgot.

Graeham seized his shirt—her husband's shirt—and whipped it over his head. He tore off Prewitt's braies and drawers and the bandage around his ribs, leaving himself naked save for those damned splints.

"Serjant? Please, serjant, save me."

With frantic haste, Graeham clawed at the linen strip that bound the splints together and began unwinding it. He unwound it and unwound it and unwound it, and still it kept coming, a never-ending ribbon of linen that grew and grew into a great tangled mass. He would never get it off. It would never end.

"Serjant . . . please."

Graeham leapt off the cot, heedless of the splint, which disappeared in any event the moment he hit the water. He'd expected it to be cold, but it was warm, like bathwater, and very still and quiet now. The mist lay atop it like a great, dense cloud. It was deep; he had to tread water to keep afloat.

"Where are you?" he called through the mist.

"Here."

Graeham saw a shadow up ahead; perhaps it was her. He swam toward her, the water strangely thick as he moved through it, like heated oil.

"Is that you?" he asked as he approached the nebulous figure; in the dark and the fog he could barely see her.

"Yes, it's me," she said, softly now. "I've come to you. I'll make you happy."

Dimly he realized things had gotten turned around. Now it was she who had come for him, she who was going to make *him* happy.

She had her arms outstretched to him, luminous and beseeching, but her face was still obscured by the mist. "Come."

He reached out to her—she was right in front of him now, she was inches from him—but his hands slid right off her, she was so slick and wet.

"Come to me." He saw her more clearly now. She closed her eyes, her lips half parted.

Knowing it was wrong—she was a wedded woman—Graeham bent his head to hers, wrapped his arms around her, but she slipped from his embrace like a wraith. Her body glided against his as she floated away, buoyed by the syrupy water. He felt her stiff little nipples graze his chest, felt the sleek caress of a thigh against his, and instantly grew hard.

He grabbed her, pulled her to him, felt her legs open for him fleetingly before she drifted into the dark and the mist. Thrashing in the thick water, he cried, "Where are you?"

She touched his back and he spun around and seized her, or tried to; she was so slippery, so elusive, and he needed her so desperately, needed to join with her so they wouldn't be alone anymore. Their legs pumped slowly in the viscous water, touching and parting and touching again. He tried to grip her hips to pull her to him, but his fingers wouldn't hold her.

Graeham clutched at her, frantic now, hard as steel, quivering with the need to pierce, to push. Sweat ran into his eyes as he struggled to capture her, to wrap her legs around him and ram himself into her. He thrust against her, his hands slipping and sliding as he grappled for purchase, every light brush of his erection against her driving him closer . . . closer . . .

"Please," he begged, writhing in a frenzy of need as his urgency mounted. "Please . . ."

Her gaze filled with melancholy, she dissolved, leaving him splashing in cold water, all alone.

"Joanna." Graeham sat up in bed, panting. "Jesu." His ribs throbbed from the abrupt movement; he lay back down, swallowing a groan of pain. "Jesu," he breathed raggedly, dragging trembling hands through his sweat-dampened hair.

He lowered a hand to his groin, hissing through his teeth at the sharp jolt of arousal that greeted his tentative touch. His cock strained painfully, its tip leaking through his drawers.

Swearing under his breath, he sat up—slowly this time— and muttered his Latin drill until his erection had mostly subsided. He listened carefully for sounds from the salle but heard nothing. It must be midnight by now, or even later.

Taking up his crutch, he got out of bed, crossed to the leather curtain and peeked through. It was dark in the salle; Joanna had retired for the night.

He made his laborious way down the back hall, leaning

against the wall when he got to the end. It was black as pitch back here, but by reaching out, he could feel the iron-reinforced oaken door. The bolt was secure in its slot, as it should have been. He felt for the latchstring and threaded it through the hole so it hung outside.

Returning to the storeroom, Graeham fumbled around in the dark until he located the *Roman de Brut* on the chest next to his bed. Sliding out the string he'd been using as a bookmark, he unshuttered the alley window, double-knotted the string to one of the window bars, and relatched the shutters.

Then he set his crutch on the floor and lay back down to wait.

Joanna awoke to a muffled scraping from below, which she recognized as the bolt lifting in the back door. There came a muted squeal of rusty hinges and then a thump as the door swung closed.

Graeham must be visiting the privy. She wished he would use the jake instead. After that night when he'd fallen coming back inside, she worried about his moving around on his own, especially in the dark. He could easily lose his balance in the privy. If he took a bad fall out in the croft, he could end up lying there all night.

She decided to listen until she heard him come back in, so she'd know he was all right. If she didn't hear him reenter the house within a minute or two, she would go downstairs and check on him.

"Serjant."

Another dream? "Nay . . ." Graeham moaned, shaking his head. The first dream had been maddening enough.

"Serjant, I'm here." Soft hands on him, stroking his face, his chest, lightly fondling him between his legs; he stirred, grew rigid. "Wake up, serjant."

"Joanna?" He reached for her in the darkness as he opened his eyes. But even before he touched her, he knew by her thickly sweet scent that this wasn't Joanna. And then he remembered. "Leoda."

"Would you like to call me Joanna?" She was sitting on

the edge of the bed, caressing him nonchalantly through his drawers.

"Nay." What point was there in pretending? This woman wasn't Joanna. He would never have Joanna. She belonged to Prewitt, and he was destined for Phillipa. He must stop thinking of her, stop dreaming about her.

He closed his hand over Leoda's, molding her fingers around his thickness, encouraging a firmer caress, a steadier rhythm.

"That's quite the fierce cockstand you've got there," she said approvingly. "Have you been thinking about her all night, then?"

"Don't talk about her."

"As you wish. Shall we have us a nice little tumble, then?"

"Nay." Rising onto an elbow, Graeham felt around for his purse on the floor.

"Poor pup," she said. "You're worried about your leg. I can be on top, and I'll take care not to hurt you."

" 'Tisn't that." Graeham wouldn't be able to pull out with her on top. Leoda was probably still young enough to get with child, and he'd promised himself a long time ago—when he'd first discovered the circumstances of his birth—that he would sire no bastards of his own if he could help it. He extracted three pennies from his purse, found her hand, and pressed them into it.

There came a pause as she counted the coins; he heard a soft clink as she slipped them into her own purse. "Threepence. So you're wantin' somethin' out of the ordinary."

"Take me in your mouth," he said.

" 'Twould be my pleasure, serjant."

Leaning over him, she tugged at the cord to his drawers. Someone gasped. Graeham looked toward the leather curtain to find it being held open by Joanna, radiant in the glow from the candle she held. Bright spots of crimson bloomed on her cheeks as she stared at Leoda's hands, stilled in the act of untying his drawers.

Graeham bolted upright, flinching as pain spiked through his ribs. "Mistress . . ."

The curtain fell closed. He heard her rapid footsteps in the rushes, and the squeak of the ladder as she climbed it, and let out a low, virulent curse.

Chapter 9

~⚬~

Joanna dressed with excruciating care the next morning, in a kirtle of snowy linen with intricate smocking along the neck and sleeves. Over this she layered her best tunic, a fitted gown of gleaming honey-colored silk, delicately pleated in the sleeves and skirt—her wedding gift from Prewitt, which she'd worn but the once. It laced up the sides with golden cords; she had the devil of a time getting the two sides to look even and still have the tunic fit right. The sleeves, which she left detached beneath the arms for mobility, hung in points to the floor; she wrapped them around her arms to get them out of the way.

She glanced toward the uneven little looking glass nailed above her washstand and flinched, seeing, in lieu of her own image, that of Graeham Fox lying on her storeroom cot with the whore Leoda casually untying his drawers. A sick pain squeezed her stomach; it hurt her to think of him taking his ease with that woman. Recognizing the ache inside her for what it was—jealousy—Joanna felt chagrined that she was still capable of harboring such naive romantic impulses for any man.

Don't think about it now, she told herself, sliding her feet into the gold-dyed goatskin slippers that had come with the gown. She was going to the Friday fair today. It was to be a day of pleasure and relaxation, a precious rarity, and she had no desire to ruin it by ruminating on what had transpired during the night. Tonight would be soon enough to deal with Graeham Fox.

Joanna tried on the wide, elaborately beaded girdle she'd worn on her wedding day but rejected it as unseemly for a

respectable widow. The tunic, although elegant—and flattering—was a shade of brown, and therefore acceptable,
and the shoes would barely show, but that girdle was too
ornate. And, as she recalled, hellishly uncomfortable. She
looped a narrow sash around her hips and hung a small
embroidered purse from that, dispensing with the chatelaine; she was trying to look like a princess, not a shopmaid.

Now for her hair . . . *Your hair's your best feature,* Hugh
had said. A proper widow didn't go out and about with her
hair uncovered, but there were permissible compromises.

Joanna brushed her hair until it crackled, parted it neatly
down the middle, and gathered it in two long sheafs, which
she wrapped tightly in gold ribbons. She draped a half-
circle of the sheerest linen over her head, securing it with
two discreet pins so that it fell in pleasing folds around her
face and shoulders.

Did she need a mantle? The cloak that matched this
dress had long ago succumbed to moths, and her everyday
one wasn't regal enough. She'd just have to do without;
ladies often dispensed with their mantles when it was warm
out, as it was today.

She inspected her image in the looking glass. Even dis-
counting the mantle, something was still missing. "Earrings," she murmured. She hunted up her only remaining
pair—she had sold the rest—and put them on. "You'll do,"
she informed her reflection.

Joanna came downstairs half thinking that Hugh might already have arrived to escort her to Smithfield, but he wasn't
there. The curtain across the storeroom door was closed;
Graeham might still be abed—not surprising, given his nocturnal escapade. She had time to run across the street and
visit with Olive for a spell before she left for the fair.

The poor girl had taken to confiding in Joanna about a year
ago, when her mother began her gradual retreat into herself.
Joanna hated to think of Elswyth as unbalanced, having
known and liked her for years before her sorry decline.

For her part, Joanna was happy to lend an ear when
Olive needed it. She recalled all too vividly how it felt to
be buffeted about by fate and have no one to share her
fears with, no one to counsel her.

Joanna left her shop by the front door and crossed Wood

Street, stepping carefully over the drainage channel and holding her skirts above the rutted roadbed to keep them from getting dirty. At least the ground was dry; it hadn't rained in days.

The rope maker, Halwende, appraised her appreciatively as he propped open his shop window. "Good morrow, mistress. You look like the queen herself this mornin'."

"Thank you, Halwende."

A carter hauling bolts of multicolored silks turned to gape at her as he drove past.

She knocked on the front door of the apothecary shop, which was still closed up. "We're not open yet," came a girlish voice from within.

"Olive, it's me," Joanna said, not too loudly, lest she disturb Elswyth. "Joanna Chapman."

The door squealed open. Olive peered out, her pretty young face framed by that bright froth of hair, uncovered and unbound as usual; ah, to be a maiden again. "Mistress Joanna! What brings you across the street this morning?"

"I wanted to talk to you. May I come in?"

"Of course." Olive opened the door and stood aside. "Mistress, look at you! You look so grand."

"Thank you." Joanna glanced about the shop, similar to hers in size and layout, but fitted out with floor-to-ceiling shelving, on which were arranged myriad jars and caskets. Bundles of roots, garlic, and dried herbs hung from the rafters, scenting the air with their earthy bouquet. In the center of the room, half a dozen kettles hung from a toothed rack over a tile-lined fire pit, cold at present. A work table in front of the shuttered shop window was laid out with mortars and pestles, scales, and a stack of thick little blue glass phials.

"Is something wrong?" Olive asked. Usually it was she who sought Joanna out, not the other way around.

"Nay . . . perhaps. I suppose that's what I've come to find out." Joanna lifted a phial from the stack and turned it over in her hand; a ribbon of sunlight from between the closed shutters ignited the bubbly blue glass like a jewel. Lowering her voice, she said, "You were speaking to a man in the alley yesterday afternoon, and you became upset."

"Olive!" The deerskin tacked over the doorway to the

back of the house parted. Elswyth, in a rumpled sleeping shift, stood glaring at her daughter with her intense little dark eyes. The apothecary was heavier than Joanna recalled from the last time she'd seen her close up, which had been several months ago. Her face was puffy and sallow; her hair—wiry and red like her daughter's but rapidly graying—hung raggedly about her shoulders.

"Mum." Olive wrung her hands. "You're awake."

"Aye, and the shop's not open." Elswyth's gaze darted toward Joanna, taking in her opulent attire with an expression of leeriness.

Joanna inclined her head to the older woman. "Good morrow, Mistress Elswyth."

Elswyth pointed to the phial in Joanna's hand; her fingernails were ragged and black with ingrained dirt at the tips and edges. "That's ours."

Joanna set the phial atop the others. "Yes, mistress. I know."

Elswyth speared her daughter with her half-mad gaze. "Why is the shop not open?"

" 'Tis early still, Mum."

"Open the shop."

"But I never open it this—"

"*Open it,* you lazy girl, or I'll take the paddle to you."

Olive sighed. "Yes, Mum." She looked bleakly toward Joanna.

"I'll help you with the shutters," Joanna offered, stepping outside.

"Thank you, mistress." Olive unlatched the big shutters from inside and then joined Joanna on the street. By the time they got the awning buttressed and the countertop braced, Elswyth had retreated into the house again.

Joanna took Olive's hands in hers. "Come see me when you have the chance," she said—softly, lest Elswyth was listening from behind the deerskin.

Olive squeezed Joanna's hands, her eyes filled with turmoil. "Thank you, mistress. I will."

"Anybody home?" bellowed Hugh's voice from beyond the curtain drawn across the storeroom door.

"I am," Graeham called out, sitting on the edge of his cot to pull on his braies.

Hugh ducked through the curtain and entered the store-room, looking a bit less like a paid soldier today, in a gray tunic trimmed in black braid. He still wore his sword on his hip, but so did most men of his rank, whether they had any use for it or not. Only that incongruous gold earring hinted that he might be something other than an ordinary young nobleman. "Where's Joanna?"

"I've no idea. I haven't seen her since I woke up." No doubt she'd been avoiding him. Graeham worked the braies over his hips and tied them. "She isn't here?"

"Nay."

"She must have just stepped out for a moment. I know she means to go to the Friday fair with you. Would you fetch that shirt off the peg for me?"

Hugh tossed him the shirt, then rubbed his forehead. "Where does she keep her wine?"

Graeham pulled the big shirt down over his head, breathing in its freshly laundered scent. "Suffering from the ale passion, are you?"

"Aye, I spent most of the night at the White Hart, throwing the devil's bones. Now all I've got to show for it is a blinding headache and an empty purse. I could use a bit of the hair of the dog, if you know where she keeps it."

"In the cupboard in the salle."

Hugh left and returned a minute later with a ewer and two cups.

"Don't pour any for me," Graeham said, thinking it best to keep his wits about him until he'd had a chance to apologize to Joanna for last night. "I haven't broken my fast yet. Wouldn't want to start the day off sotted."

"Why the devil not?" Hugh poured himself a cup of wine and swallowed it down in one tilt.

From the alley there came a faint clacking that grew steadily louder. "That'll be Thomas Harper, looking for his breakfast." Graeham hauled himself to his feet. "Do you know Thomas?"

"A rather monstrous-looking leper?"

Graeham nodded.

"I met him the last time I was in London. Poor wretched bastard."

"Don't let him hear you say that." Graeham unshuttered the alley window just as Thomas in his black cape and straw hat came into view, shuffling along with his walking staff. "Good morrow, friend."

"Serjant!" Smiling, Thomas looked from Graeham to Hugh. "I know you. You're the brother."

"I am indeed." Hugh maintained a neutral expression in the face of Thomas's disfigurement, Graeham was gratified to note. " 'Tis a pleasure to see you again, Master Thomas."

Laughing raspily, Thomas pointed a gnarled finger at his ravaged face. "A pleasure to see *this*?" His one good eye seemed to focus in on the cup in Hugh's hand. "Where there's wine, Sir Hugh, I'm afraid there's little wisdom."

Hugh grinned and raised his cup. "If we're to quote old adages, I prefer *In vino veritas*."

"If Alcaeus really did write that," Thomas said, "I suspect he did so while he was stinking drunk."

Hugh made a little bow. "No doubt you're correct about that."

"Are you looking for Mistress Joanna, Thomas?" Graeham asked.

"That I am, but the shop window's still shuttered."

"She'll be back presently, I'm sure."

"I'll go wait for her out at the kitchen, then." Thomas turned and started making his way back up the alley toward the croft. "She keeps a barrel for me to sit on—I must get off these worthless feet."

When they were alone, Hugh turned to Graeham with a knowing smile. "How'd you like her?"

"Who?"

"Leoda. She was here last night, was she not?"

How could he know? "Have you seen her already this morning?"

Hugh snorted with laughter as he refilled his cup. "I've rarely seen *any* whore before nones, unless it was one I'd spent the night with. The morning hours are when they get their sleep."

"Then how . . ."

Hugh nodded toward the window. Graeham cursed inwardly when he saw the string still tied to the window bar; he hadn't thought to remove it. He hobbled on his crutch to the window and plucked one-handed at the knot in an attempt to untie it.

"I'm glad to see you finally accepted the wisdom of my advice," Hugh said from behind him. "You should put that string out at least once a week—'twill keep your bodily humors balanced."

Graeham grunted noncommittally, but he knew he would have no more use for this string, except as a bookmark. Far from balancing his humors, last night's aborted little tryst had left him in as agitated a state as he'd ever been plagued with.

He winced at the memory of Joanna walking in on them, grateful only that she had made her entrance before Leoda had had a chance to go to work on him. Unperturbed by the interruption, Leoda had still been eager to service him after Joanna fled upstairs, but Graeham had retied his drawers and sent her packing.

He was ashamed of himself for having summoned Leoda. It had been both dishonorable and foolhardy, a rash act born of a deep and restless hunger. In fact, no sooner had the whore left than Graeham found his thoughts straying inevitably to the woman asleep upstairs. What would it be like, he'd wondered, to feel Joanna's hands stroking him as Leoda's had, to feel her mouth on him, hot and sweet and coaxing, to feel her writhing beneath him as he filled her with his aching need? Before long, he was murmuring his Latin drill once again and cursing his unruly passions.

"So, how'd you like her?" Hugh repeated. "She's not as tight as some of the younger ones, but her moves make up for it, I think."

"I wouldn't know," Graeham said over his shoulder as he struggled ineffectually with the stubbornly knotted string.

"You tupped her, didn't you?"

"Nay."

"Then what—"

"Your sister came downstairs and walked in on us just as—"

"God's bones!" Amusement warred with horror on Hugh's face. "She can't have been very pleased."

"I don't imagine she was."

"Did she make Leoda leave?"

"Nay, I sent her away myself."

"Before she could tup you?" Hugh asked incredulously.

"I never even intended to tup her—not strictly speaking. I was going to have her in the Frankish manner."

Hugh grinned salaciously. "I've had her that way. Too bad you didn't get the chance to enjoy that talented mouth of hers. She could suck a spear head off its shaft." Abruptly he cleared his throat. "Good morrow, sister."

Graeham wheeled around to find Joanna standing in the doorway, holding a tray laden with half a loaf of black bread, a hunk of yellow cheese, two pitchers, and a cup. She stood motionless, regarding Graeham in dreadful silence, her face stained red.

Graeham closed his eyes and raked a hand through his hair.

He heard the rustle of silk and opened his eyes to find her setting the tray on the chest next to his bed. She was more incandescently beautiful than ever today, in a gleaming tunic the same sumptuous golden brown as her hair. "This is for you to eat while I'm gone, serjant," she said tonelessly.

Hugh, damn his eyes, was chuckling noiselessly, as if it were all some great jest.

Graeham swallowed, not knowing what to say, but knowing he must say something. "Mistress . . ."

"We should be going, Hugh." Joanna turned and swept out of the storeroom, leaving the tantalizing scent of wildflowers and spring grasses in her wake.

"I've never seen so many people here," Hugh said as he guided Joanna by the arm through the cacophonous throng that had gathered in Smithfield for the Friday fair.

"Nor I. Must be the weather."

A diverse assortment of Londoners—nobility, merchants, clerics, peasants, and scores of darting schoolboys in monastic habits—mingled in the grassy field among foreigners speaking exotically accented Latin, Continental French and their native tongues. The Tower of Babel must have sounded much like this. One section of the huge fairground was a forest of merchants' stalls beneath boldly striped awnings. Another was set aside for the horse races and attendant wagering. Roughly in the center of the irregular field was the horse pool, a sizable pond around which were grouped the various classes of horses for sale.

Hugh led Joanna to an area devoted to farm implements and various livestock in makeshift pens—blooded bulls, mares with their foals, pigs, oxen, spring lambs, geese, even a peacock. Squinting against the bright sunlight, he looked this way and that. "I thought perhaps Robert might be here. He takes a rather keen interest in farming."

Joanna stopped in her tracks. "You mean to say you didn't arrange a time and place to meet him?"

"I've never been much for planning, Joanna—you know that." He gave her that boyishly crooked grin before continuing. "Watch where you step."

Wrapping her trailing sleeves around her arms, she followed him past displays of sickles and scythes, wheelbarrows and felling axes. "Look at me." She held out the skirt of her fine silken tunic, the hem of which was already stained. "I went to all this trouble to look presentable for this fellow. I even left my shop closed on a Friday, and for what? This entire day will go to waste."

Hugh sighed. "You've been prickly as the Devil all morning, Joanna. Does it have anything to do with . . . that business about Leoda?"

She looked past him, her gaze falling on the tidy cluster of stone buildings on the perimeter of Smithfield that housed St. Bartholomew's hospital. Graeham Fox would be recuperating there if she'd refused his four shillings; perhaps she should have.

Hugh cleared his throat. "They never actually—"

"I know that." She'd heard Leoda leave by the back door shortly after she'd gone upstairs. "That doesn't make it all right."

"You must understand," Hugh said, "that Graeham is a healthy young man, with the needs and appetites of any—"

"I understand that perfectly well," she bit out. "What I don't understand is how he could have had the *gall* to bring that woman into my home. Whatever could have possessed him?"

"Well . . ."

"It shows exceedingly poor judgment, if you ask me."

Hugh rubbed his jaw in that way he had when he was uneasy. "Yes, well, I suppose it does. Certainly it does."

"You put him up to it, I assume."

A gasp of nervous laughter escaped him; his ears pinkened.

"Don't try to deny it, Hugh."

Contritely he said, "All right, I did encourage it, but only because . . ." He shook his head. "Two months is a damnably long time for a man to go without . . . release of that sort, Joanna."

"If he's such a slave to his . . . his carnal drives, then perhaps he should have boarded somewhere else. I'm a respectable widow. I can't have him bringing loose women into my home."

Turning on her heel, she strode away to watch a woman in a clay-spattered kirtle throwing cooking pots on a kick wheel.

Hugh came up behind her. "Are you going to make him leave?"

Frowning, she lowered her gaze, discovered a smudge of manure on the tip of one of her gold slippers, and rubbed it off on the grass. She *should* make him leave, despite the money she would lose. The house would feel empty without him, but she was used to being alone. There were worse things than loneliness.

She gravitated toward a table on which were stacked willow baskets, pots of honey, and freshly pressed cheeses wrapped in leaves. A bored-looking young girl swept a branch back and forth over the cheeses to discourage flies from settling.

"Joanna?" Hugh persisted. "Are you going to make him—"

"I don't know," she said sullenly. "I think so. Probably."

Sighing, Hugh offered her his arm again and led her to the horse pool, circling it at a distance to watch prospective buyers poke at the horses' hooves and pull back their lips. The smell of horseflesh competed with the savory aroma of sausages grilling in a pit nearby. One of the men inspecting the horses turned to look at Joanna, his gaze crawling over her elegant attire with all-too-penetrating interest.

"God's bones, it's Rolf le Fever." She turned away.

"Who is Rolf le Fever?" Hugh asked.

"A man whose nose I almost cut off once."

"That fellow over there in the scarlet and purple? From the looks of him, you should have finished the job."

"Sometimes I wish I had. They'd have hanged me, but at least I would have enjoyed some measure of revenge."

"Revenge for what?" Hugh asked, spearing le Fever with a chillingly black look—a reminder to Joanna that her good-natured brother had, deep down inside, the heart and soul of a warrior.

"He's the reason I can't sell silks by the yard anymore."

"I thought that was because you couldn't join the Mercers' Guild."

"Of which Rolf le Fever is guildmaster. After Prewitt died, I worked out a way to import silks without traveling abroad—by employing other silk traders as agents for me. I went to the silk traders' market hall—le Fever has an office there, behind the merchants' booths—and I told him I was going to petition to join the guild. He told me the decision would rest with him, and at first he seemed . . . sympathetic, congenial. But as we spoke, he kept moving closer to me. I didn't like the way he looked at me, like Petronilla when she's toying with a mouse, and once or twice he found excuses to touch me . . ."

A feral little growl rose from Hugh's throat.

"He said that women could do quite well in trade if they understood that it's simply an exchange of one thing for another, that there's no such thing as true generosity in business. If, for instance, one party grants a privilege to another party, he naturally expects some sort of repayment."

"Naturally," Hugh gritted out.

"He wasn't so bold as to come right out with it, not at first, but I knew what he was up to—he'd sniffed around me before, while Prewitt was still alive. He complimented my beauty, said he'd admired me for years. He asked me to remove my veil so he could see what color my hair was."

Hugh swore under his breath. "Did you?"

"Of course not—and it seemed to provoke him. He

backed me against the wall, looking me up and down as if I were standing out in front of some Southwark stew."

"Did you cry out for help?"

" 'Twas midday, the dinner hour. There was no one else there. But I got away before he could do anything."

"How?"

"He put his hand on my breast. I put my dagger in his nostril."

"Ah." Hugh grinned approvingly. "Good choice. A man as vain as that strutting peacock would sooner lose his . . . privy parts than his nose."

"I walked away unviolated from the market hall that day, but he saw to it that the guild rejected my request for membership."

"Little surprise in that. There—that's the horse Graeham is selling." Hugh pointed to a petite chestnut tethered with the other palfreys—docile creatures suitable for ladies or children.

"Why on earth was he riding a palfrey?"

"He wasn't. His mount was a fine sorrel stallion."

"Why did he have two horses?" she asked. "And one of them a lady's horse?"

"I don't suppose we'll ever find out, given that you're sending him back to St. Bartholomew's." Excusing himself, Hugh paused to admire the destriers—brawny creatures bred for size and trained to remain steady in the face of battle cries and volleys of arrows.

Joanna claimed a nearby tree stump, slipped off her shoes, and flexed her stocking feet in the cool grass. Resting her chin in her hand, she gazed at the little chestnut palfrey as it drank from the horse pool.

I'd take off my clothes, Graeham had said, *and wade in, and let the water envelop me. 'Twas heaven.*

Closing her eyes, Joanna tried to envision the boy Graeham, swimming in this pond all alone in the middle of the night. Instead she saw Graeham the man, stretched out on her store room cot with the whore Leoda leaning over him.

"Just like Prewitt," she whispered, opening her eyes. A young woman passing by with a basket full of flatcakes cast her a curious glance. She closed her eyes again.

This time it wasn't Graeham she envisioned with the black-haired whore but her husband. Not that he'd ever bedded Leoda, but he might have. He'd bedded everyone else.

For the hundredth time, she wondered how she could have succumbed to Prewitt Chapman's calculatingly smooth charms. Granted, she'd been young and terrified at the prospect of being cast away from Montfichet for refusing to marry Nicholas. Her father would kill her, he'd said— and from the savagery of some of his past beatings, she'd believed he was capable of doing it.

Prewitt had happened upon her just when she'd been most desperately in need of a savior. If only she'd had the wit to see how transparently he set about casting himself in that role. When he stole into her little tower bedchamber a mere two weeks after their first meeting, begging her to come away with him and be his wife, she was ecstatic. She would belong to the darkly handsome Prewitt Chapman, with his yearning eyes and ardent declarations and be forever freed of her father's tyranny in the bargain. Not once did she pause to consider how the marriage would benefit Prewitt.

If only Hugh had been in London during Prewitt's clandestine courtship. Her brother would have seen it all; he would have warned her about her suitor's ulterior motives. But Hugh was off fighting in Ireland. By the time he came home that summer, Joanna was married and living in Prewitt's shabby little flat in that tumbledown tenement on Ironmonger Lane—all alone, for her new husband had departed for Sicily within days of the wedding.

Hugh was outraged to find his gently bred young sister married, abandoned, and living in squalor. He knew intuitively what Prewitt was and why he'd married her. Despite the silk merchant's elegant dress and manners, he had nothing. He'd jumped at the chance to unite himself with Lady Joanna of Wexford, only to discover afterward that her father would slaughter them both if he got his hands on them. Hugh made inquiries regarding annulment, but the Church would not allow it.

Joanna, still fancying herself in love with her husband and unwilling to believe that he had married her only to advance himself, declined Hugh's offer to hunt Prewitt down and disembowel him for her. Hugh had to go abroad again, but before he left, he bought her the house on Wood

Street so she would have a decent place to live and a shop with which to support herself. It pained her to have to accept it, but she couldn't remain in that hovel on Ironmonger Lane. She vowed most solemnly never to take anything from him again—ever.

Like a fool, she continued to believe the best about her ne'er-do-well husband even after he returned from Sicily that fall. He'd become distant with her—impatient, distracted. Joanna attributed his ill temper to shame over his inability to provide for her. After all, what man wanted to live in a house his brother-in-law had bought?

It was shortly before he was scheduled to go abroad again that she came home from marketing one afternoon thinking the house was empty, only to hear Prewitt upstairs, groaning. Fearful that he might be sick, or hurt, she dumped the capon she'd bought on the table and raced up the ladder, heart pounding.

Chapter 10

❦

Even now, almost five years later, Joanna's stomach clenched at the memory of how she'd found him—how she'd found *them*, Prewitt and the poulterer's wife.

Halfrida was on her hands and knees on their big bed, naked but for her striped woolen stockings. Joanna had always thought of her as being only somewhat plump, but without her clothes she looked enormous—white and fleshy and obscene, her pendulous breasts swaying in rhythm with Prewitt's thrusts against her. He knelt behind her, his tunic discarded, his trouserlike silken chausses around his knees, his shirt gathered up in one hand while the other gripped Halfrida's sturdy buttocks.

Halfrida had her head down, her coarse yellow hair hanging about her face. Prewitt watched himself pound into her, his face reddened, his breath coming in harsh grunts. They didn't notice Joanna standing there at the top of the ladder, reeling with repulsion and the shock of betrayal.

Prewitt must have sensed her presence, because he looked up and saw her. His eyes widened slightly, but he didn't so much as slow down. "Jesus, Joanna," he panted, "are you going to just stand there and watch?"

Halfrida looked up abruptly, squealing when she saw Joanna. But then Prewitt started laughing, and so did she, her big white body jiggling with her giggles as he continued tupping her.

Joanna stumbled down the ladder and fled outside. She walked swiftly down to Newgate Street, weaving her way blindly around pedestrians, horses, and pigs, then east to Aldgate Street, growing breathless as the street rose toward the apex of Corn Hill. She turned right onto Gracechurch Street and followed it all the way down to the Thames.

The waterfront was a raucous hive of activity that afternoon. Sailors cursed as they pulled reluctant stallions up a gangplank and into the hull of a ship docked nearby; fishwives barked their prices; gulls shrieked.

Joanna set off across London Bridge, thinking it might be quieter over the water; it was. Halfway across the dilapidated old wooden bridge, she paused and leaned over the rail, shivering as the cool, river-scented breeze ruffled her veil and kirtle.

Hundreds of boats of all types were moored in the quays and in the huge river itself. The great white Tower of London rose in the distance, just inside the southeast corner of the city wall. Lord Gilbert and Lady Fayette had escorted her to the Tower last year, when Eleanor of Aquitaine was in residence, introducing her to the queen as their future daughter-in-law. Joanna had presented Queen Eleanor with an embroidered purse, blushing with pride when the queen praised her handiwork. She supposed she would never set foot in the Tower again.

Hugh had been right all along, of course. Prewitt didn't love her. He'd married her purely because she was the daughter of Lord William of Wexford, the irony being her sire's complete renunciation of her as a result of that marriage. Now Prewitt had no use for her anymore, except for occasional sexual relief—a function it seemed she shared with others. She was nothing to him but a thing to be exploited for his own ends. First her father had used her for his purposes, and now Prewitt; it was as if she existed purely to facilitate the aspirations of grasping men. She burned with shame to think how gullible she'd been, how easily led down the path to her own ruin.

Dropping her gaze to the water lapping against the piles below her, she wondered how deep the great river was here, in the middle. If she happened to fall in, would she drown? She couldn't swim. She imagined some earnest undersheriff informing Prewitt that his wife had thrown herself off London Bridge in despair. Prewitt would sink his face into his hands. The undersheriff would offer fatuous words of comfort and then depart.

Alone, Prewitt would uncover his face. And smile.

The bells of St. Magnus Martyr, located at the London end of the bridge, rang vespers. Joanna retraced her steps down the bridge toward the little church, drawn by the comforting notion of sanctuary within its thick stone walls.

It was cool inside the deserted chapel, and dark, and blessedly quiet. Joanna knelt in the straw before the altar and crossed herself, beseeching God for strength and direction.

Direction toward what? she fancied the Lord asking her. *What is it you want?*

To be free of Prewitt. That was what she wanted with all her heart. Annulment was impossible, but perhaps they could live apart—although she hated the notion of leaving their home. In truth, it was *her* home; Hugh had deeded it to her. She couldn't sell it without her husband's permission, though, and he might choose to keep it for himself. It disgusted her to think of his having sole use of it, and besides, where would she go? Even if she'd been willing to swallow her pride and throw herself on her father's mercy, he would never take her back. Neither, of course, would Lord Gilbert.

She could try to force Prewitt out of the house, but the law was on his side; if he didn't want to go, he needn't. He could live there forever, forcing her to share his bed, even beating her if he were so inclined, and no one would lift a finger to stop him. And if she *could* talk him into leaving, she would be left with no resources. The income from Prewitt's silk importing was modest at best, but it was better than nothing.

Could life be made tolerable if they continued living together? Perhaps. After all, he would be abroad more often than not. But his visits home would be unendurable.

The sobering truth was that many women were forced to endure the unendurable when it came to marriage. No wonder so many widows had an air of contentment about them. If men knew how attractive many of their wives found the prospect of life without them, they might become nervous.

Joanna smiled at the crucifix above the altar as a possibility began forming in her mind. More than a possibility—a resolve. Whispering a quick prayer of thanks for the Lord's guidance, she left the church, finding that night had fallen. Mindful of her newfound resolve, when she came upon a cutler's shop in East Cheap, she spent all the money in her purse on a dagger in a tooled scabbard, which she hung on her girdle.

On arriving home, she discovered Prewitt sitting at the table in the salle in his shirtsleeves, his back to her, a ewer of wine in front of him. He glanced over his shoulder. "It's past suppertime. Where have you been?"

Joanna fisted her hands in the skirt of her kirtle. "Is she gone?"

"Aye." He lifted his legs over the bench and sat facing her. Those striking brown eyes that had always captivated her so now lit with malicious humor. "But before she left, I worked up quite an appetite." Nodding toward the capon on the table behind him, he said, "Cook that, and be quick about it."

In the beginning, Prewitt had been adoring, almost worshipful, then apathetic. This brazen new hostility made her scalp tickle with foreboding.

Licking her dry lips, Joanna said, "When you proposed to me, you swore you'd always be faithful."

Prewitt smiled as if at a dim-witted child and swallowed down some of his wine. "I tend to spout all manner of mawkish drivel when I'm in the throes of passion."

"You never felt passion for me."

Lounging back against the table, he said wearily, "Men aren't subject to the same sorts of romantic infatuations as women. We have drives that are altogether more . . . elemental. If you weren't so young and pampered and witless, you'd know that."

Joanna had never felt the sixteen-year difference in their ages more keenly, for if he thought of her as a witless child, it was only because she'd behaved like one—until now. She forced herself to walk right up to him, chin high. "You didn't marry me to serve any drive other than your cold ambition. I'm not so witless that I haven't figured that out."

He reached behind him for the ewer and poured some more wine into his cup. "Are we going to have supper or not?"

Joanna drew in a steadying breath. "I'm not going to

make supper for you anymore, Prewitt. Or breakfast or dinner."

His eyes widened. "You damn well will."

"And you can't sleep with me in the solar anymore," she added, struggling to keep her voice even. "From now on, you'll sleep in the storeroom."

"The *storeroom*." He laughed harshly; there was a hysterical edge to it. "You insolent little bitch. Who do you think you are, ordering me out of my own bedchamber?"

"It's my bedchamber," she said quietly, cursing the strain in her voice. "This house belongs to me."

"You're my wife," he gritted out between his teeth, the wine cup trembling in his hand. "You belong to me. You're required by law to bend to my will. I damn well *will* sleep in the solar if I'm so inclined. And I will fuck you morning, noon, and night if I'm so inclined. And in between, if I choose to fuck someone else, I will fuck her when and where I please, and you have naught to say about it."

"This is my house," Joanna repeated shakily.

"Over which I exercise complete authority. If I decide to oust you from here and keep it for myself, I can. Or perhaps I won't keep it. Perhaps I'll rent it out instead." He raised the cup to his lips again, looking around the salle as if appraising it. "After all, I spend most of my time abroad—what need have I of a house like this? Or even the shop—I can sell my silks out of the market hall, as I did before. I'd make quite a tidy profit. Don't know why I haven't thought of it before."

"Because it isn't your house to rent out." She took another bold step toward him. "It's mine. You have some control over it, but you're not allowed to dispose of it without my consent, and you can't make me leave here, either—Hugh told me so."

"Husbands dispose of their wives' property all the time without their consent."

"Aye, but if the husband dies, the wife can get her property back. It's the law."

"I'm young and healthy."

With a feigned display of composure, she said, "Young, healthy men have mishaps all the time."

"Oh, you'd like that, wouldn't you?"

"Perhaps I would."

"You goddamned spoiled little bitch." Prewitt flung his cup aside, wine spraying into the rushes. He seized her by the waist, slammed her to her knees in front of him. "How dare you?"

Joanna's head whipped to the side as he slapped her. Her cheek burned. *Don't cry. Keep your head.* She tried to get up, but he dug his hands into her shoulders to immobilize her. His legs pressed against her on either side; she felt trapped.

"You think you're still Lady Joanna of Wexford, don't you, you coddled, impudent—"

"Let go of me." She tried to pull his hands off her shoulders, but he was too strong.

"Well, you're mine now, milady." Prewitt tore her veil off and grabbed a fistful of her loosened hair. *"Mine."* He squeezed her breast hard; she cried out.

Still clutching her painfully by the hair, he pulled his shirt up and started untying the drawstring of his silken chausses, snug over his erection. Joanna knew what he wanted. She'd done this for him before, at his insistence, not particularly enjoying it but considering it an act of love.

This would be no act of love.

"You're mine to do with as I please," he said breathlessly, drawing her head down toward his lap. Joanna smelled Halfrida's musky scent on him, and the bile rose in her throat. "And right now," he said, "it pleases me to give you something better to do with your mouth than threaten me."

Joanna slid her new dagger out of its sheath and aimed it at her husband's groin. "Take your hands off me, Prewitt." Meeting his astonished gaze, she added, "You wouldn't want a mishap."

He released her and sat back, eyeing the steel blade with wide-eyed outrage, his erection rapidly waning. "Where the bloody hell did you get that? Get it away from there!"

"As you wish." Joanna rose to her feet, removing the blade from his groin and resting its tip lightly against his throat. She leaned in just a bit, forcing him to bend backward over the table. "The more I think about widowhood," she said conversationally, "the more I like the idea of it."

His eyes rolled white, like those of a spooked horse. Suddenly his expression transformed, rage sweeping in like a storm cloud to banish his fear. "You bitch."

He rammed a fist into her belly, dropping her to the floor. The dagger flew out of her hand. For a panicky moment she couldn't breathe, but then her wind—and her resolve—returned. Fighting pain and nausea, she fumbled in the rushes and found the dagger. She scrambled to her feet, gasping, her hair in her face, one arm wrapped around her middle.

He sneered at the weapon quivering in her hand. "You're sorely mistaken if you think that protects you. I'm half again your size, and I can defend myself as well as any man."

"I daresay you can." She smiled. "When you're awake."

His eyes slowly widened as he absorbed her meaning.

"If you even think about making me leave here," she said, "I suggest you sleep lightly at night."

In the end, Prewitt not only abandoned any idea of casting Joanna away but chose to sleep in the storeroom. For five years, whenever he was in London, he shared her home but kept largely to himself. They ate separately and rarely spoke. Many nights he never came home, which was fine with Joanna. Their relationship became one of commerce and was actually quite mutually beneficial; he shipped the silks to London, she sold them, and they both lived off the modest proceeds.

Joanna could have carried on like that for many more years. But then had come that package from Genoa, wrapped tightly in crimson silk—how strangely appropriate—and sealed with the insignia of the city government. Prewitt was dead. God knew she didn't miss him, but she missed his damned silks. Until Graeham had arrived, with his four shillings, she'd been at her wits' end, wondering how she would manage to keep her home. . . .

Until Graeham had arrived.

Joanna recalled the sordid and all too familiar little scene she'd encountered last night after she'd come downstairs thinking he might need help. She still *was* a witless child, at least when it came to men. *We have drives that are altogether more elemental.*

Joanna hated for Graeham to remind her of Prewitt, but when it came to sex, it seemed that men—most men, any-

way—were insatiable and indiscriminating. If a woman was
convenient and a man felt he could get away with it, he would
use her to assuage his lust and not think twice about it.

Use her . . . Shivering, Joanna wrapped her arms around
herself. *Never again* . . .

Hugh seemed to think marriage to the right sort of man
would solve all her problems. He had a point in that a man
of means wouldn't be using her for her family name, as
Prewitt had. And not all married men strayed; some took
their vows to heart. Hugh had told her that Robert had
been a faithful husband to Joan. The right husband could
save her from penury and ease her aching loneliness. The
right one. Not another charming silk merchant.

Nor a certain equally charming but unlanded serjant,
with his earnest blue eyes and reckless curiosity.

Are you happy?

No, not him. Certainly not him.

"Hugh—is that you?"

Hugh turned from the fine destrier he was admiring to
find Robert of Ramswick grinning at him. "Rob!"

The men greeted each other with slaps on the back. In
his black, unadorned tunic, Robert looked rather like a
fresh-faced young deacon. He'd never been one to advertise his wealth.

"I thought I might find you with the beasts of war."
Robert glanced around. "The lady Joanna, is she . . ."

"Right over there." Hugh pointed through the crowd
toward his sister, sitting on a tree stump, her chin in her
hand, her eyes closed. One sleeve was still rolled around
her arm; the other dangled in the grass. Her linen veil was
askew, one of the pins that secured it having come loose.
And on top of it all, she was in her stocking feet.

Robert shaded his eyes as he studied her. Chuckling, he
said, "She was that way as a girl, wasn't she? Something
always a bit undone."

All Robert knew of Joanna since he'd last seen her years
ago was that she'd married a silk trader who'd died. He professed not to care that Joanna had married beneath her. His
primary concern was finding a good mother for his children.

It seemed odd to think of Robert as a widower with two

daughters. Although he was three years Hugh's senior, his boyish face and close-cropped sandy hair made him look younger. And, too, there was a rather appealing unworldliness about him, with his devotion to the land and his deep-rooted sense of right and wrong. In many ways he was Hugh's complete opposite—strange that they'd become such fast friends.

"I thought you were going to bring your girls," Hugh said, looking about. "Where are they?"

"Over there somewhere." Robert pointed toward the food vendors, whose booths were next to those of the foreign merchants. "Margaret's buying them some sweetmeats."

Hugh frowned. "Your cousin Margaret?"

"Aye. She came to Ramswick to take care of the girls after Joan and Gillian died. I thought you knew."

"Nay—she wasn't there when I came to visit you."

"She'd taken the girls to London that day. Well—are you going to reintroduce me to your lovely sister?"

Hugh brought Robert over to Joanna. "Are you awake, sister?" he asked with a tug on one of her braids.

Without opening her eyes, she muttered, "Bugger off."

Jesus have mercy.

Robert said, " 'Twould be a grievous disappointment to me if you made us bugger off, my lady."

Her eyes flew open. "Oh! L-Lord Robert?"

He bowed. "A pleasure to make your acquaintance again, Lady Joanna."

She bolted to her feet, hastily smoothing her gown and rearranging her veil. On the pretext of helping her, Hugh slid the other pin out and snatched the pointless thing off her head.

"Hugh!" She reached for it, but he stuffed it in his purse.

" 'Tis a sin to cover hair as beautiful as yours."

"A mortal sin, my lady," agreed Robert.

Joanna glared beneath her lashes at her brother as she slid her feet back into her slippers.

"Papa! Papa!" A towheaded little girl in a billowing white kirtle came running up to Robert, arms outstretched.

He swept her up, grinning. "This is my daughter Catherine. Catherine, say hello to Sir Hugh and Lady Joanna."

The child, who was perhaps five, turned and pressed her face into the crook of her father's neck.

Robert made a sound halfway between a groan and a chuckle. "What sticky confection have you painted your face with, then?"

"Fried fig pasties," offered a young woman—Margaret—striding up to them with a younger girl—a baby, really—in her arms.

Robert presented Margaret and little Beatrix to Hugh and his sister. The lady Margaret was much as Hugh remembered her from their youth—comely and pink-cheeked, with warm hazel eyes. Her modest wool tunic and mantle looked like something a widow might wear, but her light brown braids were uncovered; although nearly thirty, she was a maiden, having refused all offers of marriage.

"You had a fried fig pasty?" Robert asked, taking Catherine by the chin so he could inspect the shiny film on her face.

She nodded vigorously.

"May I?" He licked a bit of the sticky residue off her fat cheek; she shrieked with laughter. "Mmm . . . delicious."

The younger child strained in his direction, her chubby arms extended. Robert lowered Catherine to the ground and took the plump little girl from his cousin. His gaze lit on Margaret's mouth, and he smiled. "You enjoyed the pasty, too, I see." Settling Beatrix on his hip, he reached out and wiped his thumb just below his cousin's lower lip. Margaret met his gaze, the pink in her cheeks heating up. They both quickly looked away.

Joanna cast Hugh a swift, speculative look.

"Well!" Hugh clapped his hands together, forcing a smile. "Who'd like to take in the horse races?"

"He loves her," Joanna told Hugh as they strolled past the canopy-shaded tables laden with goods from foreign ports . . . supple leather shoes from Córdoba, indigo from Jerusalem, glassware from Venice, pelts of sable and ermine and vair from the Northlands . . . and everywhere, perfuming the air like incense, vast arrays of fragrant spices from remote and wondrous lands.

"He does not love her," Hugh said.

"Have you been watching them this afternoon? The little looks and gestures? Look at them. They look like a family."

Robert and his cousin wove through the crowd ahead of them, Beatrix limply asleep on her father's shoulder, Catherine sucking listlessly on two fingers as Margaret led her by the hand. It was midafternoon, and the children were exhausted.

"They can never be a family," Hugh said, pausing to admire a display of rare and costly goods from the Far East—carved ebony, pearls, lapis lazuli, ambergris, musk. "She's his third cousin."

"Third cousins marry all the time," she said. "So do second cousins." Although the Church condemned marriage between people related in the seventh degree or closer—sixth cousins—the restriction was widely overlooked. "Is Robert that devout?"

"His parents are, and Robert is devoted to them."

"But if it weren't for them," she persisted, "would Robert have married Margaret?"

Hugh sighed heavily. "They were in love once—a long time ago. They were young. It's been over for years."

Joanna watched Robert guide Margaret to a table overseen by a brown-skinned infidel selling sugar, wax, ivory tusks, paper, and various exotic fruits and nuts. Robert rested a hand on his cousin's back as he pointed out two little monkeys chattering away in a cage.

"They live under the same roof," Joanna said.

Hugh shrugged. "You live under the same roof with Gracham."

Her cheeks stung. "'Tisn't the same. The serjant and I . . . we would never . . ."

"And neither would Robert and Margaret. Even if he were still in love with her, he has too much honor to compromise her, knowing he could never marry her."

"Couldn't he get a papal dispensation?"

"About eleven or twelve years ago, he petitioned the Roman curia, but they turned him down. He and Margaret were heartbroken, but they got over it. He allowed his parents to betroth him to Joan, and he was a good husband to her."

"He should have wed Margaret without the pope's blessing."

"He was content with Joan."

"Some people have the gift of persevering in the face of adversity," Joanna said, echoing what Graeham had told her about herself. "One makes the best of a bad situation. But he should have married Margaret."

"Perhaps, but that's all in the past." Hugh took Joanna by the shoulders and bored his gaze into hers. "He wants to remarry, Joanna. This could be a wonderful opportunity for you."

"You told me he's remarrying because his children need a mother. But they've already got Margaret, and they seem to adore her—as does he. Why should he feel compelled to replace her with a wife?"

Hugh shrugged. "I don't know. He *is* a man, after all, with a man's needs. Does it really matter? He wants a wife, and he seems willing to consider you. He's a good man, of noble blood, with an important holding. He'd make you a wonderful husband. Don't discourage him just because you fancy he's still in love with Margaret. That's over and done with."

Up ahead, Robert transferred the sleeping Beatrix to Margaret's shoulder and gave some coins to the infidel merchant, who plucked three oranges from the pile on his table and handed them over. Stepping back, Robert tossed the oranges into the air and juggled them as expertly as any jongleur, to the evident enchantment of his cousin, who rewarded him with laughter and praise. Catherine chortled sleepily, one arm wrapped around Margaret's legs, those two fingers still firmly lodged in her mouth.

Robert grinned with pride in response to Margaret's delight. Never once did he look in Joanna's direction.

Chapter 11

❧

Graeham spent the day contemplating his idiocy while keeping a halfhearted watch on Rolf le Fever's house.

Late in the morning, the shutters over the solar window opened. Graeham sat up in bed, his ribs smarting. Those shutters had been closed since he had arrived there, but it was, after all, an unusually warm day. The maidservant Aethel stood at the window, running a rag over the sill as she chatted with someone—her mistress?—over her shoulder. She walked away from the window, and for a short while Graeham saw nothing but part of the paneled walls and raftered ceiling of the solar.

Presently Aethel reappeared, shaking her head and gesturing toward the window. She clasped her hands in prayerlike supplication, smiling in a pleading way toward the room's other occupant. Finally, with an expression of resignation, she pulled the shutters closed.

Graeham watched and waited, but the solar window did not reopen. At nones he shuttered the alley window. Olive arrived at the le Fever house with her tonic and left, after which he unshuttered the window, needing all the fresh air he could get in this heat.

Eventually he sank back onto his bolster of pillows and resumed his pitiless self-chastisement, uninterrupted by human contact, for neither Thomas nor Leoda happened by that afternoon. More likely than not, Leoda was plying her trade at the Friday fair. Graeham smiled, recalling how he and the other boys used to linger at the fair until late afternoon, when the whores began circulating. They were easy to spot, with their painted faces and brazen dress. The boys would whisper together about the things these women did for money in the woods nearby. Sometimes the whores would catch them staring, and wink, or beckon them seductively; the boys would turn and scatter like mice.

Shortly after St. Mary-le-Bow rang vespers, the black-and-white tomcat, Manfrid, jumped onto the alley window's deep sill and poked his big head through the bars. He still did that from time to time, as if hoping that Graeham would have disappeared. Joanna once mentioned that the storeroom had been Manfrid's favorite refuge before Graeham appropriated it.

On seeing him, Manfrid started backing away. Graeham clicked his tongue and the cat stilled. With slow movements, Graeham reached out to the tray on the chest and lifted a bit of cheese. Holding the crumb toward the animal, he clicked his tongue again.

Manfrid looked at the cheese, then at Graeham, then again at the cheese. He backed up a step.

Graeham tossed the cheese onto the floor beneath the window. The cat settled down on the sill and regarded it for some time with an expression of feline wistfulness. At long last, he leapt down, sniffed at the morsel, and ate it.

Before Graeham could offer him another one, he jumped back onto the sill and disappeared into the alley. Graeham's disappointment disgusted him. Was he truly so bored and lonely that he craved the company of that pathetic creature?

The family in the stone house punctuated the tedium by launching into an especially theatrical row, which culminated in the son's furious departure from the house, accompanied by a slamming door and bellowed epithets.

In the ringing quiet that followed, Graeham's thoughts returned to his ill-advised visit from Leoda and its likely ramifications. By the time the low afternoon shadows began merging into twilight, he had convinced himself that Joanna was going to kick him out of her house—and who could blame her?

The more full the cup, Brother Simon used to say, *the more carefully one must carry it.* Fortune had smiled on Graeham when Joanna had consented to let him live here.

But he'd been careless with his bounty, and now he would surely lose it.

He would let her keep the four shillings, he decided. It was entirely his fault the situation hadn't worked out. Joanna had maintained her end of the bargain—and graciously.

He would miss her.

"Shit."

"That's a bad word."

Graeham turned toward the alley window to find a small, remarkably grimy face staring at him through the bars. It was a boy, judging from his tattered red cap, from which sprouted a few blond wisps. He couldn't have been more than nine or ten; only his head showed above the windowsill.

"I suppose it is a bad word," Graeham admitted, "but I didn't realize there was a child lurking about to overhear."

The boy's gaze fell on Graeham's splinted leg. "What happened to you?"

Graeham shifted on his cot to face the child. "I met some bad men."

His young visitor nodded sagely. "There's lots of bad men in London. You've got to keep your wits about you." Despite his appearance, his speech wasn't as coarse as that of the lowest classes.

"Verily. What's your name, boy?"

"Adam."

"I'm Graeham Fox."

"Fox—for your hair?"

Graeham smiled. "For my cleverness."

" 'Tis good to be clever. 'Tis better to be clever than to be comely. Me mum always told me so." A hint of melancholy shadowed Adam's expression.

"Your mother," Graeham said quietly, "is she . . ."

"We live over in the Shambles," Adam said quickly, peering this way and that through the bars to get a better look at the storeroom. "Me pa's a meat butcher. Me mum, too."

"Ah." From the boy's neglected appearance, Graeham would have taken him for the child of a beggar, or at best a carter—someone of that ilk.

"Is this where you live, then?" Adam asked.

"For the present." Perhaps just until Joanna returned home this afternoon.

"It looks right cozy."

"It is."

A noise from the front of the house drew Graeham's attention. The door opened and Joanna entered the shop, along with her brother.

A flash of movement and the soft pat of footsteps made him turn back to the alley window. Adam was gone.

Graeham heard whispers from the direction of the shop. Joanna and Hugh stood very close, conferring together quietly; Graeham wondered if they were discussing him. Hugh did most of the talking, while Joanna contemplated something round and brightly colored that she held in her hand. Hugh's voice rose; he said something that sounded like, "It's a good match, Joanna."

"Shh!" Joanna looked toward Graeham for the first time; so did her brother. He led her out to the dusky street with an arm around her shoulder and continued his mysterious exhortations. She nodded somewhat grudgingly. He leaned closer and spoke again, gripping her upper arms. "Yes, all right, I'll think about it," she said, loudly enough for Graeham to hear.

Hugh patted her hair—she'd dispensed with her veil, Graeham saw—kissed her cheek, and left. Joanna watched him walk away, then reentered the shop, locking the door behind her. For one weighty moment her gaze met Graeham's across the length of the house.

She came toward him, and his heart beat a little faster, but she merely walked into the salle and placed the object she'd been holding in the middle of the table. It was an orange, Graeham saw. There were two tallow candles in iron holders on the table. She fetched the fire iron and lit them; golden light swept the early-evening dimness from the room.

He took hold of his crutch and hauled himself to his feet. "Mistress Joanna."

She looked at him, somewhat apprehensively. Christ, but she was beautiful today, painfully beautiful. If gold could tarnish to a slightly darker shade, but keep its brilliant luster, it would look like her hair. Her gown was the same striking color, giving her the aspect of a statue cast in bronze, save for the womanly softness of her face and hands.

Graeham limped to the doorway, gripping its frame to help support himself. "I'm sorry," he said softly. She regarded him with such hushed intensity that he had to look down. "I . . . violated your hospitality." Tempted to summon clever words to mitigate his transgression, he shook his head. "There are no excuses. I'm sorry."

When he looked back up, she was studying her fingertips, resting on the table. "I know that you're . . . lonely for female companionship. But this is my home, and—"

"It was wrong," he said earnestly, taking a step toward her and capturing her gaze. "It doesn't matter why it happened. I knew better, but I did it anyway, and now you're . . . we're . . ." He raked his hair out of his face in frustration. Why did his gift for words flee him in her presence?

He took another few halting steps in her direction. "Tell me what to say to make it all right," he implored, abashed at the faltering edge of desperation in his voice, the tightness in his chest. She was going to make him leave. He didn't want to leave. He wanted to stay here, with her. "Tell me and I'll say it."

She wouldn't look up.

"Joanna . . ."

She looked up then. He'd never called her by her Christian name before. Her eyes searched his. He didn't even try to school his features, though he knew he should. Let her look into the empty place inside him, let her see the terrible void. *But please, God, don't let her make me leave.*

Lowering her gaze, she reached out slowly and lifted the orange from the table. Hesitantly she said, "I . . . got this at the fair. Robert—Robert of Ramswick, a friend of Hugh's—he gave it to me. I haven't had one since Montfichet." A little shyly, she looked at him and asked, "Would you share it with me?"

The air left Graeham's lungs in a shaky exhalation; relief galloped through him. She wasn't going to make him leave.

He could stay. "Yes. Yes. Yes, I'd love to share it with you."

She smiled tentatively. He grinned like an idiot.

A knocking came at the back door. "Mistress Joanna! Mistress, it's me—Olive."

"Ah, Olive," Joanna said. "I told her I wanted to speak to her. She must have seen me come back." She set the orange on the table and started toward the back door.

Graeham picked up one of the candles and hobbled back to the storeroom. "She mustn't see me."

Joanna paused at the entrance to the hallway. "Why ever not?"

Fool. Thinking fast, Graeham said, "Too many people know I'm staying here as it is. 'Tisn't good for your reputation for it to be obvious you've got a man living with you."

"A week ago, you argued that my reputation wouldn't suffer from your being here because you were crippled, and just a boarder. Have you reconsidered, serjant?"

Propitiously, Olive chose that moment to resume her knocking. "Mistress? Are you there?"

"You'd better let her in," he said and ducked into the storeroom, drawing the curtain behind him.

He found Petronilla on the chest, dining on the remains of the cheese. "Scat!" She leapt down and darted out through the curtain. To his surprise, when he came farther into the room, he saw Manfrid sitting on the windowsill. "At least you've got some manners," he muttered, lowering himself to the edge of his cot and setting his candle down.

From the back door came muffled voices—Joanna greeting Olive—followed by footsteps heading into the salle. Through the leather curtain he heard Joanna say, "Let me take your mantle, Olive. Have a seat. Would you like some wine?"

"Nay, nothing for me, mistress. I just . . . I don't mean to impose on you."

"You're not imposing. I asked you to come."

"It's just that . . . my mum . . . I can't talk to her. She's gotten even worse of late."

"I know."

There came a pause. "Begging your pardon, mistress, but what's that?"

"It's an orange. Have you never seen an orange before?"

"Nay. Is it for eating?"

"It's a fruit. They grow them . . . well, I'm not sure where they grow them. Somewhere very far away. Smell it."

After a moment, Olive said, "Oh, isn't that lovely? There's an herb that smells a little like that."

Graeham pinched a bit of cheese off the block and tossed it to the floor by the window. Manfrid jumped down, ate it, and looked at him expectantly.

He tossed another piece a little closer to himself. The cat hesitated, then padded over to it and ate it as well.

Olive was telling Joanna how much she appreciated having her to talk to. "You've been so kind to me, mistress. You always have time for me. And you always know what to tell me. You always know what's what."

"Not always."

"Aye, I've never known a woman so wise in the ways of things. I wish my mum was more like you."

"Well . . ."

"I wish *I* was more like you. I wish I was strong like you."

"You're strong, Olive."

"Nay, I never could have gone through everything you've been through and kept my chin up like you have. Especially after you found out your husband was—"

"Olive, we . . . we don't need to talk about me."

"Did I say something wrong, mistress?"

"Nay, of course not. I just—"

"Is it because I said that about Master Prewitt? I didn't mean to stir up sad memories. I was that sorry when I found out what happened."

"Olive, please . . ."

The girl groaned remorsefully. "There I go, me and my mouth. I'm sorry, mistress. Sometimes I don't know when to hold my tongue."

Something tickled Graeham's bare foot—Manfrid's whiskers. He broke off another crumb of cheese and held it toward the cat in the palm of his hand. Manfrid stared at it as if he could make it leap off Graeham's hand by sheer force of will.

"Olive," Joanna said, "why don't you tell me what's troubling you?"

Manfrid gazed at the cheese. Olive lapsed into silence. Graeham sighed.

"There's this man," Olive said, so softly that Graeham could barely hear her. "I can't tell you who he is."

"Why not?"

"There'd be trouble if it was found out . . . what's transpired between us."

"What *has* transpired between you, Olive?"

When Olive finally spoke, her voice was damp and hoarse. "I love him, mistress. And . . . and he loves me."

"That shouldn't be cause for tears," Joanna said gently. "Here—dry your eyes."

Olive muttered a watery thank-you. " 'Twouldn't be cause for tears, if only . . ." She sighed heavily. "If we could marry."

"Why can't you marry?"

"We can't." The girl broke down, her words consumed by sobs. "We can't, we can't."

"There, now. Shh . . . it's all right. Everything will be all right."

"I know I should forget him. Nothing can come of my feelings for him. I try. I do try, I really do, but every time I see him, it's as if . . . as if my heart's being squeezed tight by a fist. That sounds very fanciful, I know, but I'm not clever with words. I don't know how else to say it."

"You said it just fine. I know exactly how you feel."

"You do?"

This time it was Joanna who took her time answering. Graeham looked toward the leather curtain, waiting for her to speak. "Yes," she said quietly. "Yes, I do."

Manfrid nudged Graeham's hand with his wet nose, and he realized his fingers had curled into a fist around the bit of cheese. He opened his hand and the cat ate the tidbit, then licked Graeham's palm with his raspy tongue.

Olive sniffed. "I must go. Mum doesn't know I'm here. Thank you, mistress."

"I've done nothing."

"You listened."

"But I didn't help you."

"There's no help for me," Olive said, calmer now, "unless I can manage to put him out of my mind. But you let me talk, and that's something. If it weren't for you, my troubles would just fester inside me, like . . . like a bad tooth that never stops aching. You can't imagine what it's like to have no one to turn to."

"Yes," Joanna said. "I can."

Graeham heard footsteps as Joanna escorted Olive to the back door and let her out. He pressed himself into the corner until the girl had passed outside both windows, then grabbed his crutch and stood up.

Manfrid mewed.

"Help yourself to the rest of the cheese," Graeham said magnanimously and made his way back out to the salle.

Joanna was sitting at the table, puzzling over the orange. "I can't remember how to get the peel off. I suppose a servant always did it."

"Give it here." Sitting opposite her, Graeham took the fruit and pierced the skin with his teeth, then loosened a section of its rind with his thumb and peeled it away.

Joanna closed her eyes and inhaled as the orange released its exotically sweet fragrance. Graeham was reminded of how she'd looked last night, transfixed with pleasure as she breathed in the herbal steam rising from her bath. He wondered if she looked that way when she was making love.

Christ, man, that's the last thing you should be wondering about. Hadn't his unruly imaginings caused enough trouble already? He'd best keep his passions firmly tethered during his stay here. There would be plenty of time to unleash them once he was wedded to Phillipa.

"His name is Damian," Graeham said as he methodically stripped away bits of peel and white pith, which rose in a little pile on the table in front of him.

"Whose name is Damian?"

"Olive's secret lover."

"How do you know?"

"I heard her with a man in the alley, remember? She called him Damian."

"Damian . . ." Joanna gaze became unfocused. "There's a priest at St. Olave's named Damian."

"A priest!" Graeham remembered the black-cloaked man walking away from the alley after his clandestine meeting with Olive. "I suppose he could be a priest. They have their human weaknesses like anyone else."

"And that would account for why they can't marry. But I just can't see a man of Father Damian's age taking up with a sixteen-year-old girl."

"How old is he?"

"Of middle years. Perhaps as old as fifty."

Graeham shook his head. "This Damian, he sounded young."

"It's not him, then. Ah—there's a young man in the neighborhood, Lionel Oxwyke's son. Master Lionel is a money changer. He's one of the wealthiest men in West Cheap—in all of London, for that matter. He lives in thăt big stone house on Milk Street next to le Fever's."

"The one that was built from paving stones?"

"That's the one. No doubt you've heard them screaming at each other."

"Those fights are one of my major sources of entertainment." Graeham removed the last of the peel, split off a section, and handed it to Joanna.

She held it in front of the candle's flame, her shimmery brown eyes taking his breath away. "It looks like a jewel," she said.

Don't stare at her, for pity's sake. Graeham loosened a section for himself. "I seem to recall Olive saying something about Damian's father. I got the impression he would disapprove if he knew about them."

"I'm quite sure he would. Who knows—perhaps that's what they've been fighting about. Those spats started up only a few weeks ago." Joanna brought the orange section to her mouth and lightly licked it, her expression one of rapturous anticipation. She closed her mouth over it, juice trickling over her lips as she bit it in half.

Jesu, don't stare. Graeham looked down at his own orange section, only to find he'd crushed it in his hand. He shoved it into his mouth and chewed; seeds crunched between his teeth.

Joanna plucked a seed from between her lips and placed it daintily on the table. "Damian is Lionel Oxwyke's only son, and his betrothal was negotiated years ago. Master Lionel contracted for him to marry the daughter of another money changer, the only one who's even richer than he is, outside of the Jewry. The girl is only nine, though, so they have to wait another three years before the Church will permit her to marry."

"But this Damian is formally betrothed to her?"

"As far as I know. Damian's father would be livid if he proposed to marry someone else. And Master Lionel is not the type of man one likes to anger. He's of a choleric temperament, much like my own sire. They say he suffers from an excess of yellow bile, which keeps his stomach too hot, and that's why he's got such a foul disposition." Joanna slid the other half of the orange section between her lips.

Don't stare, don't stare. "That's it, then." Graeham pulled off another wedge and handed it to her, cursing the adolescent thrill that coursed through him when their fingers touched. "That's why Damian and Olive can't marry."

He ate another section, frowning as he tried to recall the conversation he'd overheard in the alley that day. "There was something else . . . something she didn't want him to know, but that he already knew. It seemed to distress her greatly."

"Her mother's madness?"

"Is her mother mad?"

"Not mad, perhaps, but . . . in the grip of a powerful melancholia. Sometimes even . . . bereft of her senses, it seems."

"Has she always been this way?"

"Nay, only in the past year or so. Olive thinks her mother had been involved in an unhappy love affair, which I suppose is possible. Elswyth is a handsome woman for her years—or she was, before she let herself go to pot."

"And you think that's what Olive wants to keep hidden? That her mother is unbalanced?"

"I know she wants to keep it hidden. When she first confided in me about Elswyth, she begged me not to tell anyone—and not just because of the shame of madness. As an apprentice, Olive is only supposed to assist her mother in preparing the tonics and elixirs and so forth, but for months she's been doing it all herself—her mother's unfit to do it, and she's long since lost interest. She sleeps till midday, then scratches about in the medicinal garden out back—even in the middle of winter, when nothing's growing. If that came to light, they could lose the shop. Naturally it would upset her for Damian to know about her mother. She'd have to wonder who else knew."

Graham pondered this as he ate another orange section. "I suppose . . ."

"But . . ." she prompted, eyeing him astutely.

He shook his head. "That's not quite what it sounded like to me."

"What did it sound like?"

"As if . . . as if Olive's secret had to do with *her*."

"If her mother's gone mad and she's left running the shop, I think that has very much to do with her."

"Yes . . . I'm sure you're right." He handed her another slice of orange.

"No, you're not." She smiled at him as she ate the fruit.

Later that evening, as Graham was readying himself for bed, he heard a tapping on the closed shutter of the alley window. "Serjant?" came the feminine whisper.

He unlatched the shutters and opened them. "Good evening, Leoda," he said softly; Joanna was still awake, working on her embroidery in the shop.

The whore smiled; she was prettier at night, younger-looking. "I missed you today. I was at the Friday fair."

"So I gathered. Did you do well?"

"Made sixpence, but I'll never get my kirtle clean. I hate doing it in the woods." She smiled seductively. "How about a bit of company again tonight?"

He shook his head. "I'm afraid not, Leoda. That won't happen again."

"I'll be quieter coming in. She'll never know."

He took her hand in his. "It's really not wise for you to keep coming around, Leoda."

"Even during the day?" she asked forlornly. "Just to talk?"

"Even during the day. I'm sorry about it, too. I've enjoyed our talks."

"You don't want her to see me about."

"Before last night, it wouldn't have much mattered if she had. But now, I'd feel . . ." He shook his head.

"You're worried she'll toss you into the street if she sees me."

Oddly, that hadn't even occurred to him, although she probably would. "I'm worried about her feelings, mostly."

"Her *feelings*." Leoda smiled knowingly. "Ah, it's about feelings, is it?"

Absurdly, Graeham felt a rush of heat in his cheeks. "Nay, it's . . . not that way between us. She's a wedded woman."

For a long moment Leoda contemplated her hand in his, her conflicted expression gradually giving way to one of determination. Looking up, she said, "Joanna Chapman's no wedded woman, serjant."

"What are you talking about?"

"She's a widow."

"Nay, you just think that because her husband's never about. He spends most of his time abroad."

"He was stabbed to death last summer by some Italian whose wife he'd been diddling. Sir Hugh told me himself, just the other day." She smiled a little sadly. "He asked me not to mention it to you."

Graeham stared at her blankly, recalling hints and implications, things he'd heard and dismissed . . . *I was that sorry when I found out what happened.*

Of course. Of course.

Leoda squeezed his hand. "I thought you had a right to know."

"Thank you."

"I'm sure she has her reasons for keeping it from you. You shouldn't be cross with her over it."

"I'm not," he said honestly—for how could he fault her for her prevarications when he was guilty of the same sin himself? He'd fabricated his reasons for being in London and wanting to stay in her home. He'd lied to her outright dozens of times in an effort to conceal the secret of Ada le Fever's parentage. Joanna's one simple deception was relatively benign by comparison.

"I promised Sir Hugh I wouldn't tell you," Leoda said.

She added despondently, "He'll not be payin' me any more of his afternoon visits—he'll be that vexed at me."

"I won't tell him you told me. I won't even tell him I know."

Her eyes lit up. "Truly?"

" 'Twould ill repay you for confiding in me."

"You *are* a good man. I knew it from the first." She stroked his cheek with her free hand. "I've been pleased to know you, serjant."

"And I you." He kissed her hand and released it.

She sauntered away, blowing him a kiss over her shoulder.

Chapter 12

◆❦◆

"Mind if I join you?" Graeham limped into the shopfront, where Joanna had repaired, as usual, after supper.

"No . . . no, of course not." She hung a lantern on the chain dangling over her linen-draped embroidery frame and took a seat on the little folding stool in front of it. "There's no place for you to sit, though."

"This will do." He sat on a large chest tucked beneath the shuttered front window, stretching his splinted leg out to the side so he could lean back against the wall.

In the three weeks he'd been living here, he'd rarely set foot in this part of the house. During the day he was wary of being seen, especially by Olive, whose apothecary shop was directly across the street. At night he generally retired to the storeroom to read by candlelight before turning in, while Joanna worked on her embroidery.

He'd always felt a little hesitant about imposing himself on her while she was occupied with such a solitary, creative pursuit. And, too, he'd never been one to depend on the company of others, a trait he'd grown smug about over the years. But that smugness evaporated when it came to Joanna Chapman. He savored her company, reveled in it, craved it. Tonight he felt damned near starved for it.

She lifted the linen dustcover from her embroidery frame, revealing an untouched length of white silk twill waxed around the edges and lashed tight to the wooden struts. A basket sat on the little table next to her. Pulling it closer, she sorted through its neatly packed supplies—needles on a parchment card, various fringes and braids, brushes, a measuring rod, clay jars, quills, a number of short sticks wound with colorful silken threads, and for some reason, a feather duster.

Joanna chose a goose quill and a piece of willow charcoal from the basket. She broke off about an inch of the charcoal, pared down one end with a penknife, and inserted it in the tip of the quill.

"Clever," Graeham said.

"One of Lady Fayette's little tricks." With this ingenious charcoal pen, Joanna began sketching a design of curved lines and circles onto the silk. He watched her in profile, her brow furrowed in concentration as she worked.

She had removed her veil before coming in here to work, not realizing that Graeham would follow her. The amber lamplight ignited the gold in her hair, tendrils of which had sprung loose from her single braid to curl around her cheeks and nape. She wore her violet linen kirtle tonight, which was as plain and patched as her two woollen gowns, but a bit more pleasingly snug around her breasts and waist and hips. Graeham contemplated the elegantly sensuous curve of her back as she leaned over her work.

Two weeks had passed since the Friday fair and the revelation about Joanna's widowhood—a fortnight of interminable days and long, lonely nights on his solitary little cot. Sometimes, after Joanna climbed the ladder to the solar at night, he would lie very still in the dark, listening for the groan of certain floorboards as she trod upon them, the faint squeak of the bed ropes—apparently directly above him—as she lay down and shifted to get comfortable.

After giving it some thought, he'd decided not to tell her that he knew about Prewitt's death—not just for Leoda's sake, but because he understood and sympathized with her determination to pass herself off as a wedded woman. Undoubtedly the pretense made her feel better about his staying here; insulated by her presumed matrimony, she could keep him at a respectable—and safe—distance.

Curious as to what pains she'd taken to maintain her deception, Graeham had several times casually mentioned Mistress Joanna's husband to Thomas Harper, whereupon the leper had swiftly changed the subject, clearly discomfited; no doubt she'd asked Thomas not to reveal her widowhood to Graeham, just as Hugh had asked Leoda.

Suspicious of everyone now, Graeham had even broached the subject of Prewitt Chapman with young Adam, who'd taken to coming around from time to time, but the boy had clearly never even heard of the man, nor met Joanna.

Deep inside, Graeham wanted her to tell him the truth, to look him in the eye and say, "I'm a widow—no man has a claim on me." His heart wanted this, ached for this . . . but he was old enough to know better than to trust the impulses of his heart. His rational mind knew far better. Joanna had constructed this subterfuge for a reason, and a good one. She was well advised to keep Graeham at a distance; as an unlanded soldier, he could only worsen her already dire prospects. As for Graeham, he'd best remember that he was, for all intents and purposes, a betrothed man. He had no business cultivating an infatuation with Joanna Chapman when he would soon be wed to someone else—a wedding he mustn't jeopardize, lest he forfeit the estate that came with the lady Phillipa's hand.

Striving to keep his mind off Joanna, Graeham had spent the past fortnight maintaining his vigilant surveillance of Rolf le Fever's house, an effort that seemed more futile with each passing day. Ada le Fever's sickroom window remained shuttered, while her husband came and went as if naught were amiss. One night he'd spirited a woman through the back door and up to his bedchamber, not bothering to shutter the window while he'd coaxed her out of her sable-trimmed mantle, jeweled cap, and opulent tunic; her beauty had been marred by pockmarked cheeks, but she'd been buxom, with striking white-blond hair. She'd laughed as he tied her to the bedposts—at which point Graeham had shuttered his own window, ashamed of having watched as long as he had.

He wondered if the guildmaster ever climbed the stairs to the solar, where Ada le Fever passed her days and nights. When was the last time he had actually seen his ailing wife in the flesh?

Joanna's drawing was taking form as a tree with gracefully drooping branches on which were suspended a dozen or more weighty spheres.

"A fruit tree?" Graeham inquired.

"An orange tree." Her shoulders rose in a small shrug. "I've been thinking about oranges of late."

He smiled; for some reason that pleased him. "What is it going to be when it's done?"

"A scarf."

"You draw beautifully," he said, leaning closer for a better look. Her lines were light, fluid, and executed with a dexterity born of long practice.

She glanced at him from beneath her dark lashes. "Thank you."

"Do you always create your designs this freely? Just . . . thinking them up and sketching them out like this?"

"Oh, no—generally I use a pattern. I've been collecting them for years. Some I made myself, and others were gifts from Lady Fayette. They're in that box on the floor." She smiled. "Would you care to choose a border for this scarf?"

"Me?"

"Yes, you. Go on—open the box and take a look."

Graeham lifted the box—a large, flat document chest—onto his lap and flipped open the leather-hinged lid. Stacked on top were a number of stencils cut from white silk.

"The borders are underneath," she said.

Setting the stencils aside, Graeham found sheets of parchment scraped extraordinarily thin and oiled to make them transparent. Each one had a repetitive image inked onto it—flowering vines, networks of circles, interwoven knots, grape clusters, fleurs-de-lis, scrolls, circular medallions, stylized leaves, and various geometric patterns. Holes had been pricked along the outlines of the images; traces of chalk and charcoal clung to the templates.

"That"—she nodded toward the wall hanging above her—"will give you an idea of how those borders will look once they're stitched." The banner of ivory silk was embroidered in a variety of different designs. All the borders were represented, as well as a number of animals—a bird with a nestful of young, a rampant lion, an eagle, a squirrel collecting acorns, a frolicking monkey, a peacock spreading its tail, and a dragon spewing fire. There were crosses, saints, angels, lovers, beasts, flowers, a king and queen, and, interestingly, a woman bending over an embroidery frame.

"What is that hanging for?" he asked. "Why did you make it?"

" 'Tis a sampler of my work," she said, still sketching away. "If a customer wants something special, she can pick the design and I'll embroider it."

"You take commissions?"

"No, not really. I mean—I do, I have. I made a very elaborate pair of cuffs for Alderman Huxley last year and a purse for his wife. But most of my customers aren't interested in more than a new pair of garters or a hair ribbon. And even if they were, they wouldn't be able to afford my prices. Work like that is time-consuming, and I charge good coin for it."

"Then it could be very lucrative work for you—more lucrative than the shop—if you could cultivate the right customers."

She glanced at him. "A while ago—it was during the Friday fair, actually—I got to thinking about the time I visited the Tower of London as a girl. There were beautiful embroidered cushions on all the chairs and benches, and decorative hangings on the walls. The queen and her ladies had the most exquisite panels and bands sewn onto their tunics—satin stitched in gold with hundreds of pearls and garnets and silver plaques sewn in. And they all had such lovely girdles and purses."

"Ladies like that could afford to commission pieces from you."

"I know. And I've been thinking about showing my sampler and some of my best pieces to the ladies at the Tower, but . . ." She shook her head and frowned at her drawing.

"Why don't you? You'd do a far sight better than selling the occasional ribbon or scarf out of this shop."

"It's . . . you'll think it's silly."

"No, I won't."

Joanna gestured toward the sampler. "Have you picked a border?"

"You can't change the subject that easily, but yes, I've picked one. The one that looks like knotwork."

She smiled. "Perfect."

He felt a ridiculous surge of pride.

"Would you find me the template for that one?"

Sorting through the templates, he said, "Your embroidery is worthy of the queen herself. A royal commission could feed you for years."

"Well I know it."

"Then why do you hesitate to show your work at court?"

She plucked the worn-down bit of charcoal out of the goose quill and put it away, then took a shiny black raven quill out of the basket and proceeded to sharpen its point. "It's because of the change in my circumstances," she said without looking at him, seeming a little embarrassed. "At fourteen I was presented at court. I met the queen. To return at one-and-twenty as a tradeswoman . . ." She shook her head. "It shouldn't shame me, but it does. Perhaps I just need a little longer to work up my courage . . . or to grow so desperate that I don't have any choice."

He handed her the template and set the box back on the floor. "Allowing desperation to take over is rarely a successful strategy, no matter what your goal."

Joanna sighed. Opening a jar of ink, she charged her quill and began tracing over the lines of her charcoal drawing, quickly but flawlessly. "There's another problem. The ladies of the court aren't going to be content with what I do—plain silk thread on twill and damask. They like ornaments sewn into their embroidery, and fancy ones—pearls, enamels, jewels set in gold. I don't have the money for that sort of thing. Gold thread is just as dear. It's made by winding strips of gold by hand around a core of silken threads. The silkwoman gets more for an ounce of it than I get for a scarf like this."

"The queen's ladies must have gold and jewels?"

She cast him a doleful glance. "Gold and jewels are all they know, serjant, all they've ever known. These are the daughters of the most noble families in the kingdom. A merchant's wife—even an alderman's wife—might be content with silver thread and spangles, but not these ladies."

"Spangles?"

"Little metal ornaments—they can be had fairly cheaply, and if they're applied well, the effect isn't too tawdry. There are also little glass beads from Venice that can be bought at the Friday fair—they're a passable substitute for precious gems. I've used them on some of my girdles."

"And merchants' wives find these compromises acceptable?" Graeham asked, as an idea began to take shape in his mind.

"They have no choice. Gold and gems are generally out of their reach. Even if they aspire to look like nobility—and most of them do, it seems—their husbands simply can't afford it."

Graeham sat forward, infused with excitement; this could work. "Have you considered . . . seeking commissions from the wives of the more well-to-do merchants here in West Cheap?"

She studied her completed ink drawing with a critical eye. "I already do. If they come by the shop and ask for something special—"

"Nay, I mean actively soliciting them—going to their homes with your samples. Most of them probably have no idea the level of work you're capable of. If you came to them in their homes, the way their dressmakers do, and talked to them, found out what it is they really want, you'd soon have more commissions than you could handle."

She plucked the feather duster out of her basket and swept the charcoal dust from the silk, leaving a clean, precise ink drawing.

"You wouldn't have to travel farther than Milk Street," he said. "There's the wife of that moneylender with the evil temper . . ."

"Lionel Oxwyke's wife?"

"Aye—she could afford your work." Graeham strove to keep his tone nonchalant, not wanting to seem overeager; she mustn't suspect that this idea would be of any benefit to him. "And what about the wife of that guildmaster who lives behind you? The woman with the head cold."

"Ada le Fever?"

"Aye."

"Absolutely not." Joanna stood and walked to the rear of the house, down the hall, and out the back door.

Graeham muttered an oath and slumped against the wall. It would serve his cause well if he could talk her into visiting Ada le Fever. Afterward he could question her and possibly get a better idea of the situation in the guildmaster's household—the nature and severity of Ada's malady, whether she would be capable of travel if he could find a way to get her out of there. Any information was better than what he'd been able to come up with by spying through the storeroom window.

Joanna could be very useful to him. She could be his eyes and ears and legs . . . if only he could convince her to seek out Ada le Fever's patronage. That the scheme might very well serve Joanna's purposes as well as Graeham's was an added benefit, but he didn't delude himself that his motives for proposing it were altruistic. Graeham was consumed with his mission; if he could use Joanna to implement it, with or without her knowledge, he would; any advantage to her was entirely secondary.

When she returned, she was carrying a rag and a wooden bowl of water with a sea sponge in it, which she set on the work table before taking her seat. "I'll do it."

"You will? You'll go to see Ada le Fever?"

"Not her. But I'll pay a call on Rose Oxwyke, and perhaps Elizabeth Huxley, the alderman's wife—she likes her finery. And there are one or two others. With the rent you've paid me, I can buy some silver thread and spangles and—"

"What's stopping you from going to see Ada le Fever? Her illness?"

"Her husband." Rising, she lifted the embroidery frame from the trestles and turned it over, exposing the reverse side.

Interesting. "You don't care for him?"

"He stole my livelihood from me just because I wouldn't—" She cut herself off with a sharp look toward Graeham.

"Stole your livelihood? How so?"

Joanna squeezed the wet sponge into the bowl. "I . . . went to him for a favor once."

"What kind of favor?"

She chewed on her lip as she rubbed the sponge over the silk, dampening it. "I wanted to be admitted to the Mercers' Guild."

The pieces were falling into place. "Isn't your husband a member of the guild?" he asked, half hoping she would tell him the truth about her husband if he pressed her, knowing he shouldn't want that, that it could only bring trouble.

Luckily, she had more sense than he did. "Yes," she said as she returned the sponge to the bowl and flipped the frame back over. "He is. I wanted to join also, just because . . . because I did. But le Fever, he . . . he had conditions."

Of course—the lecherous worm. "Conditions you refused to meet."

"I should say so." Taking her seat, she extracted a blunt, soft-looking brush from her basket, dipped it in the ink, and blotted it on the rag. With deft strokes she gradually shaded in the trunk of her orange tree.

Manfrid entered the shopfront through the open alley window. On seeing Graeham, he leapt onto the chest next to him and threw himself on his back, displaying his vast white belly as he gazed imploringly at Graeham.

"Yes?" Graeham said in the low voice the cat seemed to find reassuring. "And what, precisely, is it that you want?"

Manfrid stretched luxuriously, throwing his head back as he writhed in delicious expectation.

"What's that? I don't quite follow you."

"Stop teasing the poor creature," Joanna chuckled, "and scratch his stomach."

"I don't want him to start thinking I'm at his beck and call."

"Aren't you? 'Tis a wonderment how he's taken to you." With a mischievous smile she added, "And how you've taken to him. I wouldn't have thought it would be worth your trouble to befriend such a . . . *useless* creature."

Graeham held his hand poised above Manfrid's enormous stomach, eliciting a purr of astonishing volume and resonance. "Sounds like cart wheels on gravel."

Joanna grinned as she added whisper-soft shadows to the tree and its fruit, making it stand out in astonishing relief from the surface of the taut silk.

" 'Tis a miracle, how you do that." Graeham stroked the downy fur of the cat's underbelly; he squirmed in hedonistic abandon.

"All it takes is a good squirrel brush and a steady hand."

"You shouldn't dismiss your talent so cavalierly. You're a remarkable woman—an extraordinary woman."

She made no response to this, seemingly absorbed in her

work, but spots of pink bloomed on her cheeks. Graeham kicked himself; he should be finessing her into visiting Ada le Fever, not flattering her like some lovesick suitor.

Changing tack, he said, "You're not just talented, you're very strong, especially for a woman—independent, self-reliant."

"I've had to be."

As have I. Perhaps that was what drew him to her, the shared sense of isolation, of having no one to rely on but oneself. For all the advantages of being unfettered by others, it was a lonely way to live. He wondered if she ever lay awake at night, listening for sounds from below.

"You *are* strong." He lightly scratched Manfrid's throat. "Which is why it surprises me so for you to cower before this Rolf le Fever as you do."

"Cower!" She whipped around to face him, her eyes glittering with outrage, as he knew they would; they were really much alike, he and Joanna Chapman.

"Yes, cower. This man intimidates you so thoroughly that you won't even attempt to approach his wife. He's defeated you without even trying, while you just sit back and let it happen."

She turned back to her work, but her brush was unmoving in her hand. For a moment Graeham feared that she might ask him where, precisely, his interest in these matters lay. She might have, if she'd had an inkling of his ulterior motive for wanting her to visit the le Fever house—but as far as she knew, Graeham had never heard of Rolf le Fever before fate landed him in her storeroom while he was en route to visit kinsmen in Oxfordshire.

Joanna would assume that Graeham's only interest lay in helping her. An uneasy little rivulet of contrition wormed its way into his belly.

"You're right," she said soberly. "He's coercing me without even knowing it, and I'm letting him do it. It's just that I swore I'd never have anything more to do with that man. He just wanted to . . . to use me, the same as every other man I've ever known. Except for Hugh." With a tentative glance in his direction, she added, somewhat shyly, "And you, of course."

The little worm of contrition grew into a hissing serpent, squeezing him until he felt sick with guilt. But all he said was, "Thank you, mistress. I appreciate that."

Chapter 13

❧

Graeham watched through the rear window the following afternoon as Joanna knocked on the back door of Rolf le Fever's house, lugging a leather bag containing her sampler and her best pieces—a beaded girdle, an elaborate scarf, and a fringed purse.

The door was opened by the shiny-faced kitchen wench, wiping her hands on her apron. She nodded as Joanna spoke to her, then turned and retreated into the house. A minute later, Graeham saw the kitchen wench through the window of the second-floor sitting room, where Rolf le Fever was meeting with some men. He snapped at her; she flinched as she spoke, pointing outside.

The guildmaster crossed to the window and leaned out, his eyebrows quirking when he saw Joanna. He disappeared from view. A few moments later he appeared at the back door.

Leaning against the door frame, his arms crossed, he spoke to Joanna while slowly surveying her up and down. Graeham's hands clenched into fists. Suddenly it seemed like very poor judgment on his part to have urged her to go there.

Joanna had her back to Graeham, but from le Fever's expression of weary forbearance, it was clear that she was entreating him to let her pay a call on his wife. He shook his head resolutely and backed up, his hand on the door.

She took a step forward and said something else, pointing to her bag.

Le Fever held up a hand, his attitude irate, his voice so loud now that Graeham could make out a word here and there. From what he gathered, the guildmaster was telling

Joanna that his wife had no use for her "cheap frippery" and that she should leave or he would have her bodily ejected from his property.

He slammed the door shut.

Joanna stood there for a moment, then turned and started back through the stable yard. As she passed through the opening in the stone wall, she paused, her hand on the iron gate, her countenance meditative. Presently her expression lightened; she smiled slowly.

Graeham assumed she would cross the croft and enter the house through the back door. Instead, she headed for the alley. Wondering what she had in mind, he grabbed his crutch, struggled to his feet and unlatched the alley window—having shuttered it after nones, as usual, pending Olive's daily trek to the le Fever house—but he was too late. Joanna had already passed.

Limping to the salle, he watched through the front window—she'd closed the bottom shutter but left the top open for air—as she crossed Wood Street and entered the apothecary shop. She was in there so long that his broken leg started aching. He leaned against the wall, his gaze trained on the window, waiting for her to come out.

When she did, she was wearing Olive's dark green mantle. "What the devil . . . ?" Graeham murmured as she raised the hood of the heavy woollen cloak, pulling it low to shade her face, and started back across Wood Street. She still carried her bag of wares; in her other hand was something small that flashed blue in the afternoon sun—no doubt the phial containing Ada le Fever's tonic.

She disappeared into the alley. Graeham turned and hobbled back into the storeroom. By the time he got there, she was crossing le Fever's stable yard.

Byram emerged from the stable, leading le Fever's black horse by the reins. Glancing at Joanna as she walked up to the back door, her head down, he called out, "Afternoon, Olive. You can go on in."

She raised a hand in acknowledgment, opened the door, and disappeared inside.

"You clever girl," Graeham whispered, sinking onto the cot.

*   *   *

Closing the door behind her, Joanna found herself in a hallway leading straight ahead the length of the house. To the right, through an arched doorway, she saw part of a sunlit room that must have been a kitchen, judging by the pots and utensils hanging from the rafters. The plump kitchen wench who had greeted her at the door earlier stood with her back to her at a work table, singing as she chopped.

An oaken door stood open to her left. Through it, she saw kegs of ale, barrels of wine, and a number of ewers, goblets, and cups on shelves. In a corner of this well-stocked buttery she spied what she was looking for—the service stairwell.

She climbed the stairs quickly but stealthily, praying that she wouldn't bump into Rolf le Fever before she had a chance to find his wife and talk her into a commission. As she passed the second level, she heard men's voices, including le Fever's, and crossed herself. *Please, God, don't let him find me here.*

Pausing on the third-floor landing, she listened for sounds on the other side of the oaken door, her spirits sinking when she heard nothing. Olive had told her she'd find the mistress of the house in the solar, nursing her stubborn cold. If she wasn't here, Joanna would have to return home, defeated.

She knocked softly on the door.

"Aethel?" came a reedy voice from within. "I thought you'd gone marketing."

Joanna cracked the door open. The great chamber, with its tightly shuttered windows, was so dim that it took her a moment to spot the narrow, uncurtained bed on the opposite wall. A woman lay propped up on pillows beneath a coverlet, observing her with an expression of bewilderment.

" 'Tisn't Aethel, mistress," Joanna said, stepping into the room and closing the door behind her. It was warm in here, and stuffy, despite the room's size. "My name is Joanna Chapman. I live behind you."

Joanna crossed the room, feeling decidedly uneasy to be here in this woman's private sanctum, uninvited, having gained access by subterfuge. She began to wish she hadn't done it, not because of the risk of discovery but because she was violating the privacy of this stranger. Most likely she wouldn't be entertaining these misgivings had she found Ada le Fever dressed and sitting up, rather than abed in her night shift.

The darkly paneled walls were bare of hangings, the wooden floor devoid of rushes, the furniture minimal. A carved wooden crucifix hung over Mistress Ada's bed, and a book with a cross stamped into the leather-bound cover sat on a shelf beneath it. There was an almost empty bowl of what looked like broth on a little table next to the bed and a cup of water. Were it not for the chamber's spaciousness, it might almost have looked like a nun's cell.

Ada pointed toward the blue glass phial as Joanna approached the side of the bed. "Is that my tonic?" she asked in a very soft, girlish voice.

"Aye. Olive . . . asked me to bring it." In truth, Olive had seemed confounded by Joanna's request to borrow her mantle and deliver Mistress Ada's medicine. But once Joanna had explained what she was about, the girl had agreed readily enough, on one condition. *Have her take the tonic while you're there, so's you can bring back the phial. Mum counts those phials twice a day—they're that dear.*

Joanna set her bag on the floor and took a seat in the chair next to the bed, trying not to stare at Ada le Fever. She was young, much younger than Joanna had realized— or perhaps it only seemed that way because she was so dreadfully thin. Her face looked white as chalk in the half-light, an effect intensified by the sharp contrast of blue-black hair worn in two tidy braids. She had enormous, dark eyes with shadows beneath them, as if someone had smudged a bit of charcoal there.

Joanna tried to reconcile this pale, fragile creature with the vibrant young woman she'd seen last summer, gardening behind her house. She'd struck Joanna as extremely pretty then, in a delicate, rarefied way. Now she just looked sick.

Very sick.

"If you can help me to sit up," Ada said weakly, "I'll take the tonic." She spoke the Continental dialect of Norman French, rather than the anglicized version that was in common use in England, and with a refined manner of speech that signified gentle birth.

Sliding an arm beneath Ada's shoulders, Joanna urged her into a sitting position and uncorked the phial. The tonic smelled pleasantly minty. She held it out to Ada, but the young woman shook her head. "I'll drop it if I try to hold it. My hands . . . they don't always do what I want them to."

Joanna supported Ada and held the phial to her mouth while she drank its contents, taking small sips that were clearly difficult for her to swallow. When it was empty, Joanna helped her to lean back against her mound of pillows.

"There, now," Joanna said, switching to the classic French she'd been tutored in by her father's clerics. "That will make you feel better."

Ada shook her head listlessly. "I feel even worse after the tonic."

"Worse?"

"For a while. I get to feeling cold all over, and numb in my mouth and throat—and sometimes I get nosebleeds. Master Aldfrith says it's just the medicine doing its job."

"Master Aldfrith the surgeon?"

"Aye, my husband sent for him when I first took sick. He still comes round from time to time. Sometimes he brings his son-in-law."

"Is his son-in-law a surgeon too?"

"No, he's a mercer—or wants to be. Master Aldfrith's trying to get him into the guild, but Rolf says he's too inexperienced."

From the looks of her, Ada le Fever needed a proper, university-trained physician, not the neighborhood bonesetter. "What does Master Aldfrith say is wrong with you?" she asked.

"A rheum in the head. They linger like this sometimes, he says."

"I see." But Joanna had never known anyone to waste away like this from a head cold.

"Master Aldfrith told Olive what kind of tonic I need, and she brings it to me every day. He says I'll feel better very soon."

"How long have you been taking it?"

Ada frowned in concentration. "Since Christmastide. How long ago is that?"

"Almost six months."

Ada turned her head toward the wall.

"I know what you need," Joanna said cheerily, rising and crossing to the window on the back wall. "A bit of fresh air and sunshine."

"Nay."

"Aye, it's too dark in here, and dreadfully warm. I don't know how you can bear it." Joanna unlatched the shutters and threw them open. When she turned around, she saw that Ada had an arm thrown over her face.

"Close it," Ada pleaded. "The light hurts my eyes."

"You'll get used to—"

"No, I won't. Close it—please."

Joanna shuttered the window and returned to stand at the side of the bed, where Ada was rubbing her eyes with trembling hands. She was trembling all over, Joanna saw; her body was racked with shivers. "Are you cold?"

"Aye," she said, turning onto her side and tucking her legs up.

Joanna covered Ada with the extra blanket that had been folded at the foot of the bed. "You should see a physician."

"Nay. Rolf . . . my husband . . . he says it isn't necessary. 'Tis but a rheum in the head, he says. Master Aldfrith says so too—and he's a surgeon."

"Still, I think you should ask to see—"

"I did—the last time Rolf was up here, back before Lent. But he won't send for one. He says physicians charge too much and that I'm not really as sick as I seem, that I'm just . . ." Ada let out a shaky breath. In a tone of weary defeat, she said, "He says I'm just melancholy, and making too much of a head cold. They both do, Rolf and the surgeon." She shook her head. "I'm sorry. You don't want to hear these things."

"I don't mind. Is it true? Are you melancholy?"

Ada closed her eyes and nodded.

"Do you think that's all that's wrong with you?" Joanna asked. "Apart from a head cold?"

Ada shrugged. "Perhaps. I suppose so. Master Aldfrith, he tried to explain it to me, but it's so confusing, all that business about humors and the stars and the balance of earth and water and fire and so forth. My sister, Phillipa, would understand—she's very clever—but I just can't make sense of it. Apparently it has much to do with an excess of black bile. That's what's making me melancholic—that's why I think I'm sicker than I am."

"Ah." Joanna couldn't completely discount the theory. If the soul was ailing, could not the body suffer as well?

"Rolf says it has naught to do with humors and such. He says I want attention and . . . and pity and . . . and . . ." She shook her head. "You didn't come here to listen to this. I have no one to talk to except for Aethel, my maid—that's why I'm subjecting you to this. You want to leave, and I'm—"

"No, I don't." Neither did she intend to solicit a commission from Ada le Fever; she was far too ill to take an interest in a new seat cushion or purse. Lifting the book down from the little shelf over the bed, she opened it and found it to be a psalter.

"My uncle gave me that," Ada said. "He's a canon of Notre Dame."

"It's beautifully done," Joanna said, admiring the gilded capitals and borders on the neatly inked pages of tissue-thin vellum. "Do you read from it often?"

Ada shook her head. "My eyes . . . it hurts to read. I used to, though. I love the Psalms."

"Would you like me to read to you?" Joanna asked, taking a seat.

"You can read?"

"Aye."

Ada looked at her speculatively. "You don't seem like any merchant's wife I've ever met."

Joanna smiled. "Nor do you."

Ada returned her smile. "Yes, I'd like for you to read to me. I'd like that very much."

The bells of vespers were pealing when Joanna left the le Fever house, stealing out the same way she'd stolen in. She had just enough time to pay a call on Rose Oxwyke before heading home to start supper.

There was a lovely garden behind the Oxwykes' grand

stone house, with a slate path leading to the back door. Joanna was halfway down the path when the door opened and young Damian Oxwyke emerged, wearing his black mantle and felt hat, his jaw set, his eyes glinting.

Joanna nodded as he passed her. "Good afternoon, Master Damian."

"Mistress," he muttered, slamming the gate on his way out.

From the back stoop, Joanna watched him stalk across the croft and into the alley. Turning toward the door, she raised her hand to knock, but hesitated when she heard the muffled bellowing of Lionel Oxwyke's voice from within. "He's been sneaking over there to see her! He didn't even try to deny it!"

His wife said something in a high, wheedling tone that Joanna couldn't make out.

"Of *course* my bloody stomach is bothering me," he raged. "It's on fire, and it's that boy's fault."

Rose Oxwyke tried again to placate her husband, but he would have none of it.

"Damn him for his impudence!" the money changer roared. "Damn him! Damn him to hell!"

Joanna turned around and walked swiftly away. Perhaps she would try to visit Rose Oxwyke some other time—some time when her husband wasn't home. Of course, if this fruitless afternoon was any indication of the kind of success she would have seeking commissions from the local matrons, she should simply abandon the idea right now. She'd closed her shop all afternoon for what was beginning to look like a doomed enterprise.

But if she couldn't find some better way to support herself than the shop, what would become of her once Graeham Fox's four shillings ran out? Penniless women did not fare well anywhere, particularly in a city like London. No wonder so many women ended up spreading their legs for tuppence. Could Joanna make her living that way if the only option was starvation? If things kept on as they were, she would find herself facing that choice by next winter.

According to Hugh, all she needed was to marry the right man, and her problems, financial and otherwise, would disappear. The more she thought about it, the more sense it made. Perhaps she shouldn't be so quick to dismiss Robert of Ramswick as a potential husband; he hadn't contacted her since the fair, but Hugh assured her he meant to. She'd been humoring Hugh when she told him she'd think about Robert's suit—if and when he broached it—but upon reflection, there was a measure of merit to the idea.

Or there would be, if it weren't for the lady Margaret.

Thinking to return the mantle and glass phial to Olive, Joanna didn't head directly home, but went instead to the apothecary shop. The shop window was open, but there was no sign of Olive. Joanna entered the stall and looked around; it wasn't like Olive to leave things unattended. Setting the phial and her bag on the work table, she unpinned Olive's mantle and hung it on its peg by the doorway that led to the back of the house.

The deerskin over the door was open just an inch or two; through this gap, Joanna could view the length of the house to the rear window that looked out onto the walled medicinal garden in back. Elswyth, in her grimy night shift, was kneeling in the garden, clawing away at the dirt.

Joanna turned to leave, stilling when she heard whispers from beyond the curtained doorway, a feminine voice—Olive's voice—saying, "No . . . please . . . no."

Joanna unsheathed her dagger, drew a fortifying breath, and whipped the deerskin open. Olive gasped. She was standing against the wall, pinned between the arms of a dark-haired young man in black—Damian.

"Mistress Joanna!" Olive gaped at the dagger.

"What's going on here?" Joanna asked.

"Nothing. Please . . . put that away. He's not hurting me."

"*Hurting* you! Oh, Christ." Damian turned and paced away from her. "I can't bear this any longer, Olive. Sneaking about this way—"

"Then stop coming here, Damian," the girl pleaded.

"I can't. I love you."

"Damian, please . . ."

"Come away with me."

"No, Damian, please."

"Olive—"

"It's impossible. You know that."

"Because of Father? My betrothal to that . . . that child?"
Olive glanced uneasily toward Joanna. "Not just that."

He closed the space between them swiftly, taking Olive's
face between his hands and saying softly, "I've told you
before—I don't care about that. You weren't to blame. You
were coerced. 'Twas—"

"Please, Damian." Olive closed her eyes, her hands fisted
in her kirtle. "Please go."

"Olive—"

"Please." Opening her eyes, she laid a hand gently on
his cheek. "Please. Please."

A tear slid from her eye. He brushed it with his thumb,
lightly kissed her damp cheek, her forehead. "I won't give
up, Olive," he said, and left.

Olive slumped back against the wall, her eyes closed,
tears trailing down her face. Sheathing her dagger, Joanna
plucked her handkerchief from her sleeve and handed it to
Olive. "Are you all right?"

Olive nodded as she dried her face. "It's impossible. He's
just having trouble accepting it."

"Judging from those tears, so are you."

"It can't be that way between us."

"Has he tried to . . . take advantage of you?" Joanna
asked. "Does he want you to be his mistress?"

"Nay. He's never touched me. He wants me for his wife."

"Verily?"

"I can't marry him. It's impossible. Impossible."

"What was it he said you weren't to blame for?"

In a teary whisper, Olive said, "Something that can never
be undone, much as he would like to think it can." Sighing,
she folded the damp handkerchief in a neat square and
handed it back to Joanna. "How did you find Mistress
Ada?"

Joanna let Olive change the subject, knowing she would
just withdraw further if she pressed her. "Very ill."

"That's a bad head cold she's got." Smoothing her hair,
Olive returned to the storefront.

Joanna followed her. "That's no head cold."

"Well, Master Aldfrith says she's melancholic too, like
Mum."

"Perhaps." Joanna lifted the empty phial that had contained the tonic and inspected the few drops remaining in the bottom. "Master Aldfrith prescribed this medicine, did he not?"

"That's right."

"Do you mind telling me what's in it?"

" 'Tis an ordinary cold remedy—an infusion of yarrow with a bit of mint and honey to soothe the throat. We sold a great deal of it over the winter—I brewed up four pintes at a time."

"Yarrow? That's all?" There were few more benign or commonly prescribed herbs than yarrow.

"That's all."

"Is it possible to consume so much yarrow that it would . . . make someone even sicker?"

Olive shook her head. "Yarrow's not like that. Wormwood is, and valerian, and . . . well, many herbs will sicken you if you get too much—kill you, even. But not yarrow. Why?"

Joanna shook her head. "No reason. I just thought perhaps . . . but obviously I was wrong."

" 'Tisn't my tonic making Ada le Fever sick, mistress. 'Tis an overabundance of black bile doing that."

"Perhaps," Joanna said. But if Master Aldfrith was so sure of what was ailing Ada le Fever, why couldn't he manage to cure her?

Chapter 14

~

Not wanting to appear too interested, Graeham waited until after supper, when Joanna sat down at her embroidery frame, to question her about her visit to Ada le Fever.

"How did it go today?" he asked as he lowered himself onto the chest against the front wall, a cup of wine in his hand.

She sighed as she took her seat, inspecting the orange tree painted on the silk, and the knotwork border with which it was embellished, with a critical eye. "Not well." Plucking a needle off its parchment card, she threaded it with brown silk.

She'd kept her veil on tonight, for he'd made the mistake of telling her at supper that he would be joining her again. He missed seeing that extraordinary hair glimmer in the lamplight, like rippling waves reflecting a fiery sunset. But even with the veil, it was, as always, a struggle to keep from staring at her like a besotted youth.

"No one commissioned anything from you?" he asked, although he'd surmised as much from her solemn demeanor when she came home this afternoon. She hadn't even smiled when he'd suggested she take up burglary, so ingeniously had she gained access to le Fever's house.

"Nay, no commissions." She retrieved a leather thimble from the basket and fitted it over her finger. "I never even got to show my samples."

"What happened?"

She pierced the silk from underneath, on the edge of the orange tree's trunk. "Mistress Ada is too ill to have any interest in such things, and Mistress Rose was preoccupied with trying to soothe her husband's temper."

"Ada le Fever is ill?" He raised the cup to his lips, watching her over the rim.

"Aye, very ill—thin, wasted," she said, swiftly tracing the outline of the tree with a line of neat stitching. "She's confined to a bed in her solar. A rheum of the head, supposedly, plus an excess of black bile, according to Aldfrith."

"Aldfrith—the fellow who set my leg?"

"The same. Her husband thinks she's just looking for attention and pity."

Graeham took another slow sip of wine. "What do you think is wrong with her?"

"I think if she has an excess of anything, it's exposure to Rolf le Fever."

"You don't think he's . . . doing anything to harm her, do you?"

"Not unless . . ." She frowned; the needle flashed. "Nay, I have no business speculating on—"

"You can speculate. Is he doing her harm?"

She looked at him curiously before returning her attention to her orange tree. "His mere presence in that house must worsen her melancholia—perhaps even cause it. But there's no reason to think he's actually hurting her. She showed no sign of bruising. And she said he hadn't even been up to the solar since before Lent—that would be more than three months ago."

"How did she appear to you?" he asked.

Joanna shrugged without looking up. "As I said, very thin—although I know she's getting nourishment. There was a bowl of broth on the table, and she'd eaten it. She was deathly pale, with dark circles beneath her eyes. Despite that, she's a pretty little thing. Enormous brown eyes, raven hair."

Graeham's gaze lit on the gleaming raven's quill in Joanna's basket. It hadn't occurred to him that Lord Gui's twin daughters might be black-haired. Lord Gui had described Phillipa only as comely. The baron's legitimate issue—like him and his wife—were quite fair, so Graeham had always pictured his future bride with golden hair and sky-blue eyes.

"She's very petite, very delicate," Joanna continued, well

into the painstaking process of outlining the orange tree's drooping branches. "I felt like an ox next to her."

Laughter burst from Graeham at the notion of Joanna Chapman comparing herself to a draft animal. Never in his life had he known a woman more exquisitely graceful, more innately feminine.

More desirable.

More unattainable.

Don't think about her, Graeham scolded himself. *Think about Phillipa.* He could summon a mental image of his betrothed now, thanks to Joanna. It was an appealing image. She was petite; small women could be quite attractive. And although many men seemed to prefer blond women, some of the prettiest women Graeham had ever known were black-haired. Her eyes were brown . . .

Like Joanna's

No. No woman had eyes like Joanna's. When Graeham married Phillipa, he would have to forget Joanna's eyes. Or try to.

Refocusing on his inquiries, he asked, "Is she in any . . . real danger from this illness, do you think?"

"You mean, do I think she's going to die?"

Graeham took a deep breath and tossed down the rest of his wine. "Aye. She's not . . . I mean, she didn't seem . . ."

"As if she were on her deathbed? Nay—not as yet, anyway."

Graeham sighed with relief.

"She was conversing with me fairly comfortably," Joanna said as she methodically stitched the branches. "And she's still eating. And she takes her medicine without complaint, even though she doesn't like how it makes her feel afterward."

"She doesn't? Do you . . . happen to know what's in it?"

Joanna glanced briefly in his direction. "According to Olive, 'tis but an infusion of yarrow."

"Yarrow," he mused. "That should do her no harm."

"No real good, either, if she's as ill as I think she is."

The severity of Ada's illness could be a problem. "Does she ever get out of bed?" he asked.

"I don't know. I doubt it."

"But if she had to . . ." he began. "If she had to, say, travel . . ."

"Travel? Where?"

"I don't know. Anywhere. Say she had to take some sort of journey. Do you think she'd be up to it?"

"On that palfrey you brought for her?"

"Hugh sold the palfrey. I'll have to—" *Shit.*

Joanna stuck her needle in the silk and turned on her stool to face him. She was not smiling.

Graeham closed his eyes and sank back against the wall. "I suppose I was a bit too obvious."

"More than a bit."

He opened his eyes. She still wasn't smiling.

"Did you suspect," he began, "before tonight . . . ?"

She pulled the thimble off and absently fiddled with it. "Nay, you were very smooth. Some men are skilled at deception, serjant. You're one of them."

"Mistress . . ."

"Granted, there were hints that things weren't as they seemed. There was that palfrey. No soldier rides a palfrey. It's a lady's horse. And before that, I remember thinking it was awfully strange for you to be searching for an inn in West Cheap when you already had accommodations, seeing as you were just passing through London on your way to Oxfordshire. But you don't even have any relatives in Oxfordshire, do you?"

He raked a hand through his hair. "Nay."

"You were in West Cheap because of Ada le Fever. You came to London because of her."

"Aye," he said hesitantly, loath to reveal more than he absolutely had to.

"You came to take her away. Back to Beauvais?"

"To Paris."

"Are you in love with her?"

He sat forward. "Nay!"

"You crossed the Channel to steal her away from her husband," she said impassively. "You're still trying to find a way to do it, despite . . ." Her eyes narrowed on him. "That's why you wanted to live in my house. That's why it was worth four shillings to you. You needed a convenient lair—a place to hide out while you planned a way to abduct

Ada le Fever from her home. You've been using my store-room as a hunting blind!"

"Mistress . . ."

"You have, haven't you?" she demanded furiously. "Tell me the truth for once, damn you."

He sighed heavily. "Save for your somewhat sinister insinuations, yes. You're right. I've been keeping watch on that house for the reasons you've surmised—I need to get Ada le Fever away from there. But not because I'm in love with her."

She regarded him skeptically.

"I've never even met the woman." He rubbed the back of his neck as he pondered how much to tell her. "I was sent here," he said carefully, "by a kinsman of hers, someone who's troubled about her welfare. He has reason to believe that her husband may be mistreating her."

"Why?"

"She stopped writing letters about six months ago."

"That's when she took ill," Joanna said. "I'm sure she simply hasn't felt up to it."

"There wouldn't be such concern if it weren't for le Fever himself. He regrets the marriage and has done naught but heap abuse on his wife since bringing her back to London."

"What manner of abuse? Beatings?"

"Apparently not—not bad ones, at any rate. He insults her, threatens her."

"Threatens her?"

"Says things that could be perceived as threats," Graeham hedged.

"And what, pray," Joanna asked with grim humor, "has he done that would set him apart from the general run of husbands?"

"You already know what a debaucher he is. It seems he's had numerous liaisons with other women."

"I'm still waiting."

He was stabbed to death last summer by some Italian whose wife he'd been diddling, Leoda had said of Prewitt Chapman. Graeham suspected that the marriage for which Joanna had sacrificed so much had been a grievous disappointment to her.

"Rolf le Fever flaunts these trysts within Mistress Ada's

hearing," Graeham said. "It seems he takes special pride in seducing the wives of important men, and he's not as discreet as he might be. I myself saw him bring a woman up to his bedchamber and . . . disport himself with her while his wife was asleep upstairs. From the way this woman was dressed, I'd say she was a matron of high rank."

"What did she look like?"

"Very blond hair, almost white. Rather generously proportioned."

"Pockmarks?"

"Aye."

"That's Elizabeth Huxley, the wife of the alderman for our ward. John Huxley is not a man to trifle with. If he knew about this, he'd take measures."

"Would he have le Fever killed, do you think?"

"Or at the very least, gelded," she said. "Le Fever must know this—he's no fool."

"Men tend to lose perspective in matters of the heart."

"Women lose perspective in matters of the heart," she said dryly. "Men are enslaved to the whims of another organ entirely."

He nodded to acknowledge her point, while trying not to smile. Given her mood, he'd best conduct himself soberly.

"Who is this kinsman who sent you here?" she asked.

"I'm not at liberty to reveal that."

Joanna dropped the thimble into the basket, her jaw set.

"He asked me to bring her back to Paris," Graeham said. "And I intend to find a way to do that, despite my leg. That's . . . as much as you need to know."

Her eyebrows shot up. "And 'tis your place, I suppose, to determine what I need to know about schemes being perpetrated from within my own home."

"I'm not perpetrating anything, mistress. I'm trying to rescue an ailing woman from a miserable marriage."

"Why?"

"It's as I've said," he answered impatiently. "Her husband mistreats her, she's ill . . . and who knows but that he may intend her some real harm."

"Nay. Why are you really doing this? Why did you come all the way to London on this mission for some mysterious kinsman? And why is it so important to you?"

He just stared at her, wishing she weren't so damned insightful.

"What do you stand to gain," she asked, "by bringing Ada le Fever back to Paris?"

He shrugged, looking away from her. "Do I need to gain anything by it, other than the satisfaction of having helped a woman in need?"

"Are you so chivalrous, then, that you'd go to all this effort for no reward at all?"

"Perhaps I am." To reveal his upcoming marriage and the land that went with it would compromise Lord Gui's anonymity. That wasn't the only reason he was loath to tell her about Phillipa, but it was the reason he clung to, the one he told himself was important enough to justify the fabric of lies he continued to weave around himself and Joanna Chapman.

She lied to me by not revealing her husband's death. She's lying still. But that was a simple lie, and a benign one— wise, even. Graeham's lies were complicated and rooted in self-interest. There was a profound difference.

"Your motives may be selfless," she said, "but I doubt it. You've a personal interest in this mission. Otherwise, it wouldn't be so critical to you that you'd sacrifice your honor for its success."

"Sacrifice my honor!"

"You came into my home," she said quietly, "and deceived me."

"Mistress . . ."

"And, worst of all, used me. This grand idea of yours, this plan for me to seek commissions from the merchants' wives, it was all a ploy to get me into Rolf le Fever's house so I could spy for you, wasn't it?"

Graeham grappled for words; why was his tongue so clumsy in her presence?

"I was your agent," she said. "Your unsuspecting pawn. I was to take stock of the situation in that house and report back to you. Only I had no idea this was my true purpose. I daresay it must have amused you when I agreed so readily to do your bidding."

" 'Twasn't that way, mistress."

"Do you deny that you sent me over there to act as your

eyes and ears? That you *used* me, exploited me, without my knowledge or permission?"

He dragged both hands through his hair. " 'Twas the only way." In frustration he added, "It still is. I know you hate me for having misled you—"

"Lied to me."

"Lied to you," he corrected, dismayed that she didn't deny hating him. "And I don't blame you. But I still need you. I need you to go back there—"

Her jaw dropped. "You can't be serious."

"Don't do it for me," he said. "Do it for her—for Ada le Fever. Help to rescue her from that insect she's married to."

"You're smooth, serjant, but not that smooth."

"Mistress—"

"First you lie to me. Then you have the gall to make pronouncements about how much I need to know. Now you actually expect me to go back to that house—"

"Don't you care at all what becomes of that woman? Le Fever once told her he wished he could be rid of her. For all we know, he may have plans to do just that."

"Loathsome though Rolf le Fever may be, there's no reason to think he intends any harm toward his wife. He doesn't care enough about her to harm her. He hasn't even seen her in over three months. She languishes in her solar while he dallies with the local matrons. If he wanted to remarry, I could see him thinking about . . . doing away with her. But as it is . . ." She shrugged. "I won't do it. I won't go back."

"Think about it," he entreated. "Please."

"I've thought about it." Joanna stood and brushed off her skirt. "The answer is no."

Graeham grabbed her hand as she turned. "Mistress . . ."

"Let go of me, serjant." She tried to wrest her hand from his; he closed both hands around hers, immobilizing her.

"I just want you to consider—"

"Letting you *use* me? I'm sick to death of being manipulated by ambitious men. Let *go* of me!"

He tightened his grip, implored her with his eyes to look at him. "I'm sorry I kept the truth from you," he said, wishing he didn't have so much to apologize to this woman about, but most of all wishing he didn't have to continue deluding her.

"I'm sure you're sorry now," she said, "knowing you can never regain my trust. 'Twill make it that much harder for you to trick me into any more of your clever schemes."

Her hand felt silky within his, except for her slightly calloused fingertips, and so very warm. He found himself caressing her palm, her fingers, seeking her heat and her irresistible womanly softness.

"Please," he murmured. "I need you."

She closed her eyes, her chest rising and falling more rapidly now, in time with his.

"Don't walk away from me," he said softly. "I've made mistakes. Perhaps I'm still making them— I don't know. I just . . . I feel desperate."

She opened her eyes, shook her head.

"I need you," he said earnestly.

"I can't—" Her voice snagged; she was shivering. "I can't let this happen." She met his gaze. "I can't."

"Joanna . . ."

"I can't let you use me, serjant," she said in a trembling voice. "Not for . . . I can't. Please let go of my hand."

He hesitated, feeling his need grind away at him like an empty belly, never filled. Yes, he needed her, and not just because of Ada le Fever.

"Please," she said quietly. "Let me go."

He released her hand. She turned and walked into the salle. A moment later he heard her climb the ladder.

He lay awake that night long past midnight, listening to the muted squeak of her bed ropes above him as she tossed and turned, and wondering how everything had managed to get so complicated.

Chapter 15

~

Graeham watched Joanna through the rear window the next day as she labored over the weekly laundry under a sultry noon sun. She'd stripped the sheets off his cot as she did every Sunday morning, bundling them up with his shirts, braies, and drawers, her shifts and the rest of the household linens. Hauling them to one of the two big wooden laundry troughs out back, she set them to soak in hot water, caustic soda, and wood ashes while she attended Mass at St. Peter's, on the corner of Wood and Newgate.

Upon her return, she'd rolled up her sleeves, tied an apron around her hips, put another kettle on to boil, stretched a clothesline from the house to the kitchen, filled the second trough with hot water, and set herself to pounding, rinsing, and hanging up the wash—a production that Graeham knew from having watched it three times before would occupy her at least through the early afternoon.

Did she know he was watching her? Would she care anymore?

She'd grown cool toward him. Graeham missed her smiles, her little nervous gestures, that heady awareness between them that always left him a little light-headed. He loved that feeling.

He hated that feeling.

So damned complicated. "Too damned complicated," he whispered out loud, watching sweat bead up on Joanna's face and chest, dampening the edges of the coverchief wrapped around her head and forming a dark patch between her breasts.

She had on the violet kirtle today, the linen one that

laced up snugly in back, conforming all too well to her
high, round breasts and slender waist. Its neckline was deep
and wide, extending to the curves of her shoulders and
revealing the top of her sleeveless undershift, embroidered
in white on white. As she bent over the trough, Graeham
could see the sweat-sheened upper swells of her breasts.
He imagined sliding a hand beneath the layers of linen to
cup the damp flesh; it would fit warm and soft and perfect
in his hand; her nipple would graze his palm right in the
center, where it was ultrasensitive.

Instantly aroused, Graeham closed his eyes and sank
back onto his little pile of pillows to whisper his Latin drill.
He had no business imagining such things about Joanna
Chapman, especially in the absence of any outlet for his
passions. She was unavailable to him. He would never
have her.

And it was for the best.

In command once more of his unruly body, he picked up
Geoffrey of Monmouth's *History of the Kings of Britain,*
found his place with that piece of string he wished he'd
never laid eyes on, and read several pages without absorbing a single word.

Giving up, he returned his attention to the window. Joanna pulled a sodden sheet from the rinsing trough, twisting
and folding it to squeeze out the water. A tendril of bronze
hair escaped her coverchief to curl rebelliously over her
forehead; it looked so haphazardly pretty, Graeham had
to smile.

Behind her, walking up the alley from Milk Street—his
expression lighting when he saw Joanna—was a young
cleric.

Or Graeham assumed he was a cleric until he got closer
and it became evident that his tunic wasn't black after all,
but a very deep purple, and that his short, sandy hair was
untonsured. Nor was he quite as young as he'd appeared
at first glance.

Pausing at the edge of the croft, he wiped his forehead
on his sleeve and propped his hands on his hips to watch
Joanna, standing with her back to him, wring out the damp
sheet. He looked slightly amused and all too interested.

Graeham's hackles rose. Grabbing his crutch, he hauled

himself to his feet just as the stranger said, "I thought Sunday was supposed to be a day of rest."

Joanna wheeled around, almost dropping the damp sheet. "Lord Robert!"

She knew him. And he was a lord.

Robert. She had mentioned that name once; it was when she brought the orange home from the Friday fair. *Robert—Robert of Ramswick, a friend of Hugh's—he gave it to me.*

"You look as if you could use some help, my lady."

My lady? Graeham sank back onto the cot, his gaze riveted on the couple in the croft.

"Nay!" Joanna protested as Robert approached her, reaching for the sheet. "You'll get that fine tunic wet."

" 'Twill cool me off—it's hot as the devil today." Robert took the sheet from her, shook it out, and slung it over the clothesline. "You ought not to do work like this, Lady Joanna," he said as he adjusted the damp linen on the line and smoothed it down. "Why don't you send your laundry out?"

She dried her hands on her apron and tucked the stray hair back under the coverchief, to Graeham's disappointment. "I can't afford to send it out."

Graeham admired her candor. The tendril of hair popped out again; he smiled.

Robert nodded, looking a little dismayed at the notion of "Lady Joanna" being too poor to afford a laundress.

They regarded each other in ponderous silence.

"Well," she said.

He squinted at the sun. " 'Tis a hot one."

"Would you like a drink of water?" she asked.

He brightened. "Aye. Very much."

She fetched a ladle from the kitchen, filled it from the well, and handed it to him. He drank the water in one tilt, sighed, and returned the ladle to her.

"Some more?" she asked.

"Nay. That was . . . fine. I'm . . . fine." He nodded.

She smiled tentatively.

He returned the smile.

Graeham clenched his jaw until his teeth throbbed.

"My lady," Robert began, taking a step toward her.

"I . . . I'm not quite sure how to go about this. By rights, I should, well, I should speak to your father, negotiate this through him."

Joanna's eyes widened. She glanced toward the window, meeting Graeham's gaze for a mere instant before Robert took her hands, drawing her attention back to him.

"But I know about your father," Robert said, "about how things have been between you since . . ."

"My lord . . ."

"So I asked Hugh to take care of it, but of course, he just laughed at me. He told me I should speak to you directly, so . . . here I am. I suppose you already know what I want to—"

"Not here," she said.

He looked toward the house. "Inside?"

"Nay! Not in there. Let's go for a walk." Clearly flustered, she fumbled with the knot of her apron. Graeham sympathized with her plight; how could she let him overhear this fellow's marriage proposal when she was supposed to be still married? At the same time, something inside him was curling up in anguish. *No!* he wanted to scream. *You can't marry him! I won't let you!*

Idiot! As if he could offer for her, would even want to offer for her, considering what he'd be giving up. He should be happy for her. It was a good match for her—superb.

Be happy for her, he told himself as he watched her walk away with Lord Robert, rolling down her sleeves. He must forget what he wanted and couldn't have, what he thought he needed but must live without. He must put aside his fevered dreams, his restless longings, disregard that void inside him that she could have filled, and find it within his heart to be happy for her.

Standing alongside Robert in a grassy field at the edge of the Walbrook, which flowed southward through the middle of the walled city, Joanna gazed downstream at three girls of about eight or nine cavorting in the shallow water. They giggled and shrieked as they chased and splashed each other, not caring that their humble kirtles were soaked through.

"They're trying to stay cool in the heat," Joanna observed.

"Gillian used to do that." Robert's smile was shaded with melancholy. "On hot days she would wade into the fish pond in naught but her shift. Her mother would scold her, but I always took her side. I used to do the same thing when I was her age."

Gillian had been only ten, and he'd adored her. He pulled her body from the river himself.

"I'm sorry," Joanna said, touching his arm. "It must have been . . . I'm sorry."

"I try not to think about it," he said. "I'll never get her back."

Curious, Joanna thought, that he said "her" and not "them." But then, his marriage to Joan had been but a union of duty; Gillian had been his firstborn, his flesh and blood.

"I've still got two other daughters to think about," Robert continued. He took Joanna's hand. "They need a mother, my lady."

They need a mother, not I need a wife.

"I would be deeply honored," he said, "if you would consent to marry me."

She took a breath. " 'Tis I who am honored, my lord—especially considering . . . that our stations have grown apart in recent years."

"That means naught to me. You're a lady in every way that counts—more so than those silly young girls my parents have been trotting out."

"Ah. Prospective brides?"

He nodded ruefully. "And not one over fourteen, nor with a whit of sense. I have no intention of giving my children over to the care of another child."

Quietly she said, "What of the lady Margaret?"

He released her hand. "What of her?"

Choosing her words carefully, Joanna said, "She's wonderful with your daughters, and they're obviously very attached to her."

Robert shifted his gaze to the three girls romping in the stream. "She's always loved children."

"I was wondering, if you do remarry . . . if we were to

marry . . ." Joanna hesitated, then forged ahead. "Would Margaret remain at Ramswick?"

He looked sharply at her. "Nay. 'Twouldn't be . . ." Clearly unsettled, he looked away. " 'Twouldn't be necessary, for one thing." *'Twouldn't be right.* Joanna suspected that's what he'd been about to say. "The girls would have you to provide for them as a mother would. They wouldn't need Margaret."

"Will she return to her family, then?"

He shook his head, gazing across at tiny St. Stephen's Church, built right on the bank of the stream. "We've discussed it, she and I. When I marry, she'll take holy vows."

"She's going to become a nun?"

He nodded without looking at her; a muscle tensed in his jaw. "A teaching nun, so she can be with children."

"I . . . didn't realize she was that pious."

Robert didn't answer that, nor did he look at her.

"Catherine and Beatrix will miss her," Joanna said.

"Children adapt—better than we do." Smiling in a way that looked forced, he took her hand again. "You're a good woman, Lady Joanna, and I would like you to marry me. I'll be the best husband to you I can be. I'll never . . ." He paused, seemingly discomfited. "Hugh told me about your husband. I would never treat you like that."

"I know that. 'Tisn't in you."

"You needn't give me your answer today," he said. "I know there's much to think about. You'll be uniting yourself not just with me but with my children—and with Ramswick as well. 'Tis a farming manor, and I tend to get the earth under my fingernails. I dress in braies and russet shirts, like my villeins, and I'm afraid there's always a bit of manure on me somewhere."

She laughed; it sounded like heaven after Prewitt. "I wouldn't try to change you, if that's what you're worried about."

"I didn't think you would."

Perhaps, she reflected, that was one reason he'd chosen her over the vacuous young girls his mother and father had tried to betroth him to. Not that his parents didn't still wield a powerful influence over him, for it was because of them that he continued to forsake Margaret, but at least he'd decided to select his own bride this time.

He took her other hand and faced her squarely. "May I kiss you?"

"Aye."

Leaning down, he pressed his lips lightly near the edge of her mouth but not actually touching it. She felt a little ticklish warmth, the light scrape of his jaw against hers, and nothing else. Her heart didn't speed, her breath didn't quicken. She didn't want more.

Graeham Fox didn't even have to touch her to make her hunger for more. She had but to stand near him, and the very air between them crackled, like the atmosphere before a violent storm. The few times they'd been in physical contact, she'd felt the lightning charge of his touch right down into her deepest, most hidden places. When he looked at her, her skin prickled hot beneath her clothes.

Robert of Ramswick, handsome though he was, and noble of character, did not have the power to make her quiver with longing. Could she learn to love him? Possibly; she liked him immensely. At the very least, she would grow quite fond of him. How could she not? He was as nearly perfect a man as she'd ever known.

Robert would never use or exploit her—except as a substitute mother for his children, and he'd been frank about that from the beginning. And she couldn't imagine his ever bringing another woman into their home. He was incapable of such base behavior. She would never have to bear that pain again.

"I'm bringing the girls into the city on St. John's Eve to see the Midsummer Watch," he said. "That's the four-and-twentieth day of June, ten days from now. Is that enough time for you to make up your mind, do you think?"

"Aye—you'll have your answer then."

He smiled. "You'll join us for the festivities, won't you? You and Hugh?"

"Aye, I'd like that."

"Shall we meet at nones at the cross in front of St. Michael la Querne?"

"We'll be there."

Chapter 16

~

"I'm going marketing," Joanna told Graeham the next morning, a bald lie. *If he can lie straight-face to me, I can do the same,* she rationalized, but lying always had made her queasy.

"What about the shop?" he asked, wiping his razor on his washrag. It was beyond her how he managed to look so devilishly handsome when his face was half covered with soap lather.

"I'll just open it a little later than usual. I don't get that many customers this early in the morning. As a matter of fact," she added, fiddling nervously with the handle of her marketing basket, "now that money's not such a problem, I thought I'd start opening it later every day so that I'd have more time beforehand for my chores and errands."

"Makes sense." He hunkered down to peer into the little propped-up looking glass, raised his chin, and skimmed the blade over his throat.

"Just so you know where I am," she said, backing out of the storeroom. *Shut up, you dunderhead. Just shut up and leave.*

He looked at her without pausing in his shaving, holding her gaze for a moment that seemed just a hair too long. "Thank you."

Leaving by the back door, she detoured to the kitchen, in front of which Thomas Harper sat, his empty bowl in his lap, having finished the porridge she'd poured for him earlier.

"More porridge, Thomas?"

"Nay, mistress." He patted his stomach. " 'Twas quite

enough. I'm just resting here for a while before I have to get up and start trekking about."

"Sit there as long as you like," she said, ducking into the kitchen. People like Thomas didn't have too many places to sit, because no one wanted to touch anything that had been touched by a leper, so Joanna had set a barrel out in front of the kitchen that could be his alone. She kept a bucket of fresh water next to it, which Thomas used for drinking and washing.

In the cool, dim stone kitchen hut Joanna wrapped a hunk of rye bread and a piece of cheese in waxed linen and set them in the bottom of her basket. Ladling some porridge into a small iron pot with a tight-fitting lid, she tucked it in next to the other food. She filled a goatskin flask with well water and put that in, covering the contents of the basket with a napkin.

"Who's the food for?" Thomas asked when she came out of the kitchen.

"Shh." Joanna glanced toward the storeroom window, wondering if Graeham was watching her from within; he was hard to see from outside. "A friend," she whispered. "I don't want the serjant to know."

Thomas frowned. At least, she thought he did; it was hard to tell, what with his disfigured face. "There's a great deal you don't want him to know, it seems," he said softly. "I don't like keeping secrets from friends, mistress. Especially when it's another friend asking me to keep the secret. Secrets are naught but lies one is too cowardly to tell outright."

Joanna nodded, touched despite Thomas's gentle censure that he considered her a friend. "I know. I'm sorry. I won't put you in this spot again."

His one good eye took on a faraway look. When he spoke, his voice was low and raw. "Seven years ago, when the first few sores appeared on my face, they wrapped me in a shroud, read the burial service over me, and pronounced me dead to the world. I was told I might never again enter a church or monastery, an inn or tavern or bakehouse, a shop, a mill, a home such as yours—anywhere healthy people might be about. I'm not to bathe in streams nor walk on narrow footpaths. I'm forbidden for the rest of my earthly existence to eat with others, take a child in my arms, make love to a woman."

Joanna was speechless; Thomas had never discussed his plight with her, except to make light of it.

"That's the worst of it," he said. "Not being able to touch, or be touched. The rest . . ." He shrugged. "One learns to make do. But to be so . . . apart from others that you can't reach out and take someone's hand . . ." He shook his head. "Of course, even if someone did touch me, I wouldn't feel it, the condition I'm in—but at least I'd know I was being touched. I never gave much thought to being close to people when I was healthy. I took it for granted. You may find this hard to believe, but there was a time when I didn't lack for the company of women."

"I don't find that hard to believe at all," she said.

" 'Twas the harp, I think—women were drawn to the music. Everywhere I played, ladies were eager to grant me their favors. I fell in love with one once, in Arundel. Her name was Bertrada. She wanted me to stay there and marry her."

"What happened?"

"I was young and arrogant and foolish. Much as I loved her, I decided I wasn't ready to settle down. I liked traveling about, playing my harp in grand castles and seducing beautiful women. So I pushed Bertrada away, using lies and secrets. It worked—I was a free man again. I missed her horribly, but I kept telling myself that someday, when I was ready to be tied down, I'd meet another woman, someone just as sweet and giving and quick-witted. Four years later, the first signs of my disease appeared. The service of the dead was read over me and I was told I could never touch a woman again—unless, of course, I was already married to her. But I'd seen to that, hadn't I?"

"Oh, God, Thomas."

"Not a day goes by that I don't think about Bertrada of Arundel, yearn for her, all throughout the day. At night I can't get to sleep unless I imagine her arms around me, her head on my shoulder." He chuckled grimly. "Who knows—if I'd stayed in Arundel and married her, I might never even have come down with this cursed affliction."

"I am sorry, Thomas."

"I didn't tell you this to solicit your pity."

"I know why you told me. It's just that . . . my situation . . . it's different. It's complicated."

He smiled, more or less. "It's always complicated. That's the kind of creatures we are." Planting his staff in the dirt, he raised himself awkwardly to his feet. "I must be off. If I sit still too long, someone might decide to dig a hole and bury me with the trash."

After bidding good-bye to Thomas, Joanna walked down the alley to Milk Street, through Rolf le Fever's front gate and straight up to his bright-red front door, hesitating only when she came face-to-face with the iron knocker—a rather lascivious looking gargoyle with a long, curved tongue.

Looks like le Fever. That thought gave her the courage to knock on the door. A plump maidservant answered. "Good morrow, mistress."

"Good morrow. I'm here to visit with Ada le Fever."

The maid looked nonplussed. "Mistress Ada, she can't receive visitors. She's that ill."

"I know she's ill. I'd still like to—"

"Aethel, who is it?" called a man from within—Rolf le Fever.

Aethel closed her eyes briefly in a way that implied both resentment and fear. " 'Tis . . . a visitor for Mistress Ada, sire."

Joanna heard footsteps pounding down the stairs, and then Rolf le Fever shoved Aethel aside and said, *"You."*

Joanna raised her chin. "I've come to—"

"Tradesmen—and -women—enter 'round back."

"I'm not here as a—"

"But don't bother coming 'round there," he added with a sneer. "I told you, we have no use for your wares."

He slammed the door shut. From inside came his footsteps on the stairs.

Raising her voice so it would carry through the thick oak door, Joanna called out, "I suppose I'll just go and visit my friend John Huxley, then."

The footsteps ceased at the mention of the alderman le Fever had cuckolded. Presently she heard them again, much slower, as they descended the staircase. The door swung open. The guildmaster scrutinized her with his queer crystalline eyes, as if he were trying to read her very thoughts. "I didn't realize you and Alderman Huxley knew each other."

"Aye, we're old friends," Joanna lied, both proud and ashamed of her newfound skill at fabrication. "We met when I served the baroness Fayette de Montfichet." They had, but she'd been a child; he would hardly remember.

"You know," le Fever said, "when I saw you at the Friday fair, in your finery, it occurred to me that perhaps you'd discovered there was more profit to be made on your back than bending over that embroidery frame of yours. Is it John Huxley who's keeping you, or someone else?"

"I'm no man's leman," she said.

"Come now." His strangely lucid gaze crawled over her, making her shiver. "A pretty wench like you, you must have men begging to slide their swords into that sweet little sheath."

"When they do, I can generally find some convenient place to slide my sweet little dagger," she reminded him.

"I should have let you cut me that day," he said in a menacingly soft voice. " 'Twould have been worth losing my nose to watch you choke to death at the end of a rope."

Joanna marshaled her features, unwilling to give him the pleasure of seeing how unnerved she was. "I'd like to see your wife now. Or, if she's so indisposed that she can't receive me, I'll go pay a call on Master Huxley. We always have so much to talk about." She smiled.

Le Fever's already pale face lost a bit more of its color. Turning away, he said, "Go ahead up there. She's damned poor company. You two ought to get along fine."

When Joanna arrived home later that morning, she found Master Aldfrith in the storeroom, substituting new, shorter splints for Graeham's old ones. Hugh was there, too, holding in place the new splints—which came up only to Graeham's knee—while Aldfrith wrapped his leg in linen.

The serjant was clad in his drawers and nothing else; the bandage around his ribs had been removed. Joanna hadn't seen him in a state of undress since he came here over three weeks ago, and the sight unsettled her. His confinement and its attendant inactivity had in no way diminished his musculature. He had a soldier's body still—powerfully proportioned, lethally hard.

Merely being in his presence made her feel starved for air. She tried not to look at him, lest she stare. The last thing she wanted was for Graeham Fox to find her ogling him.

"How does that feel, then?" Aldfrith asked as he tied off the linen bindings.

Graeham sat up and gingerly lowered his resplinted leg over the side of the bed. He stood with the help of his crutch and flexed his leg at the knee. "Stiff."

"Your muscles have tightened up from disuse. You'll be able to get about better with this half splint than with the old one, though. And then, in another month or so, perhaps it can come off altogether."

"And you'll be good as new and on your way to Oxfordshire," Hugh said.

Graeham exchanged a look with Joanna. They hadn't discussed what to reveal to Hugh about his purpose for being in London.

Joanna took the decision out of his hands. "Not Oxfordshire," she said.

Hugh looked back and forth between them. "I beg your pardon?"

"I was never on my way to Oxfordshire." Graeham lowered himself to the side of the bed. With a glance toward Aldfrith, who was packing up his supplies, he said, "I'll explain later."

"He's healing nicely, mistress," Aldfrith declared. "You'll have him out of your hair in no time."

"I'm glad he's doing well." From the corner of her eye, Joanna saw Graeham watching her in that penetrating way he had that made her shiver hotly. He'd seemed pensive since Robert's visit yesterday. She wondered at first about how much he'd overheard, but on reflection she'd swept those worries from her mind. Surely if he'd figured out that she'd been keeping Prewitt's death from him, he would have told her. No doubt he would have relished the opportunity to rub her nose in her own duplicity after the way she'd reproached him about his.

As Graeham was paying Aldfrith for his services, Joanna

said to the surgeon, "I was by to see Ada le Fever . . . recently."

"Were you now?" Aldfrith counted the coins under his breath. "You're a friend of hers, then?"

"Aye," she said. Hugh frowned in confusion; Graeham smiled.

The surgeon shook his head as he stowed the silver in his purse. "Poor woman's been indisposed since Christmastide. Master Rolf called me in. Said she had a rheum in the head, which she did."

"Are you sure it was just a rheum in the head?" Graeham asked.

Aldfrith shrugged. "She was sneezing and sniffling something fierce when I first looked in on her."

"She's not sneezing anymore," Joanna observed.

"An excess of black bile is complicating things," Aldfrith said, "but Master Rolf assures me it's just a head cold."

Graeham said, "Master Rolf assures you? You're the surgeon."

"I've no call to start questioning Master Rolf's judgment. He lives with the woman." To Graeham he said tersely, "I'll be back in a month to take that splint off. Send for me if you have any problems in the meantime."

After he left, Joanna said, "He wants le Fever to let his son-in-law into the Mercers' Guild. That's why he's toadying up to him, I'll wager. He'd say Ada le Fever was suffering from an excess of . . . of monkeys living in her head if it would keep him on le Fever's good side."

Graeham grinned. "Monkeys living in her head?"

Hugh shook his head in evident exasperation. "Will someone please tell me what you're talking about?"

Joanna and Graeham filled Hugh in about his mission— or as much of it as Graeham was willing to disclose—and her visit to Ada le Fever on Saturday. She declined to mention this morning's visit, not wanting Graeham to know that she intended to pay a call on Ada every day, bringing food she'd prepared with her own hands. Thinking of that bowl of broth, she'd beseeched Ada to eat and drink only what she brought to her from now on, forgoing anything from her own kitchen.

Despite what Joanna had told Graeham about le Fever's

having little reason to harm his wife, the fact remained that
he was an unprincipled wretch. Who knew what he was
capable of? She would bring Ada safe food and keep an
eye on things in the le Fever household, but to her own
ends, not Graeham Fox's. She cared about Ada's welfare—
how could she not?—but she'd be damned if she would
serve as Graeham's spy after the way he'd made her his
unwilling pawn.

Hugh was unamused by Graeham's deception, but, being
Hugh, he let it pass when it became clear that Joanna had
put the matter behind her. Her brother was never one to
hold a grudge.

"I didn't know what to think when I got here this morning and saw that the shop wasn't open yet," Hugh said.

"I . . . went marketing," Joanna said, dismayed that her
net of lies was growing to encompass Hugh, as well.

"Yes?" Hugh nodded toward her empty basket. "Didn't
find what you went out for, I take it."

Graeham was looking at her, his gaze too inquisitive,
too discerning.

"Nay," she said, backing out into the salle. "If you'll
excuse me, I . . . I have to open the shop now."

Chapter 17

❧

"What'cha doin'?"

Graeham looked up from reading the *Mystère d'Adam* by the dying afternoon light to find the small, sooty face of another Adam peering in through the bars on the alley window. The boy materialized every few days for a bit of idle conversation, always vanishing in a heartbeat.

"I'm reading," Graeham said.

"You can read?"

"Aye."

"You a cleric?"

"I was educated to be one, but I became a soldier instead."

"Wish I could read."

"You're young. You can still learn."

Adam snorted. "Who'd teach *me* how to read?"

That was a good question. "How do you spend your days, Adam?"

The boy shrugged. "Roamin' around here and there. I do odd jobs sometimes, for money—mending clothes, weeding folks' gardens . . ."

"Mending? You can sew?"

Spots of pink appeared beneath the filth on Adam's face. "Boys can sew, too."

"I suppose." But not many of them did.

"That lady," Adam said, inclining his head toward the front of the house, where Joanna was waiting on a customer. "Is she your wife?"

"Nay."

"Sweetheart?"

Graeham sighed. "Nay."

"Do you have a sweetheart?"

"Nay." He'd never even met Phillipa, so she could hardly qualify as a sweetheart.

Adam squinted at him. " 'Tisn't boys you fancy, is it?" *"What?"*

"There are men who like boys," Adam confided in a tone that suggested Graeham might find this revelation hard to believe.

"Yes, I know," Graeham said, "but I assure you, I'm not one of them."

"Good," the boy said without a trace of humor. "I didn't think you were. There aren't really many of that sort. Most of the . . . the bad men . . . they go after girls."

"So it would seem."

"If that lady isn't your wife or your sweetheart, why are you living here?"

It was a good question, given Graeham's lack of progress in advancing his mission. A week had passed since Joanna's visit to Ada le Fever, and although he'd broached the subject several more times, he'd had no luck in convincing her to go back. Her attitude toward him had thawed a bit since their quarrel Saturday over his "using" her, but they had yet to regain the rapport he'd felt previously. And he missed it.

Most days he didn't even see her till midmorning, when she came back from her daily marketing trip—curiously empty-handed more often than not. She'd open up the shop then, and for the rest of the day they would scarcely interact at all, save for two cursory meals featuring little in the way of conversation.

He shouldn't pine so for her company, shouldn't strain for glimpses of her, shouldn't listen for the squeak of her bed ropes when she retired at night. She was betrothed by now, or would be soon enough. So was he.

This was lunacy.

"Does she, do you think?" the boy was saying.

"What?"

"Does she have any odd jobs for me?" he said. "The shop lady."

"Her name is Joanna Chapman," Graeham said. "And I

doubt it." A model of frugality, Joanna did everything herself.

"Do you, then?" Adam asked. "I'm fresh out of silver."

"That depends," Graeham said. "What can you do? Besides sew and garden? I've no use for those skills."

"I can deliver messages, fetch water from the river, mind the cook pot, mind children, keep a fire going, go marketing, feed pigs and chickens . . ."

"Go marketing?"

"Aye. Do you need someone to market for you?"

Graeham closed the book and set it on the chest. "Nay. Mistress Joanna does it in the mornings. That is, I think she does. It's what she says she does."

Adam looked at him as if he were daft.

"I wonder . . ." Graeham began. "Do you think you could . . . follow someone?"

"Follow?"

"Trail behind them without being seen. Take note of where they go and what they do and report back to me."

"Sure, I suppose." Shrewdly Adam added, " 'Twould cost you, though."

Smiling, Graeham reached for his crutch and rose from the cot, a maneuver that had become much easier since his splint was shortened last week. He dug four pennies out of his purse, hanging on a peg, and handed them to Adam. "Will that do?"

"I should say so!" the boy exclaimed, gaping at the coins. "Who is it you want me to follow, then?"

With a quick glance toward the shopfront—Joanna was still dealing with that customer—Graeham said, "Mistress Joanna."

The boy cocked his head as if he hadn't heard right.

"I want you to do it tomorrow morning." Graeham sat on the edge of the cot. "She leaves here by the back door very early and walks up to Milk Street. She comes back around terce. I want you to stay behind her, keeping in the shadows so she doesn't see you, and find out where she goes. Don't lose sight of her. Then come back and tell me where she's been. Think you can do that?"

"Nothin' to it." Adam slipped the coins into a little pouch tied around his waist.

"Whatever you do, don't let her see you." God forbid she caught him spying on her—but the more he'd thought about it, the more he realized he had to find out what those mysterious morning trips of hers were about.

"Don't worry. I'll keep myself well hidden." Nodding toward the stack of books on the chest—the result of Hugh's latest trip to the used-book store—Adam said, "So, where'd you learn how to read?"

"Holy Trinity."

The boy brightened. "That priory against the wall near Aldersgate?"

"That's right."

"I sleep there sometimes, in the stables."

Carefully Graeham said, "When I first met you, you said your parents were butchers and you lived in the Shambles. And then, last week, you said something about needing to get to Fleet Street before the gates closed, and when I questioned you, you said you lived there."

"We moved."

"Why would you sleep in Holy Trinity's stables if you had a home to go to, Adam?"

The boy backed away from the window.

"No, Adam, don't go." Graeham grabbed his crutch and bolted to his feet. The abrupt movement woke Manfrid, who'd been stretched out luxuriously across the foot of the bed. Startled, the cat jumped up and darted away.

Adam tensed as if he were about to do the same.

"Do you like sweetmeats?" Graeham asked. "I've got a piece of pine nut candy from the bakeshop that I've been saving. 'Twas meant to be dessert after dinner today, but I was too full for it." He lifted the treat from the chest and limped to the window, with Adam regarding him warily. "You may have it if you'd like."

Adam eyed the honeyed confection with longing. "Me mum said I was never to take sweets from men."

"I'm not one of those men, remember?"

Adam hadn't taken his eyes off the candy. Graeham moved closer, holding it between the bars. Quick as a squirrel, the boy reached out and snatched it from his hand.

"Your mother sounds like a wise woman," Graeham said, leaning on his crutch.

"She was." Adam sniffed at the candy, then took a bite from the corner.

Was. "Your father . . . is he dead, too?" Graeham asked.

Adam looked at him as he chewed. He nodded slowly.

Graeham sat down on the edge of the cot with his crutch across his lap. "Why didn't you want me to know?"

"No one knows," Adam said around a mouthful of the sticky delicacy. " 'Tisn't safe."

Graeham nodded as if this made sense to him, but in truth he was stumped. "Why don't you start at the beginning, Adam? Where did your parents live when they were alive? What part of London did you grow up in?"

Adam stared at him as he ate, his eyes filled with suspicion.

"You have to be able to trust someone, Adam," Graeham said soothingly. "I only want to help you."

Adam swallowed and licked crumbs off his lips. "I didn't grow up in London. Me pa, he was a free bondman in Laystoke Manor, just north of here."

"A farmer, then?"

"Aye, with his own furlong in the village field," Adam said. "He grew oats and peas and beans, mostly, but I had my own little patch at the end where I got to plant whatever I wanted. I grew lettuce, leeks, onions, and cabbages. And I kept watch over me little brothers and sisters."

"It sounds as if you liked it there."

"A far sight better than I like it here, I can tell you. On the farm, you could breathe. In London . . ." Adam shuddered. "There's a new bad smell everywhere you turn, and some of them, you don't even know what they are. Others, you wish you didn't know. On the farm, if you smelled somethin', you knew what it was, and most likely you could just wipe it off your foot and be done with it."

"What brought you here?" Graeham asked.

Adam took another bite. "There were too many of us, me brothers and sisters and grandparents. One furlong, it wasn't enough to feed all of us and still make our rent at harvest time. I was the oldest child, so I was picked to come to London and apprentice to Mistress Hertha, the weaver."

"You were apprenticed to a weaver?" Graeham asked. Weaving was women's work.

"I liked the weaving," Adam said. "And Mistress Hertha, she was all right. Only I didn't much like that husband of hers."

"Did he beat you?"

"Nay, he . . . looked at me."

"*Looked* at you."

" 'Twas the way he looked at me. And once, he walked in on me when I was takin' me bath. Tried to help me wash up—that's what he called it. I splashed soapy water in his eyes, but that only made him mad. So I told him me pa was a bear of a man and would come to London and wring his neck if he didn't leave me be. So he left me be. For a time."

Graeham steeled himself; he'd come this far. "What happened?"

Adam ate the last of the pine nut candy with a melancholy expression. "The yellow plague came to Laystoke. Killed me whole family."

Graeham groped for words. "All of them? Everyone?"

"Me mum, me pa, me six brothers and sisters and most of me kin. 'Cept for me uncle Oswin, 'cause he's too mean to die."

Graeham closed his eyes briefly. "I'm sorry."

"They're in heaven now. They're at peace."

"Yes, of course. Still, I'm sorry. What became of you?"

"Mistress Hertha's husband, well, he figured he could have his way with me now that me pa wasn't around to stop him."

Graeham's fist clenched.

"But I wasn't about to wait around and let it happen."

"So you ran away."

"Aye."

"And now you're living on the streets."

Adam shrugged.

"And sleeping . . . where? Stables, alleys, doorways?"

" 'Tisn't too bad now that it's getting warm—and I'm small, so folks don't notice me."

"Why don't you throw yourself on the mercy of one of the almshouses?" Graeham asked.

"Bad people go to the almshouses. I don't like to be where they are."

There's lots of bad men in London, Adam had said once. *You've got to keep your wits about you.*

" 'Twas clever of you to dress like a boy," Graeham said.

Adam—or whatever her name really was—stilled in the act of licking honey off her delicate but grimy fingers. "As you say, most of the bad men are after the girls."

The child wiped her hands on her braies. "How'd you know?"

" 'Twasn't any one thing. You really make a very convincing boy."

"Thank you."

"What's your name?" Gracham asked. "Your real name."

"Alice."

"What a lovely name."

Alice smiled prettily—too prettily, for she suddenly looked every bit the little girl she was, despite her woolen cap and the film of dirt on her face. Sooner or later, some "bad man" would notice that pretty smile and figure it out. Graeham didn't like to think what would happen then.

"You ought not to be living on the streets the way you do," Graeham said. "Especially being a girl and all."

A movement from the salle caught his eye. Joanna was bringing the stein of ale he always liked around this time of day. He wondered how she would feel about taking in yet another stray. Alice could sleep on a pallet in the salle, or possibly even in the solar, if Joanna didn't mind.

"I mustn't let her see me," Alice said. "She might recognize me tomorrow morning if she happens to notice me while I'm following her."

"Don't worry about that," Graeham said, much less concerned now with keeping tabs on Joanna than with making sure little Alice didn't spend another night on the streets.

"There's someone I want you to meet," he told Joanna as she entered the storeroom.

"Who?" She looked around, mystified.

Graeham turned toward the alley window. Alice was gone.

Squatting on a limb of the big tree overhanging Joanna Chapman's kitchen hut and shielded from view behind a

screen of newly sprouted leaves, Alice of Laystoke watched
the back door open. Mistress Chapman emerged wearing a
shapeless brown kirtle, her hair veiled, a marketing basket
over her arm.

Finally! Alice had been waiting in this tree since dawn,
eager to earn those four pennies Graeham Fox had paid
her yesterday, one of which she'd spent last night on a ham
pasty and a sweet wafer, her best meal since leaving Mistress Hertha's. Shortly after she'd climbed up here, the serjant had limped out on his crutch wearing naught but a
pair of baggy linen underdrawers, which he'd started untying even before the privy door swung closed behind him.
Mistress Joanna had come out in her wrapper for the same
purpose a while later, fetching a bucket of well water on
her way back inside.

After that, all had been quiet for some time. Alice had
watched the rising sun illuminate the thatched roofs of
West Cheap and majestic St. Paul's Cathedral on Ludgate
Hill . . . and waited. Now her waiting was over. Mistress
Joanna was walking away from the house and down the
alley toward Milk Street, her stride swift and purposeful.

Alice waited until her quarry was almost out of sight,
then swung off the branch and dropped to the ground.
Hearing her name hissed, she turned. At first she didn't see
anyone, but then she noticed movement in the small, deep
rear window of the house. It was Graeham Fox, gesturing
her to come to him.

"I can't," she whispered back, pointing toward Mistress
Joanna, who was walking rapidly down the alley. "I'll
lose her."

Alice darted into the alley just in time to see the shop
lady turn left onto Milk Street at the end. She glanced in
Alice's direction just as she disappeared from view; Alice
hoped she hadn't noticed her, but even if she had, she
wouldn't take much note of one scruffy little girl—*boy*. She
must remember that she was a boy now and act the part.
No more being careless. Not all men were good, like Serjant Fox.

At the end of the alley, Alice peeked around a tall stone
wall that separated the alley from a fancy blue-and-red
house. Mistress Joanna opened the front gate and walked

through it. A moment later, Alice heard a knocking, followed by muffled voices and a door opening and closing.

The Church of St. Mary Magdalene stood directly across from the blue-and-red house. Alice ran across the street and into the deep, arched doorway of the small stone church. Crouching in the concealing shadows, she trained her gaze on the fancy house, unnerved by the carvings that surrounded her in the entryway—a saintly figure being accosted by beasts with snarling, wolflike heads. She stuck her tongue out at them, then concentrated on ignoring them.

The waiting was the worst part of it, she decided, growing fidgety as time crawled by. Following someone wasn't that hard; sitting and doing nothing was excruciating.

She bolted to her feet when the front door opened and Mistress Joanna appeared, glancing around as she passed through the gate; Alice pressed herself further into the shadows. The shop lady retraced her steps, turning right onto Milk Street and then again around the high stone wall, disappearing into the alley.

When she was out of sight, Alice dashed across the street and into the alley—only to come face-to-face with Mistress Joanna glaring down at her, hands on hips, her basket looped over her arm. "Why are you following me?"

Alice squealed and spun around. Her legs pumped wildly, but she didn't go anywhere; the shop lady had her by the back of her shirt.

"Not so fast, young man. I want to know why you've been following me."

"Let me go! I didn't do nothin'."

"Ah, but you did. And I want to know why."

Whatever you do, don't let her see you. Alice hadn't been careful enough; she'd been caught. The serjant would be disappointed in her. He might even want his fourpence back.

"Let me go!" Alice swatted at the shop lady's hand, but she held tight to the shirt. The child kicked, as hard as she could.

That did it. Mistress Joanna cried out as Alice's foot connected with her leg. Her grip on the shirt loosened.

Alice turned to run.

Hands grabbed at her. Her cap was yanked off; she felt her braids spring out.

"What the devil . . . ? Wait!"

Alice sprinted into Milk Street, but her progress was aborted by arms wrapping around her and lifting her off the ground.

"Not so fast," Mistress Joanna said as she carried Alice, kicking and flailing, back into the alley. "We need to have a conversation, you and I."

Alice struggled mightily, but the shop lady had her in an iron grip. She carried her calmly up the alley, saying, "Serjant Fox told me there was a little girl named Alice running about dressed as a boy. That would be you, I assume."

"Let me go!" Alice geared up her nerve to say a bad word. "You bitch! Let me go!"

"I think not."

Alice looked up as they crossed the croft to Mistress Joanna's back door. She looked toward the little rear window, dreading what she would see. Sure enough, Graeham Fox was there, watching her being lugged like a sack of turnips.

Mistress Joanna carried her into the house, down a hallway, and through a leather-curtained doorway into the little storeroom-turned-bedchamber. Serjant Fox was sitting on the edge of his cot, his expression doleful. "Good morrow, Alice."

"I'm sorry, serjant," Alice said as Mistress Joanna plunked her on her feet and gave her back her cap. "She saw me. I can give you three of your pennies back, but I spent the fourth."

"Your pennies?" said Mistress Joanna.

Graeham Fox closed his eyes briefly. Realizing what she had done, Alice felt her stomach constrict in a knot of remorse. She pulled her cap back on, shoving her braids beneath it.

The shop lady walked up to Serjant Fox. "Your pennies, serjant?"

He lifted his crutch and pulled himself to his feet. "Mistress . . ."

"I take it you paid this child to follow me."

He sighed.

"I might have known."

"I needed to know where you've really been going every morning," he said. "And don't tell me you've been marketing, because you hardly ever bring anything back."

"She went to the red-and-blue house!" Alice offered, thinking he might let her keep the money he'd paid her if she gave him the information he'd been seeking.

The serjant smiled slowly. "I thought that might be it."

Mistress Joanna gave Alice a look before returning her attention to Graeham Fox. "You are sorely trying my patience, serjant." She wasn't acting angry, but how could she not be?

Alice swallowed hard. They were both mad at her now— and at each other, as well. She'd mucked things up badly. Digging the three remaining pennies out of her purse, she held them out to the serjant. "Here. I got caught, so . . ."

"Keep them," he said. "I don't want them back."

Somehow that made her feel even worse. She returned the money to her purse and edged toward the doorway.

"You could have simply asked me where I was going," said Mistress Joanna.

"Would you have told me the truth?"

Unseen by the shop lady and the serjant, Alice pulled the leather curtain aside.

"That's not the point."

"Mistress . . ."

"I'm going to continue my visits to Ada le Fever, but don't think for a moment I'm doing it for you, serjant. And don't expect me to spy for you or report back to you, because I won't."

"I understand," he said, with a hint of smugness. "But I also know that you've got far too much honor and compassion to keep quiet if you suspect any wrongdoing on the part of Rolf le Fever. You'd report to me rather than let any harm come to his wife."

Alice slipped through the curtain, raced up the hall and out the back door. It banged behind her.

"Alice!" Graeham Fox called from inside.

She heard Mistress Joanna say, "I'll go after her," but she knew she had too much of a head start to be caught— not by a woman.

"Alice!" the serjant yelled through the window. "Come back! Please!"

But Alice knew, as she sprinted away, that she would never go back there, ever again. She'd caused enough trouble for those people. No use sticking around to cause more.

Chapter 18

❦

"Thank you for seeing me, Brother Prior," said Joanna early that evening as she was ushered into the office of Simon of Cricklade, prior of Holy Trinity.

"Not at all." Brother Simon circled his desk and gestured Joanna into one of two high-backed chairs facing each other in a corner of his office. He sat in the other, adjusting his black, cowled habit so that it lay smooth over his lap. "When I was told it was Graeham Fox who had sent you, I knew I had to see you. I haven't seen the boy since he left here eleven years ago . . . although I don't suppose he's a boy any longer."

Brother Simon's office, austere yet strangely elegant, suited him perfectly. The prior was old, very old, with snowy hair beneath his skullcap and translucent, softly fissured skin. Yet, despite a slight palsy in his head and hands, his movements were smooth and graceful, his back straight, his gaze astute—and kind, which served to put Joanna at ease even though she'd never set foot in a monastery before, much less had an audience with its chief administrator.

The prior turned to the young monk who'd escorted Joanna into his office and said, "Spiced wine, if you please, Brother Luke."

Brother Luke nodded and retreated from the chamber, closing the door softly behind him. The prior sat back in his chair and crossed his legs. "I'm sorry Graeham couldn't come himself. A broken leg, you say?"

"Aye, the work of robbers."

Brother Simon shook his head. "This can be an unkind city."

"He asked me to convey his best wishes and tell you that he's planning to visit you before he returns to Beauvais next month."

"I'd like that."

"The reason I came here," she said, "is to ask for your help in locating a child."

"A child. One of my boys?"

"Nay, 'tis a girl—though she dresses like a boy for safety. She's orphaned and homeless. Her name is Alice, but she goes by Adam."

A soft knock sounded at the door. "Come," said Brother Simon. The young monk entered with a tray of warm spiced wine in a ewer, which he poured into wooden goblets before taking his leave.

"I hope you don't mind," said the prior as he handed a goblet to Joanna. "I like my wine heated even in the summer. Old men need all the warmth they can get."

"I don't mind at all." Joanna lifted the goblet to breathe in the exotic blend of cinnamon and cloves and good red wine.

Brother Simon took a pensive sip. "I'm afraid I don't quite see how I can be of help in this matter, mistress. We're a very insular community here. If you need assistance in searching the city for the child, you're best off notifying the ward patrol to keep an eye out for her."

"I did," she said, "before I came here. But she's a slippery little thing, and she looks like a thousand other ragged young boys. The reason I came to you is that she sometimes sleeps in the stables here."

The prior's eyes lit with amusement. "Yes, the brothers tell me they often come across waifs asleep in the empty stalls. I've ordered them to be undisturbed."

"If they find a child of about nine or ten in a ragged red cap, Serjant Fox and I would very much appreciate being informed. And if you could manage to detain her . . ."

"I don't think that should be a problem."

"You might be surprised," Joanna said, but she felt a rush of relief at his easy cooperation. "I live on Wood Street, the first house after the alley near the corner of Newgate."

The prior took another sip, eyeing her over the rim of his goblet. "And where does Serjant Fox live?"

"With me." A wave of heat consumed Joanna's face. "That is, he's renting my storeroom. While his leg heals. He sleeps there."

Brother Simon nodded, almost smiling; Joanna knew he suspected that their relationship wasn't innocent. "I find it hard to think of Graeham Fox as a soldier. I spent fourteen years trying to prepare that boy for a career in the Church. He was bright enough, certainly, one of the cleverest boys we've ever had here. Always poring over books in our library."

"He still reads a great deal."

The prior nodded sagely. " 'Tis a favorite pastime of people who enjoy solitude—or have simply grown accustomed to it. Graeham was never one to rely on others, for companionship or for any other reason—most unusual in a place like this, where the boys tend to run in packs. Not Graeham. If he needed something done, he did it himself. If he was bored, he found ways to amuse himself." A spark lit his eyes. "There's a door in the city wall within our property—did you know that?"

"Nay." The only openings in the wall that Joanna knew of were the seven well-guarded gates.

"It's close to one end of the boys' dorter. The justiciar lets us keep it—on condition we lock it at night—because it provides access to a field we maintain outside the wall. Graeham somehow found a way to unlock it. On hot summer nights he would often steal out of the dorter when everyone else was sleeping and use that door to get out of the city. Then he'd walk the mile or so to Smithfield and go swimming in the horse pool. 'Twas the type of thing a group of boys might do for a lark, except that Graeham did it regularly, and all alone."

"He told me about the horse pool," Joanna said. "I don't think he realizes you knew about it."

"He who lives long sees much," the old man chuckled. "There is little that's happened at Holy Trinity over the half century I've been here that has escaped my notice, mistress."

"You said you tried to prepare Graeham for a career in the Church. Are you disappointed he didn't become a cleric?"

"Actually, I'd always hoped he would take monastic vows, but I would have been content if he'd entered minor orders. At one time, he intended to, but . . ." He shrugged and set his goblet down. "I should have known he'd find another path. He never felt a sense of belonging at Holy Trinity. The other boys respected him, but they never quite accepted him as one of their own. I think it was because he'd grown up here and had no other home. They didn't quite know what to make of him. I know many of them suspected he was in a position of privilege, granted special favors, that sort of thing—entirely untrue, of course, but the rumors did their damage."

"He was brought up here from infancy, he said. That's unusual, isn't it?"

"Aye, but given the circumstances . . ." The prior spread his hands. "His father was in quite the quandary. He contributed generously to the priory in return for the boy's upbringing, of course, but that wasn't why I agreed to it. I hated to think what might become of the infant if we didn't take him in. Babes born under those circumstances ofttimes simply"—Brother Simon's expression became grave—"disappear."

"What circumstances? Was he . . ."

"You don't know? I assumed . . ." The prior shook his head disgustedly. "Forgive me. The older I get, the less circumspect I become. I tell my boys that the best part of wisdom is discretion, but 'tis a lesson I'd do well to relearn myself."

She captured the old prior's gaze and held it. "I'd like to know, Brother Prior."

"Then you'd best ask Graeham," he said.

Should I? Joanna wondered as she walked home in the gathering twilight. And if she did, would he confide in her?

Their relations had been strained following Saturday's row, but had gradually warmed over the past six days. She'd tried to cultivate her anger toward him, to nourish it into an ongoing undercurrent of vexation, but like her brother, she found it difficult to hold a grudge.

She couldn't even manage any real wrath over his sending Alice to follow her this morning. What could she expect, after having lied to him about her morning excursions? And wasn't she lying to him still, about Prewitt? How could she hate him when she'd been so baldly dishonest to him?

She wished she *could* hate him. It would be better by far to detest Graeham Fox than to think of him . . . the way she often found herself thinking of him. He was a distraction she couldn't afford, especially while she was trying to come to a decision about Robert. St. John's Eve was a mere five days away.

As Joanna made her way to Wood Street, a steady rain began to fall. She was glad she'd worn her mantle but sorry she hadn't thought to substitute wooden pattens for her leather slippers, which were soaked through by the time she got home. She entered her house through the back door, having left the latchstring out, and kicked the sodden slippers off in the hallway. She'd assumed Graeham was in the storeroom, but when she crossed the lamplit salle to hang up her wet mantle, she saw him in the shop, leaning on his crutch over her embroidery frame.

He seemed to be studying something in his hand, although she couldn't see anything there. The rushes crackled beneath her bare feet as she approached him; still, he didn't seem aware of her until she entered the shop, but then he spun around. "Mistress."

"Serjant." She looked at his hand; he had her leather thimble on his little finger.

Following her gaze, he sheepishly pulled the thimble off and returned it to the basket. "Did you get to speak to Brother Simon?"

"Aye. He was most cooperative. He'll send word if Alice shows up in the stables."

Graeham nodded distractedly as he reached for a cup of wine he'd set on Joanna's work table. He brought the cup to his mouth and drained it, his movements slow and deliberate, his gaze slightly unfocused.

"How much have you had to drink?" she asked.

"Not nearly enough." He hobbled past her, through the salle and into the darkened storeroom to refill the cup from a ewer on the chest next to his cot.

Joanna hadn't seen him drink to excess since that first

night, when he was trying to deaden himself to the inevitable pain of having his leg set. She followed him as far as the storeroom doorway. Cautiously she asked, "What's troubling you, serjant?"

Graeham tossed down his wine. "Aside from the fact that there's a little girl all alone on the streets of London tonight and not a bloody thing I can do about it?"

"I spoke to the ward patrol. I went to Holy—"

"It's raining, for Christ's sake!" Graeham sat on the cot and tried to lean his crutch against the wall near the head of the bed, but it clattered to the floor. He growled an oath.

Joanna crossed the little chamber and crouched to pick up the crutch as Graeham leaned over to do the same thing. They collided, awkwardly but gently. His arm brushed her breast; his hair swept her face.

Unbalanced by drink, he closed a hand on her shoulder and squeezed his eyes shut. "Dizzy," he muttered.

"I'm not surprised," Joanna said, trying to keep her voice steady as her heart rioted from his touch, his nearness, his scent. *Fool.* She lifted the crutch and rested it against the wall. "You should lie down."

"I should drink some more wine."

"Why don't you lie down for a bit first?"

Grumbling, he let her help him to stretch out on the cot. The muscles of his arms and shoulders shifted like moving stone beneath the soft linen of his shirt. He was looking at her with that lazy intensity that left her breathless.

"There, now," she said brusquely as she straightened up. "Just rest a bit, why don't you? I'll put this away."

She lifted the ewer and turned toward the door, halting abruptly when he reached out and seized the embroidered sash tied around her hips; the keys on her chatelaine jangled. "Don't go," he said.

She just stared at him, her chest rising and falling too quickly, her heart pounding.

"Sit with me," he said softly, his voice only slightly slurred from drink. "Put that down and sit with me. I won't drink any more. I just want . . ." He closed his eyes. His hand fisted tightly around the sash, his knuckles pressing into her hip. "Please just sit with me."

He tugged downward on the sash. Joanna set the ewer

on the chest and sat on the edge of the cot, turning to face him. He didn't release the sash, as if he thought she might flee if he did. It unnerved her to be tethered next to him on his bed in the dark this way.

Outside, the rain intensified, battering the latched shutters of the rear window in an incessant barrage. Graeham eyed the trembling shutters, his brows drawn together. She knew what he was thinking.

"She'll find shelter from the rain," Joanna said.

He looked at her.

"Alice knows the streets, serjant. She knows where to sleep in bad weather." Joanna forced a smile. "Mayhap she'll decide this is a good night to spend in the stable at Holy Trinity—in which case, we'll see her again soon enough."

"If the brothers don't muck things up," Graeham said. "And if they can hold on to her once they find her."

"I'm sure they'll handle it just fine."

"I'm not. *Damn* this leg of mine. If I weren't a helpless cripple, I could go out looking for her myself. Hell, I would have caught her as she was running away. I hate having to depend on other people for things I ought to be doing myself."

"Brother Simon said that about you."

"What did he say?"

"That you were never one to rely on others, for anything. He said if you needed something done, you did it yourself, and if you were bored, you found ways to amuse yourself." She smiled. "He knew about the door in the wall and the nighttime trips to the horse pool."

Graeham regarded her incredulously. "He didn't."

"He did."

"By the Rood," he chuckled. "I should have known."

"I'm glad to see your spirits improve," Joanna said shyly.

He smiled at her in that drowsy-eyed way of his. " 'Tis your doing. Just having you here, so close, makes me feel . . ." His expression sobered. Still gripping her sash, he draped his free arm over his eyes and sighed. "I'm drunk."

"Perhaps you should try to sleep."

"Nay. You must tell me what else he said."

"Brother Simon?"

"Aye. He told you about the horse pool." Graeham uncovered his eyes and looked at her. "What else did he tell you about me?"

Joanna averted her gaze. "He said you were a clever boy, very bright, and that at one time you'd wanted to be a cleric, but then you chose a different path."

"It chose me. What else?"

"That you tended to keep to yourself."

"Ah. Did he tell you why?"

Joanna hesitated. "He said the other boys didn't quite know what to make of you, because you'd been brought up there from the time you were an infant."

Graeham's gaze searched hers, his eyes luminous in the dimly lit room. "Did he tell you why I was brought up there?"

"Not in so many words. He . . . hinted about the circumstances of your birth. I gathered you were . . ." How did one say it politely?

"A bastard. A rich man's bastard, evidently."

"Yes, Brother Simon said your father made a generous contribution to the priory as compensation for your upbringing."

"Twelve marks a year, plus the cost of wet nurse for the first two years."

"Twelve marks!" Graeham Fox's father must have been very wealthy indeed. "Who . . . Nay, 'tis none of my affair."

"Who is my father?" Manfrid jumped onto the cot and settled down between Graeham and the wall, nosing Graeham's free hand. The serjant gently scratched his head; Manfrid closed his eyes and purred ecstatically. "I've no idea."

"Brother Simon never told you?"

"Nay, he was sworn to secrecy, but there was a time—before I stopped caring—that I used to plead with him to tell me. All he would reveal was that I was sired by an important man on a gently bred woman to whom he wasn't wed. I take it I was something of a potential embarrassment to everyone involved. I suppose I should be grateful I was sent to Holy Trinity. 'Twould have been easier and cheaper to simply leave me out in the woods."

Joanna rubbed her arms.

Graeham's hand slid along the sash, the backs of his fingers stroking her hip through her kirtle. "You're shivering. I can feel it."

"It saddens me to think of an unwanted baby."

His eyes grew hard. "It more than saddens me. I'll never . . ." He looked away self-consciously.

"Yes?"

He sighed. "I promised myself long ago that I'd never sire a bastard. Every child deserves parents who want him, and a home to call his own."

How, Joanna wondered, did a man lie with women and avoid siring bastards? The answer came to her in a remnant of overheard conversation . . . *I was going to have her in the Frankish manner.* And there were other ways a woman could satisfy a man without fear of pregnancy—as Joanna knew well from the things Prewitt used to make her do. No doubt the handsome, blue-eyed serjant was well acquainted with all the more sinful variations of lovemaking.

A devilish impulse made Joanna say, "Had you become a monk, as Brother Simon wished, 'twould have solved the problem of siring bastards."

Graeham gave her wry look. " 'Twasn't a solution that held much appeal for me. By the time I was fourteen, I knew I could never spend the rest of my life in a monastery. I decided I'd take minor orders. Clerics live with certain restrictions, but at least they get to live in the world."

"And those restrictions are often ignored," Joanna said, thinking of the many clerics in lower orders who enjoyed the privileges of laymen, including wives. Even deacons and priests often kept mistresses. "What happened when you were fourteen?"

Graeham loosened his grip on the sash, absently rubbing his thumb over the embroidered surface, the movement of his hand a gentle and mesmerizing caress against her. "My father instructed Brother Simon to send me to Beauvais so that I might serve his old friend Lord Gui as a lay clerk. I was outraged. I'd expected to be tonsured that summer and go to Oxford to study theology and dialectic, but my sire insisted that I spend two years serving his lordship first. Without his money, I couldn't afford to pay my teachers, so I had no choice but to concede to his wishes. I arrived in Beauvais filled with resentment and determined to be the worst clerk I could be, so that he'd send me packing and I could go to Oxford."

"Yet you stayed for . . . how many years?"

"Eleven."

"And not as a clerk. Were you truly that bad at it?"

"Not on purpose." Graeham smiled; his fingers glided back and forth along the sash, over her hipbone, grazing her belly, raising shivers wherever they touched. "Lord Gui took a liking to me, and I to him. I didn't have it in my heart to serve him poorly, so I tried to do my best. I wrote his correspondence and delivered his messages—but whenever he could spare me, I'd be at the sporting field, watching the men-at-arms go through their training exercises."

"Ah."

"I can imagine how I looked to them—this unworldly boy in a black habit gazing in awe as men swung their swords and axes and charged each other on warhorses. One afternoon Lord Gui brought me over to his master-at-arms and ordered him to instruct me in small weaponry and the art of defending myself with my fists and feet. I was thrilled, and my enthusiasm made me a diligent student. Within a year, I was wielding swords and hurling lances from horseback—and Lord Gui had found another clerk to take my place."

"What happened when your two years were up?" Joanna asked.

"His lordship offered me a position with his corps of soldiers, and I accepted unreservedly."

"Did you ever ask Lord Gui who your father was?"

Graeham's expression sobered. "Once. He told me my father had made him vow on a holy relic not to reveal his identity. He said it vexed him to have to keep this secret, but he had no choice. I never asked him again. I told myself I didn't care. If he didn't want me . . ." Graeham turned his face toward the wall, his jaw set.

Joanna touched his hand. "I'm sorry."

He withdrew his fingers from beneath her sash and closed his hand over hers. Joanna's heart raced as he brought her hand to his face. Her knuckles brushed his mouth, and for a breathless moment she thought he might kiss her hand, but he didn't. Closing his eyes, he murmured, "I love the way you smell."

He opened her fingers and laid the flat of her hand against his warm face; she hitched in a breath at the strangely erotic sensation of needle-sharp stubble against her tender palm. All she could hear was the drumming of the rain and her own erratic breathing.

He pressed her hand to his cheek, rubbed against it. "God, I wish . . ."

"Yes?" she whispered unsteadily, her heart like a fist in her chest.

He opened his eyes and looked at her, the heat in his gaze giving way to something that looked like resignation. "I wish I hadn't gotten so bloody drunk," he said, releasing her hand.

Joanna stood, smoothing her skirts awkwardly as she strove for composure. "You should sleep it off, serjant. I daresay you'll feel better in the morning."

"I daresay," he muttered.

"Well." Joanna crossed to the doorway and began drawing the leather curtain across. "Sleep well."

"Mistress." He raised himself on an elbow.

"Yes?"

He seemed to be having trouble finding his words. Presently he sighed and lay back down. "Good night, mistress."

"Good night, serjant."

Chapter 19

❧

Newgate Street was so crowded with St. John's Eve revelers that it took Joanna and Hugh twice as long as it should have to make their way from Wood Street to the cross in front of St. Michael la Querne. The small church, tucked into a fork in the road at the apex of Ludgate Hill, was dwarfed by St. Paul's Cathedral, rising in dignified splendor right next to it.

Shading her eyes against the midday sun, Joanna scanned the hordes of people milling about, looking for Robert and his daughters. It was as mixed an assembly as that at the Friday fair, most of them dressed in their holiday finest. Not wanting to wear the honey-brown silk again, Joanna had chosen her least patched kirtle—the blue one—but embellished it with her best girdle and purse. Over her braids she wore a crisp linen veil secured with an embroidered ribbon.

"There they are." Hugh pointed to an audience that had gathered around two jongleurs acting out a little *comédie* involving a priest selling an indulgence to a portly and pompous "Sir Alfred." Standing at the edge of the crowd were Robert, his daughters . . . and Margaret. Sir Alfred, cleverly maneuvered into sacrificing his riches in order to avoid the pains of hell, began extracting bags of silver from beneath his overtunic, thus shrinking his considerable belly. Robert and his cousin laughed along with everyone else. They caught each other's eye, as if to share the jest. Catherine was sucking on her two favorite fingers; Beatrix was squirming.

Hugh cupped his hands around his mouth. "Robert!"

Robert turned, smiling when he saw them. Margaret turned, too. Her smile faltered when her gaze lit on Joanna.

She knows, Joanna thought. *She knows he asked me to marry him.* How would Joanna feel in such a situation? How would she act?

Margaret caught Joanna's eye and smiled—just a small smile, and perhaps a bit strained, but Joanna had to admire her for it. She was going to get through this with her head held high; she would survive it, with grace. *Some people have the gift of persevering in the face of adversity.*

Could Joanna display such strength of character if the situation were reversed—if the man she loved were preparing to wed another woman? She immediately pictured Graeham Fox kneeling at the altar next to some faceless woman and felt a sickening ache in her belly—in her very soul.

And she wasn't even in love with Graeham Fox, merely . . . infatuated with him. Fascinated by him. Obsessed with him.

But not in love.

"Papa, look! Look!" cried little Catherine, pointing to an acrobat executing feats of contortion on a long pole held aloft by two colleagues, all of them in parti-colored tunics and fanciful hats. A crowd had formed around the troupe, performing in front of the tanners' market hall on the corner of Newgate and St. Lawrence. The child hopped and bobbed excitedly as she angled for a better view.

"Here you go." Robert lifted his daughter onto his shoulders, holding on to her stockinged legs. "Is that better?"

"Oh, yes!" She clapped her hands, screeching with delight. "Beatrix, look!"

But Catherine's little sister was taking her midafternoon nap on Margaret's shoulder, arms and legs hanging limply, little pink mouth half open, oblivious to the chaos surrounding her. Newgate Street had been a riot of noise and roiling crowds since before nones; judging from past midsummer celebrations, the merrymaking would continue through the night, curfew being lifted for the Feast of St. John the Baptist.

Every house and shop in West Cheap and Corn Hill—in

fact, most of the dwellings in London—were bedecked with garlands of Saint-John's-wort, white lilies, green birch, and fennel. Lanterns dangled among the boughs and branches, to be lit at sundown, along with the bonfires being built at regular intervals along the city's major thoroughfares.

The daylight hours were a time of feasting, the more affluent citizens having set out tables laden with sweetmeats, pasties, and ale, free for the taking. Tonight would come the much-anticipated Midsummer Watch, an annual parade by London's most prominent citizens.

Joanna, standing with Hugh at the edge of the acrobats' audience, shaded her eyes and peered farther down the street to see what entertainments awaited them. On a platform erected at the corner of Ironmonger Lane, two dancing girls in filmy silks leapt and spun. Farther down, in front of tiny St. Mary's Church, was a fellow coaxing tricks from a trained bear.

Joanna's gaze was drawn to a momentary flash of red in the crowd surrounding the bear and his master. She instantly thought of Alice and her tattered red cap. Five days had passed since the morning the child had disappeared, and there'd been no sign of her since. Neither the ward patrol nor Holy Trinity's Augustinian brothers had reported seeing her. It was as if she'd simply vanished. Joanna suspected the child wouldn't be found unless she wanted to be found, and she prayed nightly for her safety. Graeham was still morose about it; he blamed himself for driving her away.

Joanna kept her gaze trained on the audience around the bear, many of whom were children, but the bit of red she'd seen before did not reappear.

"What are you looking at?" her brother asked her.

Joanna shook her head somberly. "Nothing."

Later, while they were watching a trickster perform sleights of hand, she saw it again, a flicker of red at just the right height to be a child's cap, about twenty yards down the crowded street. It appeared and disappeared in the blink of an eye. She stilled, her gaze riveted to the spot where she'd seen it.

Hugh smiled indulgently. "Nothing again?"

Robert, guiding Catherine by the hand, came up behind her. "My lady? Is anything amiss?"

She shook her head, still staring. Presently it appeared again, a spot of red in the throng. It *was* a cap, she saw—a child's cap. A moment later its owner turned toward her, just briefly, but long enough for her to see his face.

Her face. "Alice," she whispered, her heart skittering.

Hugh and Robert exchanged a look.

"It's Alice, Hugh—the little girl I told you about, the one who ran off last week."

"Where?" Hugh squinted down the street.

"There—see? The red cap." Joanna lifted her skirts and threaded her way swiftly through the crowd as the red cap winked in and out of sight. Should she call out to her or sneak up on her? She seemed to be moving away quickly. "Oh, God, I don't see her anymore," Joanna said despairingly.

"I'll get her." Hugh sprinted off, disappearing among the swarming celebrants.

"Who is she?" Robert asked.

Joanna told Robert and his cousin what she knew about Alice.

"A little girl sleeping on the streets." Margaret, still holding the slumbering Beatrix, curled an arm protectively around Catherine. "How awful."

Hugh reappeared, holding Alice tucked beneath an arm like a kicking, thrashing little demon. "Put me down, you . . . you . . . damned *mongrel*!"

"If you want to call people bad names," Hugh said mildly, "I'll teach you some better ones than that."

"Please don't," Joanna said.

The child ceased her struggles and looked up, wide-eyed. She was as filthy as ever; her cap was askew, one long braid trailing out of it. "Mistress Joanna."

"Hello, Alice. I was worried I'd never see you again."

Alice squirmed against Hugh's grip. "Would you tell this . . . *bastard* to put me down?"

" 'Bastard,' " Hugh mused. "That's an improvement over 'mongrel,' but I'm sure you can do better."

"This *gentleman*," Joanna said, "is my brother, Hugh of Wexford. You may call him Sir Hugh. And this is Lady

Margaret and Lord Robert. And I have no intention of asking my brother to put you down until you give me your word you won't run away."

"I give you my word," Alice said quickly.

"Swear on this," Hugh said, taking one of Alice's grubby hands and wrapping it around the crystal knob on the hilt of his sword. "There's a bit of hay from the manger of Bethlehem in this crystal."

Alice gaped at it.

"An oath taken on this relic is binding before God," Hugh intoned, his manner so absurdly grave that it was all Joanna could do to keep from laughing out loud. "If you break such a holy vow, the Lord will find a way to punish you. Now, do you swear before Almighty God and all the saints that you'll stay put after I release you?"

"What'll you do to me if I don't?"

"Find some rope and tie you up, I suppose."

Alice sighed heavily. "I swear it."

Hugh set her down and dusted her off. She jerked away from his touch and stuffed the braid back under the cap, her exaggerated scowl vanishing when she caught sight of Beatrix, blinking in wakefulness on Margaret's shoulder. "A baby."

Margaret smiled. "Do you like babies?"

Alice nodded, transfixed by Beatrix.

"She's my sister," Catherine proudly announced.

Alice smiled at the younger girl. "She's very pretty. So are you. How old are you?"

Catherine held up five fingers. "How old are you?"

"Ten. What's your name?"

"Catherine. What's yours?"

"Alice."

Catherine frowned in evident puzzlement. "You don't look like a girl."

Alice hesitated, then pulled off her cap and stuffed it under her belt; her untidy braids sprang free.

Catherine giggled in delight. "Why do you dress like a boy?"

Alice frowned, obviously at a loss as to how to explain it to such a young child.

"I'll bet I know." Robert squatted down next to his

daughter. "Do you remember how your sister Gillian used to wear braies and shirts when she went for long rides?"

Catherine nodded. "Mummy used to scold her for it, but you didn't."

"Yes, well, Mummy and I didn't always agree about Gillian, but we both loved her very much. Gillian felt braies were more practical than skirts when it came to riding." Casting a meaningful glance toward Alice, he said, "Perhaps that's why Alice wears braies—because they're practical."

Taking the cue, Alice said, "Aye, that's just it. They're practical."

"Can I wear braies, Papa?" Catherine implored. "Please."

Margaret arched an eloquent brow and looked at her cousin as if to say, *See what you started?*

"Perhaps someday," Robert hedged as he rose to his feet. "When you go for long rides."

"Do you ride much?" Catherine asked Alice.

Alice shook her head. "I used to ride our mule sometimes, when I lived in Laystoke. I had a sister your age, and she rode behind me."

Catherine pouted. "Papa says I'm too young to ride."

"I just don't want any accidents," Robert said. "I wouldn't want you . . . getting hurt." From his grim expression, Joanna knew he was thinking of the wife and daughter he had lost.

"What if Alice rides with me?" Catherine asked.

Robert and Margaret exchanged a pensive look.

"I don't live near you," Alice told the little girl.

"Where do you live?" Catherine asked Alice.

Hesitantly Alice said, "Here in London."

"Whereabouts in London?"

Alice chewed on her lower lip.

Joanna was wondering how to redirect Catherine's interrogation when Robert asked, "Who wants some sweet wafers?"

"Me!" Catherine shrieked happily, clapping her hands.

Beatrix slapped her pudgy hands together and squealed in jubilant imitation of her sister.

Alice brightened and started to say something, but swiftly

collected herself, as if she weren't sure the invitation had been meant to include her.

"Alice," Robert said, touching her shoulder, "why don't you take Catherine over to where they're handing out the wafers"—he pointed to a table across the street—"and get three of them, one for each of you?"

"Aye, milord!"

As the two girls set off hand in hand across the street, Margaret turned to her cousin. "She even looks a bit like Gillian, doesn't she, Robert?"

Robert nodded slowly as he gazed at the grimy little girl in boy's clothing. "A bit."

"May I speak to you alone, my lady?" Robert asked quietly.

This was the moment Joanna had been waiting for uneasily all day. Now, as the setting sun stained the sky orange and the lanterns along Aldgate Street flickered to life one by one, he had evidently decided it was time for her answer.

"Yes, my lord. Of course."

Hugh and Margaret, standing with the three children in the crowd surrounding a raging bonfire, glanced toward them as Robert led her around the corner of St. Mary Street. Hugh caught her eye and winked, apparently gratified that his scheme to betroth her to Robert was bearing fruit. Margaret looked away, her face horribly void of expression.

St. Mary Street was lined with houses that leaned so far out over the rutted dirt lane that it seemed as if they were holding each other up on either side. It was dark here, and much quieter than Aldgate Street. Two little boys sped past them on their way to the festivities; otherwise it was deserted.

They walked slowly, and in silence, until Robert touched her arm and they turned to face each other. He took a breath. "Have you thought about . . . what I asked, my lady?"

She nodded and looked down, her arms wrapped around her middle. "I'm deeply honored that you want me to be your wife, Lord Robert. I like you very much, and your children are delightful. But I can't marry you."

After a long, hushed moment, he said softly, "May I ask why?"

Graeham Fox's image materialized in her mind's eye. *Are you happy?* But this wasn't about Graeham. She wouldn't let it be. Mostly it was about Margaret.

Joanna looked up and met Robert's gaze. "Your cousin."

Robert briefly closed his eyes. "Margaret . . . I told you, she'll be leaving Ramswick after I get—"

"I know." Joanna rested a hand on his arm. "She'll be taking holy vows. But you still won't stop loving her."

He just stared at her. "I . . ." He shook his head. "Nay, you don't understand. It can't be that way between Margaret and me. She's my cousin."

"Your third cousin. And I know you wanted to marry her once."

"The Roman curia refused to sanction it."

"You should have married her anyway. You still should."

He shook his head, his expression conflicted. "My parents—'twould kill them."

She allowed herself a wry smile. "I somehow doubt that."

"No, you don't know them, my lady. They're terribly devout. They've been talking about taking vows, both of them. If I were to disregard the Church's authority in this matter, it might literally kill them."

"I thought it might kill my father when I married Prewitt Chapman. It made him angry—furious—but he's still alive."

"And still not speaking to you." Robert looked abashed. "Forgive me, my lady. 'Tis none of my affair."

Joanna took both of Robert's hands in hers. "Just because my father repudiated me doesn't mean your parents will do the same. William of Wexford has yellow bile flowing through his very veins. He lives for spite. From what I know of your parents, they seem like good people. They *will* forgive you."

"But they'll be shocked, hurt . . . angry."

"Are you worried that your sire will disinherit you?"

Robert shook his head. "All I care about is Ramswick,

and he deeded it to me outright. It can't be taken from me."

"Then let them get angry. They love you. They'll get over it."

"What if they don't?"

"Have you *never* done anything against their wishes, even when you were a boy?"

"Nay—never."

Joanna laughed. "Then I think you're a bit overdue. You must make up for the oversight in some significant way. Marrying the lady Margaret should do it."

"If I married her," Robert said, " 'twould be like betraying my mother and father."

"So instead you choose to betray Margaret."

He blanched and withdrew his hands from hers. "*Betray* her!"

"You're betraying the love you share with her—a love that will never die, no matter how much you want it to. How do you think she feels right now, knowing you've asked me to marry you?"

"She accepts it. She told me."

"Just as you would accept it if she were to marry someone else, I suppose."

"She's not going to get married. She's going to become a nun."

"But if she *were* planning to marry—to unite herself with some other man, to speak vows with him, to share his bed—"

"She isn't!"

"You'd not feel so complacent then, I'll wager."

"I'm not complacent, for pity's sake," he ground out.

"Accepting, then," Joanna said, finding it interesting to see the phlegmatic Robert's face begin to flush, a cord swelling on the side of his neck. "You wouldn't like it if she were to consent to a marriage proposal from, say . . . Hugh."

"Hugh!" Robert exclaimed, looking so stricken that Joanna was tempted, but for only a moment, to reassure him with the truth—that Hugh was far too free-spirited ever to bind himself in matrimony to anyone.

Instead, she found herself saying, "I shouldn't have mentioned anything. Forget I—"

"Hugh?" Robert seized her by the upper arms, actually hurting her with the violence of his grip; interesting. "Has he asked Margaret for her hand?"

"Nay. My lord, let go of me. You'll leave bruises."

He released her abruptly and stepped back, his expression one of outrage. "Is he going to?"

Joanna averted her gaze. "I shouldn't have said anything. 'Twas indiscreet of me."

"Is he?" Robert's hands curled into fists. Joanna hoped Hugh and Robert didn't end up coming to blows over this little game of hers, but it was a chance she was willing to take.

"My lord, please," Joanna said, backing away. "I shouldn't have spoken."

"Tell me!"

"I can't." That was no more than the truth, of course, inasmuch as there was nothing to tell.

"Jesus Christ," he muttered, pressing his fists to his forehead. The profanity surprised her, coming from the highly principled Robert of Ramswick.

"We must be getting back to the others," Joanna said.

He stood with his hands on his hips, his eyes closed, his chest heaving.

"My lord?"

"Go," he said. "I'll meet up with you."

Turning, she lifted her skirts and sprinted back to Aldgate Street.

"They're coming! They're coming!" squealed Alice and Catherine as the distant thudding of drums grew steadily louder, signaling the approach of the Midsummer Watch down Aldgate Street. The procession had commenced at St. Paul's on the city's west side and passed through West Cheap along Newgate Street. Now it was proceeding through Corn Hill along Aldgate, to terminate in front of Holy Trinity on the east side.

Night had fallen some time ago, the bonfires serving not only to dispel the darkness but also to impart an atmosphere of pagan wildness to the revelry. The wine and ale flowed freely. Whores, cutpurses, and mischievous boys wove their way through the masses lining the parade route. Young men and women danced in the streets, kissing openly and pairing off in darkened doorways and alleys when the kissing wasn't enough. It was a night of riotous celebration and unfettered passions.

Alice and Catherine had been inseparable all afternoon and evening. Seeing Alice interact with the little girl—playing with her, herding her here and there, wiping her face—made Joanna realize how much she must miss her younger siblings, and how she must have relished the role of big sister.

Robert had been edgy and remote since rejoining them after his conversation with Joanna. He'd drunk two cups of fortified wine, glaring at Hugh when he'd made some jest about Robert's low tolerance for spirits. The festivities seemed to interest him not at all; he couldn't tear his gaze away from Lady Margaret.

"Robert doesn't look very happy," Hugh whispered to her as the parade drums grew louder, accompanied now by the trill of panpipes. They were standing with Margaret and the two girls right at the front of the crowd, where they would have a good view of the procession. Robert, who'd professed no interest in watching it, sat on the steps of nearby St. Andrew's Church with Beatrix asleep in his arms. "He ought to look happy."

"Why is that?" Joanna asked with feigned innocence.

"Because you accepted his proposal of marriage."

"Ah. Yes . . . well, about that . . ."

"Joanna . . ." Hugh groaned. "Oh, bloody hell."

"It's them! It's them! Gog and Magog!" Catherine shrieked as grotesque representations of the legendary giants crested Corn Hill and advanced toward them, surrounded by drummers, flutists, and youths bearing torches. The giants, twice the height of the men beneath their painted plaster forms, roared as they swayed and lurched down Aldgate Street.

Now came the city's most prominent citizens, led by the three men who represented London's interests with King Henry—the justiciar and the two barons, Gilbert de Montfichet and Walter fitz Robert fitz Richard—in their bejeweled finery, sweating beneath ermine-lined mantles.

Lord Gilbert had aged over the years since Joanna had served his wife at Montfichet Castle. He was as tall and regal as ever, but his great shock of dark hair had turned snowy, and his face was far more weathered than she remembered. He noticed her as his piercing blue eyes scanned the crowd, and for a moment he seemed almost nonplussed. They hadn't spoken since she'd run off to marry Prewitt six years ago after balking at a union with his son. She wondered if he knew anything of the course her life had taken since then; would it matter if he did?

She inclined her head to him. After a moment's hesitation, he returned the greeting and continued on.

The two sheriffs came next, followed by the city's two dozen aldermen in single file, along with their beadles and serjanz. Lastly came the guildmasters and other distinguished merchants, grouped together by ward. The portly money changer Lionel Oxwyke, his expression as dour as ever, recognized her and nodded. Rolf le Fever, right behind him, leered at her as if she were standing there stark naked, the icy transparency of his gaze adding an ominous nuance to the gesture. Joanna straightened her back and met his gaze squarely. He looked away.

Dancing girls and more musicians brought up the rear of the procession. As it tapered off and the crowd dispersed, Joanna noticed that Margaret wasn't with them anymore. Glancing around, she saw her walking up to Robert, still cradling the sleeping Beatrix on the church steps. He looked up when she approached, suddenly animated for the first time all evening. Sitting on the step below him, she spoke to him; he nodded.

"You're staring," Hugh chided.

Joanna spun back around, gathering herself. "Alice, Catherine, stay with me. I don't want you to get lost in the crowd."

A minute later, Margaret and Robert—with Beatrix shifted to his shoulder—joined them.

"Papa, you missed it!" Catherine exclaimed. "You missed the Midsummer Watch!"

"I saw Gog and Magog," he said. "Did they frighten you?"

"Nay. Alice told me they'd be coming, and that they were just make-believe—like big dolls."

Robert and Margaret exchanged a brief look. "Thank you, Alice," he said. "That was thoughtful."

She shrugged. "I didn't want her to be afraid."

"Alice," Robert said, "there's something I'd like to ask you. 'Tis Lady Margaret's idea, actually. Perhaps I'd best let her ask you."

Margaret crouched down so she could look Alice in the eye. "Alice, is it true you have no family—no kinfolk?"

Alice's smile evaporated. "None who'd care to claim me."

"And no home?"

The child glanced anxiously at the adult faces staring down at her. "I won't live in no almshouse."

Fearful that she might bolt, Joanna closed a hand over her arm. "No one wants to send you to an almshouse, Alice."

"I thought you might want to come live at Ramswick," Margaret said.

Catherine squealed with pleasure and clapped her hands. "Yes! Oh, yes, please! Please come!"

Alice blinked at Margaret. "Ramswick?"

"Ramswick is my manor," Robert said. " 'Tis naught but a great farmstead, really."

Alice's eyes lit up. "A farm?"

"Aye, a grand farm," Robert said proudly. "Or many small farms that make up one grand farm."

"Like Laystoke?" Alice asked.

"I know Laystoke," Robert said. "Ramswick's on a larger scale, but the idea is the same."

"You'd live in the manor house and share a bedchamber with the girls," Margaret said. With a glance at Robert, she added, "There's a bed just your size already there. It's got lovely pink bedcurtains and a feather mattress."

"Say yes!" Catherine pleaded, pulling on Alice's sleeve. "Say yes! Come live with us!"

Alice looked back and forth between Margaret and Robert, evidently mystified. "Why?"

"Why do we want you to live with us?" Robert asked. Alice nodded.

"We like you," Margaret said. "And Catherine adores you."

"Am I to be a sort of nursemaid, then?" Alice asked.

"You'd be my ward," Robert said. "I'd raise you as I would have raised . . ." His voice caught; he took a deep breath. "As I would have raised you had you been my very own."

"You'll be given fine kirtles," Margaret said, "and educated. Lord Robert's chaplain will tutor you in reading and account—"

"Reading?" Alice exclaimed. "I'll be taught how to read?"

"And how to calculate numbers," Margaret said, "and manage an estate. And when you're old enough, we'll arrange for your marriage to a wellborn man with his own holding, and you can be the lady of the manor. Would you like that?"

Alice stared at Margaret, wide-eyed. " 'Twas your idea, milady?"

"Aye." Margaret looked up at Joanna, her expression suddenly troubled. "I'm sorry. We should have consulted you, seeing as . . . well . . ."

So. Robert hadn't told her yet that she'd rejected his proposal. "There's no need to consult me," Joanna said, in a tone she hoped conveyed the significance of the statement.

Margaret stood slowly, looking from Joanna to Robert. He shook his head. They held each other's gaze for a long moment.

"Well, Alice?" Joanna prodded. "Do you think you'd like it at Ramswick?"

"Is . . . is it really all right with you, milord?" Alice asked Robert.

"It makes me very happy to think of you coming to live with us, Alice. Just as Lady Margaret knew it would." With a fond look at his cousin, Robert said, "She's a very clever woman."

"Well?" Margaret prompted, smiling at Alice expectantly.

Hugh nudged Alice. "Say yes."

Alice smiled at them, her chin wobbling just slightly. "Yes."

Catherine shrieked delightedly. "Oh, thank you, Papa! Thank you, Aunt Margaret! I have a big sister again," she said, throwing her arms around Alice. "Thank you, thank you!"

"Where's Robert?" asked Hugh as the festivities were winding down. "The children are tired. They need to go home."

Joanna, on whose shoulder Beatrix now slept, looked around at the thinning crowd. The bonfires had mostly died down to embers, but flames still leapt in the largest one, near the gate of Holy Trinity.

A couple stood near the fire, facing each other. "That's them," Hugh said.

Robert was talking, Margaret listening. He seemed very wrapped up in what he was saying, almost overwrought. His gestures grew abrupt, his expression anguished.

Margaret held her hands up. Robert took them in his and moved closer to her.

"You're staring again," Hugh said quietly.

"So are you."

Releasing one of her hands, Robert reached out tentatively and stroked Margaret's face. She closed her eyes. He spoke to her, his manner rawly earnest. She nodded and opened her eyes. Something glimmered on her cheeks. Tears.

Robert brushed the tears away with both hands. He said something to her, his gaze imploring.

She nodded. "Yes," she said. Joanna could read her lips. "Yes. Yes, Robert. Oh, yes."

Joy lit his face. He laughed, his cheeks wet with his own tears. Margaret laughed, too.

He cupped her chin, tilted it up. She gazed at him, her eyes huge. He bent his head, touched his lips to hers, drew back.

Gathering her in his arms, he lowered his head and kissed her again, a real kiss this time. She seemed momentarily stunned, but then her arms banded around him and she returned the kiss.

It went on and on. Gladness squeezed Joanna's throat, stung her eyes.

Hugh cleared his throat. "This is your doing, I assume," he said reproachfully.

Joanna turned toward her brother, amused to find his eyes shimmering wetly. "You don't seem unmoved by this turn of events."

He swiped at his eyes. " 'Tis the smoke from the bonfires."

"Ah."

"He would have made you an excellent husband, Joanna. I hope you know what a fool you are."

She sighed, thinking of Graeham Fox. "I'm afraid I've known that for some time."

Chapter 20

❧

There was something about the footsteps in the alley that made Graeham's ears twitch. Quick and soft.

He instantly thought of Alice. His chest tightened instinctively, until he reminded himself that the child was no longer roaming the streets of London, sleeping in doorways and doing odd jobs for the occasional silver penny. A week ago, she'd taken up residence at Ramswick, to be brought up by Lord Robert. Graeham was grateful beyond measure that she'd found such a good home. The most Joanna could have offered her was a pallet by the fire. As Robert of Ramswick's ward, she would enjoy a life of privilege and promise. Graeham had thanked God in his prayers for smiling on her.

The footsteps raced out of the alley and across the croft. On reflection, they were a bit too heavy to belong to a child. A woman, most likely. A woman running.

It was long past curfew. The only women who roamed the streets at this hour were whores; most of them shared a bit of their meager earnings with the ward patrol for the privilege of defying curfew. But whores didn't run. Unless something was wrong.

He blew out the candle by which he was reading, unlatched the shutters on the rear window, and peered into the darkness, wondering, given his leg, how he could be of help if some whore were being pursued against her will.

But she wasn't a whore, or at least she didn't look like one from the back. She had on a hooded mantle, despite the heat. Whores didn't like to cover up their hair and various other charms if they could help it, and they certainly wouldn't do so on a sweltering summer night like this one. When the weather forced them to cloak themselves, it was usually in some garish color that served to advertise their occupation. Graeham couldn't see much by the weak moonlight, but the mantle of the woman running across the croft looked dark.

The woman went directly to the gate in Rolf le Fever's stable yard, opened it, and sprinted up to the house. Graeham sat up straighter, suddenly alert.

He expected her to knock on the back door, but instead she crouched down and picked something up off the ground. Straightening, she stepped away from the house, drew back her arm, and threw what she'd picked up—a pebble, most likely—at the closed shutters of le Fever's bedchamber window. Squatting down, she gathered up more pebbles and hurled them one by one against the shutters. Presently they opened. Rolf le Fever, in a night shirt, leaned out and saw her.

The woman gestured for him to come down; he nodded once and closed the shutters. Light filtered through them as he lit a candle or lantern. The woman looked around furtively; it was too dark and she was too far away for Graeham to make out her features.

The door opened and le Fever appeared, hastily clad in a tunic and chausses of much more subdued hue than he usually wore. The woman said something to him and sank her face in her hands. He grabbed her arm and walked her through the gate, across the croft, and into the alley.

Through the closed shutters of the alley window, Graeham heard their footsteps slow and then stop. In a voice choked with tears, the woman said, "But, Rolf . . . I can't. I just—"

Her words were abruptly silenced. Long moments later, there came her voice again, breathless but still weepy. "Your kisses can't make this all right, Rolf. What we've done is wrong, but what you want me to do now is even—"

More silence, then a soft, feminine moan. His voice, low, inveigling. A whisper of fabric being gathered up.

"Nay, Rolf, not here." Her voice was thick and scratchy, as if she'd been crying for hours, but she sounded young.

"No one can see us," he said. "Be still. Just let me touch you . . . yes . . . ah . . ."

She gasped.

"How is this?" he asked. "Do you like this?"

"Rolf . . ." Her breath snagged on a little sob. "Rolf, please . . ."

Softly, cajolingly, he said, "Aye, you love it when I do this. You're getting wet."

"God, Rolf, not here. Let me take you—"

"I need you *now*. Feel this. Does that feel as if I could wait?"

It was quiet again for a few moments. When the kiss broke, they were both panting. "Not so hard," he protested. "Do you never learn? Yes . . . yes . . . like that. A little faster. Faster. Faster. Oh, God, stop. *Stop.*"

The window shutter jiggled as he backed her roughly against it. Graeham heard their ragged breathing, the whip-like sounds of a cord being untied, le Fever's brusque commands. "Raise your skirts—keep them up. *Up.*"

The shutter rattled as he lifted her, slamming her against it. "Wrap your legs around me. Tight. Hold on."

She sucked in a breath. He groaned. "Ah, yes. That's it. Ah." The shutter creaked in rhythm with his grunts and her soft intakes of air.

"Move against me," he said gruffly. "You know what to do, don't pretend you don't. That's it. That's it."

The shutters shook on their hinges with every pounding thrust against them; the wooden latch pin quivered. Graeham prayed it didn't snap under the strain.

The thrusts grew swift, frenzied—then the movement ceased. "Hold still," le Fever growled. "Oh . . . oh, yes . . ." He muttered lewd obscenities on a low, drawn-out moan that left him breathless.

She was weeping.

"Shit," he grumbled. "Not again."

Graeham heard him set her on her feet; they adjusted their clothing.

"Really, Olive," drawled le Fever. "You wouldn't be a half-bad fuck if you didn't burst into tears quite so often."

Olive? Olive and le Fever?

"Rolf, please," she begged. "We've got to talk about this. It's murder. It's a sin. I can't—"

"You can and you bloody well will."

"Rolf, listen to me . . ."

"I want it taken care of, do you hear? And soon. You're taking too long about it. You know what needs to be done. Do it."

"Oh, God, Rolf," she sobbed. "I can't. I can't."

Le Fever sighed heavily, impatiently. "Come here. There, now. Don't cry. I hate it when you cry. Here, blow your nose."

She did.

"Pull yourself together, my sweet. I'm sorry I spoke harshly, truly I am."

Smooth-tongued snake, thought Graeham.

"I can be such a bear," he said in a tone of oily contrition. "How do you put up with me?"

"I l-love y-you," she stuttered between little hiccupping sobs.

"And I love you, too, Olive. Deeply. Unbearably. Our future together means everything to me—which is why you really have no choice but to take care of this."

She sniffed.

"I know you understand," he said soothingly. "You're just a little balky, which is natural. But it's the only way. Isn't it?" After a pause, he said, softly but firmly, "Isn't it, Olive?"

"Y-yes."

"Say it," he murmured.

"It . . . it's the only way."

"That's right. That's right. You have everything you need in the shop, don't you? All the ingredients?"

"There are just two, and yes, I . . . I have them."

"And you know there's no other way. You know it has to be done."

"I just w-wish it didn't."

"Of course you do. And I hate it as much as you do. But we have no choice, do we? Not if we want to be together. You want to be my wife, don't you?"

"More than anything."

"Go then," he urged. "Prepare the mixture. Do what you have to do. Now, before you lose your nerve."

She drew in a shaky breath. "All right. All right, Rolf. I'll do it."

"That's my girl," he said. "By this time tomorrow, 'twill all be over. And you'll see it was the only way. You'll see."

Graeham heard them kiss, and then her footsteps receded toward Wood Street. A few moments later, le Fever turned and walked away in the other direction. Graeham watched him slip back into his house.

Levering himself off the cot with his crutch, Graeham made his way to the leather-curtained doorway and paused. All he had on were his drawers, because of the heat, but Joanna always seemed a bit agitated when he was in a state of undress. He snatched that day's shirt off the floor by the bed, pulled it on and limped into the salle.

Fumbling in the dark for the fire iron and flint, he lit the candle on the table, startled to find Petronilla blinking at him from the windowsill. He crossed to the ladder that led to Joanna's solar and hesitated, wishing he didn't have to wake her up, but mostly wishing he didn't have to drag her into this any more than he already had.

He swore softly under his breath, then called out, "Mistress Joanna?"

Silence.

"Mistress, wake up. Please. I need you."

From the back of the solar came the squeak of the ropes supporting her mattress. "Serjant?" she said groggily. "Are you all right?"

"Yes. I just need you for something."

He heard her feet on the floor and imagined her climbing out of bed naked. The image aroused him deeply despite the urgency of his objective. With a mental shake, he reminded himself that she was, by now, a betrothed woman. And he was as good as betrothed to Phillipa.

But that didn't stop him from wanting her, with every breath he breathed. He would never stop wanting her. Long after he'd left here and settled in Oxfordshire with Phillipa, he knew he would still dream of Joanna Chapman, still long for her. She'd gotten into his bones, she flowed red-hot in his veins, she haunted his waking thoughts and nightly dreams. He could no more forget her than his heart could forget to pump, his lungs to breathe.

She descended the ladder quickly, clutching the skirt of her white silk wrapper, her great shimmering swath of hair rippling around her like old gold come to life. Sleep had made the blood rise in her cheeks and heated her skin, intensifying its wild, rain-soaked scent.

Graeham's heart stilled in his chest. He hadn't seen her in such sweetly alluring dishabille since the night he'd watched her getting ready for her bath. That had been more than a month ago, but every detail of that stolen memory was etched indelibly in his mind's eye from having been examined and reexamined during long nights on his lonely cot. He recalled all too well how her fingers had shaped the heaviness of a breast through her shift, how her nipple had pushed against the threadbare linen, how her hand had traced a path lower still . . .

He raked his fingers through his hair, trying to ignore the heat pumping through his loins and grateful that he'd bothered with the concealing shirt. "I'm sorry to awaken you, mistress."

"What's wrong?" She glanced at him—his bare legs, his rumpled shirt—and pulled her wrapper closed across her chest. The silk stretched taut over her breasts, molding to their lush contours, their delicate tips.

Graeham sighed. "Perhaps nothing's really wrong. More likely, a great deal is."

"What happened?"

"I overheard a couple in the alley just now. Rolf le Fever . . . and Olive."

"Olive? Perhaps . . . perhaps she was bringing him some tonic for his wife."

"Mistress, there's only one reason for a man and a woman to meet in an alley in the middle of the night."

She shook her head. "Nay. Olive and le Fever? You're imagining things."

"He tupped her against the wall," Graeham said shortly.

The flush spread from Joanna's cheeks to encompass her face. "Perhaps it wasn't really Olive. Perhaps—"

"I heard her voice. She was crying, so I didn't recognize it right off, but after he called her Olive, I realized it was her. I had the impression they'd . . . been intimate for some time."

"Oh, my God." Joanna crossed to the table and sat on the bench, looking dazed and sad. "What about Damian? He loves her, and . . . I thought she loved him."

"Perhaps she does," Graeham said. "Matters of the heart are rarely simple. Usually they're quite complicated . . . often unfathomable."

She looked up and met his gaze then. Graeham thought about the awareness that enveloped them, the ponderous weight of things felt but unspoken, like a cloud swollen with rain waiting for a spark of lightning to make it burst forth.

Joanna was the first to avert her gaze. "You said you needed me."

"I do," he said softly. Too much, for far too many reasons.

She glanced at him. "What is it you need?"

Refocusing on the matter at hand, he said, "I'd like you to go across the street to the apothecary's."

"Right now? At this hour?"

"Aye. She's over there mixing up some—"

"No."

"No? But—"

"You seem to have forgotten," she said, rising to her feet, "that I don't exist to spy on my neighbors for you."

Graeham groaned. "Mistress, I'm sorry about what happened before, but this is important. At least I'm being honest with you and not sending you over there on some other pretense."

"That's something, I suppose. But I promised myself that I'd never let you use me again, for . . . for anything. And it's a promise I intend to keep." She turned toward the ladder. "Good night, serjant."

He hobbled after her on his crutch and closed a hand around her waist as she stepped on the first rung. "I know you care what becomes of Ada le Fever—otherwise you wouldn't visit her every morning as you do."

"What of it?" She lowered her foot, her back to him, her hands still gripping the ladder. He felt the tension in her and curled his arm around her waist, telling himself it was because he didn't want her dashing upstairs, where he couldn't follow her. Her belly was warm and flat through the slippery silk; her scent made him light-headed. He wanted to pull her warmth against him, bury his face in her hair, press against her, into her.

Graeham swallowed hard, striving for some command over himself. "You bring her food every day. I know it's because you're worried that she's being poisoned."

"Let go of me, serjant," she said a little breathlessly.

He tightened his arm around her, moved closer, felt the heavy satin of her hair against his face, the silken glide of her wrapper brushing his bare legs. "You'll just climb that ladder if I do."

"I won't. I promise."

Graeham released her reluctantly, letting his hand slide slowly around her waist and linger momentarily on the firm curve of a hip before he backed away. It had been almost like holding a lover; he would never have an excuse to hold her that way again.

She turned without looking at him and rubbed her arms. "I did think about poison in the beginning. I thought if she only ate what I brought her, she might recover. But she didn't."

"You suspected her tonic, too, didn't you?"

"At first, but it's just an infusion of yarrow."

"If Olive was telling you the truth."

Joanna looked at him sharply. "Olive is no murderess, serjant."

"Olive is an impressionable young girl, mistress. And Rolf le Fever is not above using her to his own ends."

"Those ends being murder?"

"I heard her speak that very word tonight."

Joanna studied him for a long moment, then crossed to the bench at the table and sat. "Tell me."

"There was something he wanted her to 'take care of, and soon.' He told her it was taking too long, that she knew what needed to be done and should just do it. She said it was murder."

"Oh, Olive, Olive . . ." Joanna murmured, absently crossing herself.

"She agreed to it because he said it was the only way they could marry."

Joanna closed her eyes and rubbed her forehead.

"With Mistress Ada out of the way," Graeham said, "Olive and le Fever—"

"He would never marry her. He'd choose someone who could advance his station—a girl from the minor nobility or perhaps the daughter of a rich and respected merchant. Not a humble apothecary's apprentice."

"Olive doesn't know that. She's entirely in his thrall."

"Poor Olive."

" 'Poor Olive' may be over there right now concocting a fatal dose of whatever it is they've been slipping to Ada le Fever all along. Le Fever had probably wanted it to look like a slow, natural death, but now the time has come to finish her off."

Joanna shook her head resolutely. "I can't believe it. I don't believe it."

"Nevertheless," Graeham said, coming to stand over her, "le Fever sent her back to the shop to 'prepare the mixture,' as he put it—before she lost her nerve. He said by this time tomorrow it would all be over. I assume he means for Olive to put the final dose in the tonic she brings tomorrow afternoon."

Joanna was still shaking her head. " 'Tisn't possible. It can't be. Olive . . . she couldn't do such a thing."

"I'm all too afraid she could."

"What do you want me to do?" she asked woodenly.

"Go to the apothecary shop and see what she's up to," Graeham said.

"Just show up there in the middle of the night?"

"Tell her you need something . . . a sleeping powder. Look around, take stock of what she's doing and how she's acting. Question her, if you can do it without raising her suspicions."

Joanna's brow furrowed. "I'd feel so treacherous, misleading her that way."

"I can't go myself," Graeham said. "There's my leg, and—"

"I know, I know."

"Would you rather I sent for the sheriff?" Graeham asked, although he preferred to avoid that until it became absolutely necessary, lest it compromise the secrecy of his mission.

Joanna shook her head and stood. "Nay—not yet. If this isn't what it looks like—if Olive is innocent—I don't want the sheriff getting involved."

He'd hoped she would feel that way. Joanna plucked her mantle off its peg and pinned it over her wrapper. Graeham followed her into the shop, where she slipped her feet into the wooden pattens she kept by the front door.

After she left, he held the door open a crack and watched her sprint across the street and knock on the door of the apothecary shop, which glowed from within. The door opened. Olive looked surprised to see her; even from this distance, Graeham could see that the girl's eyes were puffy, her nose red. She had something in her hand—a wooden pestle. Joanna said something to her. She held the door open for Joanna to enter, then closed it behind her.

Graeham stood watching the shop until his leg began to ache. It was hot for this time of night, even in July. Sweat trickled beneath his shirt, which clung damply to his chest. Manfrid, who had been outside, came and rubbed against his legs before squeezing between them and into the shop.

It was taking too long. Why was it taking so long? Something was wrong. He should never have sent her over there. She was in danger. There was murder being planned, and he had thrust her right in the midst of it without sparing a thought for her safety. He'd been complacent because it was just Olive, and he couldn't see her hurting Joanna, but if the girl was capable of poisoning Ada le Fever, she was capable of anything.

He opened the door and stepped into the street just as Joanna came out of the apothecary shop. Hurriedly he ducked back inside. When she reentered the shop, he let out a sigh of relief. "I was worried about you."

"Not too worried to send me over there." She pulled off her pattens and swept past him into the salle.

Graeham followed her, his leg throbbing. He sat at the table and leaned his crutch against it. "Did she tell you anything?"

"Nay. She was too distracted. She prepared the sleeping powder as if she were in a trance. I'd be afraid to take it in case she made a mistake with the ingredients." Joanna tossed a little parchment-wrapped packet on the table.

"What was she doing when you arrived?"

"Grinding up herbs."

"Did you recognize them?"

"Nay."

Graeham cursed inwardly.

"Do you?" Withdrawing an arm from beneath her mantle, she held up two bundles of dried herbs tied with string.

"You . . . you *took* them?"

"Aye." She laid the bundles on the table; one had large leaves, one small. "If these really are the ingredients of a poison, I thought 'twould be best to get them away from Olive before she . . . does something foolish."

Graeham lifted first one bundle and then the other, bringing them to his nose; he didn't recognize them either by appearance or by smell. "She may have more than just these two bunches."

"I know." Joanna unpinned her mantle and hung it on its peg, wiping a hand over her damp forehead. "I thought of that after I took them. Still, it might give her pause. She might rethink what she was about to do."

"Or she might go to le Fever tomorrow and report the theft, whereupon he might decide you're a threat to his little scheme." Graeham shook his head. "I can't fault you for taking these herbs—I might have done so myself. But I hope you haven't put yourself in any danger because of it."

Returning to stand over the table, Joanna lifted one of the sinister bundles and twirled it slowly. "It's Ada le Fever I'm worried about. We should send for the sheriff first thing tomorrow morning."

Graeham sighed, then nodded grudgingly. He no longer had any choice but to enlist the sheriff's aid if he wanted to ensure Ada's safety. If he weren't a damned cripple, he would go over there right now and take her out of that house, but as it was . . . "You're right," he said. "I hate to do it, but . . ."

"Why?" she asked. " 'Tis the sheriff's responsibility to investigate matters of this sort. Why would you hesitate to summon him?" She looked down at him in obvious confusion, the firelight making sparks of gold flicker in her brown eyes.

"When I was sent here to bring Ada le Fever back to Paris, I was cautioned to proceed with discretion."

"Ah, yes." She plucked off a leaf and crushed it under her nose. "The things you're 'not at liberty to reveal.' "

Graeham's ears grew hot. He was ashamed, he realized, of having withheld so much from her while enlisting her aid to the extent he had. She'd resisted being his pawn, yes, but in all respects, save one, she'd proven herself completely worthy of his trust and confidence. The one exception was her prevarication about her husband's death, but it was an innocent lie. She was a beautiful widow living alone. He couldn't blame her—or her brother—for perpetrating a falsehood meant to keep the young soldier under her roof at a distance.

But he could blame himself for keeping things from her that she had every right to know, given the extent to which he'd involved her in this complicated little intrigue.

"I haven't been fair to you," he said. "You've earned the right to know more than I've told you. You've earned the right to know who sent me here."

Joanna grew very still and quiet for a long moment. She laid the herbs back down and sat—not opposite him, as usual, but right next to him on his bench. "Who sent you here, serjant?"

" 'Twas my overlord, Baron Gui de Beauvais."

Her brows drew together. "Why did you not want me to know that?"

"Because"—Graeham took a deep breath—"Ada le Fever is Lord Gui's daughter."

She still looked puzzled.

"His illegitimate daughter," Graeham said. "No one knows—aside from their uncle, who raised them in Paris."

"The canon," Joanna said softly. "Ada told me her uncle is a canon of Notre Dame."

"That's right. And, of course, Rolf le Fever knows. He found out shortly after the wedding. 'Tis why he hates his wife so much, why he started heaping threats and abuse on her. The marriage was meant to reflect well on him, and all it brought him was—as he puts it—a shameful little secret to keep."

Joanna nodded. "Yes . . . that makes sense, knowing him. So Lord Gui began to worry that he'd go beyond mere threats and abuse—as, indeed, it seems he has—and enlisted you to rescue his daughter before real harm could come to her." She shook her head. "Rotten timing, those robbers smashing your leg before you had a chance to get her out of that house."

"I don't think they were mere robbers."

"Nay?"

"I'd been to see le Fever that afternoon. He was reluctant to let his wife leave with me, but I talked him into it with a bit of blackmail and the promise of fifty marks—or so I thought. He told me to return at compline and he'd have her ready. Olive was there, delivering Ada le Fever's tonic. I asked her to prepare enough for the journey and have it there by compline."

"Olive was there? She saw you, then, and she knew you'd come to take Ada away. That's why you didn't want her to see you here, because she knew you weren't just some fellow who ran into a bit of bad luck on his way to Oxfordshire."

"That's right. I went back at compline, of course, only to be lured into the alley by some knave representing himself as Byram, who knew why I was there. He and his two cohorts had been lurking about waiting to smash my head in and take the fifty marks. They got the silver and my mount, and if it weren't for your brother, they might have sent me to my maker that day."

"You think le Fever hired them to ambush you?"

"Aye. I think he wanted the money without the indignity of losing his wife."

"One would think he'd have been eager to see her go, regardless of the indignity."

"Don't forget, he'd been having her poisoned since Christmastide, just waiting for the right time to finish her off. He wanted her dead, so he could remarry someone more suitable—not packed off to Paris, with everyone wondering why her father had felt the need to fetch her back."

"Pardon me for saying so, serjant, but it strikes me as

awfully poor judgment on the part of your Lord Gui to have married his daughter off under false pretenses."

"It was. He admits as much himself. And I must confess to some measure of disappointment with him when he told me what he'd done. The very fact that he'd kept two daughters tucked away in Paris all those years was rather sobering. I wondered if all important men had secret bastards hidden away."

"*Two* daughters? Oh, that's right—Ada has a sister. She mentioned her once. Phillipa—isn't that her name?"

A thrumming panic gripped Graeham at the sound of his future wife's name on Joanna Chapman's lips. "Yes," he managed. "Phillipa. They're . . . they're twins."

"Does Phillipa's husband know the truth about her birth, or was he kept in the dark, as well?"

This was his chance to tell her everything, to reveal the terms of his reward, to be as candid as she deserved. Graeham's heart thumped in his chest as he pondered how best to say it . . . *Phillipa isn't married, not yet. I'm to be her husband. We'll be wed as soon as I bring Ada back to France.*

"Serjant?" Joanna's shoulder brushed Graeham's as she turned toward him; silk against linen; soft woman-flesh against muscle; warmth against warmth. God, she smelled so good; he wanted to drown himself in her hair, bury himself in her body. "Is something wrong?"

Graeham plucked a leaf off one of the bundles of herbs and ground it into dust between his fingers. "Phillipa isn't married yet," he said, his voice strangely distant and hollow, as if he were listening to someone else speak. "I'm . . ." He looked up and met Joanna's glimmery, molten gold gaze, and it was all he could do to force air into his lungs, much less speak.

"Well, I hope Lord Gui is more forthcoming with his next son-in-law than he was with the last one," she said with an arid smile.

"I'm . . ." Graeham shook his head, disgusted with himself, with the situation. He tore off another leaf. "I'm sure he will be."

She regarded him in that insightful way that he found

both disarming and unnerving. "Lord Gui must trust you very much, to have told you this."

Graeham crumbled that leaf, and another, without looking at her. "He was . . . almost like a father to me during my adolescence."

"Almost?"

Graeham thought about it. "I respected him. I still do, despite . . . his lapses in judgment and the infidelity. I harbor a great deal of affection for him, and I like to think the sentiment is mutual. He's been good to me, given me opportunities, but . . ."

"But?"

He did look up then. "I still sleep in the barracks. I still exist to do his bidding, same as his other soldiers. I'm not his son, just . . . a favored retainer. I try not to forget that."

She nodded thoughtfully.

"Your storeroom really is the first private place I've ever had to call my own," he said. I've never had a home in the true sense, nor any kind of family."

"I'm sure you've felt the lack of those things very keenly," she said. "But growing up the way you did—having only yourself to rely on—did have some benefits. You became independent, self-reliant. Those are admirable qualities."

"I know. I've greatly admired them in you."

She lowered her gaze, letting that statement hang heavy in the air between them.

"We're much alike, you and I," he said quietly, acutely aware now of her shoulder pressed to his, the soft caress of her silken robe along the side of his leg. "You must have noticed."

She nodded, her gaze fixed on her hands, resting on the table in front of her.

"I know we've had our differences," he said, feeling as if he were falling, slowly but dizzyingly, into some dark abyss filled with mystery and promise, and taking her with him. "But when I talk to you, I feel as if I'm talking to . . . a friend, someone whose soul is attuned to mine. I know you've felt the same loneliness I've felt, the same sense of isolation."

With a kind of drunken recklessness, he reached for her hand and took it. She still wouldn't look at him. Through the serpentine tendrils of hair cloaking her chest, he saw the rapid rise and fall of her silk-clad breasts.

He squeezed her hand. "I'm sorry for the lies," he said, meaning it—especially the one last, tenacious lie of omission about Phillipa. "I'm sorry for everything I've done to push you away."

"I haven't been truthful with you, either." She curled her fingers around his. "I need to tell you something, something I should have told you in the beginning."

"Mistress . . ."

"Nay, let me tell you—please. I feel a little silly now, for having kept this from you, and . . . and a little ashamed."

"You don't—"

"I've been letting you think I'm a married woman, but I'm not. I'm a widow. My husband . . . he died last year in Genoa."

"I know."

She stared at him. "You don't know."

"I do," he admitted. "I've known for . . . some time now."

"How long?" she asked in a thin voice.

"Since the day of the fair."

"The Friday fair?"

He nodded.

"You've known since the Friday fair?" A shrill note of anger joined the incredulity in her voice. "That was a month ago!"

"Mistress," Graeham soothed, feeling as if he'd played a particularly idiotic move in chess, one from which there was no turning back, "I understood why you—"

"Have could you have gone on letting me pretend, after you knew?" she asked in a quavering voice.

"Mistress, please . . ."

"You *knew*." Her eyes shone too brightly; patches of red stained her cheeks. "You knew all along. All this time . . ."

He tightened his grip on her hand. "Please listen to me."

"I feel like such a fool. I can't stay here and . . . I can't." She jerked her hand out of his and stood. "Good night, serjant."

"Nay!" Graeham gripped her around the waist with both hands. "Stay. Please just—"

"Let me go!" she said fiercely, prying at his hands. "I'm humiliated enough. Don't make me stay here and—"

"Joanna—"

"Let go of me." She slammed her fists into his arms.

He released her. Bracing his hands on the table, he rose awkwardly to his feet. "Joanna, stay. I just want to—"

"Leave me alone." As she turned, he grabbed her arm. She wrenched away from him, her robe sliding off one shoulder, and wheeled around.

"Joanna!" His splint and the lack of space between the bench and the table put him off balance, but as she turned her back to him, he seized her shoulders. One was uncovered; he felt a moment's disorientation to be touching her bare flesh, warm and firm and damp with sweat.

Twisting around, she struck out at him. One fist caught him on a forearm, the other on the side of the shoulder. They weren't hard punches, but they were enough to upset his footing.

He toppled sideways, overturning the bench and landing painfully on its underside. Cursing at the sudden jolt to his leg, he rolled off the bench, both hands wrapped around his splint.

"Graeham!" She knelt over him, her hair brushing him in slick, heavy waves as she softly touched his splinted leg. Despite the situation, it gratified him on an elemental level to hear her call him by his Christian name. "Oh, God, I'm sorry. Are you all right?"

Gritting his teeth, he nodded, stretched his leg out, managed to sit up.

"Thank God," she said. "I . . . I didn't mean to hurt you. I've never hit anyone . . . I'm just . . . I can't . . . I have to go." She started to rise.

"Nay." He caught her around the waist and threw her down in the rushes.

With a gasp of outrage, she tried to sit up. He pushed her back down by her shoulders.

She tried to roll out from under him, but he shoved her flat on her back, lowering himself onto her to hold her still.

"Let me go!" She thrashed and squirmed, pushing against his chest. "Get off me!"

"Nay." He banded his hands around her wrists and

pinned them amid the great corona of golden hair blanketing the rushes, but still she writhed against him, trying desperately to pitch him off.

Her wrapper had loosened further in their tussle, exposing her upper chest and arm on one side. He could see the creamy rise of a breast, its nipple barely concealed by the disarrayed garment. With every heave of her chest, every arch of her back, the swath of silk threatened to slip away from the taut nub and reveal what he'd only looked upon in his inflamed imaginings.

Desire, hot and heavy, unfurled in his loins, pushed against her. In her struggles, she didn't seem to notice.

"Joanna, stop this," he said, his hair falling in his face as he tried to capture her fierce gaze with his. "Stop—"

"Why?" she cried. "Why didn't you tell me you knew I was widowed?"

Softly, searching her eyes, he said, "I was waiting for you to tell me."

Chapter 21

❧

I was waiting for you to tell me. Oh, God.

Joanna gazed into Graeham's luminous blue eyes, her heart drumming in her chest. His hands were like bands of iron around her wrists, his body heavy and solid as he pressed her into the prickly rushes.

He had one leg, the splinted one, nestled between hers. In the juncture of her thigh and hip she felt, through her silken wrapper and his linen undergarments, a rock-hard column of heat.

She closed her eyes to escape his penetrating gaze and this heart-pounding tempest of sensation, but that only heightened her awareness of him . . . his damp male scent, the rhythmic whisk of his shirt against her chest with every breath he drew—breath that tickled her face, her lips, growing hotter, closer.

She opened her eyes, lost herself in an intensity of blue. He was close, so close. There was no turning back.

He touched his lips to hers and she fell, tumbling slowly, into heat and inevitability.

It was an ungentle kiss, dark and rough and full of need, and—oh God, oh God—she gave herself to it, surrendered her mouth to him, his lips hot and demanding, his tongue and teeth devouring her.

He released her wrists and closed his hands around hers, tightly, possessively. She squeezed them back. *Possess me.*

He parted her thighs with his good leg. Still kissing her, he pressed against her, hard. And again.

Yes. Joanna moved against him, against the slide of his rigid flesh on her yielding softness. She throbbed where he thrust against her; her body wept for him, damp through the silk, straining, pushing, trembling.

Please. Oh, God.

He broke the kiss, gasping, released one of her hands and untied his drawers with frenzied haste, his fingers fumbling, grazing her through the wet silk, a fluttery caress.

She breathed his name like a plea, helpless in her need, felt his hands warm and rough as he yanked her wrapper open, just enough, felt the satin length of him hot and taut against her inner thigh, the head slick and ready.

And then he took her mouth again, gripping both of her hands hard, harder, every muscle in his body straining as he readied himself and drove in.

Her flesh burned as he stretched her open. So tight. It had been so long. She tensed, a startled little whimper rising in her throat.

Half-buried within her, he rose on his elbows, his eyes full of concern. "Joanna? Are you—"

"I'm fine." She squeezed his hands, moved against him, her need for him, for the fullness of him inside her, so overwhelming that she didn't care about the discomfort. She relished it, because it meant he was claiming her, taking her body as he had taken her soul.

He drew back and thrust again slowly, and again, a sinuous tightening of his hips that quivered through his torso, his shoulders, his hands. Each determined stroke pushed deeper, easing her open, invading her inch by inch.

The initial pain of penetration dissolved into a different kind of ache, a hot tingle, a breathless gathering up that made her moan and clutch his hands.

He reared up, his thrusts growing swifter, more erratic. His damp hair swung above her, sweat dripping from it; his breathing grew harsh, frantic. The rushes crackled beneath them.

Needing him deep, deep, as deep as he could go, she wrapped her legs around him, arched against him.

"Oh, God, don't," he said, his gaze unfocused, his body shuddering. "Joanna, don't."

"Why? What—"

"It feels too . . . I can't . . . oh, God . . ." He tucked his wet face in the crook of her neck, groaning raggedly. Joanna felt the tremors course through him, felt the fury of his release deep within her, and savored a sense of completeness that made her want to weep.

"I'm sorry, Joanna," he whispered against her neck as he lay heavy on top of her, still holding her hands.

"Why?"

"Because I meant to . . ." He sighed. Levering himself up, he slid his hands out of hers and framed her damp face with them. "I didn't want to finish inside you." He studied her eyes, waiting for her to understand.

I promised myself long ago that I'd never sire a bastard.

"Ah." She frowned as it fully dawned on her. "Oh. 'Twas my fault, wasn't it?" She uncurled her legs from around his waist. "Because I—"

"I loved it," he said, smoothing a hand down her hip and leg with a reassuring smile. "Too much. And that's the other thing I'm sorry about. I finished too soon."

Joanna blinked in confusion. "Too soon?" How could a man finish too soon? He finished when he finished, and then it was over.

Graeham peeled a wet strand of hair off her cheek, kissed the spot where it had been. "I didn't wait for you."

"Me? You mean, to . . ." Nonplussed, Joanna contemplated the novel idea of having a lover who gave a thought to her pleasure. Prewitt had had her every way a man could have a woman, but never once had he touched her for her pleasure, only for his. Afterward, when he was asleep, she would sometimes slide her hand between her legs and give her body the relief it craved, but she always felt vaguely ashamed afterward, and lonelier than ever.

Still buried inside her, Graeham raised himself on one arm and slid aside the loosened edge of her wrapper, exposing her left breast in its entirety. His eyes glittered as he closed his hand over the sweat-slicked flesh, caressing it in a way that made her purr like a cat having its throat stroked. He tugged on her nipple, sparking a little spasm of pleasure where they were joined.

Graeham felt it, and responded with a spontaneous flexing of his hips, stroking her deliciously from within, although his erection was waning. He continued this gentle thrusting as he untied the sash of her wrapper.

Throwing the silken robe open, he gazed on her with that look of drowsy desire she'd become so familiar with. "How beautiful you are, Joanna."

"Let me see you, too," she pleaded, tugging at his shirt. "Take this off."

He managed to peel the sodden garment off, wiped his face with it and tossed it into the rushes. His chest and shoulders, gleaming with sweat, enthralled her. Joanna caressed him as she'd wanted to for weeks, savoring the planes and ridges of his hard-packed muscles beneath her hands.

He glided his hand downward, over her stomach, to the patch of hair now tangled with his, all the while moving within her in a steady rhythm that she couldn't help matching. At first his touch was light and airy, maddeningly so.

She closed her hands over his shoulders, writhed unselfconsciously.

Only when she begged him to did he intensify the caress, lightly probing and stroking, but always backing off just as satisfaction beckoned, until she was thrashing beneath him, moaning like a woman possessed.

She threw her head back, trembling. "Oh, Graeham . . . oh, please . . ."

With a groan, he sank deeply into her, pulled out, and plunged in again, still touching her as before. Even as she teetered breathlessly on the edge of climax, some part of her was dimly aware that he'd regained his erection. He was making love to her again without even uncoupling from the first time.

She cried out rawly when she fell over the edge, lost in pleasure that exploded over and over and over, stoked by the driving rhythm of his thrusts. As her climax ebbed, he fell on her and kissed her deeply. His body slid against hers in an ever-quickening rhythm, sweat trickling between them, his restless hands in her hair, on her breasts, her hips.

Joanna clung to him through a second shattering climax as her fingers raked his hair, his back. There was a violent energy to their lovemaking that made her feel wicked and beautiful and filled with utter abandon.

As her pleasure subsided, he seized her hips, his face darkly flushed, a low, almost pained sound rising from his throat. Swiftly he slid out of her, leaving her shockingly empty. He thrust against her once, twice, then stilled, taut and quivering, holding her so tightly she could barely breathe. Heat pumped wetly between them, then he sank, panting on top of her.

A few moments later, after she'd caught her breath, Joanna said, a little shyly, "I . . . I didn't know men could do that—make love twice in a row that way."

Raising his face from the crook of her neck, Graeham chuckled. "Neither did I," he said, and kissed her soundly.

"I've never been in such a big bed," Graeham said later that night, after they were settled upstairs in the solar.

It was a surprisingly beautiful chamber, airy and whitewashed and inviting. Her bed was enormous, with a leather mattress and white curtains they'd drawn around them. Candlelight glowed through the curtains, burnishing her lush body, curled up with his in a comfortable, naked embrace. He basked in the soft weight of her against him, the coolness of the linen sheets beneath them, and most of all the sense of intimate companionship that was so novel to him, and so wonderful.

"You were mad to insist on coming up here," she murmured against his chest. "I thought you were never going to make it up that ladder."

He trailed a hand through her extraordinary hair, heavy silk falling through his fingers. "I wanted to sleep with you."

"You must have wanted it a great deal. You grimaced with every step."

There were still a few rushes caught in her hair. He pulled one out and dropped it onto the rush-covered floor. "I've never slept with anyone before."

She raised her head to look at him. "Never?"

He shook his head. "In the dorter at Holy Trinity, and now in Lord Gui's barracks, everyone has his own cot—no bigger than the one downstairs in your storeroom. I've never shared a bed."

"Not even . . ." She looked away from him and resettled her head on his shoulder. "Not even when you were with a woman?"

"Oh, I've tupped in beds, of course," he said. And many other places—behind Lord Gui's wash house with the laundresses, in pantries and butteries with the serving wenches, in dark Paris doorways with whores—but he knew better than to think Joanna wanted to hear any of that. "But when the tupping was over, I always left."

"Your lovers never wanted you to stay?"

"They weren't 'lovers,' Joanna, they were just . . . accommodating women."

"Prostitutes?"

"Sometimes," he said, uncomfortably aware that she might be thinking of Leoda. "More often than not, just women who gave themselves freely. They never meant anything to me. Sex with them . . . it was more a bodily function than anything else, a way of gaining relief. It wasn't like it was with us, downstairs. That was . . ."

"Magic," she said softly.

He curled his arms around her and kissed her hair. "Aye. And you're a witch who's caught me in her spell. A beautiful, wanton witch."

"Wanton!" She buried her face against his chest. "Nay."

He chuckled at her foolishness. "Wanton in the best way. You felt so . . . unbridled in my arms, so responsive and unrestrained. And I felt the same way—you made me feel that way. 'Twas the first time I've ever lost that sense of being separate and apart. You made me feel as if I were one with you—that we were a single being, together. Does that make any sense?"

"Aye. I felt the same."

"I'm afraid I wasn't very gentle," he said, remembering how she'd reacted when he first entered her. She was as tight as a virgin, or how he imagined a virgin to be, never having lain with one. He'd never been with a woman whose body fit so snugly around his. It felt incredible—so hot and tight and slick—but it unnerved him, too. "Did I hurt you? I hope I didn't hurt you."

"Nay—not at all."

He knew she was just saying that to spare his feelings. "It must have been a long time since you were with a man."

"Five years," she said. "I caught Prewitt in this bed with the poulterer's wife and banished him to the storeroom."

He chuckled. "I'd wondered what he'd done to deserve such a fate. I suppose I should have known. There was no one, then, even when your husband was abroad for months at a time and you were all alone?"

"Nay. I was a married woman."

"In name only."

"It still would have been adultery. And, by and large, men steered clear of me, because I was a wedded woman."

"They didn't keep their distance once you were widowed, I'll wager."

"Nay, but I kept my distance from them. Most men just want an uncomplicated tumble with an experienced woman. They want to *use* me, same as I've been used all my life—and just for sex. Some of them are married, betrothed. . . . All they want from me is my body, and only for as long as it takes to ease their lust. I despise the notion of being used that way. The very idea makes me sick."

Some are married, betrothed . . . Graeham felt a little red-hot stab of contrition deep in his stomach. He was all but betrothed to Phillipa. Yet . . . wasn't Joanna betrothed as well? Surely it would be official by now.

He cleared his throat. "I know about Robert of Ramswick."

She twisted her head to look at him. "What about Robert of Ramswick?"

He brushed a lock of hair off her forehead, striving for a gentle, nonjudgmental tone. After all, was he not also guilty of infidelity to his betrothed? "I know he asked you to marry him, Joanna."

Her eyes lit with comprehension. "That day he came here while I was doing laundry. You overheard . . ."

"Enough to know what he was about." He embraced her tightly, possessively, and nuzzled her fragrant hair. "I hate to think of you as his wife—as any man's wife but—" *But mine?* He squeezed his eyes shut against the impossibility of their situation and the pain he knew would come eventually. "I'm happy for you that you'll be wed to a man of such high rank. That is, I want to be happy for you. I'm trying to be happy for you, but—"

"I'm not betrothed, Graeham." She twisted around so that she was lying on her stomach, her legs entwined with his, her breasts resting on his chest, soft and heavy, and looked him in the eye. "Not to Robert, nor anyone else."

"But didn't he ask you—"

"Aye. I turned him down."

"Truly?" As gratifying as this news was, it was also somewhat perplexing—even astounding. Robert of Ramswick was young, handsome, and judging from his willingness to take little Alice into his home as a ward, a very good man indeed, a man worthy of Joanna. On top of it all, he was a landed lord. Marriage to him could have rescued Joanna from the poverty into which she was slipping all too quickly. "Why did you turn him down?"

"Aside from the fact that I'm not in love with him?"

"That wouldn't have stopped you from entering into such a favorable marriage." One thing Graeham had learned about Joanna Chapman was that she was a pragmatic woman, a woman who did what had to be done, who stiffened her backbone and persevered. It was one of the qualities—the many qualities—he admired about her.

"Nay—that wouldn't have stopped me," she admitted. "But as it happens, Robert is in love with his cousin. He only asked for my hand because he needed a mother for his children, and he thought it would kill his parents if he married Margaret. I'm happy to report that he came to his senses." She smiled in a way that made her look like a self-satisfied little girl. "They were formally betrothed in a ceremony in Ramswick's chapel a few days ago. Hugh went. They're to be wed in the early part of August."

"What of Lord Robert's parents?"

"Robert was right that they would object to the marriage, but they didn't have any luck talking him out of it. Hugh says they attended the betrothal ceremony—still very much alive—so I suspect they just need time to get used to the idea." She frowned. "How could you have thought I was betrothed to Robert after . . . what happened downstairs?"

"I . . . suppose I thought you were too . . . swept away by passion to be thinking of him."

She smiled a bit sardonically. "In my opinion, passion is something one must give oneself permission to be swept away by."

He shook his head, grinning. "Sometimes I think you're *too* pragmatic."

"No, really. I wanted you tonight, desperately. I've wanted you ever since you came to live here."

"Really?" Graeham said, absurdly gladdened that the passion that had consumed him day and night for the past six weeks had not been unrequited.

"But no matter how deeply I desired you," she said soberly, "I would never have acted on that desire had I accepted Robert's proposal of marriage. Infidelity to your betrothed is still adultery. The Church says so, and it's what I feel in my heart. It's betrayal. It's wrong."

Graeham felt a little pinch of guilt deep in his stomach. He'd always loathed the idea of infidelity—not so much because of the Church's condemnation of it, but because of the circumstances of his birth. Once he spoke the words "With this ring I thee wed, and with my body I thee honor," he would honor with his body only the woman who wore his ring, forsaking all others.

He supposed he'd always intended to be faithful to his betrothed even before they exchanged vows at the church door. Certainly he had. It was the right thing, the honorable thing, and he was an honorable man. Yet he'd spared not a thought for Phillipa when he tore Joanna's wrapper open and took her on the floor of her salle.

Of course, there were mitigating circumstances. He'd never met Phillipa. He had no feelings for her, no sense of devotion or attachment that made it seem like betrayal to bed someone else. And, too, their betrothal was as yet informal; no contract had been drawn up, no betrothal ceremony conducted. Yet were those not mere formalities? He and Phillipa were promised to each other. In the eyes of both of them, they were already betrothed.

Making love to Joanna was, indeed, a form of infidelity, in spirit if nothing else. Graeham did feel a twinge of guilt, but no real shame, no sense that he'd sinned in any meaningful way. How could he feel remorseful to have shared his body, his soul, with a woman he loved so deeply, so . . .

"Oh, God." He couldn't love her, mustn't love her, yet of course, he did. How could he not? Part of him rejoiced to have found a soulmate; another part—the part that craved a proper home and family and the land to make it possible—felt a sense of dread at this new turn of events.

This could not end well, the two of them. The only way he could be with Joanna would be to reject Phillipa's hand in marriage and the Oxfordshire estate that came with it, withdraw from Lord Gui's service, and return to England. He would be a landless soldier with no overlord, no money, no prospects. He would have Joanna—if a woman like her was willing to settle for a penniless cur with no property of his own—but he would lose his hopes, his dreams, his very future.

"What's wrong, Graeham?" Bracing herself on an elbow, Joanna tenderly stroked his face, her breasts lightly brushing his chest.

He closed his eyes, still so deeply moved just to hear his name on her lips at long last . . . awed to finally be able to take her in his arms and unite his body with hers. "Nothing's wrong," he lied. "Just keep touching me and everything will be all right."

She shifted just slightly, which brought the silken curve of her hip in contact with his quiescent manhood. As she kissed and caressed him, her subtle movements against him rekindled his former arousal. He stiffened, rose. Joanna felt it and sat over him, straddling his lap and guiding him to her damp little entrance. She sighed, her head thrown back, as she lowered herself onto him in increments, her womanly chamber stretching gradually to accommodate him.

She looked so golden and enchanting and provocative making love to him this way—but it was dangerous. "You should let me be on top," he said. "Otherwise I won't be able to pull out."

"I'll take care of that," she said. "You tell me when."

"What a capable woman you are," he said, threading his fingers through her hair to pull her down for a kiss. "How did I ever get along without you?"

"Are you happy?" she asked as she tupped him, the bed ropes squeaking with each slow, luxurious stroke, her body undulating gracefully atop his, her hair cloaking both of them like a silken mantle.

Once it had been his "presumptuous question." Now it was hers. He smiled, caressing her back, her hips, her firm round bottom as it rose and fell, coaxing him closer and closer to an ecstatic crisis of the senses. "Aye. Deliriously happy. Are you?"

"Oh, yes. God, yes. If I could stay like this forever, here, with you, just like this, no past, no future, just the two of us, I think I'd be happy forever."

"So would I," Graeham said, wishing with all his heart that it could be so and wondering for the thousandth time how everything had gotten so wonderfully, terrifyingly complicated.

Chapter 22

~

"There's something I'd like to ask you, Ada," Joanna said as she spooned the last of the porridge she'd brought into her new friend's mouth the next morning. "You may think it a bit odd."

Ada swallowed with difficulty, coughed and said, "What is it?"

"It's about your husband."

"Rolf?"

Joanna nodded as she tucked the empty porridge pot back in her basket. She was loath to tell Ada too much right now, when there was nothing the ailing woman could do about it but lie in this bed and fret. Earlier, before Joanna had left for her daily visit to the le Fever house, she'd paid a young boy a penny to deliver Graeham's note about the planned murder to the sheriff who lived closest to West Cheap.

"I can't tell you anything about Rolf," Ada said. "I haven't seen him since before Lent."

"I know. But when he was still visiting you up here, did he . . . seem like himself? Was he acting unusual at all?"

Ada stared tiredly at nothing for a moment and then shook her head. "He always acted unusual, to my way of thinking. I've never understood him. Why?"

Joanna shrugged and fiddled with the basket, tucking the napkin back over it with exaggerated care. "I suppose I just think it's odd that you haven't seen your own husband in four months." Thinking of Graeham, she added, "I'd hate to go that long without seeing my husband."

They'd been up all night, whispering together and making love; many times they'd resolved to go to sleep, but then one of them would say something that got them talking again, and as they talked, he would slowly caress her with those gentle, clever hands, and she would end up reaching for him. They never did get any sleep, and this morning Joanna was as tired—and happy—as she'd ever been.

"I thought you did used to go that long," Ada said, "when Master Prewitt was abroad. You told me just last week that you didn't miss him at all."

"Ah."

"Ah," Ada repeated with a gently mocking little smile. "I feel the same way about Rolf."

The two women laughed together companionably, but it seemed to take the wind out of Ada; her head fell back listlessly onto the pillow. It pained Joanna to watch someone she'd grown to care for waste away like this.

"Some water?" Joanna offered.

Ada shook her head weakly. "Too hard to swallow. Would you read me some Psalms?"

"I'd be happy to."

Joanna read for longer than usual, apprehensive about leaving Ada alone in this house, knowing what she now knew, even though Ada wasn't in any immediate danger; it was still quite early in the morning, and the adulterated tonic was presumably to be administered later this afternoon. Nevertheless, Joanna had resolved to return and keep watch over Ada after she spoke to the sheriff.

As Joanna read, Ada's eyes drifted closed; so did Joanna's. The only thing that kept her awake was anxiety over Ada. She kept glancing nervously at the sleeping woman's chest to make sure it continued to rise and fall; it did.

When she returned the psalter to its little shelf, Ada opened her eyes. "There was something," she said in a soft, muddled tone.

Joanna sat back down and took Ada's hand, which felt terribly small and cold and fragile. "Go back to sleep."

"There was something Rolf did," Ada said, enunciating the words slowly, "that I thought was unusual. 'Twas spring—after Easter, but before Pentecost, I think."

"That would have been about a month and a half ago,"

Joanna said. "I thought you hadn't seen your husband since before Lent."

"I haven't. But one day—'twas in the afternoon—Aethel came up here in quite a state. She said that Rolf had ordered me to dress for a journey, and she was to pack my things. He said someone would be coming for me."

That was the day Graeham came to take her away and was attacked in the alley, Joanna realized.

"Aethel helped me to get dressed," Ada said, "and she put all my things into traveling bags. I was bewildered at first, but then it occurred to me that perhaps my father had summoned me home. I was so excited to be leaving this house. Even though I was ill and I knew the journey would be hard on me, I was thrilled to be going home. I sat over there, at the window that overlooks the street, and waited." The spark in her eyes dimmed. "But no one ever came."

Tempted though Joanna was to fill in the missing details for Ada, she knew this wasn't the time. And, too, this revelation was raising disturbing new questions in Joanna's mind.

"I waited until the bells of curfew were rung, and then I waited some more, looking out at the dark street," Ada said sadly. "Finally Aethel convinced me to get undressed and go to bed. I never did find out what happened that day."

Ada was shivering; she was cold again. Yawning, Joanna tucked the blanket around her. "I must go now, but I'll be back later this morning."

"You're coming back?" Ada looked pleased; she must get lonely.

"Aye—just to keep you company. Get your rest. And remember—don't eat anything that's brought to you, or drink anything, or—"

"So you've told me a dozen times this morning," Ada said with an indulgent smile.

"And if someone brings you your tonic—Olive or your husband or anyone, even Aethel—"

"I know. I'm not to take it." Ada's brow knitted. "What has you so troubled, Joanna? What's wrong?"

Joanna brushed some stray hairs off of Ada's cheek. "I'll

tell you later, when everything's resolved. You're tired now."

Ada nodded and closed her eyes.

"Sleep," Joanna said as she turned to leave. "I'll be back as soon as I can."

When she returned home, she found Graeham in the shop stall talking to a bearish fellow with silver-threaded black hair whom he introduced as Nyle Orlege, an undersheriff dispatched by the sheriff in response to their note.

"Good morrow, mistress," said the gruff-voiced Nyle, who got right to the point. "If the serjant has explained it correctly, a woman's life may be in danger."

"That's right."

The undersheriff scratched the graying stubble on his oversized jaw. Iron manacles and chains hung on one side of his belt, a gigantic sheathed knife on the other. "And you two think it's the husband and his doxy that are poisoning her."

"I hate to think of Olive as being involved in this," Joanna said, "but I admit it doesn't look good. She's not evil, though, just young and impressionable."

"She seems to be entirely within Rolf le Fever's power," Graeham said, touching Joanna's arm comfortingly. "He coerced her."

"Probably," Joanna added.

Graeham regarded her with a look of puzzlement.

"Probably?" The undersheriff turned to Graeham. "You seemed pretty sure of things in your note—came right out and accused the man of attempted murder."

"Is there something I don't know?" Graeham asked Joanna.

"Perhaps," she said. "It might mean nothing, but it struck me as odd." She told the men what Ada had revealed about the mysterious journey she'd been readied for that had never taken place. "If le Fever had been in the process of poisoning his wife to death, he would hardly have wanted her to leave with Graeham. 'Twould have made more sense to finish the job and be done with her for good."

"Aye, but assuming he did want to finish her off," Nyle said, "he very well may have hired those churls to ambush the serjant so he couldn't interfere—and he'd get the fifty marks, to boot."

"Yes," Graeham said, "but then why did he prepare his wife for a journey? You're right, Joanna. The pieces don't add up."

"Well, it's my job to make them add up," declared the undersheriff. "But I've got to proceed with caution, you understand. Rolf le Fever is an important man in this city. Can't be making wild accusations with no proof."

Graeham picked up the two bundles of herbs from the table and handed them to Nyle. "Surely any good apothecary can identify those and tell us whether they're poisonous."

"Undoubtedly," Nyle said, "and if they are, that implicates the girl, but there still won't be any proof that le Fever put her up to it. What I've got to do—what *we've* got to do, because you two are the accusers, so I want you there—is to go across the street and question this Olive. A confession would go far toward making my job easy, and if we can get her to reveal le Fever's role in this, all the better." He opened the door and led the way out. "Come along, then."

"Can you make it across the street, do you think?" Joanna asked Graeham as he limped on his crutch toward the door. He wore his heavy riding boots, she saw; it was the first time he'd had them on in the six weeks he'd been here.

"I made it up that ladder, didn't I?" With a glance outside to make sure the undersheriff had his back to them, he leaned down and kissed her, quickly but thoroughly. "As Brother Simon used to say, to him that will, ways are not wanting."

Graeham's will may have been strong, but by the time he finally made it across Wood Street—with Joanna supporting him on one side and his crutch on the other, Nyle Orlege was already inside the apothecary shop, interrogating a cowed and wide-eyed Olive.

"Mistress Joanna!" the girl exclaimed when she and Graeham appeared. "This man says he's an undersheriff. He says he might have to arrest me. Do you know—" Her

gaze lit on Graeham, recognition flickering in her eyes, still
swollen from last night's bout of crying.

"Do you remember me?" he asked.

"I . . . I think so. Weren't you at Master Rolf's a while
back?"

"That's right."

"You were going to take Mistress Ada away."

"I say, could somebody please sell me a headache powder?" asked a squirrel-faced little man standing outside
the window.

"Shop's closed." Reaching through the opening, Nyle
pulled away the support poles, causing the upper shutter
to slam slut. He raised the lower shutter and latched it to
the upper, plunging the shop stall into eerie semidarkness.

Olive wrapped her arms around herself, her panicky gaze
taking in the three of them. "What's this all about? I
haven't done anything."

"We know you didn't want to, Olive," Joanna said.

"Didn't want to *what*?"

Nyle held up the two bunches of dried herbs. "Do you
recognize these?"

Olive's milky complexion grew even paler. "Oh, God."
She backed away from them. "Oh, God." Clutching her
stomach, she said, "I feel sick. I'm going to be sick."

Joanna moved to the girl's side and sat her on a low
wooden stool. "Put your head down. That's right. Take
deep breaths."

"I didn't want to," Olive moaned, sinking her head into
her trembling hands. "He said there was no other way."

"We know, Olive." Joanna leaned over her, patting her
back. "He talked you into it. That doesn't make it right,
but 'twill help when you're tried. You might get some
lashes, but I'm sure they won't hang you, not given that—"

"*Hang* me!" Olive wailed, looking up with tear-filled
eyes. "I didn't know you could hang for . . . oh, God. Oh,
God. I didn't mean to. I didn't want to. But he said if I
went ahead and had the baby, he could never marry me,
because of the shame."

Joanna glanced at Graeham and Nyle, who looked as
confounded as she felt.

Someone knocked on the door. "Can I get an elixir of—"

"No!" Nyle bellowed.

Joanna knelt next to Olive, who was rocking back and forth as tears slid down her cheeks. "You're with child?"

Olive pressed a hand to her mouth, her eyes squeezed shut, her waxen face sheened with sweat.

Graeham handed a large tin bowl to Joanna, who thrust it under Olive's face just in time. When the girl's bout of retching was over, Graeham took the bowl and passed her a damp cloth, with which she bathed Olive's face and throat.

"Are you pregnant by Rolf le Fever?" Nyle asked her.

"Isn't that why you're going to arrest me?" she asked raspily. "Because I was going to . . . to get rid of the baby?"

Joanna, Graeham, and Nyle all exchanged looks.

Another knock sounded at the door. "Can I get some—"

"*No!*" all three of them yelled at once.

"Olive," Joanna said, "tell us what happened." Graeham handed her a handkerchief; she dabbed the girl's face with it, then opened Olive's fingers and stuffed it into her hand. "From the beginning. You and Rolf le Fever . . ." she prompted.

"Aye," Olive sniffled, wiping her nose.

"For how long?"

"Since Christmastide. 'Twas around the time his wife took sick with her head cold, because that's when he . . . he noticed me, was when I started bringing her her tonic."

"He seduced you?" Joanna said gently.

Olive closed her eyes and nodded. "At first I . . . I tried to resist him, mostly because he was a married man but also because I was in l-love with Damian. And I c-couldn't believe a man like that could see anything in someone like me. He's a guildmaster, and rich and handsome and he dresses so fine. But Rolf, he wouldn't give up. He said he loved me, he needed me. His wife took a turn for the worse, what with the black bile and all. He said it looked like she was dying, and he meant to marry me after she was gone." Olive shook her head. "I let him have his way with me. And now I'm in love with him and I've got his babe in my belly and I'm ruined."

"I don't understand," Graeham said. "He told you he couldn't marry you if you had the baby?"

Olive nodded, her gaze fixed on the damp handkerchief

as she twisted it in her hands. "I'd be a fallen woman. A man in his position couldn't marry a girl who'd had a babe out of wedlock, even if it was his. He made me promise to g-get rid of it."

"With those herbs?" Joanna asked, indicating the two bundles that Nyle still held.

"Aye."

"That's what you were talking to le Fever about in the alley last night?" Graeham asked her. "Ending the pregnancy?"

"You heard us?" Olive asked, aghast.

"Aye. I thought . . . well, I thought you were talking about something else."

"You want to have the baby?" Joanna asked her.

"Oh, yes." Olive raised her tearful gaze to Joanna. "But if you hadn't shown up when you did last night, I'd have gone ahead and got rid of it. I was that upset when I saw you'd taken those herbs. I couldn't figure out how you knew what I was doing with them. But once I thought about it, I realized you did the right thing. You kept me from a terrible sin."

Joanna was at a loss for words.

"After you left," Olive said, "I asked myself what you would do if you were in my fix. You're always so wise and strong. You always know the right thing to do. I decided you'd have the baby even without a husband, even if it meant living in shame. You'd lift your chin and make the best of it. And that's exactly what I'm going to do." Olive sat up straight and gave Joanna a watery little smile.

Joanna squeezed her hand.

"Only now I'm going to be arrested for trying to oust the babe from the womb," Olive said mournfully.

"That's not something women get arrested for," Joanna assured her.

Olive pointed to Nyle. "But he said he was here to arrest me—and he had the herbs. I thought—"

"He was mistaken," Joanna said. "We all were."

The undersheriff stepped forward. "Not necessarily."

Graeham exchanged a quick look of dismay with Joanna and rubbed his forehead.

"You two are satisfied with the wench's explanation because you know her and you're disposed to believe her," Nyle said. "But in my vocation, I've had to learn to cultivate skepticism."

"She's an innocent girl," Graeham said. "A bit impressionable, a bit lacking in judgment, perhaps, but she's young."

Joanna stood, her hand resting on Olive's shoulder. "She's certainly no murderess."

"Murderess!" Olive said.

"When did Rolf le Fever propose to you that you begin adulterating his wife's tonic with poison?" Nyle demanded, standing over the cowering girl. "Was it before or after you became his mistress?"

Olive closed her eyes. "I'm going to be sick again."

Joanna held the bowl for her and wiped her face. "Leave her be," she told Nyle. "She didn't poison Ada de Fever."

"Perhaps," said the sheriff. "But think about it. A young girl with a babe quickening in her belly, desperate to marry the father—only he's already got a wife. The girl happens to be the apothecary's apprentice. The wife's laid up with a rheum of the head. 'Tis a simple matter to lace her tonic with something that'll make her gradually sicker, and when the time comes, she gets enough to kill her, and none's the wiser. Le Fever may not even know she's been doing it. Perhaps she conjured up the scheme all on her own."

"Can you look at this trembling, weeping girl," Joanna said, "and honestly think she's capable of such underhanded doings?"

"Mistress," Nyle said wearily, "I've served as undersheriff in this city for nigh unto twenty years. I've seen grisly, cold-blooded murder done by sweet little grannies and pink-cheeked children who laughed about it afterward. More than once, I've seen men protest their innocence with tears in their eyes and their hands clutching holy relics and watched them get let go, only to turn around and murder again."

Olive leapt to her feet. "I didn't do it! I did want to marry Rolf, but I would never sully my soul with murder—never! Tell me how to prove my innocence, and I'll do it!"

Indicating the herbs, Nyle said, " 'Twill help if these are what you say they are, and not poison. I'll have them analyzed by a master apothecary. In the meantime, you're to be incarcerated at the Gaol of London—"

"The gaol!" Joanna exclaimed. "You don't have to take her to—"

"She's a suspected murderess," Nyle said, unhooking the manacles from his belt.

Olive whimpered.

"You don't need those," Graeham said. "She'll go with you quietly, won't you, Olive?"

Olive nodded vigorously. "Yes, I swear I will. Please don't chain me."

"All right, then." The undersheriff grudgingly replaced the manacles. "But if you try to escape on the way to gaol, I won't hesitate to use deadly force."

"I won't try to escape."

"What of Rolf le Fever?" Graeham asked. "You can't arrest Olive and let him off scot-free."

"I have every intention of questioning Master Rolf," Nyle said. "He lives in that blue-and-red house on Milk Street, yes?"

"Aye," Joanna said, "but you'll find him at the silk traders' market hall. He's there most mornings."

"I'll go to the market hall, then, after I escort this young woman to gaol. Are you ready?" he asked Olive.

The girl nodded.

Joanna embraced her. "You'll be out of gaol before nightfall. I'll make sure of it."

After everyone was gone, Elswyth pushed aside the deerskin curtain she'd been listening behind and stepped into the apothecary shop.

It was dark in here, with the door and window closed. Dust motes hovered in the narrow band of sunlight squeezing in between the window shutters. They looked like little sparkling stars; Elswyth trailed her hand back and forth through them, making them dance and spin.

The sunlight shot through the stack of blue glass phials on the work table, making them glow from within like sapphires. How beautiful they were, exquisite really. They came from Venice. That's why they cost so much. No wonder the silk merchant's widow had tried to steal one. But

Elswyth had stopped her. *That's ours,* she'd told her, and Joanna Chapman had seen she was caught and put it back.

Afterward, Elswyth had counted the thirty-four phials five times to make sure they were all there. And that evening, after her gardening, she'd counted them again, just to make sure.

That thieving bitch mustn't be allowed to get her hands on something so precious. That would be very bad, very bad.

Elswyth picked one up and looked around. The tile-lined fire pit was empty even of ashes, having been swept out that morning by Olive; the broom still leaned against the kettle rack. Hauling back, Elswyth hurled the phial into the pit, where it fractured in an explosion of startling blue shards.

She smiled and smashed another one, and another, and another, until the pit was filled with crushed glass that overflowed onto the earthen floor. Mistress Chapman would never have them now, no matter what happened.

Her breath came faster now, but because it was a tiring business, shattering thirty-four glass phials, not because she was excited or upset. The time for fury was over. The simmering rage that had bubbled and bubbled in her brain for the past year was gone now, replaced by a cold, clear certainty—a resolve that felt wonderfully sharp and hard and glittering, like the fragments of blue glass in the fire pit.

She knew what she had to do; it had come to her while her daughter was weeping over that lying, crawling whoreson who'd planted his bastard in her belly. *He's a guildmaster, and rich and handsome and he dresses so fine. . . . He said he loved me, he needed me. . . . He meant to marry me.*

Elswyth brought a sheet of parchment and a quill and the ink pot over to the work table. Uncapping the ink jar, she dipped in the quill and wrote *To Olive* at the top of the sheet.

You will wonder why I have done what I have done, she wrote in the elegant hand that had always been her pride. *That is why I am writing this letter before I do it. . . .*

Chapter 23

~

Thomas Harper, sitting in the sun on his barrel in front of Mistress Joanna's kitchen hut, inhaled the unhappy smell of scorched porridge and wondered where she was. She and the serjant both, for when he'd peered through the windows into the storeroom, he'd found it empty—the first time in a month and a half that Graeham Fox hadn't been there.

As the bells of St. Mary-le-Bow rang terce, the back door of the guildmaster's blue-and-red house opened and a fleshy maidservant emerged with a marketing basket over her arm. She exchanged a cheery "Good morrow" with the manservant mucking out the stable and left.

It was much later than Thomas usually broke his fast, and hunger ground away at his belly. He was sorely tempted to just walk into the kitchen and dish himself up a bowlful of porridge. Joanna wouldn't mind; like most learned people, she knew his malady to be less contagious than was generally believed. But if he was seen by one of the neighbors—such as the money changer's wife, casting him looks of abhorrence as she tended to her garden—he'd be put to death.

A gust of laughter wheezed up out of Thomas's chest. Ironic that a pathetic creature such as he should fear death. For what was he but the walking dead, a gradually crumbling *thing* that used to be a man. He'd managed on his own well enough until now, despite the deadening of his face and arms and legs, but soon he would lose the last vestiges of his precious independence, for the thing he'd dreaded for years was at last beginning to happen. He was going blind in his one good eye. The vision that used to be crisp as a hawk's was gradually, inexorably, growing cloudy around the edges. Soon the murkiness would shroud everything he saw, and then his world would be one of darkness and shadow.

He'd be blind *and* numb. Wherefore should he fear death?

Disgusted by his lapse into self-pity, Thomas closed his eyes and conjured up the image of the woman he'd loved and cast aside when he was young and healthy and foolish, the woman who still had the power to soothe and comfort him, even in his imagination. *Thomas, my love,* Bertrada used to whisper as she caressed his brow, kissed his cheek, took him in her arms. *I'm here for you. I'll always be here for you. And I'll always love you . . . always . . .*

"Thomas."

He opened his eyes to find Joanna Chapman and Graeham Fox standing before him, and he made himself smile. "Mistress," he said with a nod. "Graeham. I think this is the first time I've seen you out-of-doors, serjant. Didn't realize your hair had quite so much red in it."

"So it does." Joanna trailed her fingers through Graeham's hair. "It's lovely in the sunlight."

Graeham exchanged a smile with her so warm and intimate, that having witnessed it made Thomas feel like a voyeur. *Interesting.*

"How do you fare today, Thomas?" asked Graeham.

Thomas smiled. "Never better. Well, perhaps that's overstating it a bit."

Graeham's chuckle was weary, a little pained. He yawned. Joanna yawned, too.

"You two look tired," Thomas observed.

Graeham smiled at Joanna, who blushed and looked away. *Very interesting.*

"My porridge smells as if it's burned to the pot," said Mistress Joanna, entering the kitchen. "I'll have to throw it out, but it's a shame to waste the good part on top. Will you have some of it, Thomas?"

Thomas looked heavenward with his good eye, amused and touched by her efforts to make her charity seem like anything but. "I suppose I could help you out by eating a bowl of it, mistress."

As she was fetching his porridge, the back door of the blue-and-red house opened again. This time it was the guildmaster himself who stepped out, adorned as usual in his peacock-hued finery. Graeham ducked behind a corner of the kitchen and watched him closely as he walked toward Milk Street.

"Don't want to be seen?" Thomas asked.

"Not by him."

Something about the serjant's grim expression discouraged Thomas from asking any more questions.

The door opened yet again, as soon as the guildmaster was out of sight. Another plump, aproned woman emerged, the pink-cheeked wench Thomas sometimes saw chopping and singing at the kitchen window. She untied her coverchief, revealing brown hair braided and coiled around her head, which she patted. With a glance to make sure the money changer's wife had her back turned, she darted across the yard, around the pile of filthy straw Byram had raked onto the ground and into the stable.

"They should find a more discreet place to tup," Graeham said. "They're bound to get caught one of these days."

"According to Publilius Syrus," Thomas said, "God Himself decreed love and wisdom antithetical to each other."

"All too true, I'm afraid," said Graeham, suddenly melancholy.

"What's all too true?" Joanna asked as she stepped out of the kitchen with a ladle full of porridge.

Seemingly unsettled for some reason, Graeham said, "Thomas told me I looked exhausted, and I said 'twas all too true."

"You should take a nap if you can," she said through another yawn as she poured the porridge into Thomas's bowl. "I'd do the same, but Mistress Ada is expecting me to come back and sit with her, and I think it's best if I do." She touched Graeham's hand. "Try to get some sleep."

He brushed his knuckles across her cheek. "You're as tired as I am. I can see it in your eyes."

Joanna smiled. "I'll sleep after"—her gaze flicked toward Thomas and away—"after everything's settled."

"I don't like you being over there, with things as they are," Graeham said.

"Le Fever's not even home."

"Still . . . you'd best keep your wits about you."

"You worry too much." She returned the ladle to the kitchen, filled a bucket with fresh water for Thomas, and took her leave, crossing the guildmaster's stable yard and entering the house without knocking.

"If I weren't so hungry," Thomas said, groping about in his pouch for his spoon, "I'd have about a hundred questions I'd be pestering you with right now."

"Then I'm glad you're hungry." With a smile and a wave, Graeham turned and hobbled into the house on his crutch.

Thomas finished the porridge slowly, savoring it as he used to savor fourteen-course feasts. He drank some of the water from the bucket and used the rest to wash his bowl and spoon. When there was nothing more for him to do, he sat and did nothing, gratified simply to be off his feet. One of the worst aspects of this cursed malady was that it had made idleness a way of life.

Finally, when the sitting still got to be too much even for him, he rose awkwardly and crossed to the window at the back of the house to say good-bye to Graeham. At first he thought the storeroom was empty, but then he saw the young man lying on his back on the little cot, still fully dressed in shirt, braies, and boots but fast asleep.

"Enjoy your dreams, serjant." Thomas shuffled across the croft and into the alley, but stumbled back as someone—a woman—walked by without looking.

She brushed against him as she passed. Thomas's heart seized up; this was what he dreaded more than anything, that someone would touch him accidentally and he would be called to task for it.

But the woman didn't even seem to notice the contact, so single-mindedly did she stalk past. She had a ragged mane of red hair, he saw as she veered out of the alley and across the croft; not slightly rusty, like Graeham Fox's hair, but vibrant copper turning to gray. A wineskin was slung crosswise over her torso, and she held a twig broom with the sweeping end up, rather importantly, like a scepter. That was odd, but not as odd as how she was dressed—or rather, not dressed. For it seemed to Thomas that the woman's kirtle wasn't a kirtle at all, but . . .

Nay, it couldn't be. An undershift, or possibly a sleeping shift, and none too clean. The hem and sleeves were tattered and grimy, the flimsy linen so dirt-smudged that it looked more gray than white. And she was barefoot, her feet crusted with dirt.

He watched her walk purposefully up to the gate in the stone fence enclosing Rolf le Fever's stable yard, open it, and pass through. She was halfway across the yard when she paused and looked around, as if searching for something. Her gaze lit on the stable and she made for it.

Straw. She needed straw.

Elswyth saw a heap of it on the ground outside the stable and bent to collect some, but its acrid stink assaulted her nostrils and she recoiled. She swung open the door of the stable and found a wonderful great pile of fresh straw right in the middle of the aisle, a rake resting against it. As she gathered it up, she heard something like dogs panting in the heat and turned to see a man and a woman in the stall across the aisle, he lying between her bare legs, his braies around his ankles, rutting away.

Elswyth thought of Olive and Rolf le Fever doing that— perhaps in this very place—and the rage seethed boiling hot in her . . . but just for a moment, before she banished it with a reminder to herself that the time for rage was over. She knew what had to be done now.

Elswyth must have nudged the rake, because it fell to the ground with a thump.

The woman gasped. "Byram! Byram! Someone's in here."

"What?"

With a mass of straw bundled under one arm, Elswyth walked out of the stable, swung the door closed, and shoved the iron bolt across with a rusty grind.

"Hey!" the man shouted from inside. "Hey! What do you think you're doing? Come back here!"

Elswyth carried her straw to the blue-and-red house, aware now that two people were watching her openly—the leper and the money changer's wife. Other than them, she saw no one.

She opened the back door and entered the house, dark

and cool. The kitchen was to her right, empty save for a lively fire in the hearth. A good omen, that no one was home to interfere with her. It meant God was smiling on her plan.

Standing well back from the hearth because of the straw tucked under her arm, she held the broom head in the flames until the twigs caught fire. Leaving the kitchen, the burning broom held aloft, she went into the buttery. She dropped some of the straw onto the wooden floor at the base of the service stairwell and touched her improvised torch to it; it ignited in a crackle of flames.

With exquisite, clearheaded calm, she walked down the hallway to the front of the house, turned, and climbed the stairs to the third level on her bare, silent feet. Standing outside the closed door to the solar, she heard a woman's voice—that of Joanna Chapman—reciting something soft and singsongy that sounded like gibberish at first, until Elswyth realized she was speaking Latin: "No one who practices deceit shall remain in my house. No one who utters lies shall continue in my presence."

Recognizing the Psalm, Elswyth smiled. How perfectly it captured what was in her heart. Another good omen!

"Morning by morning I will destroy all the wicked in the land, cutting off all evildoers from the city of the Lord."

Elswyth dumped some more straw in front of the door and lit it, thus ensuring that both exits from the solar would be blocked by fire, then raised her makeshift torch to the thatch between the ceiling rafters. The broom's twigs were burned almost all the way down, but the thatch caught instantly; nothing burned like thatch, especially dry old reed thatch like this.

Within minutes, the fire would consume the entire roof; the house would fill with smoke; burning thatch would fall into the solar; red-hot timbers would come crashing down; there would be screams and weeping from within the blazing hellfire. Elswyth wished she could wait around to witness it, but her plan didn't allow for that.

Padding swiftly downstairs, Elswyth laid the rest of the straw at the foot of the stairs and set the burning broom on top of it, noting with satisfaction that smoke was already beginning to drift through the rear of the house.

She left by the front door, dusted off her hands, and, ignoring the stares of passersby, headed for Newgate Street and the market hall.

Graeham did enjoy his dream, for in it, Joanna was his wife. Not only that, but her belly was growing great with his child, their child. He'd never been more content.

They lived here in her house in West Cheap, or so it seemed in the beginning, but when Graeham opened the front door, expecting to confront the chaos of Wood Street, he instead found himself gazing upon the undulating landscape of Oxfordshire. The hills were a rich, damp green as far as his eyes could see, the sky so vibrantly blue that it made tears prick his eyes.

"Graeham!" came the distant, gravelly voice of a man.

Shielding his eyes, Graeham saw Lord Gui walking toward him, which surprised him at first until he realized—or remembered, because he must have known it, yes, of course he knew it—that Joanna was the baron's daughter, and with her hand in marriage he gained the Oxfordshire estate. He'd forgotten that, but it made everything so perfect, so wonderful. He needn't settle for Phillipa; he could have Joanna instead.

"Graeham, it's le Fever's house," Lord Gui said excitedly.

"Nonsense, it's mine." Graeham turned to admire his new manor house, dismayed to find it painted a garish red and blue. Still, although it might look like le Fever's, it wasn't; it was Graeham's. Smoke plumed from the chimney—his chimney—staining the sky and stinging his nostrils. Manfrid was there, on the thatched roof. He was yowling, which he never did.

"Graeham!" cried Lord Gui in his strange, thick voice, farther away now. "Graeham, come quick!"

But he didn't want to leave; he wanted to stay here with Joanna. They were lying together now, in bed, a feather mattress beneath them, white curtains enclosing them, adrift on gentle waves, blissfully naked. She kissed him, rolled him onto his back, sat over him, reached for him . . .

Yes.

Something landed on his chest, tickled his cheek, nudged his face with a cold, wet nose.

"Manfrid . . . Jesu, go away." He slitted his eyes open, swatted groggily at the cat. *Don't wake me up . . . not now.*

Manfrid butted him on his chin with his head, yowled in his ear.

"Manfrid, for pity's sake." Graeham sat up, grabbed the big tom by the scruff of his neck and tossed him off the bed.

Unusually bold, the cat jumped right back up, and then onto the windowsill, which was probably how he'd gotten in. *"Now."*

Graeham raked his hair out of his face, vexed to have been awakened when his dream was taking such a promising turn. He reached for the window shutters to lock the cat out—and stilled.

Smoke. He smelled it, he saw it. Not woodsmoke, from a chimney, but . . .

"Jesus!" Smoke rose from the roof of Rolf le Fever's house; flames ate away at the thatch. Oh, God, Joanna was in there. "No!"

He grabbed his crutch, vaulted out of bed, down the hall, through the back door. The crutch slowed him down. He hurled it aside and sprinted clumsily across the croft and into le Fever's stable yard, his splinted leg throbbing with each step. Rose Oxwyke, standing in her garden, frantically crossed herself, over and over, as she gaped at the burning house.

Flames leapt in the solar; smoke poured from the window. *"Joanna!"* Graeham screamed.

"Graeham! Thank God." Thomas, almost unrecognizable for the soot that coated him, appeared in the back door with an empty bucket, which he refilled from le Fever's private well; his walking staff lay forgotten on the ground nearby. "They're trapped up there. Both staircases are on fire and the roof's giving way. They can't even get to the windows."

Oh, God. *"Joanna!"*

A furious pounding commenced from within the stable. "Let us out!"

Graeham snatched the bucket of water from Thomas and

ran into the house, yelling, "Open the stable door. Byram can help."

"Don't go in there!" screamed Rose Oxwyke as Graeham hobbled into the smoky inferno. "You can't help them. You'll die, too."

Panic seized Graeham as he stumbled, half-blind, into what seemed to be a hallway. *"Joanna!"* he screamed, choking on the smoke that issued from both the front and the back of the house. It was thickest in back, where it billowed from the open door of a small room that was consumed in hellish flames, so he limped toward the front.

There was a staircase facing the front door; the bottom half of it and the floor beneath it were on fire. He doused the flames with water; they leapt back up. Dropping the bucket, he cursed and stomped on them with his wooden-soled boots.

"Graeham!" Thomas called from behind.

"Here, by the front door!" Peering through the smoke, Graeham saw a leather curtain hanging in a doorway off the hall. He tore it down and threw it over the flames at the bottom of the stairs, but it wasn't big enough or heavy enough to extinguish them. "Where's Byram?"

"He wouldn't come in." Thomas coughed hoarsely. "Said it was suicide."

"Damn!" A leper and a cripple trying to fight a raging house fire. "Is there another stairway?"

"Aye, I saw it earlier, but it's in that room that's on fire."

"These stairs are our only hope, then." Graeham returned to the room from which he'd stripped away the leather curtain. He squinted through the smoke, trying to determine whether he was seeing what he thought he'd seen.

Yes. The walls were lined with shelves, the shelves stacked with innumerable bolts of colorful silks. Graeham hefted an armload and carried them to the stairs.

"What are you doing?" Thomas asked as he stamped on the flames eating through the leather curtain. The rags wrapped around his feet were smoldering.

"Jesus, Thomas, get away from there! Your feet are on fire."

"I can't feel it," the leper said with strange detachment.

"Here." Graeham set the bolts of silk on the burning floor and the bottom few steps and headed back for more. "Help me. We need to smother the flames."

Thomas saw what he was doing and helped, although he could carry only one bolt at a time. Laid on the burning steps, the densely wound bolts stifled the flames enough that the two men could walk on them.

Graeham cursed his broken leg as he climbed the stairs, with Thomas right behind him, both struggling against their infirmities.

Graeham swore rawly when they got to the third level. The entire landing and the thatched roof above were on fire. In the midst of the flames, two blackened ceiling beams rested diagonally in front of the closed door, where they had fallen, further barring the way. Black smoke roiled overhead.

"Joanna!" Graeham screamed from the top of the stairs, then lapsed into a fit of coughing.

He barely heard her through the roar of the flames and the closed door. "Graeham?"

"Oh, God, Joanna!" She was alive!

"Graeham, go! You can't help us."

"No! I'm not leaving you there. I'm coming in."

Another ceiling beam crashed down in front of them; sparks exploded; thatch rained down in burning clumps. Graeham backed up a step, flinching from the heat of the flames and the knowledge of what he had to do.

He had to clear a path into the solar and get them out.

There were three fallen beams blocking the way, and that door—closed, but, pray God, unlocked. And, of course, the flames that licked the floor, the walls, those beams . . .

If he made it through to the solar at all, he'd be massively burned.

"You'll die," Thomas said.

"Most likely." But Joanna would live. Ada, too, but Graeham had fixed his thoughts on Joanna as a way of getting through this. He could do this. He *would* do this, for her.

Graeham sucked in a deep, steadying breath, but that only made him choke.

"You'll never make it," Thomas said. "The pain will get to you."

"*I've got to try!*" he screamed. "Joanna's in there!"

"I know." Thomas took off his straw hat and threw it down the stairs. He faced the burning landing with a look of determination, and pulled the hood of his cloak down over his face.

Graeham grabbed the leper's shoulder. "What are you—"

"I don't feel pain—not in my arms and legs."

"But, Thomas—"

"I'm going blind, Graeham," he said, so quietly Graeham almost didn't hear him.

"Thomas . . . Christ."

The leper smiled. "Wish me Godspeed."

Graeham squeezed Thomas's shoulder and released it. "Godspeed, friend."

Thomas hesitated only momentarily before plunging into the flames and the smoke.

Graeham couldn't watch; he closed his eyes, crossed himself. He heard a thud and a hiss of sparks. Opening his eyes, he saw Thomas moving through the flames like a dark ghost, having shoved the first burning beam out of the way. He grabbed the second with—

"Jesu! Thomas!"

—with his bare hands, his cloak on fire now—

"*Thomas!*"

—flames crawling up his legs, flickering over him as he threw the beam to the floor and seized the third—

Graeham muttered a prayer as Thomas, his cloak falling away in burning shreds, yanked on the door—

It opened. Thomas lurched into the solar, a living torch, and shrugged off the remains of his flaming cloak, but the rest of his clothes were on fire now, too, and his hair . . .

A woman screamed, and Graeham saw them through the curtain of flames on the landing, two dark forms on the floor amid the burning thatch and embers drifting down from above. They had a blanket over them. As Graeham watched, Joanna rose and threw the blanket over Thomas as he crumpled to the floor.

Graeham drew in a smoky lungful of air and held it,

shielded his face with both arms and hobbled across the burning landing, wishing to God he could run. He felt the scorching heat of the flames, hot stings on his arms and back; by the time he entered the solar, his shirt was on fire. He whipped it off and threw it aside, grateful that his heavier braies were spared.

"Graeham, your hair!" Joanna snatched off her veil as she leapt to her feet and patted Graeham's head with it.

There came a groan of splitting wood, followed by a thunderous crack as first one rafter, then another, came smashing down at the rear of the solar in a spray of sparks. A red-hot ember landed on his bare shoulder; he flinched

"We've got to get out of here!" Looking around wildly, Graeham saw that the narrow bed against the wall was untouched by flames. Limping over to it, he hauled the mattress off, dragging it through the doorway and onto the landing. "Come on! We haven't got long."

"Thomas can't walk!" Joanna said. "Neither can Ada."

"I can make it," Ada said weakly, struggling to her feet. She looked so young, so frail, but very determined.

"Joanna, you help Ada," Graeham gasped out as he wrapped the listless Thomas in the blanket. "I'll take care of Thomas."

"Leave me," Thomas moaned. His face was charred and blistered, his hair burned off.

"I can't do that, friend." Hauling Thomas onto his shoulder, Graeham herded Joanna and Ada through the doorway, over the mattress, and down the stairs, following with halting steps. From behind came a deafening crash, and another, as the roof of the solar caved in.

As they stumbled down the two flights of stairs, Graeham heard voices and the splashing of water. At the bottom, he found the front door open, and some of the neighborhood men throwing buckets of water on the fire.

The men helped them into the street, where they collapsed on the crumbling paving stones, gulping lungfuls of fresh air. Ada lay curled on her side, her eyes squeezed shut, coughing raggedly. Thomas lay still as death except for his chest, which rose and fell with every rattling breath.

Amid the mayhem of men running with buckets and shouting to each other, Graeham gathered Joanna in his arms, trembling in the wake of a tide of feeling that squeezed his throat until he could barely speak. "I was so afraid for you," he whispered into her hair, his voice hoarse, his heart pounding. "Oh, God, I . . ."

I love you. I love you so much. Too much.

He mustn't tell her, he knew, mustn't give voice to that which he had no right to feel. He could offer her nothing, promise her nothing. To declare his feelings under the circumstances would be a cruel self-indulgence that would only end up hurting them both.

The knowledge that she had a right to the truth about Phillipa and Oxfordshire, that he was honor-bound to tell her, weighed heavily on him. He should tell her to her face, but he doubted he'd be able to summon the strength for that. The less painful—albeit more shameful—choice would be to write her after he returned to Normandy.

She whispered something against his shoulder that he could barely hear over the chaos surrounding them. "I love you." Was that what she said, or was it merely that he heard what he wanted her to say, despite his better judgment?

He didn't answer her, just held her tight, wishing he never had to let her go.

Rolf le Fever, strolling through the central aisle of the cavernous silk traders' market hall, deserted for the midday dinner hour, thought he smelled smoke.

It was a common enough smell in London, what with the close-packed dwellings roofed in straw and reeds and lit with open flames. And if the weather was dry and the wind strong, a fire that might otherwise have consumed but one or two houses could sweep through the city with demonic speed, destroying whole wards before it was brought under control.

Rolf had been five years old the last time London had been ravaged by such a fire. For the next decade, his family had lived in the undercroft beneath the charred remains of what had once been one of the finest homes in London while his father worked at rebuilding his silk business—for every last bolt of his stock had burned up with the house. To be reduced to living in a cellar after knowing such prosperity had deeply shamed his parents, and the shame had rubbed off on him. As a boy, he used to dream of riches and respectability, of the grand life he would enjoy when he grew up and became a successful mercer himself—the fine house, the elegant clothes, the jeweled saddles and furnishings, and most important, the right kind of wife, a girl of noble blood.

He was successful now, by God. He had everything he'd ever wanted . . . except, of course, the right kind of wife. That lying dog Gui de Beauvais had cheated him out of that which he'd most longed for, God damn his soul to eternal torment.

Rolf paused and unfisted his hands, took a deep breath. He mustn't think of all that now. This was *his* time of day, his special time, when the mercers and their customers went home for dinner and he had the entire hall to himself. He relished having this quiet time to wander up and down the aisle and admire the dazzling silks hung like overlapping pennants in the booths to either side of the vast enclosure.

Noontime sun streamed into the booths through small windows high in the stone walls, highlighting the satin sheen of the richly hued samites and the coinlike seals woven into the ciclatons. The sunlight particularly enhanced the gossamer beauty of the sendals, airy and translucent as the wings of faeries, and the orphreys, shot through with gold and silver threads.

Rolf paused at his favorite booth, that of a Florentine merchant who specialized in silks dyed the sumptuous shades of red for which his region had become renowned. These were the silks he'd most admired as a boy, and they still struck him, every time he laid eyes on them, as almost wickedly beautiful, as if they'd been soaked in the blood of angels. They hung in all their vivid splendor from the ceiling rafters to the floor of beaten earth, dozens of them in shades of scarlet, rose, violet, vermillion, and every possible variation. He glided his hand from one to the other, watching them ripple and quiver as he stroked them.

"Rolf."

He turned, not expecting to hear a woman's voice in the empty market hall and surprised—nay, astounded—at who that woman turned out to be. "Elswyth?" He couldn't remember the last time he'd seen her. She'd put on weight, and . . .

Jesus Christ, was that a sleeping shift she had on? And a filthy one, at that.

"What the devil are you wearing, Elswyth? What are you thinking of, going out dressed like that?"

She had a wineskin looped across her chest. Ducking her head, she lifted it off and uncorked it. "I've come to toast our future together."

He snorted. "Our future? *Our* future? What are you talking about, woman?"

"Our future. You and I." She held the wineskin out to him, her eyes as oddly shiny and fixed as dark little glass beads.

"You and I?" The woman was bereft of her senses; there could be no other explanation. "Elswyth, you and I have no future together."

"Then why did you tell me you wanted to marry me?"

Did he? He couldn't remember; he said that sometimes, to soften them up. " 'Twas a long time ago, Elswyth."

" 'Twas but a year ago, Rolf. You told me you wanted to marry me."

Rolf sighed. "Well, then, I'm sure I did at the time, but sometimes things don't work out as one—"

"I gave myself to you."

"Yes, well—"

"Because you told me you wanted me for your wife."

"Elswyth—"

"And then, not two weeks later, you left for Paris. And when you came home, it was with *her*."

He laughed bitterly. "Believe me, my dear, I'm no more pleased about that particular turn of events than you are. 'Twas a mistake, and I regret it with all my heart."

"Verily?" Her eyes lit with human animation for the first time.

"Would that I'd never met the woman, much less married her."

"She stole you from me." Elswyth stalked toward him; he backed up into the floating silken banners. "I was devastated."

" 'Twas . . . complicated," Rolf hedged, remembering

how eagerly he'd negotiated the union with Ada, sight unseen, so excited was he at the prospect of being wed to the daughter of a baron.

"She was young and beautiful," Elswyth persisted, showing her little yellow teeth, "but unscrupulous. She stole a man who was promised to another. She tempted you. You couldn't resist her."

"Quite right," Rolf said, seizing upon her rather skewed but opportune perspective. "I was as much a victim in all this as you, my dear. Now, if you'll excuse—"

" 'Tis exactly as I thought—which is why I took the steps I took."

Rolf hesitated, not sure he wanted the answer but unable to resist asking. "What steps?"

She smiled as if at a slow-witted child. "You didn't really think a rheum of the head could last six months, did you?"

Rolf stared at this demented woman in her dirt-stained shift, this . . . this *apothecary* who'd prepared his wife's tonic every day for six months. He backed up a little further, into the cool caress of silk; she closed the distance. "That was no infusion of yarrow," he said, both appalled and impressed.

"Oh, it was," she assured him. "Olive made it up in four-pinte batches all winter."

"Then . . . what . . ."

She smiled. "Have you ever heard of woman's bane?"

"Woman's . . . I . . . I don't believe I've—"

"Most folks call it wolfsbane, or sometimes leopard's bane, but I prefer woman's bane, because it can be so handy for solving a woman's problems." She laughed; there was a slightly frantic edge to it. "It comes from the root of a plant called monkshood. The ancients called it the Queen Mother of Poisons. Do you want to know why?"

"Nay." It couldn't be. It was impossible. He'd always thought of Elswyth as rather soft and dull-witted, a woman who would yield to him and then go placidly about her business until he was ready for her again. Could he have misjudged her so dramatically?

"A tiny bit of woman's bane," Elswyth said, "a very tiny bit, can help folks to sleep and take away pain. But just a tiny bit more can make a person sicker than they've ever been, and in the proper dose, 'twill bring on a swift and rather unpleasant death. That's why Olive doesn't even know I grow it out back. I don't keep it in the shop—I go out and dig it up as I need it."

"As you need it." Rolf appraised her soiled shift, the dirt embedded under her nails and caking her feet. No doubt she'd dug up a little bit every day for the past six months.

"At Christmastide," Elswyth said, "Master Aldfrith told me your wife had a rheum of the head and needed a daily dose of yarrow. Every day, before Olive brought the tonic over, I'd set her to some chore and slip just a wee bit of woman's bane into the phial. Olive never knew. Neither did anyone else."

"And Ada just got sicker and sicker."

She laughed again, shrilly. "Don't you see how perfect it was? When the time came, I could give her enough to finish her off, and everyone would think she'd just wasted away. And with that scheming little bitch dead of natural causes, you'd be free to marry me."

"Why are you here telling me all this?" he asked, thinking it seemed foolish of her to divulge her chicanery to anyone, even him. He was convinced now that Elswyth was no fool. Mad as a ferret, mayhap, but no fool.

Elswyth's dark little eyes turned hard and glassy again. "Six weeks ago, Olive told me there was a man coming to your house at compline that day to take your wife to Paris—a serjant named Graeham Fox."

"Ah."

"Ah," she mocked. "Well, naturally, I couldn't have that. How could you marry me if you had a wife living in Paris? That bitch had to die, not just go away."

"As it happens," Rolf said appeasingly, unnerved by the lunatic glare in her eyes, "he never came back for her."

"Only because I saw to it that he wouldn't."

Rolf just stared at the woman. By Corpus, he *had* underestimated her.

"You know, you can find almost anything you want in West Cheap," she said. "I made some inquiries and found three men willing to crack Serjant Fox's skull open for the fifty marks he'd be carrying."

So that's why that bastard had never showed up that

evening. His respect for Elswyth increased tenfold. "Did they do it? Did they actually kill him?"

Elswyth smiled with her mouth but not her eyes. "He never came back, did he?"

An incredulous little giggle bubbled out of Rolf's chest. "God's tooth, woman. You'd go to such lengths just to marry me?"

"It meant everything to me. So you can imagine my dismay this morning when I found out what you've been up to with my daughter."

His giggle turned high-pitched, nervous. "I can't imagine what you're talking a—"

"I know everything, Rolf, including that she's carrying your bastard. I heard it from her own lips."

Shit. He shrugged negligently, contorting his mouth into what he hoped would look like a charming, boyish grin, although he'd never been very good at those. "What can I say, my dear? I'm a man, and Olive . . ."

"She tempted you."

"Yes. Precisely. She tempted me, and I couldn't re—"

"I still want you, you know."

Jesus Christ. "Ah. Yes. Marvelous."

"I need you," she said. "I need to be with you always. Forever."

"Well, unfortunately, there's still the little problem of my wife."

"Your wife isn't a problem anymore."

He swallowed hard. "Nay?"

"Nay. I've taken care of her, just now. She's gotten what she deserved all along."

"She's . . ." The air went out of Rolf's lungs. Could it be true? A strange giddiness overtook him. Was he free, at last, of the sickly, baseborn little wife who'd been such a vexing cross to bear?

"She's dead. You're a widower. You could remarry whenever you want." She held the wineskin out to him. "Come—drink with me to our future together."

He retreated yet further into the comforting embrace of the silken banners, eyeing the wineskin warily. Claims of devotion aside, the woman was a raving loon. "How do I know what's in there?"

Another hysterical little burst of laughter. "You think I'd want to poison you? Here." Holding the wineskin to her mouth, Elswyth swallowed down a generous portion of its contents, then handed it to him.

Reassured somewhat, Rolf took a tentative sip. It was a cheap, overly sweet vintage, but there was nothing unusual about it, no hint of adulteration. He drank more, eager to soothe his strained nerves.

"How did you administer the lethal dose of—what is it?—woman's bane?" Rolf asked.

Elswyth cocked her head as if she hadn't heard him right. "Lethal dose? No, no, no, I didn't kill her with poison."

Rolf paused in the act of squeezing more wine into his mouth. He swallowed slowly. "I don't understand. You said you were going to—"

"My plan changed," she said matter-of-factly. "Had to. The sheriff caught wind of what I was up to, so I had to come up with something different."

"Something different." The *sheriff* was on to her? Apprehension shivered up Rolf's spine, crawled over his scalp, chilling him right down to the bone. "What do you mean?" he asked, swallowing past his strangely thick tongue. "How did you kill her?"

"By fire."

Fire. That smoke. Rolf sniffed the air, or tried to. His nose and throat and mouth felt numb, dead; he couldn't smell anything. The wineskin slipped out of his fingers and fell to the ground.

"'Twas an ugly house," she said in a drunken voice, swaying slightly on her feet.

"You set fire to my *house*?" Rolf's voice was as oddly slurred as hers. He tried to grab the front of her shift, but she wasn't where he thought she was, and he ended up grasping two of the silken hangings and pulling them down. "You goddamned crazy bitch! Tell me you didn't burn down my house! And—Christ, all my silk!" He'd be ruined—*ruined,* just like his father. "Tell me, damn your eyes!"

She was laughing, damn her, *laughing,* but then the laughter degenerated into a fit of gagging. Elswyth sank to her knees, clutching her chest, her breath coming in quick, strident gasps.

"What's wrong with you?" he asked, even as his own chest tightened and his breath emerged in huffing little puffs and his vision swam and he knew oh God what was wrong oh God no, no, no—

"One of . . . the reasons," Elswyth wheezed, "they call it the . . . Qu-Queen Mother of Poisons . . . is because it's so h-hard to detect in, in, in—" Her body jerked, shuddered, her lips drawing back in a grotesque grimace, her eyes wild, blood trickling from her nose.

"No!" He was cold, so cold, an icy river crackling through his veins, his teeth clenched in agony, a mad shriek filling his ears, *can't breathe oh God can't breathe no no no no—*

Had to get help, had to get out of there. He took a lurching step and slipped on a puddle of silk, his legs wobbling out from beneath him, flailing, thrashing, hands clutching at the shimmering pennants, yanking them down around him.

He landed slowly with a hard dull silent thud, everything sideways now, silks floating over him, over both of them in celestial fluttering wings of bloodred, crimson, plum, pink, ruby . . . her face with its flat, empty eyes right there in front of his, beckoning him to join her in eternity so they could spend their future together.

I need to be with you always. Forever.

He really had underestimated her very badly.

The silk traders' market hall was unusually quiet in an odd, strained way when Undersheriff Nyle Orlege arrived shortly after his midday meal to question Rolf le Fever.

He strode through the front entrance of the massive stone enclosure to find dozens of men in fine silken tunics clustered around one of the booths, conferring in hushed tones—except for one black-haired fellow who was jabbering away anxiously in what sounded like one of the Italian dialects.

"Does anyone know where I can find Rolf le Fever?" Nyle demanded in his most booming, don't-ignore-me voice.

Heads turned, surveying him with interest, especially the

manacles and chains dangling from his belt. Looks were exchanged; slowly the crowd parted, carving a path into the booth around which they were gathered.

The first thing Nyle noticed as he walked toward the booth was that some of the sheets of red and purple silk hanging there had been torn down and lay strewn about haphazardly. He'd just about decided some drunken youths had gotten in here during the dinner hour and vandalized the place when he caught a whiff of death—all too familiar in his profession, especially in high summer, when bodies ripened within minutes.

And then he saw the legs emerging from beneath the careless heaps of silk, two sets of them, a man's in yellow silk chausses and bejeweled boots and a woman's, bare and filthy.

"Bloody hell," Nyle said.

Chapter 24

❧

"How does your leg feel?" Joanna asked Graeham as she unlocked her front door.

His splints had come off this morning. It was late in the afternoon now, and they'd had a full day, much of it on their feet. First had come Thomas's funeral at St. Giles, the lazar house where he had finally succumbed to his terrible burns after six long days—though he'd been sedated with sleeping draughts most of that time and had died peacefully. Then, this afternoon, Olive and Damian Oxwyke had been quietly joined in matrimony at the door of St. Mary Magdalene on Milk Street, and Joanna and Graeham had been there to watch.

" 'Tisn't bad at all," Graeham said, following her into the salle. Unencumbered by the splints, his natural gait was graceful in a powerful, long-legged way, but it had grown a little stiff as the day wore on.

Joanna smiled as she hung up her mantle and unpinned the veil she'd worn over her braids. "You don't need me to rub it, then?" When Master Aldfrith had removed the splints, he'd recommended a nice firm massage to ease any discomfort in the leg and had sold Graeham a liniment for that purpose. Catching her eye, Graeham had smiled and said that seemed like a splendid idea.

"Cheeky little vixen." Graeham came up behind her and cupped her breasts through her violet kirtle, caressing them until she felt breathless. Nuzzling her hair, he said, "I'm aching to be rubbed."

"No, really, if you don't want me to . . ."

With a growl of mock exasperation, he swept her up,

causing her slippers to fall off, and carried her into the storeroom, where the liniment was. It was cool and shadowy in here, the windows having been shuttered all day.

Setting her on her feet, he unbuckled his belt and pulled off his tunic. He sat on the edge of the cot—where he no longer slept, having shared her bed in the solar for the past week and a half—and tugged off his boots and chausses, leaving himself in his shirt and drawers.

"I was surprised to see Lionel Oxwyke embrace Olive after the nuptials," Graeham said, stretching out full length on the cot. "Especially given what it cost him to terminate Damian's betrothal to that young girl."

Elswyth's letter to her daughter, in which she confessed to every detail of her mad scheme to join herself for eternity with Rolf le Fever, had nevertheless made no mention of Olive's liaison with the guildmaster or her pregnancy. Damian, who knew about the illicit relationship—it was the secret Olive had been so distressed to have him unearth—proclaimed to the world in general and his father in particular that he had sired Olive's unborn child and meant to make her his wife posthaste. Lionel Oxwyke was, of course, livid about the situation, but custom and the Church were on the young couple's side; for a woman to quicken with child outside of wedlock was no grievous sin—provided the man did the right thing and married her.

"I'll bet I know why Master Lionel has warmed up to Olive the way he has," Joanna said, opening the little jar of fragrant liniment. "A few days ago, she told me she was going to concoct some sort of elixir for his stomach. It must have worked, is all I can think."

Graeham smiled. "Did you see the way Olive was looking at Damian while she spoke her vows?"

Joanna smiled. "And the way he was looking at her—aye. Rolf le Fever will be a distant memory soon enough, I think. By the time that baby comes, they'll have forgotten who really fathered it."

"Love has a strange kind of power," Graeham said. "It seems to be able to change the very nature of things, like alchemy." He met her gaze and then looked quickly away.

Joanna turned her back to Graeham and sat on the edge of the cot by his legs, facing away from him. Graeham had not spoken to her of love, had not returned her whispered declaration after they'd stumbled out of Rolf le Fever's burning house. Perhaps he hadn't heard it.

Perhaps he had.

She wouldn't say it again, she'd decided, not until she heard it from him. She knew what was in his heart; the magic that swirled around them was too powerful to be coming from her alone. He loved her. He must love her.

Perhaps it troubled him that he was a soldier, and unlanded. Perhaps he thought he didn't have any right to fall in love, or that it was unwise to have done so. Certainly it was unwise; no one knew that better than Joanna, and she had no easy answer as to what the future held for them. All she knew was that she loved him, and she couldn't fathom that he didn't love her back.

He would tell her when he was ready. Pray God he did so before he left for Paris.

He planned to leave—he and Ada le Fever—on the fifteenth of July, which was but four days hence, and had written to Lord Gui to expect them in Paris no later than the twentieth. Ada, who'd spent the past nine days recuperating at St. Bartholomew's hospital, was nearly recovered from the effects of the slow poisoning that Elswyth had subjected her to since Christmastide. Joanna visited her every day, gratified to see her cheeks blooming with color, her eyes sparkling with renewed vitality. No longer confined to bed, she'd taken to helping the nuns nurse the other patients, an activity she seemed to find great satisfaction in. Although never keen on logic and philosophy, as her sister, Phillipa, was, Ada thought she might like to study medicine when she returned to Paris. Perhaps, she'd speculated, she could even talk her papa into sending her to the great medical school at Salerno, where women as well as men were educated to become physicians.

"Joanna?" She felt Graeham's fingers, warm and rough, on the back of her neck and closed her eyes to savor the gentle caress. "You're very quiet suddenly. Is anything wrong?"

"I don't know," she said softly, but immediately amended it. "Nay. Nothing's wrong."

"Are you sure?"

"It's been a long and trying day."

His hand stroked a comforting path down her back. "Any day that begins with the funeral of a friend is trying."

Joanna nodded. She'd wept uncontrollably as Thomas's shrouded body was lowered into the ground; Graeham had held her, whispering words of solace in a voice choked with emotion.

"He died trying to save Ada and me," she said.

" 'Twas how he wanted to die, I think—not as a *thing,* eaten away with disease, but as a man, the best kind of man. He was trapped in that ruined body, but his soul is free of it now. He would want us to rejoice for him, not mourn him."

Joanna forced herself to smile. "I know that." Scooping up a dollop of the translucent balm, she set the jar on the other side of Graeham, where she could reach it, and rubbed her hands together to warm the liniment. He sighed when she smoothed her hands down his leg from knee to ankle and up again. "How does that feel?"

"I could take a firmer touch."

He'd told her that just last night, about a different kind of touch. Joanna grew warm at the memory of their uninhibited lovemaking.

As she massaged him, she felt the taut muscles of his calf gradually relax.

"A little higher," he said.

Scooting back, she dipped up some more liniment and rubbed his knee, his thigh.

Graeham lifted his shirt, untied his underdrawers, opened them; he was fully aroused. "A little higher?"

He took her hand, slick with the oily balm, and closed it over his straining shaft. She stroked him, not needing to be told to use a firm, steady pressure. During their long, breathless nights together, she was learning the appetites of his body, just as he was learning hers.

He took off his shirt, kicked off his drawers, and sat up. "Where do *you* ache?" he asked softly, pulling at the cord that laced up the back of her kirtle.

Suddenly short of breath, Joanna answered him with a sigh as he unlaced her. He peeled the gown off her shoulders, untied her shift, and tugged both garments down to her hips as she slid her arms free. Her braids hung over her chest. He gathered them behind her, untied them and trailed his fingers through her hair until it hung in a rippling sheet down her back.

Her heart thudded in anticipation when he reached into the little jar and scooped some of its contents onto his fingertips.

"Where, Joanna?" he whispered into her ear, tucking himself up behind her, his legs to either side of her, their feet on the floor. "Where do you ache?"

She gripped his thighs, waiting.

"Tell me."

She shook her head, thrumming with need but reticent, even after all those nights with him, to give voice to it.

Banding an arm around her waist, he touched a balm-slicked finger to her left nipple. "Here?"

She hitched in a breath, nodded.

His lips grazed the back of her neck, scratchy-soft kisses, one after the other, while his hand slid warm and slippery over her weighty breast, stroking, squeezing. He caressed her other breast the same way as she arched back against him, her breath coming faster, her breasts swelling beneath his touch.

"Where else do you ache?"

She whimpered, her fingers digging into his thighs.

Dipping into the balm jar again, he rubbed his fingertips together to spread the thick ointment over them and slipped his hand beneath the garments bunched at her waist.

Joanna held her breath.

His first light, probing touch incited a spasm of pleasure that made her flinch. He tightened his arm around her waist to hold her still and worked the balm into her aching flesh, at first gently, almost tenderly, then pressing into her and stroking her deep, finding her wet, so wet, his sex slick and rigid against the small of her back as he held her tight for this sweet assault.

She struggled against him, moaning, the mounting plea-sure as acute as pain. "Stop," she gasped as the pleasure quivered through her, building fast, ready to spill over. She clutched at his unyielding arm, ropy with iron bands of muscle. "Stop, wait."

"Nay," he murmured in her ear. "I want to feel you come like this." He slid his finger deep inside her, ground his palm against her.

She shouted as her climax overtook her, hard and jolting, a shock of pleasure that crested over and over as he prolonged it with his insistent caress.

Her ears rang as she slumped back against him. Swiftly he withdrew his hand and stripped off her kirtle and shift, leaving her in naught but her black silken stockings.

Scooping her up in his arms, he laid her on her side, with him behind her. He wrapped one arm around her from beneath, closing it over a breast. His other hand brushed her bottom as he reached between them. She felt his fingers between her legs, opening her, and the hot, sleek pressure of him pushing into her from behind, impaling her in one stroke, both of them slick with balm and trembling with need.

Leaning over her, he kissed her cheek, his breath harsh in her ear. "I wish I could stay," he whispered, something almost hopeless in his voice. "I wish to God I didn't have to leave you."

Finally she asked what she'd avoided asking for so long, hoping she wouldn't have to, hoping he'd simply tell her. "Will . . . will you come back?"

Graeham's hand, resting on her hip, tightened fractionally. She felt his chest rise and fall against her back. "I'll return to England in a few weeks."

"For good?"

Again he hesitated. "Aye."

"Truly?" Filled with joy, she twisted her head to look at him, but he lay down and buried his face in her hair.

"I'll miss you," he said.

" 'Twill only be for a few weeks, and then you'll be back."

He said nothing. She felt his erection wane within her.

"I'll miss you, too, Graeham, but we have four days together until you have to leave. We should make the best of that time." She took his free arm and draped it over her waist, guiding his hand between her legs.

She writhed as he caressed her, swept up once more by an unstoppable tide of arousal. From within her came an insistent thickening as he swelled and filled her. He rocked into her, deep, gliding thrusts that drove her closer, closer . . .

She clawed at the bed covers as her climax neared, cried out as it overtook her. Gripping her hip, he drove in hard, his stabbing thrusts ever more urgent.

"Oh, God, Joanna." He rolled her facedown and bucked savagely against her, one hand fisted in her hair, groaning in an almost despairing way. It seemed to Joanna that he was in the grip of something dark and desperate, an animal compulsion to mate, to claim.

All too abruptly, he uncoupled from her. Seizing her roughly, he turned her over and fell on her, an anguished moan rising in his throat as his release shuddered through him.

He shivered afterward; she held him, stroked his back, his hair.

He raised his face to look at her, there was something haunted in his eyes. "Did I hurt you?"

She smiled and laid her palm against his raspy cheek. "You could never hurt me, Graeham."

Closing his eyes, he nestled his head back in the crook of her neck. "Yes, I could."

Chapter 25

❧

"Isn't it beautiful here?" Joanna asked her brother as they strolled with the other wedding guests from Ramswick's little stone chapel, where Robert and Margaret had just been married, to a clover-festooned meadow bisected by a stream, where the bride ale would be celebrated.

"You could have been mistress of all this," Hugh said, indicating with a sweep of his hand the sprawling farmstead, green and gold and perfect beneath an afternoon sky studded with puffball clouds.

Joanna didn't need Hugh to remind her of that. She'd thought of little else since they'd arrived at nones for the wedding. Ramswick was her idea of heaven—sheep-dotted pastures, well-tended fields, woods and streams, and a lovely little village of thatched cottages. She felt a sense of peace here. She felt at home here, much more than she did in noisome, crowded West Cheap—although, of course, she'd seen to it that Ramswick would never be her home.

Nodding toward the bridal couple, walking hand in hand at the head of the procession, their heads bent together in laughter, Joanna said, "Look at them. 'Twas always meant to be. They belong here, together."

After a moment, Hugh said, quietly, "And I suppose you and Graeham belong together."

Hugh had discovered the relationship one morning when he'd arrived earlier than usual for his visit, having stayed up all night throwing dice and drinking, and found Graeham coming down from the solar in his drawers. He'd accused the serjant of reneging on his promise not to compromise Joanna and reminded him of some threat he'd once made about slicing off a certain body part and feeding it to him. No doubt he would have demanded that Graeham marry her, were it not that he'd be such an unsuitable choice for a husband. Of course, Hugh's wrath was short-lived, as usual, evaporating in the face of Joanna's indignant declaration that she hadn't been compromised or taken advantage of.

She reminded him of that now, because she sensed another of his cautionary lectures coming on. "I took a lover, Hugh. That might be sinful and it might be unwise, but I'm a grown woman, after all. I'm free to make my own mistakes."

"That's just it, sister," Hugh said, keeping his voice low because of all the people walking with them. "You've always done just exactly as you pleased, but more often than not, you've come to regret it. I just don't want you to be hurt again."

"Graeham isn't Prewitt, Hugh."

"Not in any obvious ways. God's bones, I like the man. But think about it. Prewitt laid claim to you and then disappeared abroad. So has Graeham."

"Graeham hasn't 'disappeared,'" Joanna said testily. "He had to take Ada le Fever back to Paris. That's why he was sent here in the first place, to bring her home. He's coming back in a few weeks—I told you that."

"Aye, but you didn't tell me why."

"Why?"

"He's returning to England for good, he said. Did he tell you why? Is Lord Gui releasing him from his service? Will he attach himself to a new overlord? Will he sell his services abroad, as I do?"

"Nay—I'm sure he wouldn't do that." Joanna couldn't live with that. It was bad enough having a beloved brother who was away so much, risking his life on foreign soil for other people's kings; she couldn't bear it if Graeham became a mercenary too.

"Why is he coming back, Joanna? For you? Does he have any way of making a—"

"I don't know, damn you!" A few heads turned; Joanna studied the grass beneath her feet as she walked, heat rising in her cheeks.

Three weeks had passed since Graeham had escorted Ada across the Channel; it had seemed like three years. She missed him desperately. She needed to see him, to hold him in her arms, to whisper her thrilling new secret in his ear.

"What did Graeham mean by 'a few weeks'?" Hugh persisted. "Four? Five? Six?"

"I don't know." Christ, but she wished she did. *Please, Graeham, come back to me—soon.* "Hugh, I really don't want to talk about this."

He curved an arm around her shoulder. "I know, but I have a responsibility to help you see reason about things. I'm the only family you've got anymore."

Too true. Lord William of Wexford, their sire, had been invited to this wedding, as had most of the local nobility, but he'd declined when he found out Joanna would be there. He had excised her from his world, she had no father. All she had was Hugh.

And now Graeham.

"How can it possibly work out, you and Graeham?" Hugh asked.

"Somehow it will." It had to. Joanna's hand strayed to her woozy stomach. Up ahead, she saw the meadow that was the site of the wedding feast, set up with linen-draped trestle tables beneath fluttering white canopies. Servants bustled about, laying white-bread trenchers on the tables. A bit of bread usually quelled her morning queasiness; she would nibble on her trencher.

"I blame myself for bringing him to your house that day," Hugh said.

"So you've told me numerous times. As for me, I'm very grateful to you for bringing Graeham Fox into my life." Pausing in her walking, she kissed her brother on his clean-shaven cheek. "Thank you."

"You won't thank me if he breaks your heart."

"He's not going to break my heart."

"Has he told you he loves you?"

"I told you—I don't want to talk about this."

"Ah," Hugh said sadly. "I thought as much."

"I know he loves me. I just don't want to talk about it."

Girlish shrieks advanced from behind, growing louder as

Catherine and Alice ran past, holding hands and giggling excitedly. Joanna wouldn't have recognized Alice. No longer was she the scrappy little waif condemned to fending for herself on the streets of London. She was the ward of Lord Robert of Ramswick, and by God, she looked the part, in a fine white silken tunic and a chaplet of daisies adorning her long golden hair.

"Good day, mistress!" Alice called out as she raced past with her new little sister. "Good day, Sir Hugh."

Joanna and Hugh returned the greeting, but the girls were too far away by then to hear them.

"Alice is thriving here," Joanna observed.

"You'd thrive too if you lived in a place like this."

"I suppose I would." Joanna knew she would. She longed for the quiet and serenity of the country. Every night, as she drifted off to sleep, she fancied she was in some lovely little cottage somewhere far away from the tiresome turmoil of London. In her imaginings, of course, Graeham was with her; she was his wife.

At the edge of the canopied enclosure, Hugh took her by the shoulders and gave her his gravest big-brother look. "You should sell your house and buy one out in the country."

"Don't you think I've thought of that? It won't work. I might make enough from selling that house to buy a new one, but I couldn't afford any land to go with it. I don't want some little village house all crowded in with a dozen others. I'd need some land to call my own, otherwise it wouldn't be worth it."

"Then let me give you some money, enough for a few acres and to help support you if you have trouble selling your embroidery."

"Hugh, you know I can't let you do that."

"Why not? Are you expecting Graeham Fox to come back and marry you and take you away from the city?"

"Nay . . ." Not precisely.

"Hoping?"

Aye, desperately. "It's because of what you did for me six years ago, Hugh. You bought me the house in West Cheap. You know I promised myself I'd never take your charity again."

" 'Tisn't charity. I'm your brother, for pity's sake. I have a right to try and look after you."

"I don't need looking after." And who knew what would come to pass after Graeham returned to her? She must wait for him before making any plans to leave London.

As if he'd read her mind, Hugh said, "Whether you're married to Graeham or not, you'll need a home. It's unlikely he'll be able to provide for you."

"Hugh, stop it," she said, dismayed that what he said was probably true and appalled to find the situation all too reminiscent of her marriage to Prewitt, when Hugh had had to give her the home her husband couldn't. Wresting free from of his grip, she said, "I'm here to celebrate a marriage and enjoy myself. I'm not going to talk to you about Graeham anymore."

She did enjoy herself, after she'd picked apart enough of her trencher to settle her stomach. The day was mild, the food delicious, and the music—provided by a harpist who made her think of Thomas—exceptionally beautiful. Robert and Margaret, sitting with the girls and their parents at the high table, were as adoring as love-struck adolescents.

In addition to the neighboring noblemen and their wives, every important Londoner had turned out for the wedding. The king's justiciar and his wife were there, along with both sheriffs and the two barons, Gilbert de Montfichet and his cousin Walter fitz Robert fitz Richard.

Joanna had exchanged cursory greetings with Lord Gilbert and Lady Fayette in the chapel before the nuptial Mass, feeling decidedly awkward; after all, six years ago she'd rejected their son for a silk merchant. Nevertheless, they seemed remarkably gracious, especially Lady Fayette, who took her hands and told her how much she'd missed her over the years.

Several times during the bride ale, Joanna had noticed Lord Gilbert looking in her direction, his expression inscrutable. Still, she was surprised and a bit apprehensive when he approached her table, looming over her, tall and elegant in all his white-haired, terrifying majesty.

She let out a sigh of relief when all he said was, "You look lovely today, my lady." He tilted an appreciative glance at her tunic of honey-brown silk, the only gown she owned that was suitable for such a grand occasion.

"Thank you, my lord." Joanna gestured toward the table, empty now save for her and her brother, sitting across from each other. "Will you join us?"

"I'd like that." His lordship sat on the bench next to her. "Good to see you, Hugh. I heard you were fighting in the Rhineland."

"Aye—Saxony. I'm to return in the fall."

"You don't have long, then. It's already August."

"I'll be leaving next month."

Lord Gilbert nodded, cleared his throat. He looked back and forth between them, tapping his fingertips together. Joanna and Hugh shared a surreptitious look of conjecture.

The baron cleared his throat again. "I was sorry to hear of your husband's death, Lady Joanna."

It unsettled her to hear him speak of Prewitt, after everything that had happened six years ago. "Thank you, my lord. I was sorry to hear about Sir Geoffrey," she said, referring to his eldest son, who'd succumbed two years ago to measles.

He studied his tented fingers, took a deep breath. "I wanted you to know that I understood . . . well, not then, of course. But I understand now why you . . . didn't feel that you could marry Nicholas."

Taken aback by this unexpected admission, Joanna said, "I appreciate that, sire."

His gaze still trained on his hands, Lord Gilbert said, "At the time, I must confess I was at a loss as to why you would balk at betrothal to a baron's son—even a second son. I knew about his . . . unnatural tastes, of course, but young men often outgrow such proclivities. And I thought . . . 'Twas naive of me, I suppose. Certainly it was, but I thought a beautiful young woman like you could . . ." He spread his hands helplessly.

"Change him?" Hugh put in, his crooked smile indicating what he thought of such a notion.

The baron sighed, looked sadly at Joanna. "Obviously you knew better. You were right to refuse the betrothal. We ended up marrying him off to Lord Alger's daughter, Mabila."

"I know," Joanna said.

"In five years of marriage, they've produced no children. They're miserable together, of course. He goes his way, and . . . I'm afraid she goes hers."

Hugh raised his goblet to his mouth, casting a look at Joanna over the rim. Clearly he was as puzzled as she to find Gilbert de Montfichet sharing such personal revelations with the likes of them.

"With Geoffrey gone," the baron said, "Nicholas is my heir. He's to inherit the barony. He'll be lord of Montfichet." He shook his head. "He's not a bad sort, really, despite"—he waved his hand eloquently—"his tendencies. But he's no baron. He's not a leader, he's a pleasant young fellow who likes his wine and his music and . . . other pleasant young fellows." Closing his eyes, he said, "Christ, if only Geoffrey had lived."

"It must be heartbreaking to lose a son," Hugh said. "But you have another, and he may yet surprise you. Nicholas is still young and unformed. Give him time to—"

"Two others," Lord Gilbert said quietly.

"I beg your— "

"I have two other sons—Nicholas and . . . a bastard son I've never acknowledged. I'm ashamed to say I've never even met him." Looking at Joanna, he said, "I believe you know him. His name is Graeham Fox."

The breath left Joanna's lungs in a gust. Hugh dropped his goblet, splattering the white linen tablecloth with red.

A serving wench scurried over to pour Hugh some more wine and clean up what he'd spilled. Two couples who'd been sharing their table returned, laughing as they took their seats. Suddenly they were surrounded by people and conversation.

"Do you suppose we could take a walk?" Lord Gilbert asked them, sliding a significant glance toward their tablemates. "Perhaps down by the stream."

Nodding mutely, Joanna rose and walked with her brother and the baron down to the gurgling little brook that meandered through the meadow. Hugh took his goblet to drink from as they strolled along the bank in heavy silence.

Finally Lord Gilbert said, "Twenty-six years ago, my

younger brother, Charles, was struck down while leading King Stephen's forces against the Angevins at the siege of Wallingford. Charles left a widow, Constance. She was heiress to Kilthorpe Castle, near Reading. She was . . ."

He paused at the edge of the stream, gazing into the bubbling water. "She had hair like rusted gold, and soft green eyes, and she was very charming. Quick-witted. She could always make me laugh. I'd always been . . . fond of her. Too fond, perhaps, and I'd sensed similar feelings on her part, but she was my brother's wife, and I was a wedded man, and, well . . ."

Hugh arched his brows at Joanna as he sipped from his goblet.

"Kilthorpe Castle was critical to King Stephen's defense," the baron said. "No sooner was Charles in the ground than the king chose a new husband for Constance, Brian fitz Harold, one of his best military commanders. He sent me to Constance to negotiate the betrothal, although she had little choice but to concede to it. My lady wife stayed home. She shouldn't have." He sighed. "Constance was grieving over Charles, I comforted her. 'Twas . . . complicated. I still can't explain how it happened. Perhaps it was the wine, or . . ." He shook his head. "I don't know. It just happened."

"She found herself with child?" Hugh said.

"Aye. She was my sister by marriage, promised to one of the king's most important vassals. Poor girl, she was frantic when she realized she was pregnant. There was no way she could pass the baby off as her husband's, because Charles had been away from home for months before he died. I was consumed with shame, and beside myself with worry for her—for both of us."

"What did you do?" Joanna asked.

"I told the king and Lord Brian that Constance agreed to the betrothal—as indeed she had—but that she was too deep in mourning over Charles to give herself in marriage quite yet. Lord Brian could take up residence at Kilthorpe and command his army from there, but propriety would demand that she live elsewhere until they were properly wedded."

"Clever," Hugh muttered.

"She spent her confinement at Holiwell Nunnery. That's where our son was born—in secret, of course. I arranged with the prior of Holy Trinity for the infant to be brought up there. Constance was devastated to give him up—he was her firstborn—but 'twas the only way. She returned to Kilthorpe and married Lord Brian. A year later, she died in childbirth, along with twin babes."

Hugh tried to hand his goblet to Joanna, but she waved it away. Lord Gilbert gazed at nothing with his searing blue eyes, so much like Graeham's that she wondered how she could have missed the resemblance. There were other similarities, too—that aristocratic, high-bridged nose, the chiseled cheekbones, the height, the bearing.

"For the most part," his lordship said, "I tried to forget that I'd ever sired a bastard son. Every reminder of him brought back memories of shame and grief. But when Brother Simon—he's the prior of Holy Trinity   "

"I know him," Joanna said. She and Graeham had had a lovely visit with Brother Simon before he left London.

"When he told me young Graeham intended to take minor orders, I felt I had to intervene. My youngest brother was pushed into a Church career he wasn't suited for, and it ruined his life. In my judgment, too many young men take orders without truly grasping what they're letting themselves in for—and what they're giving up. I got to thinking about it and decided that Graeham had grown up more sheltered than was healthy. Of course he wanted a career in the Church—'twas all he knew."

"That's when you sent him to Beauvais to serve Lord Gui," Joanna said.

"Aye. Gui de Beauvais is one of my oldest and dearest friends. I knew I could trust him to do right by the boy. I asked him to watch for any hint that Graeham might have an aptitude for soldiering. Of course, he did, and I assume you know the rest."

"Why are you telling us this?" Joanna asked.

"On the twenty-third of June, I received a letter from Lord Gui telling me that he'd sent Graeham to London on some important mission. 'Twas going to take longer than Graeham had anticipated, so he found lodgings in West Cheap at the home of a woman whose name was, of course, familiar to me—Joanna Chapman. Gui begged me to look Graeham up and introduce myself as his father, but it seemed like madness to break my silence after all these years. Though when I saw you the very next evening at the Midsummer Watch, my lady, I wondered if it might be a sign."

"Ah, yes," Joanna said. "I thought you looked at me rather curiously."

"I was tempted, certainly, to contact Graeham, given all the praise Gui had heaped on him, and given that Nicholas . . . well, that he's been something of a disappointment. A man likes to be able to feel that he's produced a son worthy of carrying on his lineage. Still, I wasn't convinced. Then, a few days ago, when I returned home from a hunting trip, my lady wife greeted me at the door with Lord Gui's letter in her hand."

Hugh winced and tilted the goblet to his lips.

Lord Gilbert shook his head. "The strange part was, she wasn't nearly as angry about my infidelity as about my abandoning my own son. She said the only way I could redeem myself now would be to do as Lord Gui advised and go to see Graeham. I must say, she argued her point vehemently. She wore me down. Of course, she's right—I should have claimed the boy in the beginning, not shunted him off as I did. I had resolved to come 'round to your house and meet him, when a second letter arrived from Lord Gui, just yesterday, telling me that Graeham had completed his mission and would be leaving London on the fifteenth of July."

"That's right, my lord," Joanna said. "Serjant Fox returned to Normandy three weeks ago."

"So I must go to Normandy. It's high time I made amends for having failed Graeham so miserably. I won't be able to live with myself—nor," he added with a sheepish smile, "sleep with my wife—until I meet him and acknowledge him openly as my son."

Joanna smiled. "I know that would mean a great deal to him, my lord."

"My only regret," said the baron, "is that I didn't come to my senses a little earlier. Then I might not have had to miss his wedding."

Hugh stilled in the act of bringing his goblet to his mouth. "His wedding?"

"Ah, you didn't know," the baron said with a grin. "Graeham married someone named Phillipa in Paris about a week ago. I take it she's a ward of Gui's or some such."

Blood roared in Joanna's ears.

"Are you sure?" Hugh asked.

"Lord Gui told me all about it in his letter," said Lord Gilbert. "It had been planned for some time. He set the wedding date for August second when Graeham wrote and told him he was returning."

"Jesu," Joanna whispered.

The baron seemed oblivious to her consternation. "They're going to live in England. Lord Gui is granting him an Oxfordshire estate—fifteen hides, not bad. A reward for this mysterious mission of his, apparently."

Joanna felt the cold drain of blood in her head, a roiling sickness in her stomach.

Are you so chivalrous, then, she'd once asked him, *that you'd go to all this effort for no reward at all?*

Perhaps I am.

He'd lied to her.

Not for the first time. Not for the last time.

I'll return to England in a few weeks, he'd said. Only he'd failed to mention that he would be a married man. Did he think she would consent to be his mistress?

She clutched her churning stomach. This was a hellish dream, a nightmare.

Christ, no wonder he'd never returned her declaration of love. He was using her—and God help her, she'd let him, she'd walked right into it, eyes open. From the very beginning, he had exploited her, first to advance his mission and then for sex. How could she have let it happen? How could she have lowered her guard, especially after Prewitt?

"My lady, are you all right?" asked Lord Gilbert. "You're so pale."

Joanna felt a whirling sense of unreality, as if she'd drunk too much wine. Then she felt Hugh's arm around her, guiding her along the bank of the stream to a boulder, urging her to sit, to lower her head.

The voices of the two men sounded muffled to her ears.

Hugh seemed to be telling her to take deep breaths. He was explaining to Lord Gilbert that her stomach had been troubling her today and perhaps she was ill.

If only that was all there was to it. Merciful God, what would become of her now?

Dimly she became aware that Lord Gilbert was bidding Hugh good-bye and saying he hoped she would feel better soon.

She raised her head and saw him walking away. "Wait! Lord Gilbert!"

The baron came back. "Yes, my lady."

She tried to rise, but everything twirled slowly. Hugh pushed her gently back down onto the boulder.

"I . . . I wonder if you would take a letter to Serjant Fox for me when you go to Normandy," she said.

"Certainly," said the baron. "I take it you want to congratulate him on his marriage."

"Something like that," she said. "I'll bring it 'round to you tomorrow."

"Don't trouble yourself. I'll send a servant to your house for it—say, in the afternoon?"

" 'Twill be ready then. Thank you, my lord."

"My pleasure." He inclined his head and walked away.

Hugh knelt in front of Joanna, took her icy hands and chafed them between his. "Joanna, I'm—"

"Don't tell me you're sorry," she said in a voice that sounded strangely hoarse and faraway. "You tried to warn me. I wouldn't listen. You tried to warn me about Prewitt, too, and I wouldn't listen then. This is my own fault. No one's to blame but me."

"I brought him to you, Joanna," he said, his hands closing tight around hers. "I installed him in your home. I should have known better than to trust some stranger I'd only met, just because he seemed to be a likable fellow."

"Nay," she said. "I have a weakness for men like that—handsome devils. Handsome, charming, unscrupulous devils."

"What are you going to write in your letter to him?"

"I'm going to tell him I'm moving to the country and I'll never see him again."

"Thank God! You mean you're finally going to take my money?"

"Only enough to get me settled somewhere far away from London. I wouldn't do it . . . I didn't want to do it . . . I was hoping Graeham would come back and marry me, but now I . . . I don't feel as if I have any choice, not considering . . . oh, damn it all."

"Swearing again, are you? I'll warn you—country folk don't take very well to ladies using rough language."

"I'm pregnant, Hugh."

His eyes widened in shock. He leapt to his feet, his face a mask of outrage. He spun around, fists clenched, stalked away from her and then back. "I'll kill him. I'll find him and wring his goddamned neck."

"I thought you were going to slice off his, er . . ."

"I'll do that first, and then I'll wring his goddamned neck."

"Hugh," she said, striving for calm in the face of her own tumultuous emotions, "you knew we were sleeping together."

"Aye, but there are ways to prevent . . ." He gestured in the general vicinity of her stomach. "Things a fellow can do to keep from . . . Jesu, Joanna, he should have known what to do."

"He did," she said, feeling heat flood her face. "Except, well, for the first time."

A wolflike snarl rumbled out of Hugh. "Did he know? Before he left?"

"Nay. I've only known myself for three weeks."

"Are you absolutely positive you're . . ." His gaze lit on her stomach.

"Quite." Her purgation was due the day Graeham left for Paris; never had her courses been late. And then there were her stomach troubles, the fluxes and the vomiting.

Squatting in front of her, Hugh took her hands again. "Why didn't you tell me?"

"I was waiting to tell Graeham first, when he came back. I was sure he'd marry me and we could move away from the city, and . . ." She shrugged helplessly.

"This letter you're writing to him. Don't you think you ought to tell him?"

"Nay." She shook her head resolutely. "He made it clear he never wanted to sire any bastards."

"But now that he has, shouldn't he know about it? He's a man of property now. He could provide for the child."

"Don't you understand, Hugh? He's a married man now. 'Twould be humiliating for me to force myself and my child on him, knowing he doesn't care about me, about us."

"Doesn't he?"

I wish to God I didn't have to leave you. . . . I'll miss you.

"Perhaps a little. I have no way of knowing for sure. He was always so credible when he wanted to be, so lethally charming. All I know for certain is that he didn't care enough—and that he was using me. I was convenient and willing."

"And now you're carrying his child," Hugh said.

"I'm not sorry about the baby, Hugh, in spite of everything. I want this child. I'm glad I'm carrying it. I can't stay in London now, though."

"Aye, once you start to show, you'll be the talk of West Cheap. You'll be ruined."

" 'Tisn't my reputation I'm thinking of. I don't want to raise a child in that city, and I can't bear to stay there any longer myself. The house reminds me of Graeham now. I need to get away from there."

"That's all well and good, but don't ignore your reputation. Promise me something, Joanna. When you settle down in the country, let people think you're a recent widow and that the baby was your husband's. No use making things any harder on yourself than you need to."

"All right," she said. "But you have to promise me something in return."

"What?" he asked warily.

"That you won't seek Graeham out and . . . mutilate him."

Hugh rolled his eyes and wrapped his hand around the hilt of his sword. "I swear on the baby Jesus's manger hay that I'll keep my sword away from Graeham Fox's privities."

"And your dagger."

"And my dagger."

"I know you're furious with him," she said. "Imagine

how I feel. But time will lessen our rage. I just don't want you to do anything rash in the meantime."

"Time will have no impact on the anger I feel toward that lying whoreson," Hugh said, his expression murderous.

"Nonsense. You've never been able to stay angry at anyone."

"I'll stay angry at Graeham Fox until I draw my dying breath," Hugh said grimly. "Just see if I don't."

Chapter 26

❦

An October chill was in the air when Joanna stepped out into the slanting late-afternoon sun to feed her chickens. The autumn-hued leaves on the big oaks overhanging her little wattle-and-daub cottage rattled as a breeze wafted out of the woods just beyond her front pasture.

Perhaps someday she would be able to afford a sheep or two to graze in that pasture; the wool would come in handy. She could use a few pigs, too. Pigs weren't much trouble; they could forage in the woods during the summer and feed her all winter. In the meantime she'd make do with her chickens—for she got half a penny apiece for the eggs—and her goat, which provided the milk she'd been craving in gluttonous quantities of late.

Manfrid strode in front of her as she crossed to the poultry house with her sack of feed. He threw himself to the hard-packed ground at her feet, belly up, as a silent but plaintive entreaty. Joanna crouched down to stroke his silky stomach, causing him to squirm in delight and emit that remarkable grinding purr of his.

Like cart wheels on gravel, Graeham used to say.

Manfrid had missed Graeham after he was gone. For days the big tom wandered in and out of the storeroom, as if hoping Graeham would suddenly materialize if he just kept checking.

'Tis a mystery to me why you keep him, Graeham had once said about Manfrid. *He's too timid to be of any use.* But he'd befriended him anyway, and lo and behold, he did prove to be of rather significant use eventually. For to hear Graeham tell it, it was Manfrid who'd awakened him

that eventful day when Rolf le Fever's ugly blue-and-red house had burned to the ground.

Joanna was glad she'd taken the trouble to transport the two cats to her new home. Petronilla kept the byre in back of the cottage free of vermin, and Manfrid . . . well, Manfrid was Manfrid. He kept her lap warm at night. He kept her from getting too lonely. Her few neighbors lived too far away and were too busy to visit frequently, and Hugh had set off for the Rhineland last month after making sure she was settled into her new house.

She ought to be used to being alone, after all those years of making do virtually on her own, but having Graeham around had spoiled her. God help her, she missed him more than ever, despite his duplicity and the fact that he was married and living on some grand Oxfordshire estate by now. He'd been like wine for her soul. For the first time in years, she'd felt as if she were a part of someone else, not just desired, but well and truly loved.

It had all been an illusion, of course, crafted partly out of whole cloth by Graeham Fox and partly out of her own loneliness and need.

Never again. No handsome devil would ever use her like that again. Ever.

She'd made sure Graeham Fox would never use her that way again by moving here to this remote corner of the Midlands, far from her former life. No one in London knew where she'd gone; it was as if she'd disappeared from the face of the earth. Graeham couldn't find her in a thousand years, even if he wanted to. That knowledge both comforted and depressed her.

She treated Manfrid to one last, indulgent scratch behind the ears and then stood, fighting a wave of disorientation. These dizzy spells were much less frequent now, in her fourth month, than they'd been in the beginning. In addition to all the nausea and weakness, she'd actually fainted several times. But according to the local midwife, all that would taper off completely soon, and she would have more energy than ever.

Manfrid made the funny little sound in his throat that he sometimes made—almost like a dove cooing—and leapt up, suddenly alert. If he'd been Petronilla, Joanna would have assumed there was a field mouse lurking about somewhere, but Manfrid doggedly avoided the prey that his sister found so compelling. The big cat strolled over to the dirt path that cut through the pasture and sat, staring off in the direction of the woods, his tail twitching.

Joanna turned toward the poultry house, then turned back around as something caught her eye—a movement at the edge of the woods. Squinting against the low orange sun, for the woods were to the west, she identified the source of the movement—a man on horseback.

All she could see of him was the distant, dark shape of man and horse advancing toward her along the path. She wondered who he was. Most folks around here rode mules unless they walked. Horses were a luxury.

She touched the dagger hanging from her girdle, a concession to the riskiness of living alone in relative isolation. Pray God this fellow was some local nobleman, or perhaps a priest, and not . . .

Joanna shielded her eyes, peering at the horseman's hair, gleaming rustily in the golden sunlight. It hung in waves over the collar of his brown split-front riding tunic. His long legs were encased in leathern leggings secured with crisscrossed thongs.

"Nay . . ."

Joanna focused on his face, her heart skittering in her chest. "Holy Mary, Mother of God."

The feed sack thudded to the ground.

It was him.

Thank God he'd found her.

Oh, God, why did he have to find her?

Joanna pressed a hand to her fluttering stomach, mentally scolding herself for her lack of backbone. She hated Graeham Fox. She despised him utterly for lying to her, using her, getting her with child, then leaving her to marry the lovely and learned Phillipa.

How the devil had he found her? Only Hugh knew where she was, and Hugh was in the Rhineland.

Graeham slowed his dun stallion to a walk as he got to the end of the path. Those earnest, dazzling blue eyes of his still had the power to steal the breath from her lungs, damn him. Something looked different about him; she realized his nose had a bump halfway down that never used to be there, and his forehead was marred by a livid little scar that cut through the outside edge of an eyebrow.

Reining in his mount, he said, "Joanna . . . my God, it really is you."

She wrapped her arms around herself and stared at him.

His expression sobered. He dismounted and tethered his horse to the limb of one of the oaks. Manfrid rubbed deliriously against his legs. Graeham squatted down and stroked his back. "*You're* happy to see me, aren't you, boy?"

Manfrid purred lustily. Graeham looked up and met Joanna's gaze as he petted the cat. "Christ, Joanna, I've missed you. I thought I might never see you again."

He stood and took a step toward her.

She backed up a step.

He stopped in his tracks. "I know you're . . . put out with me."

"You have no idea," she said, her voice low and unsteady.

"I just need you to listen to me." He held his palms up placatingly, started walking toward her. "Just that—hear me out."

"Roast in hell." Joanna stumbled backward as he advanced on her, his strides growing swift, determined. She backed up against the poultry house and turned to flee, but he seized her by the shoulders and pressed her against the earthen wall. She pushed against his chest, but it was like trying to budge a wall of rock.

"I can't believe it," he said, his gaze feasting hungrily on her hair, loose and uncovered, her eyes, her mouth, and lower, to her swelling breasts and the belly that pushed stubbornly against her snug violet kirtle.

He lowered a hand to her stomach, caressed the slight roundness, his expression one of wonderment.

So. He knew.

Looking into her eyes, he said, "You're even more beautiful now. I wouldn't have thought it possible."

His face was very close to hers, too close. He was bending his head to hers, his gaze on her mouth. She tried to shake her head no, but that only brushed her lips against his.

A whimper of longing rose from her as he closed his mouth over hers, his lips so warm, so demanding. He framed her face with his hands, threaded his fingers through her hair.

The world spun as he kissed her. She grabbed fistfuls of his tunic, her heart pounding, reeling with riotous emotions—love and hate, desire, bewilderment.

How could he do this to her? What kind of power did he have over her? She felt drugged by his nearness, his kiss, his warm, familiar scent that she'd missed so much.

He broke the kiss with a breathless whisper. "I love you."

"Oh, God, more lies." She covered her ears with her hands. "Stop lying to me, Graeham, that's all I ask of you."

He pulled her hands away from her ears. " 'Tis the truth, Joanna, I swear it. I should have told you long ago, but I was an idiot." Lifting her hands to his mouth, he kissed them. "I love you, Joanna. I do, I—"

"What of Phillipa? Do you love her, too, or did you just marry her for the land?"

Releasing her hands, he lightly stroked her cheek. "Joanna . . ."

"Did you seek me out thinking I'd be your leman, that you could come to me whenever the fancy struck you and I'd just spread my legs like some twopenny—"

" 'Tisn't like that, Joanna."

"Go back to your wife, Graeham." Joanna pushed against him as hard as she could. He staggered back a step, just enough for her to sidestep him.

Joanna strode swiftly toward the cottage; once inside, she could bolt the door, locking him out. She passed the sack of chicken feed lying on the ground, and automatically bent to retrieve it. As she straightened up, a resurgence of her former dizziness made everything whirl slowly.

Please, God, not now, she thought as dark spangles filled her vision and her knees gave out. *Not now.*

"Joanna?" Before she could hit the ground, strong arms banded around her, lifted her off her feet. She felt herself being cradled like a baby against his chest, felt the steady reverberations of his footsteps as he carried her, limp and half senseless, in the direction of her cottage.

Graeham kicked open the door, paused for a moment, and then she felt him walking again. He lowered her gently; she heard the crackle of straw beneath her, felt the scratchy woollen blanket that covered her little bed, the soft feather pillow beneath her head.

He stroked her forehead, her hair, and then he was gone. Feeling suddenly bereft, she forced her eyes open and saw him, clawing his hair back with his hands, looking wildly around the little one-room cottage. Spying her washstand, he crossed to it, dipped a wash rag in the bowl of water, wrung it out and returned to Joanna's side.

"Joanna, what's wrong?" he asked, sitting next to her on the bed and wiping her face with the damp cloth. He looked stricken. "Are you ill? Do you need a physician?"

She shook her head slowly. "I've had a bit of a rough time with the pregnancy," she said listlessly. "It's getting better."

His gaze lit on her stomach. He rested a hand there in a way that struck her as endearingly protective. "Is anything wrong? The baby's all right, isn't it?"

She nodded. "The midwife says everything's fine."

"You need a physician, not some—"

"There are no physicians around here, and Claennis is a very good midwife."

He smoothed his hand over her abdomen, shaping its roundness, his expression troubled. "It's been hard for you. I hate to think of what you've been through since I left." Looking around the tidy little cottage, with its whitewashed walls and jars of fall flowers scattered about, he said, "You've made the best of things, though. You always did persevere in the face of adversity. Your strength is one of the things I most love about you."

She snatched the wet cloth from his hand and pressed it to her suddenly throbbing forehead. "Don't say that."

"Don't say what?" He leaned over her, his arms braced to either side of her head, looking almost amused, the arrogant bastard. "That I love you?"

"I don't want to hear it."

"It's true, Joanna. If I had any sense at all, I'd have told you months ago. Let me tell you now."

"Why? So you can try to talk yourself underneath my skirts?"

"Ah, that again."

"I may be foolish and gullible and all too susceptible to handsome, charming devils like you—"

"I'm handsome and charming?" he asked with a delighted smile. "You love me, too. I know it."

" 'Tis your vanity speaking. How could I love a man who used me so ill?"

"I did use you ill," he admitted. "I let you give yourself to me without telling you about Phillipa and the estate in Oxfordshire. I didn't know what to do. I loved you so deeply, and I wanted you desperately, but I couldn't imagine giving up that land. Like an idiot, I used to dream about having you *and* the land, but of course, there was no way. I'm a flawed man, and I made unforgivable mistakes, for which you suffered dearly, but you still love me. I know it. I felt it when you kissed me."

" 'Twas you who kissed me."

"You returned the kiss. Now tell me you love me."

"I don't."

He leaned closer, his eyes scaldingly blue. "You do. Tell me. Say it."

"I may not have a lick of sense when it comes to you, Graeham Fox, but I do know better than to return the endearments of a married man."

"I admire your noble stand," he said dryly, "but it really isn't necessary. I'm not married."

She narrowed her gaze on him. "Yes, you are. Lord Gilbert told me you were. Lord Gui wrote him all about it."

"Lord Gui wrote him that he'd set a date. I never married Phillipa."

She blinked at him. "Why not?"

"Because I don't love her. I love you."

She regarded him in nonplussed silence for a moment and then handed him the washrag. "Help me to sit up, please."

Setting the rag aside, he scooped an arm under her shoulders and eased her into a sitting position on the edge of the bed next to him.

"What happened after you left for Normandy?" she asked him.

"All I could think about during the journey from London to Dover was you. Ada kept asking me what was wrong, why I was so preoccupied. I told her I felt ill. I did. I was sick at heart over what I'd done to you, over the prospect of losing you. 'Twas eating me up inside. The worst part came when our boat set off across the Channel. All I could think, as we pulled away from the dock, was that I might never see you again. It started raining, so they put up an awning and all the passengers crowded under it. Except for me. I stood alone at the railing and watched the cliffs of Dover disappear in the rain and wept. I don't think I've done that since I was a child."

Joanna found herself reaching for his hand.

"Lord Gui was at his brother's house in Paris when I arrived there with Ada," he said. "Phillipa was there, too. By then I knew what I had to do. I took Phillipa aside and told her I couldn't marry her, that I loved someone else and would always love her, and that I'd make a perfectly insufferable husband for anyone else."

"You did?"

"I did."

Joanna bit her lip. "How did she take it?"

"At first she was disappointed, because she'd been looking forward to studying at Oxford. Lord Gui couldn't bear to make her unhappy, so he decided to deed the Oxfordshire estate directly to her. Once she realized she could live there without being saddled with a husband, she was thrilled. The baron told me I was a fool to give up such a grand estate. I told him I was even more of a fool than that, because I was resigning from his service and returning to England."

"My God," Joanna whispered, astounded at what he'd sacrificed for her.

"Lord Gui asked me to remain with him long enough to escort Phillipa to Oxfordshire in October. 'Twould take that long to get the manor house ready for her and staff it properly, he said. I felt I owed it to him after everything he'd done for me. I spent a few weeks in Paris with him, helping him attend to business there. When we returned to

Beauvais, we found Lord—" He caught himself; his mouth quirked. "We found my father waiting there for us."

"It must have been something of a shock," she said, "finding out you were the son of Gilbert de Montfichet."

"It took some getting used to. On reflection, though, I should have suspected him—or someone of his rank. Why else would Lord Gui have been willing to betroth his beloved daughter to a baseborn serjant? In his eyes, I was Graeham fitz Gilbert, the son of a baron."

"I imagine 'twas a bittersweet meeting between you and Lord Gilbert."

"More sweet than bitter . . . until he gave me your letter."

"Ah. My letter." She squeezed his hand.

"You gave no indication of where you might have gone off to. I *had* to find you. I immediately returned to London."

"Really?"

"The fellow who bought your house told me I'd only missed you by a few days. He had no idea where you went to, and neither, of course, did anyone else. I questioned Olive and Damian, Robert of Ramswick, Brother Simon, all your neighbors . . . I was at my wits' end. I left London and spent a fortnight just riding from one village to another, asking if anyone had seen you."

"Oh, Graeham."

"Finally I had to return to Beauvais so I could take Phillipa back across the Channel. When I got there, I discovered that Lord Gui had a houseguest who'd shown up unexpectedly a few days before—one Hugh of Wexford."

She gaped at him. "Hugh?"

"He'd come looking for me while I was in England searching for you."

"*Hugh?* But . . . but he vowed that he wouldn't seek you out."

"Actually, what he swore to—as he tells it—was that he wouldn't separate me from my privy parts. And, indeed, he made no attempt to do so. He *did* try to beat me to a bloody pulp."

She reached up and touched the scars on his face. "He broke your nose."

"I returned the favor."

"You broke Hugh's nose?"

"I wasn't about to just stand there and let him pummel me to death, even if I did admire his motives." Graeham grinned. "He thanked me for it afterward. Said he'd been too damned handsome."

"That sounds like my brother. I take it you two came to some sort of an understanding."

"Aye, after I finally managed to explain to him what I've just explained to you. He cheered right up, slapped me on the back, and told me where to find you. Then he set off for the Rhineland."

Joanna laughed. "He told me he'd stay angry at you till he drew his dying breath."

"Hugh said that? He could never hold a grudge."

"I know."

Graeham trailed his calloused fingertips lightly over her face, stroked her lips. "God, it's good to see you smile, Joanna. I've missed your smile. Please tell me you don't hate me anymore."

"I don't hate you anymore. I don't think I ever did, not really—although I tried very hard to."

He searched her eyes, his penetrating gaze seeing right through to her soul. "Tell me you love me. Please."

"I love you," she said, her throat suddenly tight, her eyes burning with impending tears. "I love you, Graeham, I do."

He grabbed her and kissed her, hard.

"I never wanted you for my mistress," he whispered hoarsely against her lips. "You know that, don't you?"

She nodded.

"I want you for my wife," he said.

She nodded again; hot tears spilled from her eyes. He brushed them away with his thumbs.

"I don't deserve you," he said, "not after the way I've mucked things up. And I know you must be concerned about my prospects. There's the baby to think about, and—"

"We can live here," she said, curling her hand around his neck and kissing him. "It doesn't matter where we live. I'd live in the humblest mud hut with you. I'd sell eggs and take in laundry. It doesn't matter, Graeham. I love you. I want to be your wife."

"Truly? Even if I could offer you nothing?"

She touched her stomach. "You've already given me so much. I can't imagine anything better than to live with you right here and fill this little cottage with children. That's all I want—I swear it."

He rested his forehead against hers and grinned. "Then I suppose you'll want me to turn down the holding my father has offered me."

She felt herself gaping at him. "Lord Gilbert, he . . ."

"He said it was high time he did the right thing by me. He granted me the manor of Eastingham, not far from London. It's twenty hides of some of the best farmland in the area, with a charming little village right in the middle of it. And there are orchards, ponds, woodlands, sprawling pasturage for sheep and cows—"

"This . . . this is all going to be yours?"

"Ours. It already is. I've been there. They call me Lord Graeham."

"Lord Graeham," she said softly, disbelievingly. "Graeham of Eastingham."

"And you, my lady, are now Joanna of Eastingham. Or you will be as soon as I can find a priest to marry us. Oh, and best of all, there's a ridiculously huge manor house—a *stone* manor house, with room for lots more children than we could ever fit in here." He adopted a look of mock gravity. "But if you'd like, I'll tell him we don't want it."

"There's no need to do that."

"No, really." He rubbed his scratchy jaw against her cheek. "If you'd rather stay here, it's perfectly all right with me. I only want to please you."

"You do, do you?" She kissed him, took him in her arms.

"Oh, yes." He trailed a hand from her throat to her chest, closing it over a breast straining the confines of her kirtle. "Pleasing you is all I've been able to think about of late."

"Do you know what would please me right now, my lord?" she murmured in his ear.

"God, I hope so," he said, lowering her onto the bed.

And as it happened, he did.

Author's Note

❦

The premise for *Silken Threads* came to me while I was presenting a workshop on The Story Idea at a writers' conference. I was discussing a method of story generation popular with screenwriters wherein you take some element from an existing story—be it a novel, movie, or television show—and start playing with it. You twist it around, switching genders, time periods, or any other factors that will give it a fresh spin, then use it to launch an entirely new—and hopefully fresh and original—story. A well-known example of this is *West Side Story,* a modern *Romeo and Juliet.*

To illustrate this concept of plot-morphing with one of my all-time favorite films, I said, "For example, you could take Alfred Hitchcock's classic romantic suspense movie, *Rear Window,* in which Jimmy Stewart, sitting by his apartment window with a broken leg, tries to investigate a murder he suspects was committed across the courtyard. Instead of a modern city, you could set the story in, say, medieval London. Ooh! The heroine could be the woman the hero rents his room from . . ."

A murmur of excitement rose from the audience. "Dibs!" I shouted, and went home to pitch the idea to my editor, who was just as intrigued by it as I was.

Of course, the final result—this novel—took on a life of its own from the very beginning, and differs from the movie that inspired it in many significant ways. Nevertheless, in homage to *Rear Window,* and in light of the fleeting cameos that Alfred Hitchcock played in all of his films, I've given the great filmmaker a small walk-on role in *Silken Threads.*

He's easy to spot if you're looking for him. Just think about that famous silhouette. . . .

The current zeitgeist seems to have produced a resurgence of interest in *Rear Window*. Shortly after I finished *Silken Threads* and packed it off to my editor, the American Film Institute announced their list of the Top 100 Greatest American Movies ever made, with *Rear Window* coming in at #42. And, as of this writing, filming has just begun on a remake of the movie for ABC television, starring Christopher Reeve. Talk about inspired casting!

Steeped in the Middle Ages as I am, I'm not used to being so in tune with the ebb and flow of popular culture. Why, I feel positively trendy!

I'm always interested in feedback from readers. If you have any comments about *Silken Threads*—or if you've absolutely got to find out where in the book Alfred Hitchcock is hiding—just email me at patryan@eznet.net, or drop me a line at P.O. Box 26207, Rochester, NY, 14626. In addition, those of you online might like to check out my website: http://home.eznet.net/~patryan/

For readers who fell in love with Joanna's brother in *Silken Threads* . . . get ready for a new tale of adventure and romance by the incomparable Patricia Ryan

Hugh of Wexford is a charming mercenary content to live life without any commitments. It will take an extraordinary woman—Phillippa de Paris—to change his mind. Watch for the resulting explosion when these two opposites collide in medieval England.

Coming next year from Signet

SUSAN KING

"Masterful...brilliant...mythically lovely."
—*Publishers Weekly* (starred review),
for *Lady Miracle*